Gin Blanco has

More praise for
Elemen

WEB OF LIES

"The second chapter of the first-person Elemental Assassin series is just as hard-edged and compelling as the first. Gin Blanco is a fascinatingly pragmatic character, whose intricate layers are just beginning to unravel."

—*Romantic Times*

"A fantastic sequel in every respect. . . . This second installment is even more steamy, suspenseful, and full of mystery and adventure. Packed with pulse-pounding action and suspense, this urban fantasy truly delivers. Don't miss this series with unique world building and a complex heroine. I'm certainly caught in Estep's web, and look forward to Gin's next adventure."

—SciFiChick.com

"With each Jennifer Estep book I read I'm more in awe of her writing. She always has fresh storylines with well-developed characters. The dual plot lines are each tied up nicely in the end, yet we're left with a delicious cliffhanger that will have me first in line to read the third book in the series. . . . This is a must-read for anyone who loves urban fantasy."

—ReadingwithMonie.com

"Jennifer Estep has written one of the best urban fantasy series I've ever read. The action is off the charts, the passion is hot, and her cast of secondary characters is stellar. . . . If you haven't read this series, you are missing out on one heck of a good time!"

—The Romance Dish

SPIDER'S BITE

"Bodies litter the pages of this first entry in Estep's engrossing Elemental Assassin series. . . . Urban fantasy fans will love it."

—*Publishers Weekly*

"When it comes to work, Estep's newest heroine is brutally efficient and very pragmatic, which gives the new Elemental Assassin series plenty of bite. Shades of gray rule in this world where magic and murder are all too commonplace. The gritty tone of this series gives Estep a chance to walk on the darker side. Kudos to her for the knife-edged suspense!"

—*Romantic Times*

"The fast pace, clever dialogue, and intriguing heroine help make this new series launch by the author of the Bigtime paranormal romance series one to watch."

—*Library Journal*

"Electrifying! Jennifer Estep really knows how to weave a fantasy tale that will keep you reading way past your bedtime."

—ReadingwithMonie.com

"Loaded with action and intrigue, the story is strong and exciting. . . . With a knock-out, climactic ending and a surprising twist that I didn't see coming, I was definitely impressed. This dark, urban fantasy series has a promising start."

—SciFiChick.com

"Watch out world, here comes Gin Blanco. Funny, smart, and dead sexy."

—Lilith Saintcrow, author of *Flesh Circus*

"*Spider's Bite* is a raw, gritty, and compelling walk on the wild side, one that had me hooked from the first page. Jennifer Estep has created a fascinating heroine in the morally ambiguous Gin Blanco—I can't wait to read the next chapter of Gin's story."

—Nalini Singh, *New York Times* bestselling author of *Archangel's Kiss*

"I love rooting for the bad guy—especially when she's also the heroine. *Spider's Bite* is a sizzling combination of mystery, magic, and murder. Kudos to Jennifer Estep!"

—Jackie Kessler, author of *Shades of Gray*

"Jennifer Estep is a dark, lyrical, and fresh voice in urban fantasy. Brimming with high-octane–fueled action, labyrinthine conspiracies, and characters who will steal your heart, *Spider's Bite* is an original, fast-paced, tense, and sexy read. Gin is an assassin to die for."

—Adrian Phoenix, author of *Black Dust Mambo*

"A sexy and edgy thriller that keeps you turning the pages. In *Spider's Bite,* Jennifer Estep turns up the heat and suspense with Gin Blanco, an assassin whose wit is as sharp as her silverstone knives. . . . She'll leave no stone unturned and no enemy breathing in her quest for revenge. *Spider's Bite* leaves you dying for more."

—Lisa Shearin, national bestselling author of *Bewitched and Betrayed*

The Elemental Assassin titles are also available as eBooks

Tangled THREADS

AN ELEMENTAL ASSASSIN BOOK

JENNIFER ESTEP

POCKET BOOKS

New York   London   Toronto   Sydney

Pocket Books
A Division of Simon & Schuster, Inc.
1230 Avenue of the Americas
New York, NY 10020

This book is a work of fiction. Names, characters, places, and
incidents either are products of the author's imagination or are
used fictitiously. Any resemblance to actual events or locales or
persons, living or dead, is entirely coincidental.

First Pocket Books paperback edition May 2011

POCKET and colophon are registered trademarks of
Simon & Schuster, Inc.

For information about special discounts for bulk purchases,
please contact Simon & Schuster Special Sales at 1-866-506-1949
or business@simonandschuster.com.

The Simon & Schuster Speakers Bureau can bring authors to
your live event. For more information or to book an event contact
the Simon & Schuster Speakers Bureau at 1-866-248-3049
or visit our website at www.simonspeakers.com.

Cover illustration and design by Tony Mauro

Manufactured in the United States of America

10 9 8 7 6 5 4

ISBN 978-1-4391-9263-4
ISBN 978-1-4391-9265-8 (ebook)

As always, this book is dedicated to my mom, grandma, and Andre for everything that they do for me.

ACKNOWLEDGMENTS

Once again my heartfelt thanks go out to all the folks who help turn my words into a real book.

Thanks to my super agent, Annelise Robey, for always being so patient with me, and to my equally super editors, Megan McKeever and Lauren McKenna, for all their editorial advice, input, and encouragement. You all make writing Gin that much more fun.

Thanks also to Tony Mauro, for designing the excellent book covers. Every time I think that Tony can't possibly top himself, I get a look at the next cover and am wowed all over again.

And finally, a big thanks to all the readers out there. Knowing that folks read and enjoy my books is always humbling, and I'm glad that you all are enjoying Gin and her adventures.

Happy reading!

☼ 1 ☼

"Are you going to kill this guy? Or are we just going to sit here all night?"

"Patience, Finn," I murmured. "We've been in the car for only an hour."

"Longest hour of my life," he muttered.

I arched an eyebrow and looked over at Finnegan Lane, my partner in crime for the night. Most nights, actually. Just after ten o'clock a few days before Christmas, and we sat in the darkened front of Finn's black Cadillac Escalade. An hour ago, Finn had parked the car in a secluded, out-of-the-way alley overlooking the docks that fronted the Aneirin River. We'd been sitting here, and Finn had been grousing ever since.

Finn shifted in his seat, and my gray eyes flicked over him. The wool fabric of his thick coat outlined his broad shoulders, while a black watchman's cap covered his walnut-colored hair. His eyes were a bright green even in the semidarkness, and the shadows did little to hide the square handsomeness of his face.

Most women would be glad to be in such close quarters with Finnegan Lane. With his easy smile and natural charm, Finn would have already had the majority of them in the backseat, pants off, legs up, steam covering the windows as the car rocked back and forth.

Good thing I wasn't most women.

"Come on, Gin," Finn whined again. "Go stick a couple of your knives in that guy and leave your rune for Mab to find so we can get out of here."

I stared out the car window. Across the street, bathed in the golden glow of a streetlight, the guy in question continued to unload wooden crates from the small tugboat that he'd pulled up to the dock forty-five minutes ago. Even from this distance, I could hear the warped, weathered boards creak under his weight as the river rushed on by beneath them.

The man was a dwarf—short, squat, stocky, sturdy—and dressed in black clothes practically identical to the ones that Finn and I were wearing. Jeans, boots, sweater, jacket. The sorts of anonymous clothes you wore to go skulking about late at night, especially in this rough Southtown neighborhood, and most especially when you didn't want anyone else to see what you were up to.

Or when you were planning on killing someone, like I was tonight. Most nights, actually.

I rubbed my thumb over the hilt of the silverstone knife that I held in my lap. The metal glinted dully in the darkness of the car, and the weight of the weapon felt cold and comforting to me. The knife rested lightly on the spider rune scar embedded in my palm.

It would be easy enough to give in to Finn's whining. To slip out of the car, cross the street, creep up behind the dwarf, cut his throat, and shove his body off the dock and into the cold river below. I probably wouldn't even get that much blood on my clothes, if I got the angles just right.

Because that's what assassins did. That's what I did. Me. Gin Blanco. The assassin known as the Spider, one of the best around.

But I didn't get out of the car and get on with things like Finn wanted me to. Instead, I sighed. "He hardly seems worth the trouble. He's a flunkie, just like all the others that I've killed these past two weeks. Mab will hire someone else to take his place before they even dredge his body out of the river."

"Hey, you were the one who decided to declare war on Mab Monroe," Finn pointed out. "Correct me if I'm wrong, but I believe that you were rather eager to kill your way up to the top of the food chain until you got to her. You said it would be *fun*."

"That was six hits ago. Now I'd just like to kill Mab and give everyone in Ashland an early Christmas present, myself included." My turn to grouse.

But Finn was right. A few weeks ago, a series of events had led me to officially declare war on Mab, and now I was dealing with the fallout—and the tedious boredom of it all.

Mab Monroe was the Fire elemental who ran the southern metropolis of Ashland like it was her own personal kingdom. To most folks, Mab was a paragon of virtue who used her magic, business connections, and money to fund worthwhile charity projects throughout the city. But those of us who strolled through the shady side of life knew Mab for what she really was—the head of a moblike empire that included everything from gambling and drugs to prostitution and kidnappings. Murder, extortion, torture, blackmail, beatings. Mab ordered all that and more, practically on a daily basis. But the Fire elemental was so wealthy, so powerful, so strong in her magic that no one dared to stand up to her.

Until me.

I had a special reason to hate Mab—she'd murdered my mother and older sister when I was thirteen. And she'd been planning on doing the same thing to me and my baby sister, Bria. But first, Mab had captured and tortured me that fateful night so long ago. Which is how I'd ended up with a pair of matching scars on my hands.

I put my knife down long enough to rub first one scar, then the other with my fingers. A small circle surrounded by eight thin rays was branded into each of my palms. A spider rune. The symbol for patience. My assassin name.

And one that Mab Monroe was now seeing everywhere she went.

For the past two weeks, I'd been stalking Mab's men, getting a feel for her operation, seeing exactly what kinds of illegal pies she had her sticky fingers in. And along the way, I'd picked off some of her minions when I caught them doing things that they shouldn't, hurting people that they shouldn't. A twist of my knife, a slash of my blade, and Mab had one less soldier in her little army of terror.

Killing her men hadn't been hard, not for me. I'd spent the last seventeen years of my life being an assassin, being the Spider, until I'd retired a few months ago. Certain skills you just never forgot.

Normally, though, when I killed someone I left nothing behind. No fingerprints, no weapon, no DNA. But with Mab's men, I'd purposefully drawn the image of my spider rune at every scene, close to every body I left behind. Taunting her. Letting Mab know exactly who was responsible for messing up her plans and that I was determined to pick her empire apart one body at a time, if I had to.

Which is why Finn and I were now sitting in the dark down by the docks in this dangerous Southtown neighborhood. Finn had gotten a tip from one of his sources that Mab had a shipment of drugs or some other illegal paraphernalia coming into Ashland tonight. As the Spider, I'd decided to come down here and see what I could do to foul up Mab's plans once more, thumb my nose at her, and generally piss her off.

"Come on, Gin," Finn cut into my musings. "Make a move already. The guy's alone. We would have seen his partner by now, if he'd had one."

I looked at the dwarf. He'd finished unloading the boxes from the tugboat and was now busy hauling them over to a van parked at the end of the dock.

"I know," I said. "But something about this just doesn't seem right."

"Yeah," Finn muttered. "The fact that I can't feel my feet anymore and you won't let me turn on the heater."

"Drink your coffee, then. It'll make you feel better. It always does."

For the first time tonight, a grin spread across Finn's face. "Why, I think that's an excellent idea."

Finn reached down and grabbed a large metal thermos from the floorboard in the backseat. He cracked open the top, and the caffeine fumes of his chicory coffee filled the car. The rich smell always reminded me of his father, Fletcher Lane, my mentor, the one who'd taught me everything I knew about being an assassin. The old man had drunk the same foul brew as his son before he'd died earlier this year. I smiled at the memory and the warmth it stirred in me.

While Finn drank his coffee, I stared out at the scene before me once more. Everything seemed still, quiet, cold, dark. But I couldn't shake the feeling that something was wrong. That something was just slightly *off* about this whole setup. Fletcher had always told me that nobody ever got dead by waiting just a few more minutes. His advice had kept me alive this long, and I had no intention of disregarding it now.

Once again my eyes scanned the area. Deserted street. A few dilapidated buildings hugging the waterfront. The black ribbon of the Aneirin River in the distance. The pale boards of the dock. A lone light flickering over the dwarf's head.

My eyes narrowed, and I focused on the light. The bright, intact light burning like a beacon in the dark night. Then I looked up and down the street, my gaze flicking from one iron post to the next. Every other light on the block was busted out. Not surprising. This was Southtown, after all, the part of Ashland that was home to gangbangers, vampire prostitutes, and junkie elementals strung out on their own magic and hungry for more. People would just as soon kill you as look at you here. Not a place you wanted to linger, even during the daylight hours.

So I wasn't surprised that the streetlights had been broken, probably long ago, by the rocks, beer bottles, and other trash that littered the street. What did surprise me was the fact that there was one still burning—the one right over the van that the dwarf was packing his boxes into.

How . . . *convenient*.

"You might as well get comfortable," I said, staring at the lone light. "Because we're going to be here a while longer."

Finn just groaned.

We didn't have long to wait. Ten minutes later, the dwarf finished loading the last of his boxes into the van. Once I started watching him—really watching him—I realized that he'd been taking his sweet time about things. Moving slower than a normal person would have, especially considering the bitter cold that frosted Ashland tonight. But then again, this was far from the innocent scene that it appeared to be.

Now the dwarf stood beside the van, smoking a cigarette and staring into the darkness with watchful eyes.

"What's he doing?" Finn asked, taking another sip of coffee. "If the man had any sense, he'd crank up the heater in that van and get out of here."

"Just wait," I murmured. "Just wait."

Finn sighed and drank some more of his chicory brew.

Five more minutes passed before a flash of movement along the dock caught my eye.

"There," I said and leaned forward. "Right fucking *there*."

A figure stepped out from behind a small shack squatting at the far end of the dock that jutted out into the river.

Finn jerked upright and almost spilled his coffee on the leather seats. "Where the hell did he come from?"

"Not he," I murmured. "She."

The woman strolled down the dock toward the dwarf. Despite the darkness, the single streetlight still burning let me get a good look at her. She was petite and slender, about my age, thirty or so. She had a short bob of glossy black hair, held back with a headband, and her features had an Asian flavor to them—porcelain skin, expressive eyes, delicate cheekbones. She also wore black from head to toe, just like the rest of us.

I frowned. No woman in her right mind would walk through this neighborhood alone at night. Hell, not many would dare to do it during the day. Much less wait more than an hour in a run-down shack on a December night when the temperature hovered in the low twenties.

Unless she had a very, very good reason for being there.

And I was beginning to think I knew exactly what that reason was—me.

The woman reached the dwarf, who crushed out his cigarette. She said something to the man, who just shrugged his shoulders. The woman turned and scanned the street, much the same way that I'd been doing for the last hour. But I knew she couldn't see us, given where we were parked. The Dumpster sitting at the end of the narrow alley in front of Finn's vehicle screened us from her line of sight.

After another thirty seconds of looking, the woman turned back to the dwarf and advanced on him. For a moment he looked confused. Then startled. Then his eyes widened, and he turned and started running away from her.

He got maybe five steps before the woman lifted her right hand—and green lightning shot out of her fingertips.

Finn jerked, almost spilling his coffee again. Even I blinked at the sudden, powerful flash of light.

The dwarf arched his back and screamed, his harsh cry echoing down the deserted street, as the lightning slammed into his body. The woman advanced on him, the magical light in her hand intensifying as she stepped closer.

And she was so fucking *strong*. She stood at least a hundred feet away from me, but I could still sense the sharp, static crackle of her power even here in the car. The feel of her elemental magic made the spider rune scars on my palms itch and burn the way they always did whenever I was exposed to so much power, to so much raw magic. And she had plenty to spare.

A second later, the dwarf caught fire. He wobbled back and forth before pitching to the cracked pavement, but the woman didn't stop her magical assault. She stood over his body, sending wave after wave of lightning into his figure, even as the green elemental flames of her power consumed his skin, hair, and clothes.

When she was done, the woman curled her hand into a tight fist. The bright lightning flickered, then sparked away into nothingness, like a flare that had been snuffed out. Greenish gray smoke wafted up from her fingertips, and she blew it away into the frosty night air, like an Old West gunfighter cooling down his Colt after a shootout. How dramatic.

"Did you see that?" Finn whispered, his coffee forgotten, his green eyes wide and round in his face. "She *electrocuted* him."

"Yeah. I saw."

I didn't add that she'd used elemental magic to do it. Finn had seen that for himself.

Elementals were people who could create, control, and manipulate one of the four elements—Air, Fire, Ice, and Stone. Those were the areas that most folks were gifted in, the ones you had to be able to tap into to be considered a true elemental. But magic had many forms, many quirks, and some people could use other areas, offshoots of one of the four elements. Metal was an offshoot of Stone, and electricity was one of Air.

One that Finn and I had just seen used to deadly efficiency, thanks to our mystery woman.

I was an elemental too. In my case, I had the rare ability of being able to control two elements— Ice and Stone. But I'd never seen someone with electrical power before. And I wasn't so sure it was a good thing that I had now.

The woman stuck the toe of her boot into the man's ribs. A large hunk of his body disintegrated into gray ash at her touch and puffed up like some kind of cold, macabre fog. A sliver of a smile lifted her lips at the sight. Then she reached inside her coat, drew out something white, and tossed it down on top of his body before heading toward the van and sliding inside.

Thirty seconds later, the woman drove the van down the street, turned the corner, and disappeared from view. But instead of watching the vehicle, I stared at the burned-out body that she'd left behind, wondering what that bit of white was on the dwarf's still-smoking chest.

"You want me to follow her?" Finn asked, his hand hovering over the keys in the ignition.

I shook my head. "No. Stay here and keep an eye out."

I got out of the car and made my way across the street, slithering from shadow to shadow, a silverstone knife in either hand. After about five minutes of careful creeping and lots of pauses to look and listen, I reached the edge of the building closest to the dwarf. I crouched there in the black shadows, out of sight, until I was sure that the mystery woman wasn't going to circle back around the block and see if anyone had come to inspect her shocking handiwork. Then I drew in a breath, stood up, and walked over to the dead dwarf.

Even now, ten minutes after the initial attack, smoke still curled up from his body, the elegant, green-gray ribbons wafting up to the black sky. I breathed in through my mouth, but the stench of charred flesh still filled my nose. The familiar, acrid scent triggered all sorts of emotions that were better left dead and buried deep inside me. But they bubbled to the surface, whether I wanted them to or not.

For a moment, I was thirteen again, weeping, wailing, and staring down at the ashy, flaky ruined *thing* that had been my mother, Eira, before Mab Monroe had used her elemental Fire to burn her to death. And the matching husk that had been my older sister, Annabella. Trying not to vomit as I realized the cruel thing that had been done to them. That was going to be done to Bria and me before the night was through. Sweet, little Bria . . .

I ruthlessly shook away the memory. My hands had curled into fists so tight that I could feel the hilts of my silverstone knives digging into the spider rune scars on my palms. I forced myself to relax my grip, then bent down on my knees so I could get a better look at the white blob resting on the dwarf's back.

To my surprise, it was a single white orchid, exquisite, elegant, and petal soft in the dark.

My eyes narrowed, and I regarded the blossom with a thoughtful expression. I knew what the flower meant and exactly who had left it behind to be found. It was her calling card, her name, rank, and trademark, just as my spider rune was. Something that she'd put here to announce her presence, mark her kill, and serve as a warning to anyone who dared to get in her way.

She was taunting me, just as I'd been doing to Mab Monroe these last two weeks.

"LaFleur," I muttered, saying her name out loud.

Because the simple fact was that an assassin had come to Ashland—one who was here to kill me.

❖ 2 ❖

"You really don't know that she's here to kill you, Gin," Finn said.

After I'd examined the dead dwarf, I'd jogged back across the street and gotten into Finn's Escalade. He'd cranked the engine, and we'd left the docks and the mean streets of Southtown behind. Now we cruised through the downtown area on our way out to the suburbs that ringed Ashland.

The corporate sharks had long ago deserted the city's skyscrapers and office complexes and had gone home for the evening. The only people out on the streets at this hour were the bums who hadn't been able to find shelter for the night. A few of them huddled around trash can fires on some of the darker side alleys. Out on the main drag, vampire prostitutes wearing as little as the cold would let them trolled listlessly up and down the sidewalks, still hoping that some sugar daddy would want to get his rocks off before going back to his warm, comfortable bed. The hookers eyed Finn's vehicle with predatory interest as he drove past, their teeth gleaming like pointed pearls underneath the harsh glare of the streetlights.

"Maybe LaFleur just wanted to stiff the dwarf to get his merchandise," Finn added.

"So what? She waits in that shack on the dock for an hour until he moves those crates for her. Then she comes out and chats with him before she fries him with her electrical magic? I don't think so," I said. "The dwarf knew she was there the whole time. She was asking him if he'd seen or heard anything. If he'd seen or heard any sign of *me*. That's why he shrugged. The whole thing was a setup, pure and simple."

That was the only explanation that made sense. There was no other reason for someone of LaFleur's reputation, skills, and magic to sit in the dark for an hour. No, she'd been paid to be there—and I knew exactly who was footing the bill.

"Are you sure it was her?" Finn asked. "LaFleur? Here in Ashland?"

I nodded. "Yeah, it was LaFleur. She's the only assassin I know of who leaves a white orchid behind with her victims. It's her signature. Fletcher has a whole file of information on her."

Fletcher Lane had been the assassin the Tin Man most of his life, until I took over the business from my foster father several years ago. But Fletcher had kept up with things in his own way, including compiling information on all the other top-level assassins currently working in the trenches and those who had supposedly retired like me. Strengths, weaknesses, vices, quirks, preferred kill methods. The old man had documented everyone and everything that he could find, just in case any of the others ever became a threat to us.

It wasn't unheard of for one assassin to be hired to take out another. A few months ago, an assassin named Brutus, aka Viper, had been sent to kill me, the Spider. I'd taken a contract to off a corporate whistle-blower, only my employer had decided to frame me for the murder instead, so she'd brought in Brutus to kill me at the scene of the crime, the Ashland Opera House. Viper—so nicknamed because of the rune tattoo of a fanged snake on his neck—had gotten the drop on me and would have killed me if he hadn't stopped to brag about how much better an assassin he was than me. Talking. It was always the bad guy's downfall.

I made a mental note to dig out Fletcher's file on LaFleur. I'd seen a demonstration of her electrical elemental magic tonight, but I wanted to know what other skills she might have.

"Okay, say it was LaFleur," Finn said. "There's only one person she could be working for, given the fact that she was waiting there for you tonight, given whose shipment that was supposed to be at the docks."

"Mab Monroe." I finished his thought.

Not surprising. After all, I had declared war on the Fire elemental and her organization. But the real kicker was that a few weeks ago, I'd taken credit for killing Elliot Slater, the giant enforcer who was one of Mab's top lieutenants. Mab couldn't let the giant's death slide—not and save face with the rest of Ashland's underworld. She had to get rid of me somehow, if only to let everyone else know that she was still queen bee of the city. I'd been waiting for her to react, to make some kind of move against me, and now I knew what it was. The Fire elemental had hired LaFleur to come to Ashland and kill me.

It was a smart play. Cold, calm, logical, with a high chance for quick, lasting success. LaFleur's ambush might have worked tonight. She might have gotten the drop on me, might even have killed me, if I'd been five minutes less patient. But I'd been trained by the very best, by the Tin Man himself. Waiting out an enemy was one of the first things that Fletcher had taught me—and it had certainly come in handy tonight.

And as much as I might hate Mab, I had to admit that the Fire elemental never did anything halfway. LaFleur was one of the best assassins in the business, and now I knew that she had elemental magic at her disposal, as well as the usual assortment of deadly skills assassins specialize in. LaFleur's electrical power had felt just as strong as my Ice and Stone magic. So strong that I didn't know which of us would still be standing at the end of this little game. A troubling thought, to say the least.

"But why would LaFleur kill the dwarf?" Finn asked. "Especially if they were both working for Mab?"

I shrugged. "Who knows? Maybe LaFleur was bored after having to wait so long for me not to show. Maybe all that electrical magic makes her twitchy. Maybe she just likes frying people. Her motives aren't important. What I want to know is who set me up. Who told you about Mab's shipment of drugs or whatever was in those boxes in the first place?"

Finn didn't say anything for a moment. "You're not going to like it."

"Correction. *He's* not going to like it when I get my hands on him. Now, who told you?"

Finn looked at me. "Vinnie Volga over at Northern Aggression."

I frowned. "The Ice elemental bartender?"

He nodded. "The one and the same."

Finn was right. I didn't like it, mainly because I was friendly with Vinnie's boss, Roslyn Phillips, the vampire madam who ran Northern Aggression, Ashland's most infamous and upscale nightclub. I didn't think that Roslyn would take too kindly to my killing her favorite bartender.

I sighed. "And just how did this information get from Vinnie's lips to your ears? Did he tell you himself or was there a middleman involved?"

Information was the commodity that Finn traded in, and my foster brother had a network of spies throughout Ashland and beyond. Everyone from people he'd done favors for, to friends of friends, to folks looking to earn a few bucks by passing on what they knew about the city's power players. Finn was a master at separating the wheat from the chaff, or the solid info from the smoke screens. I rarely asked him where he got his intel from, though. I trusted Finn, and that was all that mattered to me. He wouldn't steer me wrong if he could help it.

Finn shrugged. "No middleman at all this time. I was sitting at the bar last night, chatting up all the sweet young things like usual. There was a lull in the action, so Vinnie and I started talking. He asked me if I ever, ah, imbibed something stronger than alcohol. He said he heard about some good stuff that was coming in down at the docks tonight."

I looked at Finn. "Vinnie just blurted out that he knew when and where some drugs were coming into town? That sounds like a plant to me. Like Vinnie was spreading that line around to everyone to see who might bite on it."

"I thought it was just bullshit myself, until the dwarf started unloading those boxes," Finn said.

"I think we both know it's a little more serious than that now."

We fell silent as Finn left the downtown streets behind. The metropolis of Ashland sprawled over the corner of the Appalachian Mountains where Tennessee, North Carolina, and Virginia converged. The city was divided into two sections—Northtown and Southtown—held together by the circle of the downtown area.

The docks we'd just left were firmly entrenched in Southtown, the rough part of Ashland that was home to the poor, the down-on-their-luck, and the downtrodden. Southtown was the kind of place where people would slit your throat for your shoes. Anything in your wallet would just be gravy on top of that. Gangs and junkies littered the Southtown streets, along with more traditional forms of trash.

In comparison, Northtown was the rich, genteel, refined part of town, with high-end McMansions and immaculate estates that stretched out for miles. But that didn't mean Northtown was any safer. Because the rich folks there would kill you first with kind words before they actually plunged a dagger into your back.

Middle-class suburbs with more modest homes and income levels ringed Ashland on both sides, with all the requisite schools, shops, and businesses that you'd expect to find. Which is the general direction that Finn and I were headed in now.

About ten minutes later, Finn drove his car past a massive iron gate and up a long driveway that curved by a four-story mansion. Unlike some of the others in this area close to Northtown, the home was relatively plain with a simple, sturdy, stone facade. Much like the man who lived inside. The one that I'd come here to be with this evening.

Finn grinned at me, his white teeth gleaming in the darkness. "Well, I hope you and Owen have fun on your booty call tonight, since you made me drive you all the way out here."

The Owen that Finn was referring to was Owen Grayson, the wealthy businessman I'd recently started seeing and the owner of the mansion before me. Owen had asked me to come by this evening, if I wasn't out too late killing Mab's minions. Since I wasn't covered in blood tonight as I had been for the last several, I'd decided to take him up on his offer.

"It's not a booty call," I muttered.

"Right," Finn drawled. "And I'm a eunuch."

I raised an eyebrow. "I do happen to have several sharp knives secreted on my person. So we could easily arrange that, if you really wanted to make that sort of permanent lifestyle change."

Finn shuddered. "I'd rather be dead."

He really would have. Finn had an appreciation for the

female form that bordered on obsession. Old, young, fat, thin, blond, brunette, toothless. It didn't matter to Finn. As long as it was breathing and female, he saw an open invitation to be charming and oh so suave.

"Be sure and say hello to Eva for me," Finn said in a hopeful voice.

Eva Grayson was Owen's gorgeous nineteen-year-old sister and the object of Finn's affections whenever he saw her—or at least whenever there wasn't some other, more accessible female in his immediate line of sight. Finn tended to have a short attention span where the ladies were concerned.

"I thought you'd sworn off college girls after that pair at Northern Aggression said you were old enough to be their father."

"Hmph." Finn sniffed. "I'm only thirty-two, Gin, so technically, that's not quite accurate. I'm not *that* old."

"Oh no?" I said. "You just had more than a decade on the girls you were hitting on."

But Finn wasn't bothered by my quip, because his grin widened. "Decade or not, it was a good thing that they had daddy issues, wasn't it? Because I still went home with both of them."

I rolled my eyes and punched him lightly in the shoulder. Finn just laughed.

"Seriously, though," he said after his chuckles faded away. "What do you want to do about Vinnie and the info he leaked to me?"

"We'll pay Vinnie a visit—tomorrow," I said. "After we talk to Roslyn and tell her what's going on. See what dirt you can dig up on him in the meantime. I want to know everything there is to know about Vinnie Volga before we go and brace him and see why he's spreading rumors for Mab."

And before I decided whether Vinnie was any kind of threat to me—and whether the bartender needed to get dead for being stupid enough to try and sell out the Spider.

Finn and I made plans to meet tomorrow and said our good nights. Then he zoomed his Escalade down the driveway to go back to his apartment in the city, leaving me alone in front of the house.

Instead of immediately going inside the mansion, I stood in the driveway. Listening, but not to the wind as it gusted through the trees that flanked the house, making them creak and crack and shudder. Instead, I tilted my head to one side and concentrated on the whispers of the gray cobblestones under my feet and the larger rocks of the mansion above my head.

People's emotions and actions sink into their surroundings over time, especially stone. As a Stone elemental, I could hear, listen to, and interpret emotional vibrations in the element, no matter what form it took, from loose gravel underfoot to a brick house to a granite gravestone. I could tell if a home was a happy one, if blood had been spilled in a driveway, or if someone was lurking around the side of a building with dark intentions in her heart.

Tonight the stones gave off nothing but their usual, low murmurs, telling me of the winter wind that had whipped around the mansion all day and the chipmunks that had scurried from one side of the cobblestones to the other looking for shelter from the cold.

But there was more to being a Stone elemental than just listening to rocks. My magic also let me manipulate the stone. Let me tap into the element and exert my will on it any way I wanted to, from crumbling bricks to cracking concrete. I could even make my own skin as hard as marble so that nothing could penetrate it, not even another elemental's power—a trick that had saved me more than once. And I was strong in my magic too. So strong that I could easily lash out with it and tear Owen Grayson's mansion apart one stone at a time. It wouldn't have been any harder for me than breathing. I knew from past experience that my elemental power would let me bring down all those lovely gray stones and grind them to dust.

After all, I'd done that very thing to my own home, the night that Mab had murdered my mother and older sister.

On that horrible night, I'd reached out with my Stone magic and leveled our whole house with it to try to get to my baby sister, Bria, in time. To try and save her before Mab found, tortured, and killed her. I'd thought that Bria had died as a result of my actions, that she'd been crushed to death by the falling stones. It was a cold, ugly, secret guilt I'd carried with me for the last seventeen years, until I'd discovered that Bria was still alive and back in Ashland.

I'd only been thirteen when I'd destroyed my own house. Now, at thirty, my magic was stronger than it had ever been before. And, according to Jo-Jo Deveraux, the dwarven Air elemental who healed me whenever I needed it, my power would only keep growing.

The thought always made me uncomfortable. Even now I shivered at the idea. My mother, Eira, had been the strongest Ice elemental that I'd known, but her magic hadn't been enough to save her from Mab's Fire power. Mab's flames had washed over her—hot, hungry, and unstoppable—consuming my mother until she was nothing more than a pile of smoldering ash. So I had more than a gut feeling that my own Ice and Stone power wasn't going to do me much good when I finally went up against the Fire elemental.

Sometimes, even assassins had qualms about dying.

I pushed my melancholy memories aside and stepped up to the front door. A knocker was mounted there—a large hammer done in hard, black iron. The symbol could also be found on the enormous gate that ringed the house and grounds.

The hammer was a rune, just like the scars on my palms. But whereas the spider runes branded into my hands symbolized patience, Owen's hammer represented strength, power, and hard work—all things that he knew a great deal about. Owen Grayson used the hammer as his personal and business rune. A common thing in Ashland. Elementals, vampires, giants, dwarves—most of the city's magic types used some sort of rune to identify themselves, their family, their business, or even their power.

A light burned above the front door, but I didn't see any others on inside the house, so I decided not to use the hammer rune knocker. No need to wake everyone else up. Besides, I was used to slipping into buildings in the middle of the night. It just felt more natural to me.

I held my hand out, palm up, and reached for the Ice

magic flowing through my veins. A cold, silver light flickered there, centered on the spider rune scar embedded in my palm, and a second later, I held two slender Ice picks in my hand, tools of my trade that I'd created a thousand times before.

I was the rarest of elementals—someone who could use not one but two elements. Ice and Stone, in my case. For years, my Stone magic had been the stronger of the two, due to the spider rune scars on my hands. That's because the scars were made out of silverstone, a special metal that absorbed all forms of magic, including elemental power. Like most Ice elementals, I released my power through my hands, using it to create Ice cubes, crystals, and whatnot. But the silverstone metal in my palms had blocked the easy release of my Ice power, absorbing the magic as fast as I could bring it to bear.

Several weeks ago, I'd finally overcome the block during a fight for my life against another Stone elemental. It always surprised me how easy it was to use my Ice magic now—and how it felt stronger every time I reached for it. Jo-Jo Deveraux claimed that soon my Ice power would be just as strong as my Stone magic. Another thought that made me uneasy.

Especially since my elemental magic, my dual powers, was the reason that Mab had murdered my family in the first place.

It took me less than a minute to pick the lock. Of course, I didn't really need to use the Ice picks at all, much less skulk around outside in the cold dark. Owen had given me a key to the door a few days ago, telling me to feel free to drop by anytime, day or night.

I wasn't sure how I felt about having a key to a man's home. None of my previous relationships had ever lasted long enough to get to this point. Owen and I had been together for only a few weeks, and things were moving faster than I'd thought they would between us. Then again, I wasn't sure about a lot of things when it came to Owen Grayson.

Especially the way he made me feel.

For a moment, I stood there in front of the open door, wondering whether I really wanted to go inside. Whether I really wanted to see Owen tonight. Whether I really wanted to deal with the developing relationship and deepening emotions between us.

Me, Gin Blanco, the assassin known as the Spider, hovering outside her lover's door like a nervous teenager trying to scrounge up enough courage to finally call that cute boy in her class. Finn would have laughed his ass off at me and my indecision. But I'd much rather face a dozen assassins like LaFleur any night than deal with something as tricky, convoluted, and fragile as my *feelings*.

Still, Owen had asked me to come by, and I'd told him that I would, if things didn't get too violent and bloody on my latest hit. Emotions or not, I liked to keep my promises whenever I could, especially to Owen, who had been so good to me so far, so accepting of who I was and all the ugly things I had done—that I would do again without hesitation to protect the people I loved.

So I drew in a breath, slipped inside the house, and closed the door behind me.

❊ 3 ❊

I stood in the foyer a moment, letting my eyes adjust to the shadows. The front of the house was dark, although I spotted a couple of lights burning farther back. They must have been in the downstairs living room. Faint music drifted down the hallway toward me, someone crooning the old classic "Winter Wonderland."

The polite thing to do would have been to announce my presence, to call out and see whether Owen or Eva was still up. Instead, I crept down the hallway, sliding from one shadow to the next. Being cautious, just as I had when I'd lingered outside and listened to the murmurs of the stones, checking to see if there was anyone around who shouldn't be. I couldn't afford to be careless these days. Not even here.

As I walked deeper into the house, my gaze scanned what I could see of the furnishings. Looking for anything out of the ordinary, anything out of place, anything or anyone who might be a threat to me. But all I saw was the same simple, familiar furniture. Lots of pieces done in dark, heavy woods, thick rugs on the floor, iron sculptures standing in the corners. Everything in its place for the night.

Except for me, who felt decidedly out of place.

I reached the doorway to the downstairs living room. The music was louder here, though not unpleasantly so. Still staying well back in the shadows, I peered into the room.

It looked like a Christmas fairyland. An enormous Fraser fir reached almost to the ceiling in the corner next to the gray stone fireplace. Its crisp, clean, woodsy scent tickled my nose, even out here in the hallway. Twinkling white lights had been wrapped around the tree, and a variety of jewel-colored ornaments glittered on its thick emerald branches. More decorations spread out through the rest of the room—holly leaves clustered on the mantel, candy cane–striped candles on the end tables, a fat ball of mistletoe dangling from the ceiling.

Eva Grayson stood in front of the tree, a large box of silver tinfoil icicles in her hands. Given the late hour, she wore a pair of pink flannel pajamas, cute and sexy at the same time. The fabric showed off Eva's tall, lithe figure to its full advantage. The bright color also brought out the exquisite contrast of her features—blue-black hair, blue eyes, and flawless pale skin.

Eva plucked a single icicle out of her box and tossed it at the tree. She cocked her head to one side, making sure the placement was just so, before grabbing another piece of foil and throwing it onto the tree as well.

"Are you going to put those on one at a time? Because we'll be here all night," a man's voice rumbled.

Owen Grayson moved out from where he'd been standing behind the tree, another box of silver icicles in his hand. Like Eva, Owen was dressed down for the evening in a black T-shirt and pair of gray pajama pants. The cotton stretched over his broad chest, highlighting his compact, sturdy frame, one that always reminded me of a dwarf's stocky physique. But at six foot one, Owen had more than a foot on most dwarves. He had the same blue-black hair and pale skin that Eva did, although his eyes were a light, piercing violet. His face was also blunter and rougher than hers, with a thin, white scar that slashed down his chin and a slightly crooked nose. Somehow, the small imperfections gave his face a hard, dangerous edge that only made him that much more appealing.

At first glance, most people wouldn't consider Owen to be a handsome man. Not like Finn, with his classic good looks, easy charm, and slick smile. But the more I looked at Owen, the more attractive he became to me. He was impressive in his own way, doing everything with a strong, authoritative air. I'd always been drawn to confident men, especially those like Owen who actually had something to be confident about. Even wearing pajama pants, Owen seemed ready for anything the world could possibly throw at him, from decorating a Christmas tree with his kid sister, to an unexpected business meeting, to a dangerous assassin lurking in his house. There was a quietness to Owen, a calm inner strength that I recognized and admired. He knew his power and his place in the world, and he didn't try to hide it.

And the rest of him was pretty easy on the eyes too. My gaze drifted over his broad chest once more, then down to the flannel pants that hung loosely on his hips. Warmth bubbled up in my stomach, and it had nothing to do with the orange flames crackling in the stone fireplace. Mmm. Maybe Finn would be right about the booty call after all.

"You want the tree to look good for Gin, don't you?" Eva replied, picking out another icicle to place on the green branches. "Where is she, by the way? I thought she was supposed to be here by now."

"She'll get here when she gets here," Owen replied in his deep voice. "She had another assignment tonight."

"*Assignment*. Right," Eva drawled. "You don't have to sugarcoat things for me, you know. You can just come out and say it. Gin's off killing someone. Another one of Mab Monroe's men?"

A faint wince crinkled Owen's face at his sister's blunt tone. At thirty-three, Owen was several years older than his sister and was the consummate, overprotective big brother. Even though she was nineteen, he still wanted to shield Eva from everything—including what I did late at night.

"I believe that was the plan, yes," he replied.

Owen knew that I was the assassin the Spider. He'd had his suspicions for weeks, ever since I'd gone toe-to-toe with a greedy dwarven mine owner—and had been the only one left standing at the end. A couple of weeks ago, I'd told Owen my deep, dark secret when I'd gone after Elliot Slater.

Owen had been more accepting of my past then I'd ever dreamed he could be. He knew what a dark, twisted, violent place Ashland was, and he'd done his fair share of nasty things over the years too. Just to survive, just to keep himself and Eva safe. Owen didn't begrudge me my strength, skills, or murky past, unlike another man that I'd once been involved with. His easy acceptance of me was one of the many things I liked about Owen.

We'd both agreed that Eva had a right to know about my past as well, so I'd sat her down one night and told her what I did. Eva hadn't been that surprised, especially since I'd helped out Violet Fox, her best friend, several weeks ago. Violet had told Eva how I'd saved her and her grandfather from being murdered by the dwarven mine owner who wanted their land and the diamonds he'd discovered on it. Violet wasn't the only one I'd saved. I'd also kept Eva from getting fried to a crisp by a Fire elemental who'd tried to rob the Pork Pit one night while she'd been eating in the restaurant.

Eva had been just as understanding about my past as Owen, mainly because my family wasn't the only one that Mab Monroe had murdered over the years. She'd also killed Owen and Eva's parents because of their father's gambling debt when Eva was just a toddler. The two of them had been forced to live on the mean streets of Ashland, just as I'd done before Fletcher Lane had taken me in. Now Eva treated me like a big sister—a role I wasn't sure that I was comfortable with, since I didn't know where things were going between Owen and me.

And the small fact that I hadn't even told my own sister, Bria, who I really was.

"Actually, you'll be lucky if Gin shows tonight at all," Eva said.

Owen's violet eyes narrowed. "And what's that supposed to mean?"

Eva rolled her own eyes and put a hand on her hip. "It means you've been dating her less than a month, and you already gave her a freaking *key*, Owen."

"What was wrong with giving Gin a key?" he rumbled. "It's not like I could keep her out of the house, even if I wanted to. I thought a key would make things easier, make her feel like she was really welcome here. This is the first time that I've dated an assassin. I don't want to piss her off."

I smiled at his light tone, and logic. Two more things that I liked about Owen. He didn't shy away from my past, or the fact that I could kill him as easily as sleep with him.

"Don't get me wrong. I like Gin—a lot. Certainly more than those bimbos you've brought home," Eva said.

"Hey, now. They weren't bimbos. At least, not all of them."

Eva sniffed. "When their boobs are bigger than their hair, they're bimbos, Owen. Trust me on that."

Owen grumbled something under his breath, reached into his box, and threw a wad of icicles at his younger sister. Eva snickered and ducked out of the way of the sparkling tinfoil.

"So what's wrong with Gin?" Owen asked.

Eva shrugged. "It's not that anything's *wrong* with her. But she's the Spider. Like, the best assassin *ever*."

"What's your point?"

"My point is that Gin's not the kind of woman who's going to be ecstatic when you give her a key after a few dates. There's a little bit more to her than that."

Owen frowned. "You think it was too much? Too soon?"

"Way too much, way too soon," Eva replied.

Well, I was glad I wasn't the only one who thought so, although I wasn't sure if I wanted Owen taking relationship advice from his kid sister, who wasn't even old enough to legally drink.

The two of them strung some more icicles on the tree for a minute before Owen spoke again.

"I like Gin," he said. "More than I've liked anyone in a long time. That's why I gave her the key. Because I wanted to. Because I want her to stick around."

Eva looked at her big brother. "I know. Just remember that Gin's not like anyone else you've ever dated. She's not going to act the same as the bimbos, who would have started moving their stuff in and picking out wedding dresses the second you gave them a key."

Owen's eyes narrowed, but a grin spread across his face, softening his chiseled features. "When did you get so smart?"

Eva grinned back at him. "Big brother, I've always been smart. You just failed to recognize my brilliance until now."

Owen grumbled something else under his breath and threw another wad of icicles at Eva. She laughed, dug into her box, and retaliated with her own handful. And the fight was on. The two of them slung gobs of icicles at each other, until the air sparked and flashed with the thin, silver ribbons.

I leaned against the doorway and watched them shriek, laugh, and duck around furniture as they staged their mock battle. Eva and Owen loved each other the way two siblings should. The way I loved Finn. They had the kind of easy relationship I wanted to have with my own sister. With Bria.

Too bad Bria was a detective with the Ashland Police Department. One who wanted to track down the Spider and bring her to justice for killing Elliot Slater and the rest of Mab Monroe's minions that I'd dispatched in the last few weeks.

But I wasn't here to dwell on that complicated relationship, my war with Mab, or the fact that LaFleur was in town and gunning for me. All that mattered was tonight, and this brief happy moment with the Graysons. I hadn't had many of those in my life, and I knew enough to appreciate them. To grab and hold on to and enjoy these precious moments as long as I could.

So I drew in a breath and stepped into the living room, letting the two of them see me. Eva spotted me first.

"Gin!" Eva shouted, ducking another wad of icicles. "You made it!"

Owen's head turned in my direction, giving Eva the opening that she needed to leap up onto the sofa and dump the rest of her box of icicles on top of her big brother's head.

"Ha!" she shouted in triumph. "I win!"

Owen glowered at his sister, before turning and giving me a sheepish grin. With the icicles streaming down his body, he looked like a tinfoil yeti.

I raised an eyebrow. "Sexy. Dead sexy."

Owen grinned at me through the sparkling silver strings. "I do try."

For the next hour, I helped Owen and Eva pick up wayward icicles and put them on the tree. When we finished,

Eva announced that she was giving us some private time and headed off to bed.

"Sorry about the mess," Owen said, bending down to pick a stray icicle off the rug. "I didn't mean for you to have to clean up after us."

"It's okay," I replied. "I had fun helping you guys."

Surprisingly, I wasn't lying. It had been fun doing something so simple, so normal. Something that Fletcher Lane would have considered to be *living in the daylight*, his words for having a regular life. I couldn't remember the last time I'd had a Christmas tree, much less decorated one. The old man hadn't much cared for the holiday, and Finn had always been more interested in the presents underneath the tree than what it looked like. In addition to helping me with certain things, my foster brother was also an investment banker. Finn was all about money and the shiny things you could buy with it.

While Owen salvaged a few more icicles, I wandered through the living room, staring at the decorations, enjoying the mix of red and green, gold and silver. The gleam of glass on a table caught my eye, and I picked up a large snow globe. A charming Christmas scene of a family gathered around a fireplace lay underneath the smooth, curved surface. I shook the globe. White flakes drifted up before sinking to the bottom once more. Such a small, simple thing, but it made my heart twist all the same.

My mother, Eira Snow, had collected snow globes. She had dozens of them, and I remembered running from one end of the fireplace mantel to the other, trying to make the snow swirl in the last one before the flakes in the first one settled back down. A game that I'd played with Bria when we were kids.

Bria seemed to have the same fascination with the globes as our mother. I'd seen boxes full of them the night that I'd broken into Bria's house and kept Elliot Slater and the rest of his giant goons from killing her. A few weeks ago, when Bria had first come back to Ashland, Mab Monroe had sent her giant enforcer to murder my sister. Mab had thought that Bria was a threat to her. That Bria was the Snow sister who had both Ice and Stone magic.

Mab had thought that Bria was the one who was going to kill her.

Once upon a time, an Air elemental who could see the future had told Mab that a member of the Snow family, someone who could wield both Ice and Stone magic, would kill her one day. Rather than let that happen, Mab had decided to make her own preemptive strike.

That's why she'd come to my house all those years ago. That's why she'd killed my mother and my older sister, Annabella. That's why she'd tortured me, first by duct-taping the spider rune medallion that I wore as a necklace between my palms. When I hadn't told Mab where Bria was, Mab had used her Fire magic to superheat the silverstone metal until it melted into my palms—forever marking me. Branding me as the Spider in more ways than one.

The Fire elemental just hadn't realized that I was the one that she'd really wanted to eliminate that night. That I was the real threat to her, not Bria. That I was the one with both Ice and Stone magic—magic that I was going to use to kill Mab.

The prophecy, Mab's actions, the fact that I'd survived anyway—it was all very tragic and somewhat Greek. Or maybe I thought that only because I'd just finished up a classic literature course over at Ashland Community College. We'd read tales of Oedipus and *The Odyssey*, among other things. Sometimes, I wondered if Mab and I were like two ancient Greek combatants, locked in this epic struggle, each move we made to prevent our tragic fates instead actually bringing us closer to our final, deadly confrontation.

Owen moved to stand beside me. "What are you thinking about?"

"Nothing."

I put the snow globe down on the table, turned to him, and looped my arms around his neck. I tilted up my head, and my gaze traced over Owen's features. The white scar that cut across his chin, firm lips, slightly crooked nose, and finally up to his eyes.

As always, I looked deep into his violet gaze, losing myself in the pale, amethyst color, searching for a sign, a hint, a flash of feeling that would tell me that he'd finally wised up and decided to end things with me. That Owen saw how dark and twisted I really was deep down and that it finally, ultimately, disgusted him, the way that it had Donovan Caine, the man I'd been involved with before Owen came along.

As always, I saw nothing. No fear, no condemnation, no disgust. Only acceptance.

Owen put his hands around my waist and drew me into the warm embrace of his arms. His hands moved up my back, massaging my tight muscles, before sliding down to the curve of my ass and pulling me against him, so that I could feel every hard inch of him rubbing against the junction of my thighs, even through the thick fabric of my jeans.

"Mmm," I said. "Someone's happy to see me."

Owen bent his head and pressed a soft kiss to my throat. Heat flooded my veins at the gentle contact.

"Always," he agreed.

I turned my head, and our lips met. We kissed slowly at first, sweetly, gently even. Our lips just brushing, our hands just skimming over each other's bodies. I breathed in Owen's scent, that rich, earthy aroma that always made me think of metal, something he had an elemental talent for using. But the connection between us flared too bright, burned too hot, to be contained for long.

The kiss deepened, and our tongues got involved, tasting each other. Owen's hands slid up under my shirt, gliding across my stomach. Mine drifted lower, moving across his hips. Both of us not going any farther with our teasing—at least not yet.

"You know," Owen murmured against my lips. "I think that Eva had an excellent idea about going to bed. Care to join me?"

"Why bother with bed?" I jerked my head. "I see a perfectly serviceable couch right there."

"Hmm," Owen said, grinning down at me. "Have I ever told you what good ideas you have, Gin?"

I smiled up at him. "No, but you could show me."

"Oh, I plan to. Don't you worry about that."

Owen drew me closer. His lips met mine again, and I surrendered to him for the night.

❖ 4 ❖

Since it was less than a week before Christmas, Owen was taking some time off from his various business interests, which meant that he got to sleep in the next morning. But I still had a barbecue restaurant to run, so I slipped out of bed early and took a hot shower.

Owen was still asleep when I finished getting ready. He sprawled face down on the king-size bed, a soft blanket covering his bare back, one strong arm jutting off the mattress into the empty air in front of the nightstand.

I stood there by the bed, staring down at him. Blue-black hair, rough, chiseled features, hard body. Owen Grayson was everything that I'd ever wanted in a lover. Attentive, inventive, skilled, confident. But the strangest thing was that he really seemed to care about me, Gin Blanco. The semiretired assassin known as the Spider.

After we'd finished in the living room, we'd gone into Owen's bedroom to spend the rest of the night together.

Owen had wrapped us both in a fleece blanket, and we'd sat there in front of the crackling fire, talking until the orange-red flames died down to glowing embers. We'd discussed everything from my ongoing war with Mab to my weird relationship with Bria to the new Mercedes that he'd decided to give Eva for Christmas. To my surprise, it felt good to talk to Owen, to just be with him, sex or not.

And it scared the hell out of me.

I wasn't sure if I wanted that kind of relationship with him. My former lover, Detective Donovan Caine, had burned me a little more than I'd let on to Owen or anyone else. Donovan had just never been able to accept my past as the Spider and all the bad things that I'd done over the years, all the people that I'd killed for money, survival, or something else. No matter how much he might have wanted to be with me.

I didn't want to look into Owen's violet eyes one day and see the things that I'd seen in Donovan's golden gaze. I didn't want to look at Owen and realize that my bloody past and sharp skills disturbed him the way they had Donovan.

I didn't want Owen to hate me like Donovan had.

Owen murmured something in his sleep and rolled over onto his back. I hesitated, then bent forward and traced my fingers down the side of his face. A hint of dark stubble pricked my skin, but not in an unpleasant way. Owen leaned into my touch and sighed, as though it comforted him.

I quickly withdrew my hand, not wanting to wake him or think too much about the warm softness that flared in my chest whenever I was near him. A dodged, determined, creeping sort of softness that I was struggling more and more to squash—or at least contain before it infected what little was left of my cold, black heart.

Donovan had hurt me when he'd left Ashland. But losing Owen the same way? For the same reasons? I was beginning to think that might just break me completely.

Still, I stared at Owen a moment more before turning and slipping out of the bedroom.

I spent the day cooking at the Pork Pit, the barbecue restaurant that I operated in downtown Ashland. Then I went home to change and get ready for my evening with Vinnie Volga, the Ice elemental who seemed to be part of whatever trap Mab was baiting for me, for the Spider. Just after nine that night, I pulled my Benz into the parking lot of Northern Aggression.

As its name suggested, the nightclub was located in the heart of Northtown, where it catered to some of Ashland's wealthiest citizens—or anyone who had enough cash or plastic to pay for the hedonistic delights offered inside. Blood, drugs, sex, smokes, alcohol, and everything in between. You could get it all at Northern Aggression, in whatever quantities or combinations that you wanted, for the right price.

The outside of the club wasn't much to look at, just another ordinary, warehouse-like building with a sign over the front door, that grayed out and faded into the rest of the immaculate Northtown landscape. If you'd driven by Northern Aggression during the day, you might have thought that the club was some anonymous office full of corporate drones sitting in their tiny cubicles and talking on their headsets.

But at night the place and the people inside it came alive in all sorts of ways.

I parked my Benz in one of the side lots that flanked the building, got out, and headed for the front door. An enormous neon sign hung over the entrance—a giant heart with an arrow through it. Roslyn Phillips's personal rune and the symbol for her decadent nightclub. The sign glowed red, then yellow, then orange in the night, bathing the dozens of people waiting in line below it in its bright, suggestive light.

Xavier, the guy who was Roslyn's main squeeze, stood outside the door, deciding who got into the club and who was left standing out in the cold. The giant bouncer stood roughly seven feet tall, with a strong, muscled body to match. His black eyes and shaved head both gleamed like polished onyx underneath the glare of the neon heart-and-arrow sign. Xavier held a large clipboard in his hands, checking off names on his list and taking the occasional C-note bribe to lift the red velvet rope and allow people to go inside the club.

I strolled to the front of the line, past all the men sporting sharp suits and the women wearing as little as they could bear given the chill in the December air. A few of the women gave me pointed, dirty looks, especially since I wasn't dressed for a night of clubbing.

Instead of a thigh-high miniskirt or a leather bustier, I wore my usual ensemble—dark jeans, heavy boots, a long-sleeved T-shirt, and a black fleece jacket. Since it was almost Christmas, I'd donned one of my more festive

T-shirts to celebrate—thick crimson cotton with a giant candy cane in the middle of my chest. The fabric was dark enough that Vinnie Volga's blood wouldn't stand out on it—much. Happy holidays.

And, as always, I carried my usual five-point arsenal on me as well. Two silverstone knives up my sleeves, two more in my boots, and one tucked away in the small of my back. Never left home without 'em. Not even if I was supposedly retired these days. So far, this so-called taking it easy had been far more dangerous than being the Spider full-time ever was.

I stepped in front of Xavier. "Hey, there, handsome," I drawled. "Know where I can find a party tonight?"

Xavier grinned, his white teeth gleaming in his face underneath the burning glow of the neon light. "I thought the party was always wherever you were at, Gin."

I grinned back at him. "True. But I thought that I'd branch out a little tonight. Can we talk a second?"

I jerked my head at Xavier and walked a few feet away from the front door. The giant followed me. Several people waiting in line let out soft curses, but one look at my cold, hard face and even colder eyes was enough to get them to shut their mouths.

Xavier also glowered and cracked his massive knuckles at the impatient crowd for good measure. Suddenly, nobody was even looking in our direction, much less muttering under their breath about the delay. None of the rich yuppies standing in line wanted to mess with a seven-foot-tall giant. Especially not with Xavier, who also moonlighted as a member of the Ashland Police Department. As fate would have it, he also happened to be my sister, Bria's, partner. Ah, the irony. Always out to get me.

"Did Finn call you earlier?" I asked the giant in a low voice. "He was supposed to mention that I was coming by tonight to talk to Vinnie."

Xavier nodded, his face dark and serious. The giant was one of the people who knew that I was the assassin the Spider. A few weeks ago, I'd helped Roslyn Phillips deal with Elliot Slater, the sick, twisted, giant bastard who'd been stalking her. Slater had been working up to raping and killing Roslyn, before she and I had made him dead first. Something that had ensured that Xavier was my friend for life, since he cared about Roslyn more than anything. He realized that talking was probably the last thing that I was going to do with Vinnie, but he didn't even blink at the subtle threat in my words.

"Yeah," Xavier said. "Finn called Roslyn earlier and told her about the situation. Finn's already here, and Roslyn's inside waiting for you too."

I hesitated. "How's she doing?"

Shadows further blackened Xavier's eyes, and worry tightened his face. "She has good days and bad days, you know? It's still too soon to tell, I think."

I still remembered how Roslyn had looked the night that I'd found her tied to a bed at Slater's mountain mansion. Slater especially liked beating women, and he'd already reduced Roslyn's beautiful face and body to pulpy mush by the time that I got there. Not to mention the damage that he'd already done to the vampire's psyche by stalking and terrorizing her beforehand. Roslyn had been bruised, bloody, and utterly broken—and about to be raped by one of Slater's men. It was a horrible, sickening image that I'd never, ever forget.

I'd killed the man assaulting Roslyn, cut her free, and then used some of Jo-Jo Deveraux's healing supplies to patch her up enough so she could walk out of Slater's bedroom. Killing the bastard who'd been about to rape the vampire had been easy. But putting my hands on Roslyn that night, even if it had been only to rub healing ointment on her, had been one of the hardest things I'd ever done. Because I knew that being touched was probably the last thing in the world that Roslyn had wanted then, especially since I was the reason she'd been beaten in the first place. But it had to be done to save her, and I'd made myself do it.

The way that I had so many other cold, black, hard, ugly things over the years.

"And how are you holding up?" I asked Xavier in a soft voice.

The giant gave me a small smile, but it didn't even come close to reaching his eyes. "Good days and bad days, right along with her."

I knew about those too, and I put my hand on his arm. Xavier nodded and looked away.

After a moment, Xavier cleared his throat. He stepped back over to the club, lowered the red velvet rope, and gestured for me to go inside. I nodded my thanks and stepped through the door.

It was like walking into another world. While the outside of Northern Aggression might have been bland and featureless, the inside was all rich, elegant decadence. Everything was meant to provide as much visual pleasure as possible, from the bamboo floor, to the crushed red velvet drapes that covered the walls, to the elaborate Ice bar that hugged the dance floor. The men and women who made up the nightclub staff circulated through the crowd, bearing trays filled with chocolate-dipped strawberries, fresh oysters, and tall glasses of chilled champagne. They too wore as little as was legal, showing off their hard bodies and killer curves. Most of them were vampires, all of them were hookers, and every single one wore a necklace with the heart-and-arrow rune dangling from the end of the chain, letting clubgoers know that they were on the menu too.

One waiter put down his tray, took the hand of a giggling woman, and led her toward the stairs that ran up the back wall. The second floor of Northern Aggression featured rooms that could be rented out for however long you wanted, for those who were a bit shy about fucking in the booths or underneath the tables that filled the back of the club.

I skirted around the mass of people writhing on the dance floor to a rocking song by The Pretenders and headed deeper into the club, looking for Finn. After about three minutes, I spotted him sitting with Roslyn Phillips in a booth in the back. Finn was drinking a martini, while a glass of blood sat in front of Roslyn. It took me a minute to maneuver through the thick, gyrating crowd and slide into the opposite side of the booth from them.

Finn's green eyes took in my jeans, fleece jacket, and T-shirt. "Geez, Gin," he drawled. "Couldn't you put on something a little nicer? We are at a club, you know. The finest club in all of Ashland."

Unlike my casual attire, Finn sported a dapper suit in a smoke gray color with a silver dress shirt and a matching tie. His sharp clothes only made him look that much more handsome, as did his perfectly styled hair. Finnegan Lane didn't believe in dressing down—ever. He would have happily worn a three-piece suit to bed, if only it wouldn't have gotten in the way of his nightly seduction of whatever sweet young thing he was currently romancing.

"Sorry," I said. "Unlike you, I plan on getting my hands dirty before the night is through, along with my clothes. Unless you'd prefer to be the one who talks to Vinnie?"

"Are you kidding? This is a Fiona Fine original suit." Finn smoothed down his designer tie and shuddered at the thought of blood marring the slick, expensive fabric.

Beside him, Roslyn let out a soft laugh at our bickering. I turned my attention to the vampire.

It always struck me how very beautiful she was. Even in the semidarkness of the club, she was easily the most striking woman here. Her eyes and skin were a rich, toffee color, and her black feathered hair just brushed the edge of her strong jaw. Silver glasses perched on the end of her perfect nose, and she wore a fitted pantsuit in a mint green color that showed off her exceptional figure. Great breasts, flat stomach, toned legs. The vampire had a body that most women would kill for, and she knew how to make the very most of it.

For years Roslyn had worked as a hooker on the mean Southtown streets before saving enough money to open up her own gin joint here at Northern Aggression. The madam had retired from hooking herself and was now strictly in management. She ran her own string of high-end call girls and guys out of the club and made wads of cash doing it. Still, even though she was out of that part of the business, more than a few men and women stared in Roslyn's direction, hoping to attract her gaze to their own hungry eyes.

I carefully examined her lovely features, but no marks of Slater's final, vicious attack on her remained, thanks to Jo-Jo Deveraux's healing magic. But I knew that Roslyn had scars on the inside—raw, ugly, fresh scars that might never, ever heal. Just like the spider runes on my palms would forever remind me of the night that my family had been murdered.

I stared at Roslyn a moment longer before turning and gesturing at the closest waitress. "Gin and tonic. And go easy on the tonic."

The waitress nodded and moved off into the crowd.

Finn took a drink of his martini. "About time you showed up. I've been here almost an hour already."

I shrugged. "I had to work late at the Pork Pit. We were slammed with party orders."

A few days before Christmas, and every business in Ashland was rushing to cram in their office party before everyone took off for the holiday. Sophia Deveraux and I had been cooking nonstop today, whipping up dozens of barbecue beef and pork platters, gallons of beans, mounds of French fries, buckets of coleslaw, and more. In addition to serving our regular walk-in customers.

I loved cooking, loved playing with the never-ending combinations of sweet and salty and sour. The simple process of stirring ingredients together to create something new soothed me the way that mixing bright colors would a painter. But as much as I enjoyed cooking and running the restaurant, even I was a little sick right now of peeling potatoes, shredding cabbage, and making vats of Fletcher Lane's secret barbecue sauce.

The waitress came back with my drink. I tasted the gin, feeling the cold liquor slide down my throat before it started its slow, sweet burn in my stomach.

Finn, Roslyn, and I sipped our drinks. The music of the club thumped around us, and the smell of smoke, sweat, and sex filled the air.

"So," I said after I'd drained the rest of my gin. "How are you, Roslyn?"

The vampire arched one of her perfect eyebrows. "You're actually pausing and making small talk first? Instead of immediately demanding to know everything that I know about Vinnie Volga? You're getting soft in your old age, Gin."

I winced. I hadn't always been kind to Roslyn in the past, mainly because I'd been too upset about Fletcher Lane's murder to cut the vampire much slack. The vamp talking about my being an assassin to the wrong people was one of the things that had led to the old man's death. But we'd bonded while I'd been plotting on how best to kill Elliot Slater, and I'd started thinking of Roslyn as a friend. I didn't have many of those, so each one was important to me. Looked like she didn't feel the same way, though. The knowledge stung a little more than I thought it would. So did the sharp bit of longing that went with it. It wasn't an emotion I often experienced, mainly because it always made me feel weak and needy—two things that I absolutely hated.

"Sorry," I mumbled. "If you want to get right down to things . . ."

A small smile lifted Roslyn's lips. "Relax. I'm just teasing you, Gin."

Her soft voice somehow made me feel even worse than before.

The vampire took a sip of her blood and leaned back against the booth. "As for how I'm doing, okay, I guess. Still trying to figure things out. Some days, I'm fine. Others, I can't even breathe. And nightmares. I'm having a lot of nightmares. Most of them involve Slater walking through the front door of the club, grabbing me, and beating me to death on the dance floor."

Roslyn's voice was cold, flat, and calm, just the way it had been the day that she'd told me that Slater was stalking her, that the giant was making her pretend to be his girlfriend while he worked himself up to raping and killing her. It made my heart ache for her that much more.

I knew all about nightmares. I'd had more than my share over my years, but especially since Fletcher's murder a few months ago. Living on the streets, Fletcher taking me in, my earliest days with the old man and Finn. I'd dreamed about all that and more. It was like the old man's death had opened up a floodgate of emotion deep inside me, one that I could close during the day but still had problems dealing with at night—at least until I woke up in a cold sweat, my mouth open in a silent scream.

"It'll get better." An easy lie that I'd told too many times to too many people over the years—especially myself.

"Really?" Roslyn whispered, doubt filling her toffee eyes.

I shrugged. "Well, Slater's dead and burning in hell right now. He's never going to bother you again, so it's not going to get worse. I can promise you that much."

She gave me another small smile. "I guess that will have to do for now."

It always did in Ashland.

We sat there for a few more minutes. My eyes scanned the crowd, looking through the faces, before moving on to whom I was really here to see tonight—Vinnie Volga.

One of the main features at Northern Aggression was the elaborate Ice bar that took up a good portion of one of the walls. The bar was a single, solid sheet of elemental Ice with a variety of runes carved into the frosty surface. Suns and stars mostly, symbolizing life and joy. The runes glittered like diamond chips in the Ice, making it seem more like a beautiful work of art than a functional, work- ing bar. But the Ice more than held up to all the people who sat next to and leaned on it, and the others who clustered three deep in some places waiting to get their latest round of liquid courage.

My gaze locked onto the man standing behind the bar—the Ice elemental responsible for making sure his creation stayed in one piece for the night.

Vinnie Volga had swarthy features—tan skin and a mop of curly hair that could only be described as dirty brown. A neat, trimmed goatee covered his pointed chin, although his mouth and forehead both had a pinched look to them, as though he was constantly worried about something. Vinnie was short for a guy, only about my height, five seven or so, with a thin, wiry body.

But the most striking thing about Vinnie was his eyes, which glowed blue-white in the semidarkness, thanks to his elemental magic. Vinnie held on to his Ice power at all times, even while mixing and serving up drinks. He had to keep feeding a small, steady trickle of magic into the bar, or his creation would start to melt, given all the bodies and heat packed into the club.

It's rare that an elemental can use his magic without other elementals sensing it, and Vinnie wasn't trying to hide what he was doing. Even across the room, I could feel the cool caress of his power call out to me. It made me want to reach for my own Ice magic and let the cold energy fill every part of my being, but I pushed the longing aside. I wasn't letting the bartender know that I had any kind of magic—until it was too late.

"So tell me about Vinnie," I asked Roslyn.

The vampire's eyes tracked my gaze across the club to where the bartender stood, shaking up another round of martinis. She shrugged. "Not much to tell. He's worked for me for a couple of years now. Emigrated here from Russia with his daughter. The mother died in Russia before they came to the States. Very quiet, keeps to himself. A hard worker. Always on time. Doesn't seem that interested in my girls, but he'll go out with one occasionally. I've never had any problems with him. He comes in, makes sure the bar is in one piece, mixes drinks, takes a few quick breaks to go check on his daughter, and leaves. He's the best bartender that I've ever had. I'd really hate to lose him."

I gave her a cool look. After a moment, Roslyn nodded. "But if it can't be avoided, I suppose that I can find another Ice elemental to take over for him," she said. "What I really want to know is if Vinnie's spying for Mab Monroe. If he is, he's out. Nobody who works for Mab is going to be on my staff or welcome in my club—ever."

Roslyn's toffee eyes glittered with anger, and her mouth flattened into a hard, ugly slash in her beautiful face. The vampire had just as much reason to hate Mab as I did, because Mab had been Elliot Slater's boss, the one who pulled all his crazy, twisted strings. The Fire elemental had known that Slater was stalking and terrorizing Roslyn, and she'd done nothing to stop it. As long as Slater had done Mab's bidding, she hadn't cared what he did to anyone else—or who got hurt in the process.

"What about Vinnie's Ice magic?" I asked. "Will that be a problem?"

"He has enough to keep the bar in one piece," Roslyn said. "But I think that's about it. I've never seen him do anything else with it. He's certainly not as strong as you are."

I shifted in the booth. Everybody always said how *strong* my magic was, like it was something to be proud of. But I knew that I wasn't that powerful. Alexis James. Tobias Dawson. Elliot Slater. Each one of them had come far too close to killing me in the last few months for me to believe that I was invincible. Death came to us all in the end, no matter how tough we thought we were.

Still, every time someone commented on my magic, I couldn't stop this uncomfortable shiver that swept through my body. It was like they were all setting me up for the fall that I knew was coming up fast on the day that I went toe-to-toe with Mab with my magic.

And lost.

"So can we get on with this?" Finn asked, his green eyes locked onto a redhead gyrating on the edge of the dance floor. "Because if we hurry, we can still learn everything that Vinnie knows before closing. Which would leave me plenty of time to find someone to keep me warm for the rest of the night. You wouldn't want me to be lonely, now, would you?"

I rolled my eyes. Finn's propensity to think with his dick first was going to get him into deep trouble one day. Especially since he didn't mind seducing women who were already taken. He saw a wedding ring as a challenge more than anything else. I always found it amazing that some angry husband hadn't hired me to kill Finn long ago.

But my foster brother was right. It was time to get on with things. The sooner we squeezed Vinnie for info, the sooner I could start planning how to find and take out LaFleur—before she found me first.

I'd just started to slide out of the booth when a peculiar ripple in the crowd caught my eye. A wave of people parted for someone in their midst. A moment later, a woman stepped up to the Ice bar in the exact spot where Vinnie was serving drinks.

A petite, slender woman with a short bob of glossy black hair. A wide headband of flat emeralds held her hair back off her face, so that everyone could get a good look at her delicate features. The gems winked at me underneath the black lights of the club.

Unlike me, she was dressed for a night out on the town. A tight, black, sleeveless top showed off her creamy, muscled arms, while a lime green miniskirt hugged her bony ass. Black leather boots with stiletto heels crawled up to her knees. She didn't appear to be carrying any weapons, unless she had a couple of knives tucked into her boots. But given what I'd seen her do with her electrical magic last night, she didn't really need any.

She leaned against the Ice bar and said something to Vinnie, whose head snapped up from the martinis he was making. His jaw dropped open at the sight of her and, for a moment, the blue-white glow of his Ice magic completely vanished from his eyes before sparking and sputtering back to life. The bartender's shocked reaction was understandable.

After all, he was talking to LaFleur.

✵ 5 ✵

"Fuck." I let out a soft curse.

"What are you—" Finn's eyes narrowed. "Wait a minute. Is that who I think it is?"

I nodded. "That would be her. LaFleur."

Finn let out his own curse.

Roslyn looked back and forth between the two of us. "LaFleur? As in the assassin that you guys think Mab hired to come to Ashland and kill Gin?"

"The one and the same," Finn murmured, his green gaze on the other woman. "And she's talking to Vinnie."

The three of us stared at them. LaFleur crooked her finger at Vinnie, who swallowed before moving forward. LaFleur leaned across the Ice bar a little more and whispered something into his ear. Whatever she said, it wasn't good, because Vinnie's blue-white Ice magic leaked out of his eyes once more. LaFleur was breaking his concentration with her words.

I tensed, my thumb tracing over the hilt of the silverstone knife that I'd palmed under the booth table. I wondered if the other assassin was going to kill Vinnie right here, right now, in the middle of the nightclub since no one had shown up for her staged meeting last night. Because the Spider hadn't made an appearance like LaFleur had wanted me to. She could easily kill Vinnie. One blast of the assassin's electrical elemental magic would be enough to cut through any Icy defense that the bartender might be able to muster.

That's how elementals fought—by flinging their raw power, their raw magic, at each other. By measuring their strength against each other. Dueling each other, until one person weakened, and the other's magic washed over the loser and killed her. Suffocated by Air, burned by Fire, frozen by Ice, encased in Stone. The end result for the weaker elemental was never a good one, and death by elemental magic was never pretty, easy, or painless.

But instead of forming a ball of green lightning in her hand and shoving it into Vinnie's face, LaFleur did a most curious thing. She patted the Ice elemental on the cheek, gave him a sly wink and a sexy smirk, then turned and disappeared into the crowd.

Leaving him alone and unharmed.

Vinnie blinked, then sagged against the bar as though his body were made out of water and he were melting all over the place. He stayed like that for about thirty seconds, before a waitress stepped up in the spot where LaFleur had been and slid her empty tray over to him. The waitress said something, probably telling him about her latest order. Vinnie shook his head, then picked up his martini shaker once more. But the blue-white magic flickering in his eyes was weak, dim, and faint. Whatever LaFleur had said to him, it had utterly demoralized the Ice elemental.

Since Vinnie wasn't going anywhere, I tracked LaFleur's movements through the crowd. To my surprise, the assassin headed toward the front door. Leaving. She was actually leaving. It was too good an opportunity to pass up. I wanted to see where she was off to in such a hurry.

"Watch Vinnie," I told Finn, slipping out of the booth. "Call me on my cell phone if he makes a move to leave. I want to see if LaFleur's here with anyone."

"Gin?" Finn said.

I looked at him.

"Be careful." Concern filled his face, and I knew he was thinking about LaFleur's magic. What we'd seen her do with it last night and what she might do to me tonight.

I flashed him a grin. "Don't worry about me. I always come back, Finn."

I just hoped this time it wouldn't be in a pine box.

I didn't immediately charge through the crowd after La-Fleur. Because if I were her, I would have a couple of guys stationed in the nightclub keeping an eye on Vinnie, seeing who might wander over to talk to him, and most especially who might be interested in following the assassin outside. So my first move was to make a detour by the Ice bar.

I walked down the length of it, weaving in and out of the clusters of people. Everyone was laughing, talking, drinking, and necking, so it was easy enough for me to grab a martini that a dwarf was blindly reaching for before his stubby fingers closed over it. I also swiped a pack of cigarettes and a lighter off the bar that belonged to a giant who had his back turned to them. Props in hand, I headed for the front door and stepped outside.

The night had grown even colder while I'd been in the club, and now bits of hard snow gusted along, pushed on by a breeze that slapped my cheeks and cut straight through my jeans, T-shirt, and fleece jacket. But the cold hadn't driven anyone away. The line to get inside had doubled since I'd arrived.

Xavier stood in his same spot by the door, clipboard still in hand. The giant didn't even glance up as LaFleur strolled by him. He was too busy herding the mass of people in front of him inside to care about who was leaving early.

The assassin skirted around Xavier and set off across the parking lot. Keeping one eye on her, I paused right outside the entrance long enough to light a cigarette and make sure that my martini glass was up where everyone could see it so people would think that I was here to party, despite my dressed down clothes. I also ran a hand through my dark chocolate brown hair, mussing it up, as though I'd already had a hell of a good time inside.

Then I headed in LaFleur's general direction, my steps slow and wobbly, my body swaying from side to side. Just another tipsy smoker desperate for a nicotine fix and getting some fresh air before I went back inside the club for another drink, another fuck, or whatever I was indulging in tonight. An easy enough role for an assassin to play and one that I'd used for camouflage dozens of times over the years.

I'd taken only ten lazy steps away from the building before LaFleur stopped at the edge of the parking lot. I paused as well, ambling back and forth on the fringes of a group of smokers huddled together for warmth, keeping close enough to them to look like I belonged there. Just another face in the crowd sucking down her cancer stick as fast as she could.

LaFleur stood in the shadow of a weeping willow tree, its long, delicate, swaying tendrils just brushing the top of her emerald headband. She put her back to the tree and turned to face the entrance to Northern Aggression once more. She examined everything, from the people waiting in line, to the group of smokers that I was standing with, to the flashing heart-and-arrow sign above the building. The assassin took it all in, analyzing everything just the way that I would have, looking for any threats to her, anything suspicious, unusual, or out of the ordinary.

I was glad that I'd stopped at the bar for my props. Otherwise, the other assassin would have spotted me storming out of the club after her. And then, well, things would have gotten interesting.

But LaFleur didn't see me or anything else that threatened her. Her watchful stance relaxed, and she made herself a little more comfortable against the tree, just leaning the tops of her shoulders against it, instead of the full length of her slender body.

And then she waited.

Ten . . . twenty . . . forty-five . . . I counted off the seconds in my head. LaFleur didn't move a muscle for three minutes. She could have been a statue planted under the tree for all the emotion she showed. I frowned. So not only did she have deadly electrical magic but LaFleur could be patient as well—just as patient as I could be. Mab Monroe had chosen her assassin very wisely.

I wondered what LaFleur was waiting for, though. Had she told Vinnie Volga to break away from his station at the Ice bar and come outside and meet her? Because the way he'd reacted to her had told me that Vinnie knew exactly how dangerous the assassin was. Did she really think that the bartender would want to be alone in the dark with her? Especially after her little trap down at the docks had failed to net her the Spider?

But Vinnie didn't come outside, and five minutes and three horrible, disgusting cigarettes later, I got my answer as to what LaFleur was doing lurking outside Northern Aggression.

A black stretch limo rolled through the parking lot, coming to a stop in front of her. The assassin pushed away from the weeping willow and straightened, her hands loose and open by her sides, but she made no move to step forward toward the rumbling car. My eyes narrowed. Whom was she meeting now? And why?

The driver scurried out of the front seat of the limo and ran around to the back. He opened the door and stuck his hand inside the dark depths. He helped a woman out and to her feet, then bowed and stepped back. I recognized her at once. As if I could ever forget her.

Mab Monroe.

Mab looked like she either had been or was going out for the night. The Fire elemental wore a long black evening gown with a strapless, sweetheart neckline. A matching black fur wrap was draped around her creamy shoulders.

The paleness of her skin contrasted with her hair, which was the bright, polished red of a new penny. It curled softly to her shoulders. But Mab's eyes were her most striking feature. They were even blacker than her dress and looked like two pieces of hard jet set into her milky face.

My gaze fell to the Fire elemental's throat. As always, she wore her signature rune necklace—a large ruby set in a ring of curvy, gold rays. The diamond cutting on the gold caught the light from the neon sign outside the club and made it seem that the rays were actually flickering, that they were real, burning flames. No wonder, since the necklace represented a sunburst. The symbol for fire. Mab's personal rune, used by her alone. She never went anywhere without it, just as I never left home without my silverstone knives.

I watched as Mab approached LaFleur. The assassin bowed her head respectfully to Mab, but she never took her eyes off the Fire elemental, not even for a second. LaFleur might be working for Mab, but she didn't trust her. Smart girl.

The two women put their heads together and started talking. I was too far away to hear what they were saying, and Mab wasn't the sort of person you just walked up to in the dark. I couldn't move any closer to them without attracting attention to myself. At least, not without circling all the way around the back of the club and coming at them from a different angle. Knowing my luck, they'd probably be long gone by the time I did that.

What I really wanted to know was what the hell the Fire elemental was doing outside Roslyn's club. As far as

I knew, Mab had never come here before. She and the drunk yuppies who frequented Northern Aggression didn't exactly run in the same circles.

So why would she meet LaFleur out here in the open instead of somewhere more private? What was going on between the two of them? And how much was it going to fuck up my plans to kill the Fire elemental sooner rather than later?

In the pocket of my jeans, my cell phone let out a low, steady buzz. Still pretending to be nothing more than a drunk smoker, I ambled away from the group of people that I'd been standing next to. My phone kept vibrating, so I dug it out and flipped it open.

"What?" I growled.

"We've got a problem," Finn said in my ear. "Vinnie left the bar. At least, he tried to. He didn't get five steps before three guys came out of the crowd, surrounded him, and helped him on his way."

So that's why LaFleur had come back outside Northern Aggression so quickly. She'd left her men behind inside the nightclub to watch Vinnie in case he decided to bolt. Just as I would have.

"They went out through a side door," Finn said. "From the looks of them, I think they're going to take Vinnie for a walk that he won't come back from—ever."

As I stood there listening to Finn, I kept staring at LaFleur and Mab. Emotions surged through me, and for a moment, I considered palming my silverstone knives, sprinting toward the two women, and stabbing them to death. Mab didn't have any of her usual giant guards with her. No backup, nothing. This was my chance to finally kill her. To do to her what she'd done to my family all those years ago.

My whole body burned with the need to kill her—right here, right now. *Enemy, enemy, enemy*, a primal little voice muttered in the back of my head. *Here is your enemy. In the open. Exposed. Vulnerable. Kill her now, before she leaves. Before she hurts anyone else that you love.*

But I forced the hot, aching, greedy, reckless rage aside and buried it under the cold, inescapable logic of the situation. Because the part of me that was the Spider—the cold, hard, rational, ruthless part of me that would always be the Spider—realized that attacking Mab now would be suicide.

LaFleur would be tricky enough to take out by myself. First of all, she was an assassin, trained, skilled, and deadly, just like me. She hadn't earned her stellar reputation by being weak or sloppy. But even more important than that was the fact that her electrical elemental magic had felt just as strong as my Ice and Stone power. Face-to-face, I didn't know which one of us would win. Besides, even if I killed LaFleur, that would still leave Mab to deal with. I wouldn't survive a fight with both of them—not at the same time. Together, their magic was just greater than my own.

Even if I'd been reckless enough to attack the two women, they made my decision for me. Mab gestured to LaFleur, and the two of them walked over to the waiting limo and slid into the back. A moment later, the long car pulled out of the parking lot and disappeared into the cold night. My enemies would live to see another day. And so would I.

Equal parts relief and frustration filled me. I sighed, and my breath frosted in the night air.

"Gin?" Finn's voice murmured in my ear. "Are you listening to me? LaFleur's men have Vinnie. What do you want to do?"

I snapped out of my reverie. "Tell me which way they went. LaFleur might be gone, but I still plan on having a little chat with Vinnie tonight."

❖ 6 ❖

I stubbed out my latest cigarette, walked into the parking lot, and left the pack and lighter on the hood of the closest car, along with my martini glass.

"They went out the west side," Finn said. "Through the door next to the hall that leads to the VIP rooms."

Following Finn's directions, I headed through the parking lot, slipping past rows of cars, and moving at an angle past the long line of people still waiting to get into Northern Aggression. I finally rounded the side of the building and reached one of the far parking lots. Sure enough, I spotted a group of men up ahead of me.

Vinnie Volga stood in the middle of the group, a man on either side of him, their hands on his arms, forcibly walking him somewhere. Another guy in front led the way. Every few steps, Vinnie would jerk against his captors, trying to break free, but it was no use. Both men were giants, judging by their bulky, seven-foot frames, and giants were incredibly strong, with grips like steel vises. The only way that Vinnie could wrench free from them would be to tear his own arms off in the process.

They were about two hundred feet ahead of me. I let out a soft curse and quickened my pace. I needed to get to them before they got into a car. Otherwise, I'd never see Vinnie again—alive anyway.

To my surprise, the three men didn't herd the bartender into a waiting vehicle. Instead, they reached the edge of the nightclub parking lot and kept right on walking down the street. I frowned. Where were they taking Vinnie?

"Gin? What's happening?" Finn asked.

"They're on foot," I told Finn. "Still heading west. What else is out here?"

Through the phone, I could hear the roar of the club's rocking music and Finn having some sort of muffled conversation. He must still be sitting in the booth with Roslyn.

"Roslyn says that there's a park about half a mile down the road," Finn said. "She's taken Catherine there a few times."

Catherine was Roslyn's young niece, whom the vampire adored.

"Ask her what's there," I said.

Finn murmured something else to Roslyn. Ahead of me, the men kept walking, and I kept following them, moving from the shadow of one car to the next.

"Roslyn says there's a playground with a swing set, a sandbox, and some other stuff for kids. Lots of trees, too. It wouldn't be a bad place to have a quiet little chat with someone this late at night."

"Especially if you didn't want to get blood in your car," I murmured. "Our new friends are headed in that direction. They don't seem to be in a particular hurry, so I'm going to amble along behind them. It might be nice if you could come out and join the party."

"Roger that," Finn said. "On my way."

We both hung up. I stuffed the phone back into my jeans pocket. When I reached the edge of the parking lot, I stopped, half-hidden behind a large SUV. The group of men herding Vinnie along had already crossed the street and were busy cutting through another parking lot on the other side that flanked two more industrial-looking buildings.

I shook my sleeve, and a silverstone knife slid into my hand. The hilt of the weapon rested against the spider rune scar branded into my palm. The blade was as familiar to me as my own face, and a natural extension of myself in so many ways. And now, it was time for the Spider to hunt with it once more.

A cold smile curved my lips as I stepped into the waiting darkness.

There wasn't nearly as much cover as I would have liked, but it was easy enough for me to slide from shadow to shadow without the giants seeing me. Besides, they weren't the most observant of men, more interested in making sure that Vinnie didn't break free and bolt than worried about who might be watching them. The two giants holding the bartender shot a couple of cursory looks over their broad shoulders, but that was about it. Sloppy, sloppy, sloppy.

Their casual inattention was going to be the death of them—real soon.

After several minutes of walking, the men reached the edge of the park that Finn had mentioned. An iron gate curved over the entrance, and a maple tree rune set in the middle of the design denoted it as a park, along with the name Green Acres. Just the place that I wanted to be. Old-fashioned iron streetlights lined a cobblestone walkway that led farther into the park.

I cocked my head to one side and reached for my Stone magic, listening to every part of the element around me, from the pavement and sidewalks that I'd just left behind to the cobblestones stretching out in front of me.

The pavement and sidewalks behind me only whispered of the steady grind of traffic, while the cobblestones ahead gave off low, quiet murmurs of the wind rustling in the trees, the *pit-pat* of small, eager feet, and the easy lope of animals across the grass. This was the sort of place that families came to enjoy a picnic lunch or an afternoon in the summer sun. Nothing else.

So I waited until the men were about two hundred feet in front of me, deep into the park, before following them.

I stayed off the well-lit path, instead moving from tree to tree, and keeping the men within sight. As I skulked, I also kept an eye out for LaFleur. Just because the assassin had gotten into a limo with Mab didn't mean that she wasn't meeting up with her men later. Hell, she could be on her way here right now. LaFleur might want the pleasure of killing Vinnie herself. Some assassins were twisted like that, and she'd certainly seemed to enjoy frying the dwarf with her electrical magic last night.

Finally, the men reached their destination—the playground that Finn had told me about. Since this was Northtown, the playground was a monstrous, elaborate affair, with at least ten swings, several seesaws, a large merry-go-round, and a sandbox that was almost big enough to be its own private beach. The metal gleamed a dull silver underneath the white glow of the streetlights, while the sand glinted like gold. I slithered behind the thick trunk of a maple tree so that the swing set stood between me and the men.

The giants slung Vinnie down in the middle of the sandbox. The Ice elemental bartender did a header into the ground, his face plunging into the loose sand like he was an ostrich. After a moment, he flailed up onto his knees, coughing, choking, and trying to spit out the sand all at once.

And that's when the fun started.

The giants yanked Vinnie up and started hitting him, while the third man stood back and watched. *Thwack-thwack-thwack.* The giants held Vinnie up between them, so he couldn't even curl up tight and try to protect himself. Their massive, meaty fists slammed into his chest, his face, even his balls once or twice. Vinnie groaned with every blow.

After thirty seconds, Vinnie was in bad shape. At the minute mark, he looked like he'd been hit by a bus. By the time two minutes had passed, the bus had been joined by a couple of tractor trailers.

I thought about intervening, about jumping into the mix and stopping the torture. After all, I had questions for Vinnie—questions that he couldn't answer if he was dead. But the giants weren't going for broke just yet. They could easily have killed Vinnie with one blow to the head. Quick, efficient, mostly bloodless. But instead, they concentrated their fists on his chest, hitting him hard, but not with enough force to kill. Which meant that they only wanted him bleeding and broken, not dead. Not yet, anyway.

Finally, the giants finished beating Vinnie and dropped him into the sandbox. Vinnie let out another low groan and coughed up several mouthfuls of blood. The thick gobs gleamed like wet rubies against the gold, glittering sand. The giants moved back a few steps and stared down at him with their oversize, buglike eyes. Their ham-size fists hung loose and ready by their sides, just in case Vinnie had any misguided bit of fight left in him.

The third man, the one who'd been leading the way to the playground, stepped in front of Vinnie. I mentally dubbed him Mr. Brown because everything about him was a dark sable color, from his hair, skin, and eyes to the suit, tie, and shoes that he wore. He was much shorter than the other two goons, only about six feet tall, which meant that he wasn't a giant. He smiled, and I saw the fangs in his mouth. A vampire, then. One who wasn't big on personal hygiene, judging from the yellowish tint to his teeth.

"Vinnie, Vinnie, Vinnie," Brown drawled, pacing a loose circle around the bartender, his wingtips sinking into the blood-spattered sand. "What are we going to do with you? You know, you really disappointed LaFleur tonight."

"But I did exactly what she said," Vinnie sputtered. A thick Russian accent colored his voice.

Somehow, Vinnie pushed himself up onto his knees, swaying from side to side as he tried to maintain his balance and not pass out from the excruciating pain that he had to be feeling. Blood trickled down the left side of his face, where the giants had opened a cut high on his cheek, while his right eye had already started to blacken and swell from their hard blows. Sand crusted in his dark goatee and hair, and he had his arms wrapped around his middle, as if that would ease the pain in his sure-to-be-broken ribs.

"I told everyone at the bar about the shipment of drugs coming in. And I gave you the names of all the people who seemed interested, just like you asked. Every single one of them, I swear."

"Well, Vinnie, you must not have been convincing enough because the Spider didn't show last night like LaFleur thought she would," Brown said. "Which means that LaFleur couldn't kill the bitch like she's being paid to do. Like she promised Mab Monroe that she would."

Despite the blood, bruises, and sand covering his features, Vinnie's face paled a little more at the mention of the two women. He swallowed, his Adam's apple bouncing up and down like a yo-yo in his throat.

"Let me try again," he pleaded. "I will tell more people. Many more people. I swear it."

The vampire crossed his arms over his chest and sighed. "I don't know that I believe you, Vinnie. I mean, look what happened tonight. LaFleur comes by to have a little chat with you, to tell you that no one showed up, and what do you do? Wait five minutes, and then bolt for the nearest door. Your actions don't inspire a lot of confidence."

Vinnie didn't say anything, but his face took on a greenish tint underneath the bruises. So he'd tried to run after LaFleur had come by. And, in doing so, he'd brought about this little smackdown and hastened his own death. At least, that's what he would think.

But I knew that LaFleur had just been playing with the Ice elemental. She'd come by the club with the sole intention of spooking him into doing something stupid like running just so her men could beat him. I hadn't had a chance to read Fletcher's file on her yet, but I recognized the type of person, the kind of assassin, that LaFleur was—a sick, sadistic bitch who enjoyed playing with her food before she killed it.

"It's a real shame," Brown continued. "We all know what's at stake for you Vinnie—namely, your continued existence. I just never thought that you'd do something like this, especially given that sweet little daughter of yours at home. What's her name again?"

Vinnie's face tightened. "Natasha."

The vampire snapped his fingers. "Natasha. I have to say, the first time I saw her, I wasn't exactly concentrating on her name, if you know what I mean. But then again, I like them young like that."

The vampire let out a low, evil chuckle that told everyone exactly what he'd been thinking about doing to Natasha. The harsh sound made even my skin crawl. I'd been around the block more than my share of times. I'd seen a lot of bad people do a lot of bad things, myself included. But men like Brown, who got their rocks off hurting and abusing kids, well, there was a special place in hell for them. My hand tightened around the hilt of my knife.

Despite my being an assassin, I'd never taken any real pleasure in killing my targets. They were just jobs to me, obstacles to overcome, nothing more. But tonight, part of me was going to enjoy sending Brown on his merry way. I'd consider it a public service, like putting down a rabid animal before it could hurt anyone else.

"Please, I—" Vinnie started to plead for his life, but coughs racked his body. The Ice elemental doubled over, spewing up more blood.

The vampire's eyes tracked the blood, and he licked his lips at the sight. All vamps needed blood to live, of course. To them, it was just another form of food, nutrition, something that they craved the way that normal people did potato chips. If a vamp had a hankering for a cheeseburger, he'd get a frosty glass of O positive to wash it down with, instead of a triple chocolate milkshake like the rest of us.

And that wasn't all that drinking blood did for them; vamps could also siphon strength and magic out of it. Regular, old-fashioned human blood was enough to give any vampire a little something extra, like enhanced hearing and superlative eyesight. Those who drank giant and dwarven blood on a regular basis got the inherent strength that both of those races had. Just like vamps who sucked down elemental blood got the Air, Fire, Ice, or Stone power to go along with it, depending on whom they were drinking from. Then there were vamps who were elementals themselves, who already had the magic flowing through their veins, instead of having to steal the power from someone else's blood.

But Brown wasn't ready to sink his fangs into Vinnie

just yet, because he waited until the Ice elemental quit coughing and straightened back up before he continued his speech.

"Forget it, Vinnie," the vampire said. "It's too late for all that now. Tell me, what did you think you were going to do? Go home, get Natasha, and get out of Ashland? We've had men watching your apartment all night long. And once you tried to do your disappearing act, I took the liberty of calling my men and having them scoop her up, despite her babysitter's protests. You fucked up bigtime, Vinnie, by trying to run."

The bartender didn't respond, but anguish and tears filled his pale eyes.

"We came to you with a simple plan," Brown said. "Be Mab's eyes and ears inside Northern Aggression. Watch Roslyn Phillips. See who she hangs out with. Make a list of any woman close to Roslyn who could possibly be the Spider. Pass along the information about Mab's drug shipment in order to help us trap the Spider. But you just couldn't do that, could you, Vinnie?"

My eyes narrowed. So Mab had wanted Roslyn watched. Not surprising. As the Spider, I'd publicly taken credit for killing Elliot Slater, even though Roslyn was actually the one who'd pulled the trigger, using a shotgun to finish off the giant. But Mab must have reasoned that since I'd supposedly saved Roslyn that night, I must care about the vampire. That maybe even I was her friend—or at least someone who knew her. All of which meant that the Fire elemental was getting closer to learning who I really was, if she didn't know already.

Oh, Mab didn't know that Gin Blanco was the Spider. Otherwise, she would have tried to kill me herself by now. But I often wondered if she remembered Genevieve Snow, the little girl she'd tortured seventeen years ago—and the spider rune medallion that she'd melted into my palms. The jury was still out on that one. Mab had tortured and killed a lot of people since then. Must be hard for her to remember every single one of them. Still, the Fire elemental was hunting for me now, which just gave me more reason to off Mab and her minions sooner, rather than later.

Starting with the men in front of me.

"You didn't ask. You threatened me," Vinnie said in a low voice. "Threatened to kill me if I didn't do what you wanted. Natasha too."

Brown shrugged. "Details. But you owed Mab, remember? Through our mutual Russian friends, you approached her organization for a favor, and we helped get you and your little girl into the country, green cards and all."

"But I paid her," Vinnie protested. "I paid for all that. You took everything that we had to bring us over here."

The vampire ignored his words. "And now that Mab's trying to collect on that favor you owe her, what do you do? Run away the first chance you get. Shame on you, Vinnie. Shame on *you*."

So Mab and her mob connections had helped Vinnie and his daughter emigrate to Ashland from Russia, and the Fire elemental had decided it was time to collect—in spades. Despite Vinnie's betrayal of Roslyn, I could understand his motives. He'd only wanted to protect his daughter, to keep both of them safe. I might have done the same thing in his situation. Because I'd do anything for the people that I loved. Protect them, kill for them.

I was even going to die for them, for Bria, when I finally went up against Mab.

"Since you've been less than cooperative, Vinnie, Mab's decided to pull the plug on this whole operation. Starting with you."

Despite the chill in the air, sweat rolled down Vinnie's forehead, mixing with the blood on his face. "What about my little girl? What about Natasha? She didn't have anything to do with this. Please. Leave her alone."

Brown let out another low, evil laugh. "Like I said before, I like them young. So I'm going to go pay sweet little Natasha a nice, long visit, once we get through with you. After that, well, Mab has plans for her. Big plans. Mab's starting up a new venture, you see, something that will make Northern Aggression look as tame as a preschool, and Natasha will fit in just fine there. Why, she might just even be the star of the whole show, if you know what I mean."

Grief and rage and helpless anguish filled Vinnie's eyes, along with a faint flicker of blue-white magic. Even though he'd been severely beaten, the bartender wasn't completely out of things yet.

"*Das vidania*, Vinnie," the vampire smirked, flashing his fangs and getting ready to sink his teeth into the Ice elemental. "I'll be sure and say hello to your daughter for you—after I get through fucking her."

And that was my cue to finally make my presence known. I stepped out of the shadows, walked over to the swing set, and let out a loud wolf whistle. Startled, the men's heads snapped around to me. Brown bared his fangs, while the giants' hands tightened into fists. Vinnie stayed on his knees in the sandbox, his eyes wide with surprise, fear, and just a hint of Ice magic.

I walked toward them, stopping beside the metal swing set.

The vampire's eyes narrowed as he took in my dark clothes and the silverstone knife in my hand. "Who the hell are you?"

I gave him a cold, hard smile. "The bitch who's here to kill you."

✲ 7 ✲

Recognition dawned in Brown's eyes. "You! You're *her*. You're the fucking Spider!"

"Guilty as charged," I said, flashing my knife at him. "And I'm ready to play. How about you?"

Instead of racing toward me like I thought he might, the vampire actually did the smart thing. He pointed at the giants.

"Kill her!" he yelled at them. "Now!"

The two giants charged me. Behind them, Brown started digging in his pants pocket, probably searching for his cell phone. Not good. I needed to get to the bastard before he could tell anyone else what was happening here, give someone a description of me, or worse, call for backup. Which meant that I had a minute, two tops, to take out the giants and kill the vampire.

A cold blast of magic surged through the night air, and a blue-white light flashed for a second before winking out.

Vinnie Volga reared up, a jagged Ice knife glinting in his right hand. A weapon that I'd made myself many times. Crude, but effective, as Vinnie no doubt knew since he slammed the shard of Ice into the vampire's thigh, driving it in deep and twisting it as hard as he could. The vampire bellowed with rage and crumpled into the sand, all thoughts of his cell phone forgotten. Nice move. Vinnie threw himself on top of the other man, and the two of them started grappling, rolling around and around and spraying sand everywhere.

But I didn't have time to track their progress because the giants were on me. I waited until the first one was in range, then reached over and shoved one of the metal swings at him. The giant wasn't expecting the move, and the swing caught him in the chest. Not enough to hurt him, of course, but it gave me time to dart forward, hit all the chains, and make the swings start rocking back and forth, creating a moving metal maze behind me.

Instead of being smart and going around, the first giant barreled headfirst into the row of swings, long arms outstretched, trying to get to me before I slipped out the other side. But he misjudged the arcs and ended up with his arms stuck through the different swings, the metal chains crashing and clanging together like cymbals.

I grabbed onto a swinging chain and kicked up, then out, with my feet. My boots caught the giant in the shoulder, and he spun around, twisting the chains around his torso. Instead of spinning back the other way, the giant let out a loud roar and tried to do a Hulk move to break free. But the metal was stronger than it looked, and the chains held firm.

The momentum from my kick sent me back before gravity took over and I swung toward the giant again. I used the opportunity to bury my knife in his chest all the way up to the hilt. I felt the blade scuttle off of his breast-bone before sinking deeper into his hard muscle. I yanked it out. Not enough damage to kill him, but enough to make him think about how much he was hurting.

Sure enough, the giant howled with pain and rage, baying like a wolf at the moon. He brought his fist up to hit me, but the chains wrapped around his body limited his range of motion. Still, he got a blow in on my left hip. It was just a glancing hit, but given his enormous strength, it felt like someone had slapped me with a sledgehammer. Red-hot pins of pain exploded in my hip joint.

I grunted and slashed open his stomach with my knife, going first one way, then the other with the silverstone blade. X marks the spot. Blood spewed out onto my hands and arced through the cold air, painting me with its steaming, coppery warmth.

I'd hurt him badly this time, and the giant gave up all thought of trying to attack me. Instead, now wailing and blubbering, he clutched his hands to his stomach, trying to slow the bleeding and shove everything back in where it was supposed to go. But the chains thwarted him once more, and he just couldn't get his hands up in the right place to really staunch the flow. He'd bleed out soon.

In the background, Vinnie and the vampire continued their struggle in the sandbox, still rolling back and forth, each one trying to get the upper hand.

My hip now throbbing with pain, my bloody knife still in my hand, I turned to face the other giant.

He'd been more cautious than his buddy and hadn't followed me into the swings. He stared at me a second then launched himself at one of the heavy wooden support beams that held up the whole thing—trying to collapse the entire swing set on top of me, along with his friend. The wood wasn't as strong as the metal chains were, and the beam creaked, then snapped under the giant's great strength and heavy weight. The entire structure started to slide sideways.

I threw myself forward out of the way of the flying seats and clanking chains. A second later, the whole thing collapsed in a crashing cacophony of metal, dragging the trapped giant down with it. Chains and seats piled on top of his broad back. The giant groaned but didn't get up. Well, that was one way to bury someone. I'd take what I could get.

My hands and knees sank into the loose gravel that covered the ground around the swing set, and some of the stones scraped my palms. By this point, the stones had taken on low, ugly, harsh mutters, reflecting the violence that had just happened, as the giant's blood continued to seep onto them. The gravel was just as dense as the sand in the box, which made it hard for me to scramble to my feet, as did the stabbing pain in my hip.

The second giant surged forward and clamped his hand onto my shoulder, his fingers digging into the socket like drills. The bastard picked me up, hoisted me up over his shoulder, and benched-pressed me as high as he could—a good nine-feet-plus off the ground. There was nothing I could do to stop him or make him put me down. Not from this angle. Fuck. This was not going to end well for me.

"You're going to pay for killing Olson, you bitch!" the giant screamed and threw me down as hard as he could.

I closed my eyes and reached for my Stone magic, pulling the cool power up through my veins, pouring it out onto my skin, head, and hair, letting it harden my body into an impenetrable shell.

I slammed into the closest seesaw, the whole left side of my body smacking into the metal, before rolling across the top and plummeting down the far side. It didn't hurt that badly, not like it would have if I hadn't used my Stone magic to protect myself, but it still jarred me. I still felt the hard, raw, brutal force of it. Especially in my injured hip. I gritted my teeth, ignoring the pain now shooting down into my leg and on past my knee.

But I didn't get up.

Fighting hand to hand, the giant would kick my ass now, especially since I wasn't a hundred percent anymore. Which meant that the quickest way to kill the bastard would be to surprise him. Hence my header on the gravel. The force of the fall had ripped my silverstone knife away from me, and I didn't dare reach for another one. Not yet. Not until he was in range.

Ten . . . twenty . . . I hadn't even counted to thirty before I heard his shoes crunch on the gravel. I cracked my eyes open just enough to track his movements. He came at me from the opposite side of the seesaw. The rows of seats still creaked up and down from the force of my body hitting them. My eyes flicked up at one seat wobbling just above my head.

"Bitch," the giant muttered as he neared me. "That'll teach you to kill one of us—"

I surged up, grabbed the seat, and brought it down as hard as I could.

On the other side of the seesaw, the opposing, attached seat zoomed up and clipped the giant in the chin. He groaned, staggered back, and fell—right onto the merry-go-round. The giant's head slammed against one of the metal handles with a sickening crack. Dazed, he slumped to the ground, half on, half off the merry-go-round.

I got to my feet, grabbed a knife out of my boot, and hobbled over to him. The giant's oversize, buglike eyes rolled back in his head, but he still saw me coming. He reached up, trying to keep me at arm's length, but the blow to his skull had messed up his depth perception, which made it easy enough for me to kick him in the balls. The giant howled, his hands automatically going south to cover himself from further assault instead of protecting his chest and head.

I leaned over and cut his throat.

The giant gurgled, his blood spewing out onto the sky blue paint that covered the merry-go-round. I watched him a second to make sure that he wasn't going to get back up. But his body was already shutting down from the trauma, and he didn't even try to move.

With the giants down and dying, I turned toward the sandbox just in time to see Brown, the vampire, punch Vinnie in the chest and scramble to his feet. The vamp stared at me, eyes wide in his face, as though he couldn't believe that I'd actually taken out two giants all by my little lonesome.

Then he turned and raced off in the other direction.

Fuck.

I palmed another knife, gritted my teeth against the pain pounding through my hip, and started after him. I needed to kill the vamp before he got out of the park. Before he got to a phone, called LaFleur or Mab Monroe, and gave them a description of me and what had happened here tonight.

But the relentless throbbing in my hip slowed me, and despite the stab wound in his thigh and his other injuries, the vampire was running like Death himself was after him. I supposed that he was, in a way. Still, I hurried after the vamp. It was darker on that side of the park. Maybe luck, that capricious bitch, would smile on me, and he would fall and break his ankle—

The flash of lights caught us both by surprise.

The bright glare illuminated the vampire, who was so stunned that he stopped where he was in the middle of one of the park's grassy areas, eyes wide open like a deer.

An engine revved, and a second later, a black SUV appeared out of the darkness and slammed right into the vampire. The vamp sailed thirty feet through the air before a tree trunk stopped his unnatural flight. I could hear his back break even from here. He didn't get up after that.

I was out in the open too, with nowhere to run or hide, so I stood my ground as the SUV turned and headed in my direction, its tires flattening the frosty grass. If worse came to worse, I could always harden my skin again with my Stone magic and roll out of the way of the vehicle. After that, well, I'd find a way to do something clever and deadly. I always did.

The SUV stopped about ten feet away. The glass was

tinted, so I couldn't see exactly who was inside, although I got the impression that the driver was a giant.

The passenger's side door opened, and, a moment later, a familiar, grinning face appeared over the top of the door.

"Need a lift?" Finnegan Lane quipped.

Two more doors opened on the SUV. Xavier got out on the driver's side, while Roslyn hopped out of the back. They, along with Finn, hurried over to me.

Finn stopped in front of me, his green eyes sweeping over my blood-spattered clothes and the silverstone knives glinting in my hands. Assessing what he could see of my body and injuries, just like his father, Fletcher, used to do back when the old man was my handler.

"Is any of that blood yours?" Finn asked.

"Not enough to matter."

He nodded. "Good."

My eyes cut to Xavier. "Nice driving. The vamp never knew what hit him."

The giant dug his hands into his pants pockets and grinned at me. "What can I say? I'm a closet NASCAR fan at heart."

I grinned back at him and shook my head before turning to Finn. "Well, the party's over now. I was beginning to think that you weren't coming, since I called you more than twenty minutes ago."

"Sorry, Gin," Finn said in an apologetic tone. "I would have been here sooner, but Roslyn decided that she wanted to tag along to see what was happening with Vinnie. And then Xavier saw us leaving Northern Aggression and offered to drive."

I looked over at the vampire and the giant. "You didn't have to do that, Roslyn, Xavier. Neither one of you. This is my fight with Mab. Not yours. Do yourselves a favor and don't get involved. I already know that it's going to end badly for me. Call me crazy, but I'd rather not see you two end up as collateral damage."

Roslyn stepped forward, her eyes hard behind her silver glasses, her mouth a thin, determined line in her face. "That's where you're wrong, Gin. It's our fight now too. It has been ever since that first day Elliot Slater came into my club and started stalking me."

A few weeks ago, the giant had gone to Northern Aggression to question Roslyn about how one of her heart-and-arrow rune necklaces had ended up around the neck of a fake hooker who'd killed one of Mab's flunkies. The fake hooker had been me, of course, and I'd used the necklace to sneak into one of Mab's parties so I could take out Tobias Dawson, the greedy mine owner who'd been threatening Violet Fox and her grandfather.

But the Fire elemental didn't believe that I'd died in a mine collapse along with Dawson, so she'd sent Slater to lean on Roslyn. The vampire hadn't cracked, hadn't given me up, but she'd been exposed to something much worse—Slater's creepy fascination with her.

Once again, my heart ached for everything that had been done to Roslyn, for all the pain and anguish and fear that she had suffered because of me. But being sorry didn't change the past. All I could do now was keep going until either Mab or I was dead. Maybe if I was lucky, things would end there, and I'd at least get to take the Fire elemental out with me when I kicked off to hell. And I'd have the satisfaction of knowing that everyone else I was leaving behind, everyone that I cared about, was safe from Mab—forever.

"Gin?" Roslyn asked in a soft voice, cutting into my thoughts.

I just nodded my head, accepting her help and Xavier's, at least for this night. Even though I didn't deserve it. "Thanks for stopping by. Now, let's go see if Vinnie is still alive."

I sent Finn over to the tree to make sure that the vampire was dead, while Xavier, Roslyn, and I walked back to the playground. I went first to the giant who was still sprawled on the merry-go-round. He'd bled out from his cut throat, and his body was already starting to cool, given the chill in the December air. My next stop was the giant who was buried under the remains of the swing set. He was unconscious but surprisingly still alive. I must not have wounded him as badly as I'd thought. Didn't much matter, since I pulled his head out from underneath the chains and cut his throat to finish the job.

Roslyn stood by the sandbox, looking down at Vinnie.

Disgust, horror, and sympathy filled her beautiful face, and she held her hand over her mouth like she was seconds away from vomiting. She probably was. It wasn't hard to see that Roslyn was remembering her own brutal beating at the hands of Elliot Slater. Xavier had already stepped inside the sandbox and was kneeling by the Ice elemental, who had his eyes closed and was lying on his side, curled into a loose ball.

Vinnie Volga was a mess. The giants' beating had been bad enough, but the vampire had only compounded the damage during their scuffle. Starting with his face and going down his body, there wasn't much left of Vinnie that wasn't covered with blood, blackening bruises, and crusty sand.

I looked at Xavier and raised my eyebrows.

"Still alive," Xavier said, answering my silent question. "What do you want to do with him, Gin?"

Earlier tonight, my plan had been to take Vinnie somewhere quiet and find out exactly why he'd betrayed Roslyn, why he was working for Mab, and what he might know about my real identity as the Spider. And I'd planned on getting the information any way that I had to. Just as the giants had done, truth be told. Except I would have used my knives instead of my fists.

But that was before I knew what kind of leverage Mab had on Vinnie—his daughter, Natasha—and the Fire elemental's horrible plans for the little girl. That was before I'd seen the rage, helplessness, and anguish in Vinnie's eyes as he listened to the vampire brag about how he was going to rape Natasha. That was before Vinnie had used the last of his Ice magic, risen up, and tried to take the vampire down with him. He'd tried to spare his daughter one horror, at least.

Besides, I could always kill him later, should the need arise.

"Put him in the car," I said. "Let's get Vinnie to Jo-Jo's before he dies."

While Xavier and the others loaded the unconscious Vinnie into the back of the SUV, I retrieved my dropped knife, then crouched down in the middle of the sandbox. I hadn't planned on killing anyone but the bartender tonight, but I wasn't going to miss this chance to let Mab know exactly who had taken out her men—again. It was easy enough for me to use my silverstone knife to draw my spider rune in a patch of blood-soaked sand. A couple of passes with my blade and it was done.

My eyes studied the symbol that I'd carved. A small circle surrounded by eight thin rays. It wasn't a flashy rune by any stretch of the imagination, certainly not like Mab's gold and ruby sunburst necklace. But the spider rune was the symbol for patience—something that I hoped the Fire elemental was running short on these days. Because impatience made you sloppy, and sloppy got you dead. The second she made a mistake was the second I'd make my move.

"We're ready, Gin!" Finn called out from the window of Xavier's SUV. "Let's go!"

I got back to my feet, wincing at the pain in my hip, and limped over to the waiting vehicle.

It took Xavier about twenty minutes to drive from the Northtown park out into the surrounding suburbs. The giant steered his black SUV with its now-crumpled front fender into a subdivision bearing the name Tara Heights before turning onto a street marked Magnolia Lane. I didn't have to give him directions. Xavier knew the way. We all did.

A minute later, Xavier drove up a long driveway before stopping in front of a three-story, plantation-style house perched on top of a grassy hill. The rows of white columns on the front of the house gleamed despite the late hour, and the cobblestones that made up the driveway seemed as pale as bleach in the darkness.

The four of us got out of the car. Xavier reached into the back and slung Vinnie over his shoulder like a sack of potatoes, before we all walked up the three steps leading to a wide, wraparound porch. Green, glossy kudzu vines curled around a trellis that partially obscured the porch. So did a thick cluster of rose bushes, although their branches were bare for the winter, except for the long, curved, black thorns that glittered like polished jet.

I opened the screen door. A knocker shaped like a fat, puffy cloud rested on the heavier, interior wooden door. The cloud was Jo-Jo's personal rune, denoting her as an Air elemental.

I'd just reached for the knocker when footsteps scuffled inside, the door opened, and Jo-Jo Deveraux stuck her head outside.

"I thought I heard someone out here," the dwarf said in her voice that was as light and sweet as syrup.

Despite the late hour, Jolene "Jo-Jo" Deveraux looked like she'd just finished getting ready to go out courting on Saturday night. A string of pearls hung around her throat, the same size as the pink polka dots on her fuchsia dress. Her bleached blond white hair curled around her head just so, and the perfect amount of understated makeup softened the lines of her middle-aged face. The smell of her Chantilly perfume filled the night air. I breathed in, enjoying the sweet, soft scent.

At exactly five feet, Jo-Jo was tall for a dwarf, with a figure that was still stocky and muscular despite her two hundred and fifty-seven years. Even though it couldn't have been more than ten degrees outside, Jo-Jo's feet were bare, showing off the raspberry pedicure that she'd given herself. The dwarf hated to wear socks, no matter how cold the weather got. One of the many quirks that I loved about her.

Jo-Jo stared at the five of us on her porch. The dwarf's eyes were clear and almost colorless, except for the pinprick of black at the center of her irises. She raised a tweezed eyebrow. "Quite the crowd tonight, Gin. Usually, it's just you and Finn."

I shrugged. "What can I say? I seem to attract minions wherever I go these days. Kind of like the Pied Piper."

Behind me, Finn huffed out his displeasure. "Minion? I am most certainly not a mere *minion*. Head minion, perhaps. At the very *least.*"

Jo-Jo let out a soft chuckle and stepped back. "Minion or not, why don't y'all come on in and let me have a look at that fellow there with you—preferably before he bleeds all over my front porch. I just had it painted last week, you know."

I entered the house first, trailed by Finn, Roslyn, and finally Xavier, still carrying Vinnie over his shoulder. Following Jo-Jo, we walked down a long hallway opening up into a room that took up the back half of the house.

Jo-Jo Deveraux made her living by being what she called a "drama mama." That is to say, a purveyor of all things related to beauty. The dwarf used the back half of her antebellum house as a salon, offering every purifying, exfoliating, tweezing, plucking, dyeing, curling, cutting, perming, and waxing ritual known to Southern women. And even a few that the Yankees had invented. Jo-Jo also used her Air elemental magic to augment many of the treatments, which is what made her salon so popular. Oxygen facials and other Air beauty regimens were great for smoothing out unwanted crow's feet and erasing stretch marks.

Beauty magazines, scissors, combs, curlers, hair dryers, and more filled the wide room, fighting for space on the tables and counters, along with more tubs of makeup and bottles of pink nail polish than you could find at Mab Monroe's best-stocked Sell-Everything superstore.

At the sound of our footsteps, a dog sprawled in a wicker basket by the door raised up his head. Rosco, Jo-Jo's fat, lazy basset hound. The brown and black beast gazed at us with dark, hopeful eyes. But when he realized that no one had any food that they planned on feeding him, he snorted once, put his head back down, and returned to his previously scheduled nap. Rosco didn't like to overexert himself—ever.

"Put the poor fellow over there, Xavier." Jo-Jo pointed to one of the cherry red, padded swivel chairs in the middle of the salon. "So I can take a look at him."

Xavier put Vinnie down where Jo-Jo had instructed. The rest of us made ourselves comfortable in the other chairs scattered around the room, except for Finn, who headed into the kitchen on a coffee run.

I sat in the chair closest to Vinnie's so I could keep an eye on the Ice elemental. Just because he'd been beaten to within an inch of death didn't mean that he couldn't rise up and do something stupid while Jo-Jo was healing him—like try to get away.

Once I was sure that Vinnie was out of it, I glanced around, half-expecting to see a dwarf dressed in all black come strolling into the salon. But Sophia, Jo-Jo's younger sister, didn't appear.

"Where's Sophia?" I asked.

Jo-Jo went over to the sink and washed her hands. "She went out to see a Clint Eastwood film festival at that old theater over on St. Charles Avenue. She won't be back until late."

I nodded. In addition to Sophia's Goth tendencies, she also happened to be a huge film buff.

Jo-Jo dried her hands, then clicked on a free-standing halogen light and angled it so that it illuminated Vinnie Volga's bloody face. She let out a low whistle. "Giants?"

I nodded. "Some of Mab's men. They were disappointed in Vinnie's job performance and decided to show him exactly how much."

Jo-Jo clucked her tongue and shook her head. Then she raised her hand up so that her palm hovered over Vinnie's face, not quite touching his bloody, bruised skin. The dwarf's eyes began to glow an opaque, buttermilk white, and the same sort of magical glow coated her palm. Jo-Jo's Air magic crackled through the room like lightning, making me shift in my chair.

Jo-Jo was an Air elemental, which meant that her magic was the polar opposite of my Ice and Stone power. Two elements always opposed each other, like Fire and Ice, just as two elements always complemented each other, like Fire and Air. I always felt uncomfortable when I sensed so much of an opposing element being used, even if I knew that Jo-Jo was healing Vinnie instead of hurting him. Her magic just felt wrong to me, as foreign and alien as eating fried green tomatoes would to a Yankee.

Not only that, but Jo-Jo's power also made the spider rune scars on my palms itch and burn, the way they always did whenever I was around so much elemental magic. The silverstone metal that had been melted into my flesh was highly prized for its ability to absorb and store all kinds of magic, and it always seemed to me that the silverstone in my hands actually *hungered* for power. That it was almost like a living thing, a parasite whose sole purpose was to soak up more and more magic until it just couldn't contain another molecule of power. Sort of like a greedy vampire sucking down all the blood that he could get his fangs into.

Lots of elementals had rings, bracelets, or other jewelry made out of the metal for the sole purpose of containing bits and pieces of their power in the items— power they could then draw upon at a later time. Like when they were dueling another elemental. Wear your favorite silverstone ring, have that extra bit of juice handy when you needed it to destroy your enemy. It was all just a deadly form of magical batteries more than anything else.

"So who is this guy?" Jo-Jo asked in a soft voice.

The dwarf moved her hand back and forth across Vinnie's face, not quite touching his battered features. With every pass of her hand, the swelling on Vinnie's face went down a little more, the black bruises greened out and faded away, and the bloody cuts drew together and sewed themselves shut. Jo-Jo was using her Air elemental magic to force oxygen into Vinnie's body, using her power to put all those broken molecules and blood vessels back together and make him whole once again. That's how Air elementals healed—by using all the natural gases in the atmosphere, especially oxygen.

"He's somebody who's been spying on Roslyn for Mab," I said.

Jo-Jo looked at me. "So why am I healing him?"

"Because he might have some useful information, and he seems to be in as much trouble as the rest of us."

While Jo-Jo finished healing Vinnie, I told the others what I'd overheard in the park. Everything that the vampire had said about Vinnie spying on Roslyn, about the trap LaFleur had set for me with the fake rumor about the drug shipment, and how Mab had big plans for Vinnie's daughter, Natasha.

"They said that about Natasha?" Roslyn asked. "That Mab was going to put her in some kind of whorehouse? She's eight, maybe ten. She doesn't deserve that."

Roslyn's face tightened, and she pressed her lips together, as though she was trying to keep from being sick again. Some might have thought that it was hypocritical of Roslyn to have any kind of objection about whatever sort of prostitution that Mab was involved in. After all, she ran her own stable of hookers at Northern Aggression. Most of the guys and girls at the club were vampires, just like Roslyn. The vamps pretty much owned the sex trade in Ashland. That's because for a lot of them, having sex was just as stimulating as drinking blood. Humans needed vitamins to keep going, and vamps needed sex and blood. Get laid, get your B_{12} for the day. Or something like that. For the most part, it was win-win for the vamps and their clients.

But vamp or not, everyone who worked at Northern Aggression was there because they wanted to be. Roslyn didn't force them to do anything they didn't want to, and she made sure that her giant bouncers kept the club's clients from hurting anyone. Roslyn also let her hookers keep what they made, instead of taking it all for herself like so many of the vampire pimps did on the Southtown streets. If you had to be a hooker, you wanted someone like Roslyn watching out for you, and not some gangbanger pimp who'd take all your money and then beat the shit out of you just for fun.

Jo-Jo dropped her hand from Vinnie's face. "There. He's as good as new. Your turn, Gin."

I sighed. As much as I hated being injured, sometimes I thought that getting healed by Jo-Jo was worse. But I leaned back in my chair and let the Air elemental work her magic on me.

Jo-Jo placed her hand close to my hip, and her palm began to glow milky white with her Air magic once again. A hot tingle sizzled to life deep inside my body, centered in my aching hip joint. Then another, then another. It was like being pricked with thousands of tiny red-hot needles all at once. I gritted my teeth, clamped my hands around the armrests of the chair, and suffered through it. The spider rune scars on my palms reacted to Jo-Jo's magic and began to itch and burn even worse than before, as she used her power on me. Sweat beaded on my forehead, and I bit back a primal scream. Even though I knew that Jo-Jo was helping me, healing me, the deep, dark elemental part of me wanted to lash out at her with my own magic just to get her to stop. Just so I wouldn't feel the wrongness of her power one second longer.

"Dislocated hip, some minor cuts and bruises. An easy night for you," Jo-Jo murmured.

"Yeah," I muttered. "It was just a walk in the park."

A few minutes later, the glow faded from Jo-Jo's palm, the magic evaporated out of her eyes, and she dropped her hand. I let out a quiet sigh of relief and leaned back against the chair, grateful that I couldn't feel her Air magic anymore.

I let myself relax and recover for two minutes before I sat upright again and got on with things. I turned my attention to Vinnie, who was still unconscious in the next chair over.

Normally, I would have let someone who'd been so severely injured as Vinnie sleep until morning. Being magically healed always took a toll on a person, as you went from being close to death to suddenly being healthy again. It pretty much zapped all your strength until your body could switch gears and catch up with itself again. Hell, even I would have liked to crawl into bed myself and not come out until morning. But I wanted answers, and I wanted them *now*. So I reached over and poked Vinnie in the shoulder.

It took about a minute of prodding before the Ice elemental's eyes fluttered open, and he became aware of his surroundings. Vinnie looked at Jo-Jo and frowned with confusion.

"You're welcome," the dwarf said, before getting to her feet, going over to the sink, and washing her hands again.

Vinnie sat up in his chair, his gaze flicking around the room, taking in all the beauty supplies, obviously wondering how he'd gotten from the park to Jo-Jo's salon. He froze when he spotted Xavier and Roslyn sitting together on a loveseat against the far wall. After a moment, his blue eyes cut to me, lingering on all the blood on my clothes, before going back to his vampire boss and her giant bouncer.

Vinnie opened his mouth, but I beat him to the punch.

"Before you start spouting some lame-ass lie about what you've been up to these past few days, let me tell you what we know," I said in a cold voice. "We know that you've been spying on Roslyn for Mab Monroe. We know that an assassin who goes by the name LaFleur came to see you at Northern Aggression tonight and that it wasn't the first time that you've talked to her. We know that she told you to tell everyone about a shipment of drugs that were coming in down at the docks, in hopes that the Spider would show up and LaFleur could take her out. How am I doing so far?"

Vinnie didn't say anything, but he swallowed once and nodded his head.

"Good. You've decided to be reasonable." I crossed my arms over my chest and gave him a hard stare. "Here's the deal. You tell us everything that you've told LaFleur and

Mab, and everything that they've said to you or threatened you with. And, at the end of your story, if I like what I hear, I may just let you live. So start talking."

Vinnie just kept staring at me, his eyes wide in his face.

"Now!" I barked.

The Ice elemental looked at his boss again, but Roslyn's face was even harder and colder than mine. So was Xavier's. After a moment, Vinnie slumped back against his chair.

"I didn't want to do it, Roslyn." Vinnie's Russian accent was even more pronounced than before, probably from all the stress he was feeling right now. "You have to believe me. You've been so good to me. I never wanted to betray you like this."

"I know, Vinnie," Roslyn said in a soft voice. "Now tell us what you know."

He drew in a shaky breath. "A week ago, I'm at the club, working the bar like usual. I go outside to take out the trash, and this woman comes up to me. At first I think she's just drunk or outside smoking something she shouldn't, you know? But she calls out to me, calls me by my name. And she starts telling me all these . . . things. Like what time I get off work every night, and where Natasha and I like to eat dinner. Where Natasha goes to school."

Vinnie's voice dropped to a whisper. He swallowed again and forced himself to continue.

"And then she tells me that her name is LaFleur and asks me if I've heard of her. I say no. And she says that after tonight I'll never forget her. She turns and calls out to someone, and this guy steps forward. He was just a guy, somebody that I'd never seen before. She stares at him a second and starts smiling. And then she raises her hand up, and she—and she just—"

"Electrocuted him," I finished. "Right there in front of you."

Vinnie stared at me in surprise. "Yeah, how did you know?"

I gave him a grim smile. "Because unlike you, I have heard of her. Go on."

Vinnie nodded. "Anyway, LaFleur tells me that she's working for Mab Monroe on a special assignment. To find and kill the Spider. And that I'm going to help her do this. At this point, I am freaking out. But I can't exactly leave, not without her killing me too."

He shuddered at the memory of the other assassin threatening him. Couldn't blame him for that. Not when LaFleur had thrown in a demo of her electrical magic right there on the spot.

"So she approached you about working for her. Then what happened?" I asked.

Vinnie swallowed again. "This woman, LaFleur, said that unless I wanted to end up like her friend, I was going to start watching Roslyn for her. Going to see who Roslyn was hanging out with, who she talked to at the club every night. She wanted me to make a list of every woman that I saw Roslyn with. She said that one of them had to be the Spider, and it was just a matter of narrowing it down."

Well, he'd just confirmed what Brown, the vampire, had said in the park. I didn't know if LaFleur had been ordered to do all this by Mab or if the assassin had come up with the plan all on her own. Either way, it wasn't good news for me.

"I told her that I was just a bartender, that I didn't know about anything that had happened with Roslyn or Elliot Slater or the Spider or any of it. But she wouldn't take no for an answer. LaFleur said that if I didn't do exactly what she said, she'd kill Natasha and make me watch while she did it. And then she'd kill me."

Vinnie's voice dropped to a whisper and was so soft that I had to strain to hear him. "I just—I didn't have a choice. You didn't see what she did to that man. You didn't smell it or hear him scream. So yeah, I did what she said. I started watching Roslyn. And when LaFleur came back to the club a few days ago and told me to start talking about the drug shipment, I did that too."

"Why didn't you come to me, Vinnie?" Roslyn asked. "I would have believed you. I would have helped you."

The Ice elemental gave her a wan smile. "I know that you would have tried. But Elliot Slater almost killed you, and this woman makes him look like Santa Claus. And Natasha, she comes first with me. She always has. I couldn't risk her. I'm sorry, Roslyn. So very sorry."

The vampire nodded, accepting his apology. "I know, Vinnie. Believe me, I know."

"So what did LaFleur say to you tonight?" I asked. "When she came into the club?"

Vinnie looked back at me. "She told me that no one had shown up at the drug meeting last night, which meant that I must not have done what she asked me to. She said that she was going to dance for a few minutes before she left to go over to my apartment, and kill Natasha and her babysitter. I was just—desperate. I didn't know what to do, so I left to go home and try to get to my daughter before LaFleur did. But she had men inside the club waiting for me."

"I know," I said in a wry tone. "I'm wearing little bits and pieces of them right now."

Vinnie stared at me, his blue eyes once again taking in the blood on my clothes, hands, and face. "What's going on?" he asked. "Who are you? Why were you in the park tonight?"

The bartender had been pretty out of it when I'd shown myself to Mab's men earlier, all of his attention focused on taking down Brown, the vampire, not with who I was.

So I stared at him, letting him see just how cold, flat, and hard my gray eyes really were, and made the introduction once more. "I'm the woman you're looking for, Vinnie. I'm the person LaFleur wanted you to find. I'm the Spider."

✴ 9 ✴

Vinnie looked at me a second more, then bolted out of his chair and headed for the hallway that led into the front part of the house. I sighed. As much as I liked the fact that the mere mention of my assassin name was enough to inspire abject terror in people, it was inconvenient right now. Because I needed to talk to Vinnie, not kill him. Not yet anyway.

But Vinnie didn't get far. By that point, Finn had finished his coffee run and was strolling back down the hallway, a mug of his steaming chicory brew in his left hand. He saw Vinnie heading toward him, sighed, and reached around behind his back with his right hand. Finn came up with a gun, which he leveled at Vinnie's head.

The Ice elemental froze in the doorway.

"Why don't you be a good boy, Vinnie, and go sit down," Finn said in a pleasant voice before taking a sip of his coffee. His eyes never left the other man, and his gun never wavered. Finn could be a badass when he had to, just like me.

Xavier got to his feet, walked over, and clamped his hand on Vinnie's shoulder, as a little added incentive. "If we wanted you dead, Vinnie, we would have left you in the sandbox. Relax, man. Nobody here is going to hurt you."

The giant didn't add the *not yet* part. He didn't have to.

Xavier maneuvered Vinnie back over to his original chair. The Ice elemental sank into the padded seat, a dazed expression on his face. Xavier hovered over his shoulder, in case he decided to run again.

"You're the Spider. The Spider," Vinnie muttered, his eyes flicking back to me.

"That's my name," I drawled.

He leaned forward and buried his head in his hands. Bits of golden sand fell out of his dirty brown hair and glinted on the floor. "Dead. I'm so dead. You're going to kill me, aren't you? That's why you brought me here. That's why you healed me. To question me before you kill me."

Admittedly, that had been my first plan, but now I was reconsidering things. Even assassins could be swayed from time to time.

I tilted my head to one side and gave him a thoughtful look. "Not necessarily. What I really want to know about right now is your little girl."

Vinnie raised his head out of his hands and looked at me. "Natasha?"

I nodded. "Natasha. Tell me about her."

The Ice elemental shifted in his chair. "You can do

whatever you want to me. I know that I deserve it, for spying on Roslyn like I did, for setting you up like I did. But please, leave Natasha out of it. *Please*. I'll do anything you want, tell you anything you want, give you anything you want, if you'll just let her go."

I shook my head. "I hate to disappoint you, Vinnie, but I don't have your daughter. I have no idea where Natasha is."

Vinnie's face fell. "But you—you killed those men at the park. The giants. I saw you do it. And you brought me here, you healed me. Surely, you must have Natasha here too."

"I'm sorry," I said and meant it. "But we just found you. We didn't get your daughter as well. Given what I heard the men in the park say, I'm pretty sure that Mab has her now."

Vinnie closed his eyes. His face took on a greenish tint, and a tremor shook his body. He ran a hand through his hair. More sand fell out of his dark locks and dusted the salon floor. After a moment, Vinnie put his face down in his hands again. His shoulders shook, and even though I couldn't see them, I knew that tears ran down his face. He tried to muffle a sob and couldn't. He just *couldn't*.

Nobody spoke, and the only sound was Vinnie's low, anguished cries.

"Gin?" Roslyn finally asked in a soft voice.

I glanced over at the vampire. She looked so cool, calm, and professional in her suit, but that wasn't the image of her I was really seeing. Instead, I flashed back to that night at Slater's cabin when I'd found her beaten and tied down to the giant's bed, about to be raped and murdered. All of that had been horrible enough for Roslyn, a former hooker who knew what the score was and just how twisted things could get in Ashland. I could only imagine the damage that sort of thing would do to an innocent young girl like Natasha.

"Gin?" This time, Jo-Jo was the one who murmured my name.

Gin. The shortened, bastardized version of my real name, the one I'd adopted for myself so many years ago when Fletcher had first taken me in. Three letters, one syllable. A simple name. But now, somehow, full of so many questions, so many things asked, and so much hanging in the balance—including Natasha's life.

I sighed and nodded at the other two women.

Then I leaned forward and put my hand on Vinnie's shaking shoulder. "Vinnie, I know that you're upset right now. That you've been through a lot, but I need you to focus for a little while longer. Do you think you can do that?"

I didn't know if it was fear of me or something else, but Vinnie flinched at my touch. I dropped my hand, wondering if he'd even heard me. But after a moment, his shoulders quit shaking. He wiped the tears out of his eyes and slowly raised and nodded his head.

"Good," I said. "Now, I want you to think back. This new club that Mab's opening, the one the vampire said that Natasha could be the star of. Did you hear the men say anything else about it? Where it was going to be? When it was going to open? Anything at all?"

"Why do you care?" Vinnie said. "She's not your daughter. You don't even know her—or me."

No, I didn't know Vinnie or his daughter. Didn't know them the least little bit or really care to. But I knew exactly what the Ice elemental was going through right now. All the emotions that he was feeling—and how helpless they all made him.

Instead of telling him that I understood what it was like to lose your family, I just stared at Vinnie, my mouth a flat line in my face. "Humor me."

Still, something of my pain must have flickered in my eyes, because after a moment, Vinnie slowly nodded his head.

"All right," he said. "Two nights after LaFleur first approached me, she told me to meet her at Underwood's before my shift started. She was there eating dinner with a couple of giants, Mab Monroe, and Jonah McAllister."

Underwood's was one of Ashland's most exclusive restaurants—a place that Mab liked to frequent, along with her lawyer, Jonah McAllister. Someone else I'd been having problems with recently.

"Anyway, I went inside, but LaFleur didn't want to see me right away, so I had to hang out by the bar for a while. But their table was close by, and I heard them talking. It's true. Mab is opening up her own nightclub. Some kind of underground place where anything goes—*anything*. Kids, cutting up women, whatever sick things that people would pay for. Mab kept saying how it was time for Northern Aggression to disappear—for good."

My gaze cut to Roslyn. The vampire sat on the couch, a hard look on her face, but I could see the worry flickering in her eyes. Northern Aggression was her livelihood, the way that she supported herself, her sister, Lisa, and

young niece, Catherine, the way that Roslyn was providing a better life for them. Not to mention all the people
who worked for her. All the vamps who might be hooking on the streets in the midst of all the dangers connected with that profession in Ashland, instead of being
in the safer environment that Roslyn provided.

It wasn't hard to realize what Mab's reasoning was.
Roslyn was at the center of Elliot Slater's death, and the
press has painted her as the tragic victim, the way that she
really was. All that meant that the Fire elemental couldn't
touch Roslyn right now, not with the Ashland news media
still focused on the incident. It would just be too messy,
even for Mab, especially given the fact that she also had
me, the Spider, to deal with. So the Fire elemental had
decided to go after Roslyn another way—by destroying
her business. And Vinnie and Natasha had been caught
in the middle of it all.

"So you don't know where the club might be?" I asked
Vinnie.

The Ice elemental shook his head. "No. Only that
Mab plans to start it soon. From the way things sounded,
she's hired LaFleur to run it, as well as oversee her men."

So LaFleur wasn't just in Ashland to find and kill me.
It looked as though the other assassin was also coming
on board as Mab's newest top lieutenant—a position for-
merly held by the late, unlamented Elliot Slater.

"Finn?" I asked.

My foster brother leaned against one of the salon walls.
He'd put his gun away, but he was still sipping his coffee.
The warm, fragrant, chicory blend drifted over to me.

I thought of his old man then and how he'd helped

people on the sly for years, even when he was working as the assassin the Tin Man. My mind had already been made up, of course, but thinking of Fletcher comforted me. I could almost see him behind the counter at the Pork Pit, nodding his head in approval of what I was about to do.

"Yeah?" Finn asked.

"Start digging and see what you can find out about this new nightclub. The name, where it might be located, anything useful."

If there was anyone who could ferret out the information in a hurry, it was Finn. In addition to his banking skills, he also had a network of anonymous spies and sources that any clandestine agency would be proud of. And if his spies couldn't find something out for him, Finn was more than capable of hacking into whatever computer system contained the knowledge he needed.

Finn nodded. "I'm on it."

I turned to look at Roslyn and Xavier. "You two need to be extremely careful right now. We know about Vinnie, but there's no telling who else Mab and LaFleur might have bribed on your staff. You need to discreetly nose around and figure out who you can trust and who you can't."

Roslyn and Xavier both nodded.

"Don't worry, Gin," Roslyn said. "After what Elliot Slater did to me, anybody who's working on the sly for Mab is getting booted out on her ass."

Next, I looked at Jo-Jo. "You know that Vinnie's going to need a place to stay out of sight until we can get this thing sorted out."

The dwarf smiled at me, the lines deepening on her middle-aged face. "It's a good thing that I've got plenty of extra bedrooms then, isn't it?"

Vinnie glanced at me, then the others. "What's going on? What are you all talking about?"

I stared at him. "I'm talking about you staying here where you'll be safe, Vinnie. I'm talking about getting you out from under Mab's and LaFleur's heavy thumbs. I'm talking about rescuing your daughter from whatever hellhole Mab has got her stashed in. That's what I'm talking about."

Vinnie's mouth fell open in shock. He blinked several times, as though he was thinking about speaking but the words just wouldn't come to him.

"Do you want me to do that?" I asked. "Do you want me to find your daughter? Because I was under the impression that you cared about her—a lot."

"You—you would do that for me? Try to find Natasha?" Hope brightened Vinnie's pale blue gaze.

Hope. An emotion that always kept suckering me in, time after time, despite my supposed retirement from the assassin business. Hope. The one thing that always seemed to get me into more trouble than just killing people for money ever had. Ah, hope. Sometimes, I really hated it.

"Yes."

Vinnie blinked again, and suspicion darkened his eyes. "But why would you do that? Nobody does something like that for free, and I—I don't have any money to pay you. But I can get some," he hurried to add. "I can get however much you want. I promise you that I can."

"I don't want your money, Vinnie. I have more of my own than I can ever spend."

The Ice elemental frowned at the harsh tone in my voice, but I couldn't be any gentler with him. I couldn't get his hopes up any higher than they were. Not until I found Natasha and saw exactly what had been done to her.

"As for why I would do something like this, well, there are a lot of reasons," I continued. "But mainly, because it seems to be what I do now. Don't get me wrong; I'm not promising you kittens and rainbows. Mab's men have had Natasha for hours already. There's no telling what kind of shape she's in. Do you understand what that means? How hurt she could be? Inside and out? Even if we find her, even if we get her back, she might never be the same little girl that you knew and loved before. Can you handle that? Can you give her the help that she's going to need?"

Vinnie closed his eyes a moment, but he slowly nodded.

"All right then," I said. "I'll find your daughter. I'll find Natasha. And if I can't do that or if she's already dead when I get to her, then I promise you one thing—that the people who took her will wish for their own deaths long before I am through with them. How does that sound to you?"

Vinnie stared at me with his pale blue eyes. Emotions swirled in his gaze. Fear. Grief. Anger. Anguish. Worry. Slowly, he nodded his head once more.

"Good," I said. "Then we have a deal."

❊ 10 ❊

Two hours later, I drove my Benz up a long, steep driveway lined on either side by thick stands of pine trees.
Gravel churned under my wheels, but eventually my car
crested the hill and rolled out onto the flat plateau on top
of this particular ridge, one of many in the Appalachian
Mountains that cut through Ashland like jagged teeth on
a saw.

I stopped my car in front of the large, three-story clap-
board house that perched on top of the steep hill. Gray
stone, red clay, and brown brick all mishmashed together
on the sprawling structure, along with a tin roof, black
shutters, and blue eaves. At first glance, it looked like the
house wasn't quite finished or perhaps that someone had
run out of building materials and had just decided to use
whatever was handy. Still, the uneven shapes and styles
pleased me, because this was my home now.

The enormous house had been in Fletcher Lane's family for years, and the old man had left it to me in his will, along with a sizable amount of cash. Not that I'd really needed either one, as I'd put plenty of my own money away for a rainy day. The ramshackle structure was much too large for just me to live in by myself. Half a dozen people could have comfortably roomed inside and never run into each other if they didn't want to. I probably should have boarded up the structure and moved out into a smaller apartment or town house in the city, somewhere closer to the Pork Pit. That's where I'd been living before Fletcher had been murdered. But the house was one of the few things that I had left of the old man, and I planned on staying here as long as it—and I—were both still standing.

Despite my sentimental feelings, I still parked my car and approached the front door with my usual, wary caution. LaFleur might not have trapped me the other night down at the docks, but that didn't mean the assassin wasn't still looking for me. If her resources were as good as mine were, she'd find me—sooner rather than later. And then we'd dance. But I wasn't about to give her the upper hand by doing something sloppy, like not paying attention to my surroundings. Not even here, at my sanctuary from the world.

As I walked toward the house, my eyes scanned over what I could see of the yard in the darkness. The smooth lawn stretched out for about a hundred feet before nose-diving into a series of jagged cliffs that even some mountain goats would have had a hard time climbing. Heavy clouds obscured the silver moon and twinkling stars tonight and cast the landscape in almost coal black darkness, especially up here on this high, forested ridge. The lights of Ashland gleamed in the valley below, like fireflies hovering across the surface of a quiet, murky pond.

I also cocked my head to the side and reached out with my elemental magic, listening to the stones around me—everything from the gravel under my feet in the driveway to the falling cliffs off to my right to the brick that made up part of the house itself.

The stones only whispered with their low, usual murmurs, telling me of the cold whip of the wind around the ridge, the soft scurry of animals to and fro, and the slow, crumbling passage of time. No one had been near the house all day. I would have sensed the vibration, the disturbance, in the stones otherwise, especially if it had been someone like LaFleur here to murder me in my own bed. Dark intentions like that always found their way into their stone surroundings, and the blacker your desire, the sooner it happened.

Good. I was in no mood to kill unwanted company. Not after everything that had happened tonight. Not when I knew that there was a young girl out there somewhere who might be dying at this very moment. While Jo-Jo had tucked Vinnie into bed in one of her guest rooms, Finn and Xavier had gone over to the bartender's house to confirm whether Natasha had actually been kidnapped. The news wasn't good. They'd found the babysitter tied up and stuffed in a closet. She'd told them the same story Brown had spouted at the park—that some men had stormed in, roughed her up, grabbed Natasha, and left. I had no doubt that the men had taken the little girl straight to the mysterious new nightclub that Mab was building—and all the potential horrors that awaited there.

But there was nothing that I could do to help Natasha tonight, not when I didn't even know where to start looking for her. If she made it until morning, if Finn found out something useful from his sources, things might be different. But not tonight.

Once I was certain that everything was as it should be, I stepped up onto the porch and approached the front door. Given the many additions that had been slapped onto the house over the years, bits and pieces of stone ran throughout the entire structure, including the front door, which was composed of black granite so hard that even a giant would have a tough time punching his way through it. As added insurance against unwanted intruders, rich veins of silverstone also swirled through the stone.

The magical metal would absorb a fair amount of elemental power before it began to soften, weaken, and melt, which should give me plenty of time to be somewhere else other than a sitting duck inside waiting for whoever was huffing and puffing and blowing down my door. It would take someone with major elemental magic to get through that much silverstone. Not the kind of person that I wanted coming inside the house and catching me unawares.

My security check done, I unlocked the door and stepped into the house.

I toed off my bloody boots just inside the door, then padded in my wool socks to the kitchen in the back. So many rooms had been added to the house that it was a bit like navigating through a labyrinth, except there was no Minotaur in the middle waiting to gobble me up. Halls crisscrossed this way and that, while even more passageways curved around them and led to completely new areas—or dead ends. You could wander around in here for days and still not find every room, something that was a tactical advantage for me, should someone unsavory ever come calling after-hours.

I was too tired to even think about going into the kitchen and making myself something to snack on, even though it had been hours since I'd grabbed a quick dinner at the Pork Pit. After the night I'd had, I should have showered, gone to bed, and rested up for what was sure to be a long day of searching for Natasha tomorrow.

But instead, I found myself in the den, the way that I always seemed to late at night when I had something on my mind and trouble dogging my footsteps.

The den was a comfortable room, with a couple of recliners and a worn sofa that had been around so long that each section was perfectly grooved to fit someone's ass. I plopped down on the sofa, letting my tired body sink into the thick, soft cushions, and propped my socked feet up on the scarred coffee table.

As always, my eyes lifted up to the mantel on the fireplace across from me—and the series of framed drawings that were propped up there.

I'd done the first three drawings a while back for a class that I'd taken over at Ashland Community College. I was one of the college's perpetual students, taking any and every course that appealed to me, especially those that dealt with cooking or literature, two of my passions. One of the projects in the art class that I'd audited had been to create a series of drawings, all different but linked together by a common theme.

I'd drawn a series of runes—the symbols of my dead family.

A snowflake, a curling ivy vine, and a primrose. The symbols for icy calm, elegance, and beauty. The snowflake had belonged to my mother, Eira, being the main rune for the Snow family, the one that had identified us to other elementals. The other two symbols had been fashioned into medallions that my sisters had worn. The ivy vine for my older sister, Annabelle, and the primrose for my younger sister, Bria.

But the fourth rune was relatively new. I'd done it only a couple of months ago, after Fletcher had been tortured to death by an Air elemental. That drawing was shaped like a pig holding a platter of food. An exact rendering of the multicolored neon sign that hung over the entrance to the Pork Pit. Not a rune, not exactly, but I'd drawn it in honor of the old man. Fletcher had been the only father I'd ever really known, and I'd wanted to honor him, just the way I had the rest of my family.

I stared at the runes for another moment. Then I rubbed my hands over my face, took my feet off the coffee table, leaned forward, and picked up one of two manila folders lying there. The first file had been on the table for weeks now, since it dealt with my sister Bria, but I'd retrieved the second folder earlier today from Fletcher's cluttered office in another part of the house. That was the one I was interested in tonight.

I flipped open the folder and stared at the pages of information—everything that Fletcher had ever been able to dig up on the assassin known as LaFleur. I'd seen her electrical elemental magic for myself the other night, of course, but information was its own kind of power, and I wanted to be as prepared as possible when the two of us finally danced.

Besides, I was willing to bet that wherever Natasha was, whatever dark hole she'd been stashed in, LaFleur wouldn't be too far away from it. When I found the little girl, I'd find the assassin. And then, I'd kill her—or die trying.

So I leaned back against the sofa, put the file in my lap, and started reading.

I read through all the information on LaFleur, absorbing every fact, tidbit, rumor, and sheer speculation that Fletcher had been able to piece together about the other assassin. Of course, what I was really looking for was any sign of weakness, anything that I could use against the other assassin to kill her before she killed me.

But there wasn't anything in the file to give me any hope of accomplishing that. At least, not without getting dead myself.

The file started out by listing all of LaFleur's vital stats. Height: Five foot two. Weight: One hundred fifteen pounds. Black hair. Green eyes. Asian heritage. Rumored to have some sort of tattoo on her, probably in the shape of a rune. Cliché, yes, surprising, no. As a general rule, assassins liked symbols and catchy nicknames almost as much as magic users did.

Fletcher had also pegged her age at thirty-three and concluded that LaFleur was actually part of a family of elite assassins, all of whom sold their services to the highest bidder. Included was a sheet about a brother that LaFleur supposedly had, an assassin just like her. But since the page just referenced another one of Fletcher's files, instead of spelling out the information for me here, I didn't get up and go into the old man's office to look for it. LaFleur's brother, whoever the hell he might be, wasn't important at this point.

The bottom line was that killing people was in LaFleur's blood, as much a part of who and what she was as my spider rune scars were to me. Interesting to know, but not particularly helpful when it came to actually taking her down.

So I moved on to the pages that dealt with LaFleur's accomplishments as an assassin. LaFleur had killed dozens and dozens of people over the years, everyone from common street thugs to the richest, most heavily guarded businessmen. As far as Fletcher knew, she had a one hundred percent kill rate and the exorbitant fees to match.

When success was guaranteed, you could charge whatever you wanted to for it. According to the file, LaFleur pulled down north of three million for a simple assassination. Depending on who the target was, how hard it would be to get to him, and how much someone wanted it to look like an accident, the price went up from there. Even during my heyday as the Spider, I'd only topped out at around two and a half mil myself.

"Bitch," I muttered and kept reading.

LaFleur was skilled with all sorts of weapons and was rumored to be even better at hand-to-hand combat. Naturally. She wouldn't have been much of an assassin if she couldn't kill people six ways from Sunday—and then some.

However, instead of her fists or other weapons, LaFleur mainly used her electrical magic to kill. Given the number of people she'd taken out with it over the years, Fletcher had concluded that she was an extremely strong elemental—far stronger than the vast majority of those who could tap into the more common areas, like Air, Fire, Ice, and Stone. Wonderful.

But that was LaFleur's trademark—electrocuting people and then leaving a single white orchid behind on their smoking corpses. Just like she'd done to the dwarf that she'd fried down at the docks the other night in front of me and Finn.

I wondered about the orchid, though. Lots of assassins left things behind to mark their kills. Names and runes, mostly. But even among assassins, an orchid was a strange thing to use. Mainly because they were so delicate and so expensive. Why waste all that money signing your kills when you could just draw something on the nearest wall in your victim's blood? But I'd given up trying to figure out other assassins a long time ago. Hell, I couldn't even figure myself out most of the time.

I read through the rest of the file, but nothing jumped out at me. LaFleur was skilled, efficient, and deadly, just like I was. Smart, ruthless, and brutal, just like I was. And she had elemental magic, just like I did. All of which meant that it was fifty-fifty which one of us would win against the other in the end. And with LaFleur having access to Mab Monroe's men to help back her up, well, let's just say that it didn't do wonders for my confidence about making it to Christmas without getting dead.

Bah, humbug.

* 11 *

It had been a long night, so I put the file aside, took a hot shower to wash the giants' blood off me, and then crawled into bed.

Maybe Finn would have a bright idea tomorrow about how I could find Natasha and kill LaFleur. Before we'd left Jo-Jo's, he'd promised to dig up everything that he could find on the assassin, her new job as Mab's number one enforcer, and where Mab's new nightclub might be located.

I was so tired that for once it was easy for me to put those thoughts out of my mind. I fell asleep almost immediately, but sometime during the night, the dreams took over, the way that they always seemed to these days . . .

I'd never known that I'd had this much magic before. Never dreamed that I was this strong. Never even imagined, hoped, or wished for it.

But I was. And then some.

Those were the odd thoughts that flashed through my mind in the split-second before my Ice and Stone power lashed out, reverberating through my whole house like a giant frozen jackhammer, pounding into everything that it touched.

And crumbling it all to dust.

There was a loud, violent, angry, collective roar as the stones in the ceiling above my head splintered. Seeing the long, deep cracks zigzag through the rocks was like watching spiders suddenly swarm out of a dark hole, hurrying out and out and out as fast as they could, dragging their silken strings behind them. That's what it reminded me of, as weird as it might seem.

For a moment, I sat there, stunned by what I'd just done with my magic. The terrible thing that I'd wrought with it. I'd only been trying to get free of the heavy ropes that tied me down to the chair I was sitting in. Ropes that the Fire elemental had had her giant lash around me while I'd been unconscious. Ropes that kept me from moving when she'd questioned me about Bria. Ropes that had kept me from fighting back when she'd superheated the spider rune medallion duct-taped in between my hands—her cruel, cruel way of torturing me. As if killing my mother and Annabella hadn't been horrible enough.

I didn't remember much of what happened after the Fire elemental had started torturing me. Only the red-hot, unending, searing pain as the silverstone rune melted into my hands and burned my palms. Even now, the air still smelled of charred flesh—my flesh. My stomach roiled at the acrid stench of it.

I'd been sitting here, tied to this chair, ever since, just drifting along in a dull daze of pain—until I'd heard Bria scream.

I knew what my baby sister's scream meant. That the Fire elemental or one of her men had finally found her, despite the hiding place that I'd put her in, the spot where I'd told her to wait for me while I'd gone back inside our smoldering mansion to lead all the bad guys away from her.

I'd heard Bria yell, and I knew that the Fire elemental was going to kill her, just like she had the rest of my family. So I'd let out my own scream of rage in response—one filled with all the Ice and Stone magic that I could muster.

The first chunk of the ceiling slammed into the ground beside me, snapping me back to the here and now and spraying bits of stone everywhere. Even now, in my shock and confusion, I could hear the black, angry, unending mutters of the stone—all the rage and fear and helplessness that I'd infected it with when I'd used my magic without thinking. All that coursed through the stone like a heart steadily beating, pushing my fury outward with every bloody pump. Thump-thump-thump.

Another piece of the ceiling fell. Then another, and another, until my own house was literally raining down on top of me.

And there was nothing I could do to stop it.

I couldn't even move my chair enough to try to get out of the way of the collapsing ceiling. But the stone did it for me. A large section plummeted to the floor right beside me, and the shock wave from it knocked my chair over and sent rubble flying all over me. I coughed and choked as the dust rose up like a cloud of gray death around me. I flailed around as much as I could, trying to get free from the ropes, from the chair, even though I couldn't see anything now but a thick, dull fog. Somehow, in the roaring confusion, I felt a sharp, jagged edge against my hand, a small piece of rock that had broken off into a daggerlike point.

Hope flared up in my chest, a tiny, sputtering match, and I moved my body as much as I could, trying to use the rock to cut through my heavy bonds.

To my surprise, it worked. Even as the stones rained down on top of me, I felt one of the ropes loosen. I got one of my shoulders out from under it, then my other shoulder. In the fog, I searched for that sharp point, pricking my finger on the edge of it and drawing blood. But that pain was nothing compared to all the others I'd endured tonight.

When I was sure that I knew where the point was, I maneuvered myself around until another one of my bonds was on top of it. Back and forth I rubbed first one rope, then another on top of that tiny, sharp piece of stone.

Finally, the ropes snapped free. It was too late to try to run, so I put my arms up over my head, curled into a tight ball, and protected myself as best as I could from the falling rubble.

I don't know how long it took for the house to collapse, for all the stone and wood and plaster and nails to cave in. But sometime later, the earth quit shaking, and the roar faded away. The stones still muttered around me, though, with low, dark, ugly murmurs that whispered of unending rage and pain. I might only be thirteen, but part of me instinctively knew that the sound would never, ever fade from them.

But I was somehow untouched by the falling debris. I hadn't felt any of it even hit me. My magic, I thought in a daze. I must have used my Ice and Stone magic to harden my skin, even though I didn't remember consciously doing it.

I was still alive—which meant that I needed to find Bria

before the Fire elemental and her men recovered, assuming that they'd survived the collapse of the mansion. So I forced myself to open my eyes, push the rocky rubble off my body, and get up on my trembling, wobbling legs. It took a couple of minutes before my eyes adjusted to the gray, dust-choked air. When my vision finally snapped into focus once more, I wished that it hadn't.

It looked as though a bomb had gone off inside the house. It was just a disaster. Everything crumbled and broken and shattered and torn apart. Small fires flickered here and there in the dust, licking at splintered pieces of wood, furniture, and everything else that had once been part of this room. But the worst part was the glass from my mother's collection of snow globes. The shards littered the ground like a crystal carpet, catching the light from the fires and reflecting it back to me, every sly, bright twinkle reminding me just how much I'd lost tonight.

For a moment, I just stood there, shocked by the extreme damage. Oh, I wasn't proud or vain enough to think that I'd done it all on my own. The flames that the Fire elemental had spread in her wake as she'd gone from room to room, first killing my mother and then Annabella, had definitely weakened the thick wooden beams that supported the ceiling. But still.

I'd never known that I'd had this much magic before.

Somehow, I shook off my horrified daze and started picking my way through the piles of rubble. It wasn't until I was halfway across the room that I realized my hands were still bound together by the duct tape that the Fire elemental had used to make me hold on to my own spider rune medallion while she superheated it.

So I stopped, found another jagged piece of rock, and sliced through the tape. As for my hands, they didn't want to come apart, not with the silverstone melted in between them, holding them together. The magical metal was still warm from where the Fire elemental had heated it, and I knew that if I didn't move my hands now, the silverstone would cool and they'd more than likely be stuck together forever. I couldn't stand having the metal heated again to separate them. I just couldn't.

So I sat down in the rubble next to the sharp stone, gritted my teeth, and started working the rock in between my palms. Using the daggerlike tip to help me peel my hands apart, bit by agonizing bit. It was hard, one of the hardest things I'd ever had to do, and I almost passed out again from the pain more than once. Even then, I couldn't stop the tears that ran down my face or my screams that filled the air.

I would have given up completely, huddled on the floor, and waited to die, if I hadn't been so worried about Bria. My baby sister was the only thing that was keeping me going.

I don't know how long it took me, but I eventually did it. My hands finally separated and scraped down either side of the pointed stone, drawing more blood, but I didn't care. I turned them over and stared down at the marks that now adorned my palms.

A small circle surrounded by eight thin rays. A spider rune. My rune. The symbol for patience. My medallion that I'd worn every single day. Gone now, totally destroyed, except for the horrid red, raw, ugly marks on my palms.

It made me sick.

Everything about tonight made me sick. Despite the pain,

I closed my eyes and curled my hands into tight fists so I wouldn't have to look at the marks. They weren't important right now.

Bria was. I had to find Bria before the Fire elemental did . . .

I woke up in a cold sweat, thrashing around on the bed, the spider rune scars on my palms itching and burning, just the way they had that night so long ago. Just the way they always did whenever I was reminded of that awful time.

I lie on the bed and forced myself to breathe, to let the horrible memory fade, to bottle it up and stick it in the back of my brain where it belonged. After a little while, my breathing eased, the pain faded away, and I came back to myself once more.

My eyes were just level with the nightstand, where I'd tossed my cell phone before going to bed. Spurred on by some emotion that I didn't quite understand, I reached out, flipped it open, and dialed a number I'd memorized. A number Finn had gotten for me. A number Bria didn't even know that I had.

"Hello?" Bria Coolidge's muffled, sleepy voice filled my ear.

I opened my mouth, but no words came out. They never did when my sister was around. Nothing that mattered anyway. None of the important things that I needed to say to her, like *Hi, it's Gin Blanco. Guess what? I'm really your long-lost sister, Genevieve Snow, in disguise. I also happen to be the assassin the Spider. You know, the one who recently declared war on Mab Monroe. The one that you're searching for high and low. The evil villain that you prob-*

ably want to kill yourself, since that's what good, decent, honest cops like you do.

"Hello?" Bria mumbled again. "Hellooo?"

I hung up.

Because Bria wasn't missing. Not anymore. She was here in Ashland and safe for this night, at least. And if I wanted her to stay that way, I needed my own rest. Deep, dark, dreamless sleep free of the memories that haunted me.

Figuring out where Natasha was, tracking down LaFleur, determining how I could best kill the other assassin. That was what was important. I had goals, targets, and certain things that I could do to keep my sister and everyone else I cared about safe, and maybe even save a young girl's life in the process. But to do all that, I needed to relax, rest, think, plan.

Somewhat calmer, for this night at least, I laid my head down on my pillow once more and forced myself to go back to sleep.

It was a long, long time before it actually happened, though.

* 12 *

I didn't sleep nearly as well as I would have liked to, but it was enough to get me through the next day, while I waited for Finn to see what he could dig up on Mab, LaFleur, and where the two of them might have stashed Natasha.

Late the next afternoon, I stood behind the counter at the Pork Pit, the barbecue restaurant I ran in downtown Ashland. I handed a thick wad of change and a white bag stuffed to the brim with food across the counter, along with a similarly filled box. The man took them both from me, smiled, then left the restaurant and headed back out into the December cold.

I let out a loud, long sigh and looked over my shoulder at Sophia Deveraux, who was whipping up yet another pot of baked beans—the thirteenth batch that she'd made already today, and it wasn't even time to close down the restaurant for the night.

"How many party orders was that today? Nine? Ten?"

We hadn't gotten much walk-in traffic at the Pit, not like we usually did, since people were busy shopping and getting ready for Christmas, which was only four days away now. But our takeout orders had quadrupled, along with all the ones for holiday barbecue platters that we offered for large groups and gatherings. Sophia and I had been busy all day long, getting everything ready for pickups from the restaurant, and we still had an hour to go before closing.

The storefront was empty now, except for two couples sitting at different booths. Since they'd already been served and given their checks, I was just waiting for them to pay up and leave. Normally, I would have let them linger as long as they liked, but tonight I was in the mood to hurry them along, if need be. I'd already sent the waitstaff home for the evening. They'd helped Sophia and I put together the party orders, but once that was done, there was no real reason for them to stick around with only a few customers to serve.

Sophia shrugged in answer to my question, her sharp gaze never leaving the bubbling beans in front of her. The dwarf wasn't big on conversation. She gave the pot of beans another stir, the muscles in her arm bulging with the small motion. At five foot one, Sophia was tall for a dwarf, with a thick, muscled figure that was incredibly strong—even stronger than most giants. But most people wouldn't have noticed that about her. At least, not right away.

They'd be too busy staring at the rest of her.

Sophia Deveraux had a very distinctive style about

her—Goth. We're not talking a little black lipstick here. More like the heart of darkness itself. Just about everything that Sophia wore was black, from her heavy boots to her jeans to the plain leather collar that ringed her neck. Her hair and eyes were black too, providing a striking contrast to the absolute paleness of her face—and her crimson lip gloss.

It always amazed me how different Sophia was from her older sister, Jo-Jo. At one hundred and thirteen, Sophia always reminded me of a moody teenager with her Goth wear, while Jo-Jo had already comfortably settled into her middle age with her ladylike pink dresses and ever-present string of white pearls.

Today, though, Sophia had decided to show off her holiday cheer, at least what there was of it, by wearing a pointed Santa hat while she cooked. Black, of course, with a tiny grinning skull dangling off the end of it, instead of the more traditional white fluffy ball. Merry Christmas.

I didn't have time to ponder Sophia's holiday proclivities, though, because the phone rang for what seemed like the hundredth time today. I loved all the extra business, but it had been a long day, and I was almost ready to stick one of my silverstone knives through the plastic receiver just to get it to shut up. Instead, I made myself answer it.

"Pork Pit," I said on the fifth ring.

"Tell me," Owen Grayson's low, sexy baritone rumbled through the receiver. "Do you know where I can get a good plate of barbecue?"

I leaned against the counter that ran along the back wall of the restaurant. "Sorry. I don't have a clue."

He let out a low laugh that warmed me, and I found myself smiling at nothing in particular. There was no one that I'd rather have heard from right now than him. For some reason, Owen soothed me, especially after the terrible dream that I'd had last night. I really was getting soft in my retirement, just like Roslyn Phillips had said. But right now I didn't care.

"You know, you left without saying good-bye yesterday morning," Owen said.

"I do have a restaurant to run you know," I drawled, trying to make light of the fact that I'd skipped out without waking him up.

"Was that the only reason?"

I hesitated. Owen and I hadn't been together all that long but he could already pick up on things that I wished he wouldn't—like my newfound skittishness when it came to our relationship. Or whatever we were calling it. Owen made me feel a lot of things that I didn't know if I was ready for, especially since I was in the middle of trying to take down Mab and had LaFleur and Natasha to worry about in the meantime. Emotions, feelings, letting down my guard. Those were all weaknesses that I just couldn't afford to indulge in right now. Maybe not ever.

"Yeah," I said about five seconds too late. "That was the only reason."

"No worries," Owen said in an easy voice, pretending that he hadn't even noticed my long pause. "It kept me from having to hide your Christmas present from you."

He couldn't have shocked me more than if he'd just gotten LaFleur to pump me full of her electrical elemental magic. For a moment, I just stood there, mouth open, blinking. Then reality set back in.

"Present? You got me a Christmas present?"

He let out another low laugh. "In a manner of speaking. That is the Christmas tradition."

"Oh."

I'd gotten a few small things for Finn and the Deveraux sisters, but it had never occurred to me that Owen might expect something too, given the newness of our relationship. I grabbed a nearby pen and scribbled a note down on the top sheet of my order pad. *Buy Owen Xmas present.* Too bad I had no idea what that present would be or what he would even like. Shopping had never been high on my list of priorities.

"Actually, that's why I'm calling," Owen said. "I wanted to talk to you about Christmas. I thought it might be nice if you came over."

"Oh." It seemed that was the only thing I could say. "But Christmas is family time. I thought that you'd want to spend that with just Eva. I don't want to intrude."

"You're not intruding, Gin," Owen said in a firm voice. "You are never an intrusion."

I fell silent. I didn't know about that. Having an assassin around was kind of like having an elephant in the room. It was so big that you just couldn't look away from it, even when you did your best to pretend it wasn't even there.

Owen must have taken my silence for acceptance because he continued. "I was thinking that you could ask Finn and the Deveraux sisters to join us. Maybe Roslyn and Xavier too, if they'd like. Eva plans to invite Violet and Warren Fox over. We could make it into a real holiday party."

A party? That didn't sound so bad. At least then I wouldn't have to be alone with Owen and Eva and feel like an awkward, socially inept third wheel. Killing people was far easier than making polite chitchat.

"And you could even ask Bria, if you wanted to," Owen finished.

"Oh." I was really dazzling everyone with my conversational skills today.

Owen knew that Detective Bria Coolidge was my long-lost sister and that I desperately wanted to tell her who I really was. But, of course, that I was also afraid of what Bria might do when she found out I'd been an assassin for years and that I was the Spider, the mysterious woman who'd declared war on Mab Monroe.

"Gin?" Owen asked. "Are you still there?"

The bell over the front door chimed, indicating that I had a customer, and saving me from answering him. I hoped it was the call-in order that Sophia had taken a few minutes ago so I could close my gin joint down for the night and get on with finding Natasha.

No such luck. To my surprise and consternation, Jonah McAllister walked through the door.

Despite his sixtysomething years, Jonah McAllister was still an attractive man—if you thought that having absolutely no wrinkles or natural expression in your face was something to be desired. McAllister had his chiseled features sandblasted by expensive Air elemental facials on a regular basis in order to keep his youthful glow intact. His smooth face seemed at odds with his thick coif of silver hair, which swirled around his head and gave him an elegant, distinguished air. A perfectly fitted black suit covered his trim figure, topped by a long black wool overcoat.

But more important than his slick appearance was the fact that Jonah McAllister also happened to be Mab Monroe's personal lawyer and the number two man in her organization now that Elliot Slater was dead. And he was very, very good at what he did. McAllister was known throughout Ashland for his ability to get the worst criminals off with nothing more than a slap on the wrist. Which is why he handled all of Mab's legal affairs. Thanks to McAllister's expertise, the Fire elemental had never been charged with anything, not even a traffic violation, much less taken to court, despite all the murders, kidnappings, and beatings that Mab had ordered over the years—or had simply rolled up her sleeves and done herself.

Jonah McAllister also happened to hate me, since he suspected me of being involved with his son, Jake's, death a few weeks ago. That's when Jake had come into the Pork Pit, scared and threatened my customers, and tried to rob me before I'd shown him exactly whom he was dealing with. But the punk hadn't learned from his first mistake. During one of Mab's parties, Jake had threatened to rape and murder me, so I'd stabbed him to death and left him in the Fire elemental's bathtub. Needless to say, the older McAllister had been extremely upset.

Ever since then, Jonah McAllister had kept an eye on me, trying to figure out what, if anything, I knew about his son's murder. McAllister had even had Slater and some of his giant goons attack me one night over at Ashland

Community College. Of course, I hadn't cracked under the pressure of the giants' fists, even though they'd almost beaten me to death. But that didn't stop McAllister from suspecting me. So far, the slick attorney had gotten exactly nowhere, but he hadn't given up, as witnessed by his visit here tonight. No doubt he'd dropped by just to see what other kind of trouble he could make for me.

McAllister stepped to one side, holding the door open for someone coming in behind him, and I realized that the lawyer wasn't alone. He had a woman with him, one that I recognized.

LaFleur.

❖ 13 ❖

In the split-second it took me to register the fact that Jonah McAllister and LaFleur were here in the Pork Pit, in my restaurant, in my gin joint, all sorts of scenarios flickered through my mind. Most of them involved my killing the two of them where they stood and helping Sophia dispose of the bodies.

The Goth dwarf had helped Fletcher Lane dispose of bodies for years, and I'd inherited her services when I'd taken over the assassination business from the old man. Sophia had the same Air elemental magic as her sister, Jo-Jo. Except in Sophia's case, she used her power to rip molecules apart, to break them down and tear them into nothingness. All of which was great for getting pesky little things like bloodstains off floors and walls.

My eyes strayed to the two couples still lingering over their food. Sophia and I couldn't take care of McAllister and LaFleur, not in front of four witnesses. Anyway, it was better to see what the dynamic duo actually wanted first before I made my move.

"I've got to go," I told Owen. "I just had a customer walk in the front door."

"Anyone I know?" he asked.

"Jonah McAllister. And he has the new girl in town with him."

Silence. I'd told Owen all about LaFleur and what her plans were for me the other night when I'd been at his house.

"Do you need some help, Gin?" Owen asked in a soft voice. "I can be there in ten minutes."

And this thing might be over with in one, depending on what the two of them wanted and what they knew about me and who I really was. Still, it pleased me that Owen cared enough to come, that he wanted to help me, wanted to stick his neck out for me.

I put my left hand down under the counter out of sight and palmed one of my silverstone knives. The blade was sharp enough to cut through almost anything, including McAllister's inflated ego—and neck.

"No, I think I can handle it. Sophia's here now, and Finn is on his way. Four really would be a crowd," I murmured. "Besides, they're not here to kill me. They want something instead. They wouldn't have come in through the front door otherwise. And if they knew who I really was, they would have brought some of Mab's giants along with them for backup, at the very least. Maybe even Mab herself, if she was in the mood to watch."

More silence.

"Will I see you tonight then?" Owen asked. "When it's over?"

"Probably not. I have a feeling that I'm going to be busy."

Owen blew out a tense breath. "All right. Just—be careful. And call me later, okay?"

"Okay," I said and hung up.

Jonah McAllister's brown eyes flicked over the storefront, and his lip curled up into a faint sneer, the way it always did when he came in here. With its simple, blue and pink vinyl booths, the Pork Pit wasn't exactly the expensive, elegant, highfalutin joint McAllister was used to dining in. I doubted that he ever went anywhere where the floor was covered with pig tracks done in peeling blue and pink paint, respectively, that led to the men's and women's restrooms.

Still, the lawyer carefully examined everything before his eyes slid to me standing behind the cash register, which sat on top of a long counter running down the back wall. To my left, a bloody framed copy of *Where the Red Fern Grows* decorated the wall, along with a picture of Fletcher Lane in his younger years. Both were mementoes of Fletcher that I kept in his restaurant as a tribute to the old man.

McAllister drew off first one of his black leather gloves, then the other, tucking them into the pocket of his long coat before striding toward me. His walk was just as slick and smooth as everything else about him, designed to impress and intimidate at the same time.

"Jonah McAllister," I drawled, still holding my silverstone knife out of sight below the counter. "To what do I owe this honor?"

McAllister gave me a cold, thin smile that didn't even come close to stretching his tight features or reaching his brown eyes. "Gin Blanco. So lovely to see you again. As for what I want, well, I thought that I'd show my lady friend here some of the sights of Ashland. She's new in town and trying to get the lay of the land, so to speak."

LaFleur stepped up next to McAllister, and I got my first close-up look at the assassin. She wore a pair of tight, black leather pants, topped with an expensive flowing silk shirt done in a dark green. Thin ribbons laced up the front of the shirt, giving it a bit of old-fashioned elegance. A matching green pea coat completed the stylish ensemble, along with a pair of black stiletto boots. A headband made of emeralds kept her short, black hair back off her face. An expensive bauble. I could tell that the gems were real and not just glass, because I could hear the stones whispering of their own proud beauty. A smug, arrogant sound that perfectly matched what I knew of their owner.

LaFleur had a heart-shaped face that was almost as beautiful as Roslyn's. The assassin's skin was as smooth and pale as marble—perfectly flawless. Her eyes were a bright, vivid green—the same color as the lightning that I'd seen her use to blast the dwarf on the docks the other night. Even now, her electrical magic sparked in the depths of her green gaze. Just a hint of elemental power surrounded her, the kind of faint static charge that you felt in the air right before a lightning storm, but it still made the silverstone embedded in my hands itch and burn.

As for her figure, LaFleur was petite, with a trim, athletic build. She might be thin, but there was a lean, coiled strength to her body that her expensive clothes just couldn't hide.

But the most curious thing about her was the tattoo.

It started at the hollow of her throat as a simple vine that curled up her neck until it unfurled into a single, perfect orchid. The faintest hints of green, peach, and cream-white inked in the tattoo. The artistry was exquisite in its detail, and given the petal-soft quality of La-Fleur's skin, it was almost like looking at a real flower. The steady thump of her pulse in her throat made the orchid's leaves and petals twitch ever so slightly, like it was constantly blossoming.

Well, it looked as if Fletcher had been right about La-Fleur's having some sort of tattoo. And now that I'd seen it, I knew that it was even more than that. The orchid was also LaFleur's rune, the symbol for delicate grace. That's why she always left a single white orchid behind at the scene of her kills. Because it was her mark, just the way my spider rune was to me, or Mab Monroe's sunburst necklace was to her. LaFleur left an actual flower behind instead of just drawing the complicated rune somewhere. Maybe she didn't have the artistic skill to re-create the rune, or maybe she just didn't want to take the time. After all, most assassins didn't stick around too long after their hits. That was a good way to get caught or get dead.

Still, something about the orchid tattoo bothered me. Maybe it was the way it was placed on her neck, how it curled up her skin, but I knew that I'd seen one like it somewhere before. On someone that I'd killed before—

"It's so nice to meet you, Gin," the assassin said, interrupting my thoughts. Her voice was lower than I thought it would be, with a faintly sibilant, seductive tone. "I'm Elektra LaFleur."

I kept my face smooth, as though the name LaFleur meant nothing to me. Elektra, either, even though it was an obvious play on her electrical power. What a cliché. I wondered if that was her real name or one that she'd just chosen for herself, given her elemental magic. Didn't much matter either way. She was still going to die.

I nodded my head at her, even as my thumb traced over the hilt of my silverstone knife.

At this point, Sophia had gotten interested in things. The Goth dwarf knew all about my problems with Jonah McAllister and had actually stopped stirring her pot of baked beans long enough to stare over her shoulder at the three of us. Sophia made a questioning sort of growl low in her throat, telling me that she was up for whatever I wanted to do, however I wanted to handle McAllister and LaFleur.

I met the dwarf's black gaze and made a flat, level, slashing motion with my hand, the one still holding the knife down out of sight. *No,* I was telling her. *Stay cool.* There was no real problem here—yet.

Besides, I wanted to see exactly what McAllister wanted, exactly why he'd brought LaFleur here to the Pit, before we got into anything . . . messy.

"So do we seat ourselves or is there somewhere . . . special that we need to go?" McAllister asked.

My eyes narrowed. "You came here to eat? In my restaurant?"

That was one of the very last things I'd ever expected him to say.

McAllister gave me another cold smile. "That is what one does here, is it not? I was under the impression that you were running a restaurant." His brown eyes roamed over the clean, but well-worn, interior once more. "Such as it is."

The arrogant sneer in McAllister's bombastic voice might have made a lesser woman cower. Instead, below the counter, my hand tightened around my silverstone knife.

But instead of bringing up my weapon and ending the arrogant lawyer's miserable existence, I tucked it into a slot under the cash register. There was nothing I could do but seat them. Not without creating a whole lot of trouble for everyone in the restaurant.

If it had just been me and Sophia, well, I might have brought up my hidden knife and slit Elektra LaFleur's throat with it before turning my deadly brand of attention to Jonah McAllister. But there were innocent people in here, people who had nothing to do with my feud with McAllister.

Even when I'd been the Spider full-time and assassinating people for money, I'd never killed innocents, no matter what. There were certain rules that you just didn't break, even if you were a cold-hearted bitch of an assassin like me. No kids, no pets, no bystanders. It was a code that Fletcher had taught me, one that I'd lived by for years. One that I still adhered to today—and one of the few things that was keeping McAllister alive right now.

Besides, I wanted to see exactly what kind of game the lawyer was playing, what he thought he was doing here, other than being a dick. So I leaned over, picked up a couple of stray menus, and stepped around to the other side of the counter.

"This way."

I led them over to a booth next to the storefront windows, which was as far away from the back counter, Sophia, and the other two pairs of diners as I could get them. Still too close for my liking, though.

Jonah and Elektra settled themselves in the booth, sitting on opposite sides. I handed each one of them a menu and took a step back.

"What would you like to drink?" I asked in a flat voice.

"I suppose it's too much to hope you have any sort of wine here," Jonah sneered again. "I imagine it would just be cheap swill anyway. Or worse, some sort of home-grown moonshine."

"Jonah will have an ice water with lemon," Elektra interrupted him in a smooth tone. "And I'll have a strawberry lemonade."

I raised an eyebrow, mildly surprised that she was ordering for him—and that he didn't dress her down for having the nerve to do it.

Elektra reached over and started tracing small circles with her fingertips on the back of McAllister's smooth hand. She gave him a sly smile, which he returned, before his cold brown eyes dropped to what he could see of her cleavage through the undone ribbons on her green shirt. A knowing smirk curved his tight face, like he knew exactly what was underneath the slick fabric.

Oh. So that's how it was. An interesting development. I wondered if Mab Monroe knew that her lawyer was fucking her assassin. I was willing to bet no. The Fire elemental would frown on that kind of fraternization, if only to make sure that her minions stayed loyal to her alone. Not that I imagined that McAllister and LaFleur had any kind of real love connection, but still, people would do a lot of crazy things for sex. Like kill for it.

"I'll be back in a minute to take your orders."

Jonah waved his hand at me, a clear indication that I was dismissed. Anger filled me at his arrogance, but I didn't act on it. Instead, I put the emotion aside for now. It would only motivate me that much more later, when there was no one around but me, McAllister, and my silverstone knives.

I stalked away from their booth and went back behind the counter

"Call Finn," I said in a low voice to Sophia as I grabbed a couple of glasses and filled them with ice. "Tell him that LaFleur is here and will probably be here for at least the next hour. Tell him to park out on the street and follow her and McAllister when they leave. The two of them just might lead us to Natasha. And tell Finn to bring whatever supplies he might need to finish things. I want to end this—tonight."

Sophia grunted her acknowledgment and kept stirring her beans.

I finished fixing the drinks. Then I grabbed my order pad and pen, along with the glasses, and walked back over to their booth. I plunked down the drinks, not caring that McAllister's water slopped over the side and spilled onto the table.

And neither did Elektra LaFleur.

A drop of water landed on her skin, and a green spark

immediately sizzled to life there. *Bzzzt.* The water crackled against her flesh as though she was a real-life bug zapper, and since one of my hands was down in the water on the table, I felt the shock of it zip through the liquid and up into my body. To my surprise, it *hurt,* like I'd just stuck my finger into a socket and gotten a bad jolt—one that made my teeth clench and my heart race. Startled, I looked at her.

LaFleur gave me a soft, warm smile, her eyes a much brighter green now, more electricity sparking in her gaze. She knew that she'd zinged me with her power, and she'd liked the fact that I'd felt it and that it had hurt. Maybe she'd even sensed my surprise and discomfort, given her elemental magic, the way that I could hear murmurs in stone. And I suddenly knew that's why she electrocuted people when she assassinated them, instead of using a knife or a gun. LaFleur enjoyed feeling other people's pain. She probably got some kind of high off it, like so many elementals did when they used their magic. Sadistic bitch.

"I hate winter, don't you?" Elektra said in a bored tone. "All this static electricity in the air. I'm always getting a jolt. Aren't you?"

"Sure," I muttered. "Happens all the time. What'll it be?"

Jonah McAllister ordered a cheeseburger and fries, while Elektra LaFleur opted for a barbecue pork sandwich with baked beans, French fries, and a side of coleslaw. The woman had a healthy appetite, that was for sure. I wondered where she was going to put it all on that lean frame of hers. Then again, I supposed she needed a lot of juice to fry people alive with her electrical magic.

I went back over to the counter. Sometime while I'd been talking to McAllister and LaFleur, Sophia had disappeared into the back of the restaurant. A moment later, the Goth dwarf pushed through the swinging doors and resumed her position in front of the stove.

"Finn?" I asked in a low voice, slapping a hamburger patty onto the hot griddle.

"On his way," Sophia rasped in her broken voice.

In silence, the two of us worked to get the order ready. I finished McAllister's cheeseburger, while Sophia dished up LaFleur's baked beans. I didn't look over my shoulder, but I could hear McAllister and LaFleur talking softly.

I turned around and grabbed some clean white plates to put their food on, which meant that I was facing out toward the restaurant again.

To my surprise, Elektra LaFleur had slid over in the booth so that her back was up against the storefront glass and she could see the whole restaurant. Her green eyes moved slowly over the interior, checking out every single thing inside, from the floor and walls to the long counter to the swinging doors that led to the back of the restaurant.

Finally, her eyes landed on me, and she watched me assemble the food. Her sharp green gaze took in everything about me, from the way that my hands moved to the greasy blue apron that covered my long-sleeved black T-shirt and jeans. She didn't sneer at me the way that Jonah had done earlier, though. All she did was watch me, a thoughtful, calculating expression on her beautiful face.

It was a look that I knew—a mask I'd worn on more

than one occasion. And I realized what she was doing, why she was here in the first place. She was scoping out the restaurant—and me.

Sizing up her latest target, just like assassins did.

Just like she was going to come back and kill me later.

Of course.

Jonah McAllister hated me. He had ever since I'd dared to stand up to him when he'd tried to pressure me into forgetting that his son, Jake, had tried to rob my restaurant and kill the innocent diners inside. The lawyer had wanted me to drop the charges against Jake, but I hadn't played ball, which had annoyed him to no end. Plus, McAllister thought that I knew something about Jake's murder. That's why he'd had Elliot Slater almost beat me to death a few weeks ago at the community college. And McAllister had wanted Slater to go ahead and finish the job when I'd run into the two of them again a few days after that.

That's why Jonah McAllister had come here tonight and brought LaFleur along with him. He wanted the assassin to kill me, Gin Blanco. She was in town anyway to take care of the Spider. Why not have LaFleur get rid of me while she was at it? The arrogant lawyer just didn't realize that I was the Spider as well.

A cold, hard smile curved my lips. Irony. What a bitch. But something that could actually be useful to me in this instance.

With Sophia's help, I finished the orders, grabbed the plates, and took everything over to the booth. Again, I felt LaFleur's eyes on me, watching the way I moved, calculating my strength, balance, and stamina, just the way I would have if I were looking at a person that I was planning on killing later.

I dumped the platters on the table much the same way that I had their drinks. But there was no water slopping around, so LaFleur couldn't shock me again this time. "Enjoy."

I hoped they both choked on their food, but I knew that was just too much to ask. Especially with my bad luck.

"Oh," LaFleur drawled. "We will."

I looked at her, careful to keep the calm, cold violence out of my face. LaFleur stared at me a second longer before turning to her food. Apparently she thought that she knew everything there was to know about me. She just didn't realize I could wear the mask of a simple restaurant owner as well and easily as she wore her expensive clothes. That I'd been taught how to do so by Fletcher Lane, by the Tin Man, one of the best assassins there had ever been.

One of the other couples was ready to leave, so I went back to the cash register, took their money, and sent them on their way. Then I plopped down on my stool behind the counter and picked up the latest book that I was reading, *The Iliad*. Winter classes weren't due to start back up at Ashland Community College until after the first of the year, but I was getting a head start on the classic Greek literature course I'd already signed up for.

Everything was quiet for the next thirty minutes. I read my book, Sophia cooked her latest batch of beans, the other couple gobbled up their dinner, and my enemies dug into theirs.

Finally, Jonah McAllister and Elektra LaFleur finished their meal and headed over to the cash register. McAllister reached into his wallet and handed me some bills. I was vaguely surprised that he was even bothering to pay at all, but I supposed that he wanted me to think he'd come here tonight only for the food. As if I could be that stupid.

"Keep the change, Gin," McAllister said in a smarmy, mocking voice. "Consider it an early Christmas present."

"Aw," I drawled. "A whopping thirteen cents. You're too kind, Jonah. Why, you'd put Ebenezer Scrooge to shame with your bighearted generosity."

McAllister's smooth face darkened at my insult, but LaFleur looped her arm through his, and the anger glittering in Jonah's brown eyes melted into sly certainty.

"Well, you should spend it while you can, Ms. Blanco," McAllister said. "You just never know what might happen in these uncertain times."

He and the assassin headed toward the door. Just before they stepped outside into the cold, Elektra LaFleur turned back to me, her green eyes as bright and hard as jade in her face.

"The food was excellent. I imagine that I'll be coming back here soon, Gin. Real soon."

With a smirk, Elektra walked out the door after Jonah. I watched them leave.

"Not if I kill you first, bitch," I muttered. "Not if I kill you first."

* 14 *

Sophia came over to stand beside me, her black eyes still fixed on the front door that Jonah McAllister and Elektra LaFleur had just walked out of.

"Assassin?" she rasped.

"Yeah, that was LaFleur," I said. "Did you see the way that she was checking out the place?"

Sophia nodded instead of actually answering me. The Goth dwarf spoke as little as possible, since her broken, raspy voice sounded like she'd spent her entire life downing rotgut whiskey, puffing on cigarettes, and gargling gasoline. Sophia didn't have any of those vices, at least not that I knew of, and I always wondered what had happened to the dwarf to so completely ruin her voice. But I never asked her. Whatever it was, I knew that it couldn't possibly be good. Sophia's secret pain was her own to share or not. Just like mine was.

"Problem?" Sophia asked, cutting into my reverie.

"Yeah, LaFleur's going to make a run at me here at the Pit," I said. "That's the only reason I can think of that McAllister brought her here. She was planning the best way to kill me, probably sometime in the next few days. McAllister wants me dead, and he's asked her to do it while she's in town."

"Ready," Sophia said, reached over, and squeezed.

I squeezed back and smiled at the dwarf. "I know you'll be ready. And I will be too. Elektra LaFleur's going to get the surprise of her life when she comes here to kill Gin Blanco—and finds the Spider waiting for her instead."

Sophia and I went back to work, cleaning up the restaurant for the night. The other couple paid up and left, and I was thinking about flipping the sign on the door over to *Closed* when the front bell chimed and a woman stepped inside the Pork Pit. As always, her appearance startled me and took my breath away at the same time—as well as filling me with a touch of cold dread.

Detective Bria Coolidge. My baby sister.

Like so many others moving about on the frosty streets this evening, Bria wore a long coat over a pair of jeans and thick but stylish black Bella Bulluci boots. Her V-neck sweater was a Christmas green in keeping with the season, while a gold badge winked on the leather belt around her slender waist. In contrast, her gun looked like a blob of black ink next to it.

The badge marked Bria as a detective with the Ashland Police Department, but she didn't really look like a cop. She was far too pretty for that, with her longish shag of blond hair, cornflower blue eyes, rosy cheeks, and rocking figure.

Besides the badge and the gun, Bria also wore a silver-stone medallion on a short chain around her neck. A delicate primrose, the symbol for beauty. The same rune, the same necklace, that our mother had given her as a child, one that I'd never seen her without, even now as an adult. Three rings also gleamed on her left index finger, thin silverstone bands each sporting tiny runes. Snowflakes ringed the bottom band, while ivy vines curled around the middle one. The final ring, the top one, was stamped with a single symbol in the middle—a spider rune. My rune, the symbol for patience. I supposed that the rings were Bria's way of remembering our shattered family, just as the drawings on the mantel at Fletcher Lane's house were mine.

"Gin," Bria said in her high, lilting voice. "Good to see you again."

She nodded at me, and I returned the favor. Bria and I hadn't exactly started off on the right foot. I'd first seen her a few weeks ago, the night that Slater had attacked me at the community college. To say that it had been a shock would be a serious understatement. I'd known that my sister was alive, after thinking her dead for years, but seeing her in the flesh had been something else. Enough to make me cry, especially since I'd been looking for her myself with no success. But there she had been, as large as life and back in Ashland after so many long years gone.

Bria had also been the detective assigned to find out what had happened to me that night, and she'd dogged my steps after that, trying to get me to tell her who had hurt me and why. She'd also suspected me of somehow being involved with Roslyn Phillips, of keeping the vampire's location from her when Roslyn had been hiding from Slater. But since everything had turned out all right in the end, with Roslyn living and Slater rotting in the ground, Bria's icy attitude toward me had thawed a bit. As had my wary one toward her.

"You too, detective," I said and meant it. "What can I do for you this evening?"

She moved closer, putting her hands up on the counter beside the cash register. The lights made her silverstone rings wink at me one after another, like all-seeing eyes that knew every one of my deep, dark secrets. "I called earlier. I'm here to pick up my takeout."

That must have been the order that Sophia had taken over the phone before McAllister and LaFleur had come into the Pork Pit. But she hadn't bothered to tell me it was Bria's, even though Sophia knew all about my sister. I looked at the dwarf, who gave me a small grin and went back to wiping down the counter. I supposed that this was Sophia's way of getting me to talk to Bria. The Goth dwarf could be sneaky when she put her mind to it.

"I would have been here to get it sooner," Bria said, leaning against the counter. "But I got stuck late working a case."

"Really?" I asked, moving to get the white bag that Sophia had packed Bria's food in. "Which case was this?"

As a whole, Ashland was a violent city, full of lots of powerful people with lots of powerful grudges against each other, as well as your more mundane criminals just trying to make a buck. There was so much crime here that it was hard to tell what kind of case Bria might be working. It could be everything from a domestic dispute to a gangbanger drive-by to a missing person—

"The Spider killed three more men last night. Or, at least, someone left her symbol behind at the crime scene," Bria answered.

Years of Fletcher's training kept me from showing any emotion, but once again, I cursed luck. Of all the detectives in Ashland, my sister had to be the one investigating my nighttime activities as the Spider. First, Jonah McAllister had brought Elektra LaFleur by so that the assassin could put her bull's-eye on my forehead, and now Bria was joining the firing squad. Irony was really kicking me in the teeth tonight.

"Oh." Once again, I was the conversational genius.

I set the bag of takeout on the counter between us, as if that would somehow derail Bria's train of thought. Not likely. I might not have seen her in the last seventeen years, but since her arrival back in Ashland a few weeks ago, she'd been nothing but tenacious, showing me exactly what kind of strong, confident, dedicated woman she'd grown up to be.

Then there was the fact that Bria was also one of the few honest cops in the city. With all the crime in Ashland, it was far easier for members of the police department to take bribes to look the other way than to actually investigate crimes and arrest the perpetrators. A couple of C-notes in their fat wallets made for far less paperwork. But Bria was different. She didn't turn a blind eye to crimes or bury her head in the sand—ever. Even more than that, she actually tried to help people, tried to bring some comfort to victims and put as many bad guys as she could behind bars. And now she was gunning for me, the Spider. Despite the fact that Bria knew that the assassin and her long-lost sister Genevieve Snow were one and the same.

While I admired Bria's strength and determination, her dedication to her day job also had the unfortunate reality of interfering with my plans to kill Elektra LaFleur, Jonah McAllister, Mab Monroe, and anyone else who threatened the people I loved.

Instead of reaching for the bag or digging into her jeans for some cash to pay for the food, Bria stared at me with her blue eyes—eyes that reminded me of our mother and older sister. They'd all had the same beautiful features and coloring. I was the only one who'd gotten our father, Tristan's, gray eyes and chocolate brown hair—along with his Stone magic.

My Ice magic had come from our mother, and Bria had inherited it as well. I'd seen her use her Ice power only a few times, most notably to try to save herself from being murdered by Elliot Slater and his giants. They'd paid her a late-night visit when she'd first come to Ashland a few weeks ago, but luckily, I'd been there to take care of them instead. Still, Bria's magic had felt strong to me, just as strong as our mother's had been.

"Have you heard anything?" Bria asked me in a low voice. "Any . . . talk in the neighborhood about the Spider and this vendetta that she has against Mab Monroe? Because the men that she killed last night were giants, two of them anyway, and from what I can tell, they worked for the Fire elemental."

"Why would you think that I would know something?" I asked.

Bria shrugged. "This is a popular place. Lots of people come in and out of here all day long. I thought that maybe you or one of your cooks or waitresses might have overheard something. Somebody bragging about being the Spider. Something like that."

I raised an eyebrow. "From what I read in the newspapers, the Spider doesn't seem like the kind of person to brag about what she does. She kills people and then vanishes without a trace. At least, that's my impression of her."

Bria turned around one of the rings on her index finger. The top ring, the one with the spider rune stamped on it. My ring.

"Yeah," she said in a soft voice. "That's something that I plan on talking to her about, when I find her. And I *will* find her, Gin. Make no mistake about that."

We didn't speak. Sophia continued wiping down the counter, but the dwarf kept her black eyes on the two of us, just watching.

Bria let out a long sigh and started digging into her jeans pocket. "So what do I owe you for the food?"

I waved my hand. "Your money's no good here tonight. It's on the house."

Bria shook her head. The motion made the light dance on the primrose rune around her neck. My heart twisted at the sight.

"You should let me pay you, Gin. I know how hard you work."

I held back a snort. I doubted that her tone would be so kind, so considerate, if she knew how much money I had stashed away in various bank accounts—money that I'd gotten for killing people.

I glanced at the ticket stapled to the bag. "It's a ham sandwich, beans, fries, and two pieces of strawberry pie. Don't worry. It's not going to break me. Besides," I said, thinking of Jonah McAllister and his measly thirteen cents. "A customer gave me a big tip tonight anyway. More than enough to cover your meal, detective."

She opened her mouth, but I cut her off.

"I insist," I said in a firm voice. "Think of it as an early Christmas present."

The least I could do was slip my own sister a free meal now and then. The *very* least.

"All right," Bria said, being gracious enough to take me up on my offer. "Thanks. I appreciate it."

She grabbed the bag, gave me a nod and a smile, and turned to go.

Sophia cleared her throat—loudly. I glanced over at the dwarf, and she stabbed a stubby finger in Bria's direction before stabbing it back in mine. Then, Sophia crossed her arms over her chest and gave me a flat stare. I felt like a naughty schoolgirl being chastised by her nun of a teacher. I knew what the dwarf wanted. For me to talk to Bria, to get her to stay, to do something, anything, to further our relationship, even if it was only the tiniest bit.

"Um, detective?" I said.

Bria stopped and looked over her shoulder at me.

"I know that you don't have any . . . family in Ashland." The lie stuck in my throat like lumpy gravy, but I forced it out. "I was wondering if you had any plans for Christmas."

I knew that because I kept an eye on Bria whenever

she came into the Pork Pit, trying to learn everything I could about her. Usually she brought Xavier along with her, since the giant was her partner on the force whenever he wasn't busy helping Roslyn run Northern Aggression. Finn had also compiled a fat folder of information on Bria that contained just about everything that she'd ever done in her twenty-five years.

But for some reason I just hadn't been able to bring myself to look at the file, and it lay unopened on the coffee table in the den in Fletcher's house. I didn't want to read about what my sister had been up to all these years—I wanted her to tell me herself. About her life, about her job, even about her hopes and dreams. Sappy and sentimental of me, but I didn't care.

Every time that Bria came into the Pork Pit to eat, I tried to strike up some kind of conversation with her, tried to learn more about my sister and what she'd been doing since the last time that I saw her, when she was eight years old. To let her tell me in her own words about all the things that had happened to her since that horrible night when our family had been torn apart by Mab.

From the bits and pieces that she'd told me and what Xavier had let slip, I knew that Bria had been adopted by a couple named Coolidge. The man had been a cop down in Savannah, Georgia, where they'd lived, and he was Bria's inspiration for joining the force. Her foster father had died a couple of years ago from a heart attack. Her foster mother had followed him a year later, hit and killed by a drunk driver.

By all accounts, they'd both loved Bria, and she'd loved them. I'd learned a while back that when your family had been murdered and torn away from you like mine had, you had to make a new family for yourself. Sometimes with what was left of your own flesh and blood, and sometimes with the people you met along the way. It helped to ease the pain.

Shadows darkened Bria's blue eyes, and her mouth flattened into a tight line. "I was planning on working Christmas and letting somebody else spend the day with her family since I don't really have any."

The harsh tone in my sister's voice indicated that I should drop this awkward conversation. I looked at Sophia, who cleared her throat again and raised her eyebrows, a rare show of expression from her. The dwarf didn't want me to give up. Neither would Finn, Owen, or Jo-Jo, if they'd been here. The truth was that I didn't want to give up either. Not when Bria was finally back in my life after so many years. Not when Fletcher had gone to so much trouble to make sure that I knew that she was alive and to bring her back to Ashland in the first place.

"Well, Owen Grayson is having some people over at his house," I said, taking the plunge. "Me, Finn, Xavier, Roslyn. I thought that if you weren't doing anything else, you might like to join us."

After, of course, I called Finn, Xavier, and Roslyn and asked them all to come.

Bria didn't say anything, but a sad sort of longing flickered in her blue eyes. It matched the ache in my heart.

"I'm cooking," I said, trying to sweeten the pot, so to speak. "So I can assure you that the food will be excellent."

After, of course, I told Owen that I was whipping up a Christmas feast for all the people that I hadn't actually invited over to his house yet.

Bria stared at me a moment more before answering. "I don't want to intrude," she said in a soft voice.

I smiled at her, letting a rare bit of warmth creep into my cold gray eyes. "You won't be intruding. You're Xavier's partner. You're practically family now, Bria."

Behind me, Sophia let out a soft snicker at my lame attempt to establish some sort of connection with my sister. Yeah, my words dripped with cheese, and I knew that it was amusing to see big, bad Gin Blanco reduced to pleading just to spend a few hours with her own bloody sister. But still, this comedy of errors had been the dwarf's idea to start with.

I turned and glared at Sophia. Below the counter, out of Bria's line of sight, I grabbed the silverstone knife that I'd stuck in there when McAllister and LaFleur had come into the restaurant. I brandished the weapon at the dwarf, telling her exactly what I was going to do to her if she didn't quit her giggling.

But my flashing the blade only made her snicker harder. Given her extremely thick, dwarven musculature, I could make Sophia look like a pincushion with my silverstone knives, and it wouldn't hurt her—much. At least, not as much as she'd hurt me with her fists, something that we both knew.

"I'll . . . think about it," Bria finally said.

I gave her another smile, but her lack of commitment made some of the warmth drain out of my features. "You do that."

Bria nodded at me once more, then turned and headed out of the restaurant. This time, I didn't try to call her back or stop her from leaving, even though my heart felt as cold and empty as the snowy night outside as the door swung shut behind her.

✲ 15 ✲

I stood there staring at the front door of the Pork Pit, wishing Bria would come back, wishing I could just tell her who I really was without worrying about how she would react to the information. But I didn't want to immediately lose my sister all over again when I'd just found her, which is probably how things would go if I told her I was the Spider.

I shook my head and pushed away my wistful thoughts. Now was not the time to be sloppy and sentimental. Not when I had an assassin to stalk and kill tonight, and hopefully, a little girl to rescue. So I locked the front door, dug my cell phone out of my jeans, and called Finn. He answered on the first ring.

"What took you so long?" Finn groused in my ear. "I've been following LaFleur for almost half an hour now. I got in position just like you wanted, Gin. I expected you to call as soon as she left the restaurant with Jonah McAllister."

"Sorry," I murmured. "I had one more customer I had to take care of. But the restaurant's closed now, and you have my complete and undivided attention. So what's happening?"

"Well, after they left the Pork Pit, LaFleur and McAllister got into his limo, which was parked just down the block," Finn said. "You might be interested to know that the two of them started sucking face before they even got into the backseat."

I thought of the way I'd seen Jonah look at Elektra earlier. "Yeah, they're fucking each other. What else?"

Finn huffed. "Must you always ruin my surprises?"

"Yes," I replied. "Then what happened?"

I heard Finn take a sip of something through the phone. Probably from his fifteenth cup of chicory coffee of the day. It was a wonder his stomach didn't explode from all the caffeine he sucked down on a daily basis.

"The limo cruised through downtown, going absolutely nowhere in particular, probably so Jonah and our good assassin could have a little personal time," Finn replied. "After that, the limo whisked them away to the always elegant confines of the old Ashland train yard. LaFleur disappeared into the hallowed depths. McAllister watched her go, obviously admiring her ass, then got back into the limo and rode away. I chose to stay with LaFleur, since we both know that you can stiff the lawyer any old time you want to."

"True, McAllister isn't nearly the problem that LaFleur is." I frowned. "But why did he take her to the old train yard? What is she doing there?"

Like most metropolitan cities, train lines crisscrossed

through the greater Ashland area before their slender metal rails snaked out into the more mountainous countryside. Several years ago, the city had built a fancy new complex for passenger rail service out in the Northtown suburbs that included a state-of-the-art train station, upscale shops, a couple of five-star restaurants, and several ritzy hotels.

As a result, the old Ashland train yard on the outskirts of downtown had been largely abandoned and left to rust. Oh, trains hauling coal, lumber, and other industrial products still rumbled past the area on their regular daily schedules, as it was the quickest and most direct route through town, but none of them actually stopped there anymore. These days, the train yard was a popular area for homeless bums, who liked to squat in the abandoned railcars to take shelter from the cold. At least until the cops could be bothered to come out and roust them.

"It looks to me like LaFleur's set up shop here," Finn replied. "There's a lot of activity out here, and I'm not just talking about hobos starting trash can fires. Giants moving around lots of construction equipment and building materials. Some dwarves and humans too, all working on some of the old railcars and what used to be the old train depot. Looks like they're building something brand new."

I thought about what Vinnie Volga had told me, about how Mab Monroe was planning on opening up her own nightclub in Ashland, a place that would offer absolutely anything a person's black heart could desire, no matter how twisted, perverted, illegal, or deadly it was.

"You think this is where Mab is going to establish her new business?" I asked.

Through the phone, I heard Finn take another sip of his coffee. "That thought crossed my mind as well, so I did some checking on my laptop after I realized that LaFleur was going to be here a while. Guess who just happens to have bought up all the land in the area recently, including the train yard itself."

My hand tightened around the phone. "Mab Monroe."

"The one and the same," Finn said. "Whether it's the new nightclub or not, Mab's up to something out here. And LaFleur is helping her with it."

That was more than enough reason for me to pay a visit to the area tonight. But there was something else I wanted to know before I met Finn—the reason we were doing all of this in the first place.

"Any sign of Natasha?" I asked.

I doubted that the little girl was still alive. Mab's men had probably killed her last night, since they'd been planning to do the same to Vinnie. Given what Bria had told me, the bodies of the three men I'd disposed of last night had been found at the park, along with my rune. The Fire elemental would know that I was responsible for stiffing her goons. And since Vinnie wasn't among the corpses, Mab would also realize that I'd gotten my hands on him—and that he'd probably spilled his guts to me about LaFleur and everything else that was going on.

All of which meant that there was just no reason for Mab to keep Natasha alive, except maybe for use in her sick nightclub. I had Vinnie now, not the Fire elemental, so the girl was no good as leverage anymore. But there was a slim chance that she might still be breathing—there was always a chance, even if it rarely turned out that way.

But more important was that I'd made a promise to Vinnie to do what I could to find his daughter. Or at least make the people who took her pay—with their lives.

"Not yet," Finn said. "But I'm going to take a casual stroll around the premises and see what I can see. Might be nice if you came and joined the party. You know, like you wanted me to last night at the park."

I rolled my eyes. "Must you always mock me with my own words?"

"Yes," he chirped in a happy tone. "So you coming or not?"

"Oh, you know me," I drawled. "I never miss a good party."

I told Sophia what Finn and I were going to do and asked her to tell Jo-Jo to be on standby, just in case one of us got injured during the course of the evening. The dwarf grunted at me and went home, still wearing her black Santa hat with its dangling, grinning skull. I hoped that wasn't an omen of things to come tonight. For me, anyway.

Once I turned out the lights in the storefront, I went into the back of the restaurant and grabbed a black duffel bag from behind one of the freezers. Cash, knives, clothes, credit cards, a disposable cell phone, some healing supplies, a ski mask. The bag held everything that the Spider might need for a bloody good time out on the town. Emphasis on the *bloody* part.

I changed clothes, trading in my blue work apron, T-shirt, and jeans for a pair of heavy cargo pants, boots, and a thick turtleneck. All in black, of course. I didn't really wear any other color while I was working. Few assassins did. Besides, by the time I got to Finn it would be after eight, and the night would be as dark as my clothes. Always better to blend into your surroundings, especially when you were going into hostile territory.

For the finishing touch, I put on a black vest. The garment had a variety of zippered pockets on it, which I stuffed full of my various supplies. Even without the extra gear, the vest was still heavy. That's because it was made of silverstone, just like my knives. In addition to absorbing elemental magic, the metal also had the added benefit of being tougher than Kevlar. Which meant that I could take a few bullets or blasts of magic to the chest and still come up swinging. Given the fact that I planned on killing Elektra LaFleur, I wanted every single advantage that I could get, no matter how small it might be.

When I was finished dressing, I checked my silverstone knives and made sure they were all in their proper slots. One up either sleeve, one in the small of my back, and two tucked into my boots. My standard five-point arsenal. I also fished a couple of extra knives out of the duffel bag and put those in various pockets in my vest. I had a feeling I'd need the extra weapons to take down LaFleur. The assassin wouldn't go quietly. Not with her deadly skills and electrical elemental magic. Hell, I'd be lucky if I didn't get fried in the process.

When I was outfitted for the evening, I slipped out of the back of the Pork Pit. For a moment, I stood there in the alley, my eyes flicking over the black shadows, making sure that everything was as it should be. Sophia had already left, so nothing moved or stirred in the dark night.

It was so cold that even the garbage rats had quieted down for the evening.

Still, just to be sure, I brushed my fingers against the back wall of the restaurant and reached out with my Stone magic. The red brick only murmured with its usual slow, steady, clogged contentment, matching the stomachs and arteries of so many folks after eating at the Pork Pit. Satisfied that everything was as it should be, I shouldered my duffel bag and left the restaurant behind.

It took me about ten minutes to drive to Finn's location. The old train yard was located on the outskirts of the downtown area, just on the edge of Southtown, a half-moon piece of land that curved around a high bank overlooking the Aneirin River before sloping downward and giving way to dilapidated buildings and streets once more.

I found Finn's Aston Martin parked in an alley on the far western edge of the train yard, several hundred feet from the actual start of the rail lines themselves. I whipped a U-turn and pulled my silver Benz into an alley another quarter mile out, giving us a second getaway option in case things got a little heated this evening. Then I pulled my cell phone out of my vest pocket and called Finn. He answered on the third ring.

"I'm here," I said. "Where are you?"

"On a small hill overlooking the train yard, about five hundred feet due west of McLaren Street," he said.

"I'll be there shortly."

I hung up and got out of the car. I moved quietly through the night, hopscotching from building to building, shadow to shadow, and stopping frequently to look and listen to the stones around me. But nothing moved on this cold December night, except the icy wind whipping through the streets and the few hard bits of snow that came along with it. Crushed beer cans and crumpled fast-food wrappers skittered across the cracked parking lots, pushed on by the steady breeze.

Finally, I left the streets and buildings behind and entered a more industrial area. A small knoll covered more by hard-packed dirt than actual grass sloped upward before curving around and cresting over the train yard below. Still keeping a watchful eye out, I palmed one of my silverstone knives and climbed up the shallow hill.

Two dogwood trees, stooped and gnarled by age, squatted on top of the knoll. The few leaves still clinging to the branches rustled back and forth in the breeze, threatening to fly off into the night. Finn sat against the trunk of one of the trees, sipping coffee from a metal thermos and looking down at the scene below with a pair of night-vision goggles. Like me, Finn was dressed in black from head to toe.

"About time you showed up, Gin," Finn said without looking up. "I've been freezing my ass off out here for half an hour now."

"Sorry," I said, dropping into a crouch beside him. "I had to make sure I was properly attired for the evening."

"Way ahead of you." Finn tapped on a slender metal case sitting on the ground next to him.

"You brought your rifle?"

"You bet," he said. "With the new scope that I just bought. Thought I might get a chance to test it out tonight."

Finnegan Lane could barely carve a Christmas ham with a knife, much less actually cut into a person with one the way that I could. But he was a hell of a shot, even better than me. Whether you were standing right in front of him or two hundred yards away, Finn could put three bullets through your eye before you realized that the first one had even hit you.

"Here," he said, passing me the goggles. "Take a gander at the majesty before us."

I took the goggles from him and held them up to my eyes. It took a few seconds before my vision adjusted to the greenish tinge.

Below us, the old Ashland train yard stretched out horizontally about a mile, with the left side giving way to the downtown streets once more and the right side butting up against the Aneirin River. Even from up here, I could hear the swift rush of the water as it made its journey toward the Mississippi and eventually on to the Gulf of Mexico.

Metal tracks crisscrossed this way and that in the train yard, the rails glistening like the silky, silver strings of a spider's web in the moonlight, before disappearing into the shadows. A few old railcars squatted here and there, their open doors looking like gaping maws just waiting for someone to be foolish enough to step inside so they could crunch down on them. Loose gravel covered the ground, along with a variety of junk—rotted timbers, rusted pipes, coils, and other bent, twisted pieces of metal.

I moved on, eyeing the building that lay in the center of it all. The old, original three-story train depot had definitely seen better days. All the windows had been busted out, the tin roof had long since caved in, and the porch sagged worse than a set of slumped shoulders. But Finn had been right. There was a beehive of activity around the structure. Giants moved back and forth through the area, carrying lumber, Sheetrock, power saws, and everything else you'd need to tear down or remodel a building. And the improvement project had already begun, judging from the steady *thwack-thwack-thwack* of hammers and the hoarse shouts that drifted up to us.

In the distance, beyond the depot, I spotted a few dwarves and humans working on some of the old railcars. The sparks from their welding torches flickered, fluttered, and flashed like red, white, and blue fireflies winking on and off in the darkness.

"It looks like they're remodeling the whole train yard," I murmured. "Strange place to put a nightclub, though."

Finn nodded. "That's what I thought too—at first."

I lowered the goggles and looked at him. "And now?"

Finn shrugged. "True, it's not much to look at right now, but Mab never does anything halfway. You've told me that yourself on more than one occasion."

I grunted my agreement.

"So I did some more digging and got a list of some of the building supplies that she's purchased in recent weeks. Flawless marble, platinum fixtures—it's all upscale all the way around. Even the paint has real gold flecks in it. By the time she gets through with it, this place will be swankier than a sultan's palace. It's got a nice view of the water, plus, it's only about a mile or so away from the *Delta Queen* and the Riverwalk. I'm sure Mab will get plenty of traffic from over there."

The *Delta Queen* Finn was referring to was a riverboat casino owned by underworld figure Phillip Kincaid and was one of the prime places in Ashland that folks went to lose their hard-earned money. The riverboat was nothing more than a swanky floating castle that fronted the Riverwalk, a row of upscale shops and expensive restaurants designed to siphon even more money away from those looking to have a good time at the casino.

"Then there's the added bonus of the railcars," Finn added.

"And what could that possibly be?"

Finn flashed me a grin. "Taking the show on the road, of course. Once Mab gets those railcars fixed up the way she wants them, she can load them up with girls, liquor, gambling, whatever, and roll right on over to the next city. Hell, she could go on a whole tour of the South if she wanted to. Maybe even go up north and show them Yankees a thing or two about how to have a good time."

"All of which would help put Roslyn Phillips and Northern Aggression out of business," I said.

Finn shot his thumb and forefinger at me, mimicking a gun. "You got it. Especially since Vinnie said that Mab was making her club the sort of place where anything goes. There are plenty of folks in Ashland with a lot of cash and a lot of sick, twisted vices. There's no telling how much money Mab could make off this thing, if she does it up right. And we both know that she will."

"Well, we'll just have to see what we can do about that," I said, looking through the goggles again. "What did you find out during your stroll through the premises?"

"Not much," Finn admitted. "A couple of trucks brought some more supplies in a few minutes ago, and there were just too many men roaming around for me to get very far into the rail yard. But I did see LaFleur step into that car over there. The one past the depot."

He pointed it out to me. The car was almost in the exact center of the train yard, with people moving back and forth all around it. Of course, Elektra LaFleur had gone where it would be the hardest to get close to her without being seen.

I let out a soft curse. "Why couldn't she pick a nice, dark, quiet, deserted spot to do her evil machinations in?"

"Because she's an arrogant bitch and her main goal in life is to frustrate you before she kills you," Finn quipped.

I gave him a sour look, but Finn just flashed me another grin. After a moment, though, the smile dropped from his face, and he was serious once more.

"What do you want to do, Gin?" Finn said. "Going after LaFleur down there will be risky. I'm not so sure it's worth it—especially since I haven't seen any sign of Natasha. No one standing guard, nobody carrying food anywhere, nothing."

I sighed. I'd hoped by now that Finn would have found some indication that the little girl was still alive. But regardless, I knew what I had to do.

"I know," I said in a low voice. "I know that I'm taking a big risk here tonight. But I promised Vinnie that if his daughter was still alive I'd do my absolute best to find her and bring her back to him in one piece. If there's even a chance that she's down there somewhere, then I have to go look for her. And if she's not, well, maybe I'll see just how good LaFleur really is."

Finn nodded, accepting my decision. "So what do you want me to do? Go with or stay put?"

I'd have a hard enough time slipping through the construction workers below. Two of us trying to do it would be suicide. So my eyes scanned the area once more before settling on one of the railcars that was parked away from the others. The slight rise it was perched on offered a view of the whole train yard and the added bonus of a clear, easy exit out the back. If I got caught, I wasn't dragging Finn down with me.

"Cover me from the top of that car," I said, pointing it out to him. "I'm going in to see if I can get to LaFleur."

"And if you can't?" Finn asked.

I gave him a cold, hard smile. "Maybe if I can't get close enough to kill her, I can flush her out and you can put a couple of bullets in that pretty little skull of hers. Dead is dead, remember? That's what Fletcher always told us. I don't care how LaFleur gets there, as long as we're still breathing in the end and she's not."

* 16 *

Finn and I hashed out a few quick details, like the fact that he was to get out of Dodge if things went bad for me in the train yard. Then we both pulled black ski masks down over our faces and slithered off into the night.

Back before my retirement, when I'd been killing people for money as the Spider, I hadn't bothered wearing a ski mask. Mainly, because I never left anyone alive after the fact to talk about what I looked like or give the police any sort of helpful description of me. But ever since I'd declared war on Mab Monroe, I'd worn a mask while I'd been out stalking her men. Because I had other people to think about now besides me. Finn, the Deveraux sisters, Owen and Eva Grayson, and Bria. This way, if someone did spot me, the mask would hide my face, my identity. A small precaution that I took to keep my loved ones safe.

I waited for Finn to get into position with his rifle on top of the railcar before I palmed one of my knives and headed down the hill and into the train yard itself. I made it to the first railcar with no problem and carefully, slowly, peered around the side. Lights had been strung up all around the depot so the workers could see what they were doing, which meant that it was plenty bright enough down here—in fact, much brighter than I wanted it to be.

Even more debris cluttered the ground than what I'd spotted from the hill, and I had to be careful where I stepped so as to not send metal, rocks, and more skittering off into the shadows. Underneath my feet, the gravel grumbled, groaned, creaked, and whined, just like all the trains had done so many times here over the years. The air smelled of water, oil, grease, and rust.

It took me about twenty minutes to maneuver through the train yard. I stayed well clear of the hubbub of activity around the old depot, as that would be the most dangerous place for me to get caught, and worked my way around to the railcar that Finn said LaFleur had disappeared into.

As I skulked from shadow to shadow, I also kept an eye out for any sign of Natasha. But Finn had been right about that too. I didn't see anyone standing guard outside one of the railcars, nobody taking a tray of food anywhere, and nothing else that would indicate that the girl was being held here somewhere. All the construction workers seemed focused on the depot, the railcars, and their repairs to them.

Which meant that Natasha was probably already raped, tortured, and dead.

My heart twisted at the unpleasant thought, but I

pushed it aside and kept moving. Finally, I was able slither up beside the railcar that Elektra LaFleur had entered. Since I didn't want to take a chance on anyone from the depot seeing me hovering beside the front windows, I crept around to the back, the side that faced the Aneirin River. Lights blazed inside the railcar, and I went to the window farthest back, where the golden glow was the dimmest. To my surprise, it was actually cracked open, as though someone had forgotten to completely shut it against the cold. The window was about ten feet off the ground, so I had to scale the ladder on the right side of the car to see in through it. I hung there in midair, like a spider clinging to its own web, and peered inside.

The inside of the railcar was completely finished— opulently so. Thick crimson carpet covered the floor, while the walls had been shined to a high silver gloss. A lone table covered with a fine white cloth sat in the middle of the rectangular area. A single red rose perched in a slender crystal vase on top of the table, which was set with bone china with a scarlet floral pattern swirled through it. A silver bucket of champagne chilled nearby, while a crystal chandelier dangled over the table, sending out rainbow sparks of light in every direction. An enormous bed covered with black silk sheets and crimson brocade pillows took up the back wall. All put together, the railcar looked like some kind of high-class bordello, just as Vinnie had said it would.

Elektra LaFleur lounged on a crimson loveseat in the corner, the dark green of her shirt looking particularly garish against the blood-colored fabric. She twirled a single white orchid in her hand, the same kind of flower that she'd left on the dwarf's electrocuted corpse two nights ago. I wondered whose body she planned to drop the orchid on tonight.

But what surprised me most was that LaFleur wasn't alone—Mab Monroe was inside the car with her.

Mab relaxed at the table, sipping a glass of champagne. The golden gleam of the liquid matched the play of the chandelier's lights across the sunburst necklace that ringed the Fire elemental's creamy throat. The rune's golden rays flickered as though they were actually moving, while the ruby set into the middle of the design proudly whispered of fire, death, and destruction—a sound that always made me grind my teeth.

Mab was dressed down tonight in a dark green pantsuit that made her copper-colored hair seem even redder than usual. Despite the bright lights of the chandelier, the Fire elemental's eyes were still bottomless black pools that seemed to suck the glow out of the crystals dangling above her head. I supposed it was only appropriate, since Mab herself consumed everything she came into contact with, just the way fire destroyed whatever was in its path and left nothing behind but dull, gray, useless ash.

"Well, Elektra, I have to admit that you've whipped the giants and other builders into fine shape," Mab murmured, taking another sip of her champagne. Her voice was as soft and smooth as silk delicately rasping together, but there was a clear undercurrent of power in each word she spoke. "I didn't hear any muttered complaints about working through the night the way I had before you came to town."

LaFleur gave her a thin smile. "You hired me to come to Ashland, to restore . . . morale and authority to your organization after Elliot Slater's untimely death. To help you open your new nightclub. That's what I've done. I'm mildly disappointed that I only had to kill two of your men to get them all back under control. It was hardly a challenge."

"Three, counting the dwarf you electrocuted at the docks," Mab reminded her. "Which I still think was unnecessary."

LaFleur shrugged. "Well, I couldn't have him go around talking about the fact that I was in town and hunting for the Spider, now could I?"

"No," Mab said. "I suppose not. Especially since you failed to trap and kill the Spider like you promised me."

The Fire elemental's voice was still soft, still mild, but there was no mistaking the stinging rebuke in her words. Mab was pissed that LaFleur hadn't bagged me yet. It was probably the first time in a long time that the Fire elemental hadn't gotten exactly what she'd wanted exactly when she'd wanted it. Yeah, my heart really bled for her.

Elektra recognized the barb in Mab's tone as well. Her eyes narrowed, and a bit of green lightning flickered in her gaze. Even through the metal of the car, I could feel the electrical charge in the air around her.

"Getting that bartender to mouth off about your so-called drug shipment was a solid plan," Elektra said. "It was just the kind of thing that the Spider would go after, according to what you've told me of her previous attacks against you and your organization. It wasn't my fault she didn't take the bait this one time."

Mab's own eyes narrowed at the assassin's casual insolence. "And you promised me the bitch would be dead before Christmas. Something I paid you a great deal of money to accomplish. Something you haven't done yet."

I was mildly curious as to exactly how much Mab had paid LaFleur to hunt me down and kill me. From Fletcher's file, I knew that the assassin's going rate was three million for the simplest of hits. But there was nothing simple about taking on the Spider. So how much had Mab given the other assassin to entice her to come to Ashland and try? Four million, maybe? Five? More? I would have liked to know, if only so I could tell Finn and watch his eyes gleam at the thought of that much money and what he could do with it.

"I don't like people who don't deliver on their promises to me," Mab continued in a soft voice. "I don't think I have to tell someone of your skills and qualifications what happens when one of my employees displeases me."

Black fire flickered in Mab's eyes as she embraced her elemental magic. Even though the metal of the car separated us, I could still feel the intense heat of it, pricking my skin like red-hot needles. Add it to the electrical charge of LaFleur's magic, and it made for one uncomfortable sensation. Not to mention that the feel of their power, which was so different from my own Ice and Stone magic, made a small, primal voice start muttering in the back of my head. *Enemy, enemy, enemy . . .* I ground my teeth together to keep from snarling.

Elektra kept twirling the white orchid in her hand, as though the two of them were talking about something as simple and mundane as the weather. If she was afraid of Mab and what the Fire elemental could do to her, the assassin didn't show it.

"You know, you never did tell me the real reason why you want the Spider dead so badly in the first place," Elektra murmured.

"She killed Elliot Slater and has been picking off my men like they're flies," Mab snapped. "That's why I want her dead."

Elektra tilted her head to one side and studied Mab, sly intelligence glinting in her green gaze, along with the flashing sparks of her electrical magic. "If that was all there was to it, then you would have hired someone far less expensive to come in and do the job, instead of paying top dollar for me. No, I think there's something else going on between the two of you. Care to tell me what is it?"

I studied the Fire elemental. A rare bit of emotion flickered in her black eyes, but I couldn't tell if it was annoyance at LaFleur or concern about what the assassin had deduced so far. Once again, I couldn't help but wonder if Mab herself had put two and two together yet, if she even remembered Genevieve Snow, the little girl she'd tortured all those years ago, and the spider rune necklace she'd used to do it with. She probably had. No matter how much I hated Mab, she was far from stupid or oblivious. Even though I didn't have any real information to support my theory, it wasn't too much of a stretch to think that Mab knew exactly why I was after her, especially since Bria had come back to town.

I only wondered if the Fire elemental knew that I was the one that she really wanted to kill. The Snow sister that was the threat to her, the one with both Ice and Stone magic, the little girl who had grown up with desire, skills, and perhaps even the power to kill her.

Mab's lips curved up, but the result wasn't pleasant. Death probably had a more inviting smile than she did. "I pay you to kill people, Elektra, not ask questions. If you can't remember that, then I'll find someone who can. Immediately. And don't be stupid enough to think that Jonah will step in and save you. He's just fucking you so you'll kill Gin Blanco for him."

My eyes narrowed. So Mab knew about her lawyer's plan to eliminate me and that he was getting busy with her new assassin. Interesting.

"Count on Jonah to save me? Please." Elektra let out a light, mocking laugh. "I don't need anyone to *save* me. I'm just sleeping with him to pass the time. When he bores me, and he soon will, I'll move on to someone else. As for getting rid of that little cook . . ." She shrugged. "It'll kill half an hour."

Mab took another sip of golden champagne and studied the other woman. "At least try to make it look somewhat like an accident. Blanco isn't without friends, and I have enough annoyances to deal with right now with the Spider."

Elektra tipped her head. "Of course."

Even out in the cold, I could hear the lie in her voice. There would be no elaborately staged accident. The assassin was going to electrocute me just like she did all her other victims.

Mab nodded and put her champagne glass down on the table. "Now, my sources in the police department tell me that there are no leads on the murder of my three men in the park next to Northern Aggression. Except, of course, for that damn spider rune drawn in the sandbox."

Elektra raised a black eyebrow. "Did you really think she would be careless enough to leave any evidence behind that she didn't want you to find?"

"Perhaps if you'd been there, you would have been able to take care of the problem once and for all," Mab snapped.

"You're the one who pulled me away from your men that night because you wanted an update," Elektra said. "I thought that they could handle something as simple as killing a bartender. Evidently I underestimated them. Just the way you've underestimated the Spider so far."

The two women stared at each other, magic flickering in both their gazes. The feel of their elemental power— Mab's Fire and Elektra's electricity—amped up, until the sensations crackled like invisible lightning all around me. For a moment I thought perhaps they would go at each other and use their magic to decide exactly who was the bigger bitch in the room, just like so many elementals had done before them.

But of course my luck could never, ever get that good. After a moment, Elektra dropped her green eyes to her white orchid, twirling it once more, and acquiescing to Mab—for the time being.

"I'll find the Spider. Don't you worry about that. That's what you're paying me for, and I always deliver exactly what my clients want—whether it's dead on arrival or six feet under," LaFleur said.

Mab nodded, accepting the other woman's promises—

for now. "I'll have another job for you after the Spider. We talked about it before."

"The cop? The one with the elemental magic?"

Mab nodded again.

My hand tightened around the silverstone knife in my hand. Bria. They were talking about Bria. They had to be. A couple of weeks ago, Mab had sent Slater and some of his men to murder Bria. Now she was going to put La-Fleur on the job. Another reason for me to kill them both as soon as possible.

"Consider it done. Now, on to more pressing matters. What do you want me to do with the girl?" Elektra said. "She's still sniveling away in the next car over and asking for her daddy."

My breath caught in my throat. Natasha. From what LaFleur had just said, the little girl was here and, even more importantly, still alive.

"Since Vinnie wasn't among the dead bodies at the park, I have to assume that the Spider got her hands on him and questioned him about the whole messy affair. If she's as ruthless as she claims to be, then she's killed him by now for trying to help you trap her," Mab said. "Which means the girl is of no use anymore."

"But what about your new club?" LaFleur asked. "I thought you were going to use the girl there. Make her the first star in your stable, so to speak. She should earn you quite the profit among the kid-loving crowd."

So Brown, the vampire at the park, had been right about Mab's nightclub—she planned to make it a place where anything went. Even serving up helpless kids to pedophiles just so she could make a few more bucks. The heartless, arrogant bitch. Anger filled me, the coldness of it pooling in my stomach, and my lips drew back in a silent snarl.

Mab shrugged. "Not enough profit to make it worth my while. She's getting too old for what some of my prospective customers want, and her coloring's all wrong. Besides, she's a loose end, and it's always better to cut those off before they unravel on you."

The Fire elemental stared at the assassin with no mercy or feeling of any kind in her soulless black gaze. "So kill the brat. Tonight."

❖ 17 ❖

Mab and Elektra starting talking about other things then, namely how fast they thought the construction workers could finish remodeling the old train depot and all the railcars. I hung on the ladder outside the window and considered my options.

Right now, I was as close to the two women as I could possibly get and still take them by surprise. I longed to kill them, both of them. Every cell in my body screamed at me to do it. To crash in through the window, toss my silverstone knives, and lash out at them with every ounce of Ice and Stone magic I possessed.

But the problem was that there were two of them, both powerful, dangerous elementals in their own right who were more than happy to use their magic to kill. Whereas I was out here swinging in the breeze all by my little lonesome, except for Finn and his rifle across the train yard. There weren't any windows on the side of the railcar facing his location, and as good as Finn was with his gun, even he couldn't shoot through solid metal. Not from this distance anyway, not even with the silverstone bullets that I knew he always used.

And the truth was that while I might have been able to take Elektra out by myself, I didn't have the same confidence when it came to Mab. Not after what I'd seen her to do my mother and older sister all those years ago. Throw Mab and her Fire magic into the mix with LaFleur's electricity, and I was the one who'd wind up getting dead.

But most importantly, there was Natasha to think about. A scared little girl who had already suffered who knew what kinds of horrors. And she was going to die tonight by LaFleur's hand unless I decided to go save her. *Right now.*

I hung there on the ladder for a second longer, debating my choices. Try to kill Mab and LaFleur or go save a little girl. There was no choice, really. There never had been. I might be a cold-blooded assassin, but even I still had a heart, what little, black, patchwork bits there were left of it. Besides, I'd promised Vinnie that I'd find his daughter and bring her back to him, no matter what kind of terrible shape she might be in. I didn't go back on my word—ever. Not as Gin Blanco and certainly not as the Spider.

So I hopped down from my perch on the ladder, palmed another one of my silverstone knives, and slithered off into the darkness.

According to Elektra LaFleur, Natasha was being held in the next railcar over, which stood about fifty feet off to my left and back from the old depot. Keeping to the shadows, I picked my way through the train yard, still careful not to send any of the debris littering the ground flying with my feet. It was easy enough for me to creep up to the railcar, scurry halfway up the metal ladder on the back side, and peer inside the window.

Unlike the car Elektra and Mab had been in, this one hadn't been completely renovated yet. The walls had been polished to a high silver shine, but none of the other furnishings had been put in place. The floor was bare, and only a lone bulb hung overhead.

But there was still plenty of light for me to see the two giants sitting inside, their seven-foot frames hunched over the small table that they were playing cards on. I looked at the far corner. A third, much smaller form huddled there against the wall, buried under a pile of dirty, tattered blankets.

That had to be Natasha. I watched the blankets, tracking the slight, steady lift and fall of them. She was still breathing, at least. I didn't know what kind of shape the girl was in, what horrible things had been done to her, but it didn't much matter to me right now. I'd promised Vinnie I'd do everything that I could to rescue his daughter—even if she might already be dead and broken on the inside.

The front door of the railcar was halfway open and, unfortunately enough, faced the depot where so much of the construction action was going on. Which meant I couldn't go in that way, not without drawing unwanted attention. I thought about my options, then tucked one of my silverstone knives back up my sleeve, holding one in my right hand only.

Then I drew in a breath, put my left hand up to the window, and reached for my Ice magic.

A cold silver light flickered in my palm, centered on the spider rune scar, and snowflake-shaped Ice crystals spread out from my hand, freezing the window. As always, it surprised me how much easier it was to use my Ice magic now, how much more control I had over it than before, and most especially, how much stronger it was.

But I pushed the thoughts aside and focused on the task at hand. I used only a trickle of power, as Mab and Elektra would be sure to notice anything more since they were elementals too. Still, in seconds, the entire window had completely Iced over, glass, metal frame, and all.

When I was satisfied I'd made the glass weak and brittle enough for my nefarious purposes, I let go of my Ice magic and dropped my hand. I climbed up another rung on the ladder, calculating the angles and my method of attack one last time.

Then I drew in another breath and dived through the window.

I sent out another brief burst of Ice magic as I went through it, willing the thick wall of it that I'd put over the window to shatter. It worked and took the glass along with it. I tucked into a tight ball, hit the floor of the railcar, and came up slashing with my knife.

The two giants never had a chance.

They looked up as the window shattered, startled by the sharp, sudden, unexpected noise. While they were still processing what was going on, I was already moving toward them.

With my first pass, I cut the throat of the man closest to me. Blood spattered over the cards on the table, turning them all into red hearts. The giant clutched at the crazy crimson smile on his neck, gurgling and gasping for breath, but the light was already starting to leak out of his eyes.

The second man was a little quicker. He actually made it up onto his feet before I got to him. I leaped up onto the low card table and buried my silverstone knife in his heart. He started to scream from the pain, but I clamped my hand over his mouth, yanked out my knife, and used it to cut his throat as well. His arms flailed wildly for about ten seconds before his brain quit working. He thudded to the floor and was still.

I hopped off the card table, the bloody knife still in my hand, crept over to the front of the railcar, and looked out through the partially open door. The whine of power saws and steady *thwack-thwack-thwack* of hammers filled the air. No one outside had heard me shatter the window and kill the two giants, because no one was looking, running, or pointing in this direction. Instead, the men continued with their construction work, oblivious to the danger in their midst.

I glanced over my shoulder at the two giants, but their card table had been tucked back out of sight of the open door. Their dead bodies couldn't be seen by anyone casually glancing in this direction. Satisfied that I was safe for a few seconds, I headed for the pile of blankets in the corner. Whoever was inside heard my footsteps, and the blankets shifted and then slowly lowered.

Natasha Volga peeked out from underneath the layers

of fabric, her back pressed against the wall of the railcar. She looked a lot like Vinnie, with dark brown hair, blue eyes, and a pretty, round face that hadn't quite lost that last bit of baby fat yet. She looked . . . well, I didn't know exactly how old she looked. It wasn't like I'd spent any time around kids. I remembered Roslyn saying that she was eight, or maybe ten. I also wondered if she had the same kind of Ice elemental magic as her father, but now wasn't the time to ask.

I dropped to my knees in front of her, and Natasha shrank back even more from me, as though she wanted to melt into the metal of the railcar just to get away from me. Couldn't blame the kid for that. I could only imagine how scary I looked in my black clothes, with the ski mask still covering my face. But I didn't dare take it off, not even for her.

I could also feel the warm blood that coated my torso like a crimson shroud. Still more of the sticky substance dripped off the point of my knife onto the floor of the car. It also speckled my hands as though I'd been paint-ing with it. I dropped the weapon down by my leg, but I didn't put it away. Not when another giant could poke his head inside at any second.

"Hi, sweetheart," I murmured in a soft, soothing voice. "Sorry to scare you, but I'm here to take you home to your father."

Natasha was calmer than I'd thought she'd be. Or maybe she'd been through so much already in the last twenty-four hours that she was just in shock about it all. Instead of screaming and trying to get away from me, she sat still and thought about my words.

"My—my daddy sent you? Really?" Her voice was no more than the barest whisper, and I had to strain to hear her.

I nodded. "He sure did, sweetheart. Now, let's get you out of here before more of those bad men come this way. I need you to be a good girl for me and not make a sound. Okay? If you do that, we'll both be fine, and you'll be back with your daddy real soon. I promise you that, and I always keep my promises."

Natasha stared at me for another minute before slowly nodding. I was mildly surprised that she was willing to go with me so easily, but people always said kids were smarter than you thought. Maybe Natasha realized she didn't have a lot of options. Or maybe she'd heard LaFleur and the others talk about exactly what they had in store for her.

Either way, I didn't hesitate. I got to my feet and held out my blood-spattered hand. After another moment of staring at me, Natasha reached out with her own cold, pale, trembling fingers and took mine. I pulled the little girl to her feet, and the blankets fell away from her body.

To my surprise, she still had on clothes—a pair of long-sleeved blue flannel pajamas. Whoever had taken her had stopped long enough to let her put a pair of slippers on her feet. The fluffy foam shoes were shaped like green frogs, of all things.

I examined what I could see of the girl's body. She had a puffy bruise on one cheek and some nicks and scrapes on her hands, but otherwise seemed to be in good shape.

"Natasha, has anyone . . . hurt you while you've been here?" I asked in the kindest voice that I could.

I needed to know if maybe she was bleeding somewhere that I couldn't see, if she had other injuries I hadn't noticed. Injuries that might slow us down, that might mean the difference between our getting out of here or not.

"No," she whispered. "They were waiting until the lady with the flower tattoo told them that it was okay. Some of them—touched me, though."

That was horrible enough, but at least she'd been spared the horrors of being raped by Mab's minions.

"I'm so sorry for that," I said, pulling her over to the broken window. "More than you'll ever know. But I need you to not think about that right now, okay? Just concentrate on me and do exactly what I tell you, all right?"

Natasha stared at me with her blue eyes. "Okay."

There wasn't any time to waste, so I climbed out through the broken window, reached back inside, and helped Natasha do the same. Her blue pajamas were far too light for the kind of shadow skulking that I'd had in mind, but I'd just have to make do. I always did.

Slowly, oh so slowly, I led Natasha away from the railcar. It seemed as if even more men had arrived while I'd been killing the girl's two captors, and the rail yard was swarming with people. They huddled around the depot, moved in between the railcars, and walked back and forth with supplies like busy little worker bees all scurrying to keep their demanding queen happy.

Which, of course, made it all the more difficult for the two of us to slip out of the train yard undetected. Several times I had to push the girl flat on the ground and cover her light pajamas with my black, bloody clothes, in hopes that the giants walking by would just see another shadow pooling on the gravel and not the two people trying to hide in it. But it worked, because the men walked on by and went about their business.

And Natasha was a trooper. I didn't know if she was in shock or completely traumatized or just one extremely brave little girl, because she never screamed, not even when I pushed her down onto the hard gravel that shredded her soft pajamas and dug into her hands and face. We'd made it about halfway across the yard when she looked down and saw the rust-colored stains on her pajamas—blood from the giants that had transferred from my clothes to her. She let out a little whimper then, but I grabbed her hand and pulled her along before she could think too much about the blood, where it had come from and the fact that she'd seen me kill the men it had once belonged to.

Finally, after about twenty nerve-racking minutes, I reached the railcar that was Finn's perch. I let out a soft whistle, our long-standing, prearranged signal. About five seconds later, a black shadow dropped to the ground in front of us. Finn straightened, and Natasha jerked back at his sudden appearance.

"It's okay," I whispered, squeezing her cold hand. "This is Finn. He's with me. He knows your daddy too, and he's going to help me take you to him."

Finn's eyes swept over the girl, and he gave me a questioning look.

"She's in good shape, all things considered," I said in a low voice. "It's not nearly as bad as it could have been. Now, let's get the hell out of here before they find the two giants that I just killed—"

Shouts rang up through the night. Fuck. All I'd needed

had been five more minutes, but luck had decided not to smile on me tonight.

I looked over my shoulder. Sure enough, someone had discovered the two dead giants in the railcar. The door was fully open now, and more and more men circled around that area, like bloodhounds treeing a raccoon. It wouldn't be long before they started looking for whoever had killed their buddies. Already I could see heads swiveling around in this direction.

If it had just been Finn and me, I wouldn't have been concerned. We could have melted into the shadows and gotten back to our cars before the construction workers even thought about searching the train yard. But now I had Natasha to think about too. The girl didn't have the shoes for a sprint, not to mention the fact that the giants would easily see her blue pajamas standing out against the blackness of the night. Finn or I could have carried her but not with the speed or furtiveness necessary to make a quick, clean escape. Mab's men would be all over us before we even reached the top of the hill above our heads.

Unless I did something to distract them. Unless I got them all to focus on me instead.

I took Natasha's hand and put it in Finn's. "Go with this man. Do what he says, and he'll take you back to your daddy. Do you understand me?"

Natasha stared at me a moment with her big blue eyes, then nodded.

"Good girl."

I palmed another one of my silverstone knives.

"Gin!" Finn hissed. "What the hell are you doing? We need to leave. Right this second!"

"Don't worry about me," I said, already backing up. "Just get the girl out of here."

Finn saw what I was planning and opened his mouth to protest, but I cut him off.

"Just do it, Finn. Now!"

Without waiting for an answer, I turned and ran back into the train yard.

✳ 18 ✳

Still keeping to the shadows as much as I could, I ran back the way I'd just come. By this point, more and more of the construction workers clustered around the open railcar, staring at and chattering about the two dead bodies inside.

Out of the corner of my eye, I saw the door on the next car open—and Mab Monroe and Elektra LaFleur stick their heads outside, wondering what had caused all the sudden noise. Fuck. Things had just gone from bad to worse.

The two women stepped down out of their car and hurried over to the other one to see what all the fuss was about. Even as they approached, more and more hoarse shouts filled the air.

"It's her! It's the Spider! She's struck again!"

A grim smile tightened my face. I hadn't had time to draw my rune in the giants' blood, but it looked as though I didn't need to. They already knew my name. If nothing else, this little incident tonight might make some of Mab's men think twice about working for her.

Provided, of course, that I got out of the train yard alive.

My eyes scanned over everything as I sprinted forward, searching for something that I could use as a distraction to give Finn enough time to get Natasha to safety. Something that I could make noise or a fire or perhaps even an explosion with. Finally, next to the old depot, I saw something useful—an old-fashioned kerosene lantern that someone had brought along tonight for light, warmth, or both. Even better, not too far away from the lantern was a large red plastic container that I was willing to bet was filled with something flammable.

Before I could snatch up the lantern and the container, a dwarf rounded the side of the depot and moved in between me and the objects. He rubbed his stubby fingers together, then held them over the lantern, trying to get what little warmth he could from the meager fire flickering inside the glass.

I didn't have time to be suave and kill him, so I barreled into his back like a NFL linebacker and drove my boot into the back of his knee. The dwarf screamed and did a header onto the gravel, slamming face-first into the rocks. A few heads turned in our direction at the sound, but I'd already grabbed the lantern and container and moved on. Liquid sloshed back and forth in the red plastic with every step that I took.

I leaped up onto the sagging porch of the old depot, ran across to the far side, and dropped to one knee. Lights blazed all around me now, but I was partially hidden by the dilapidated porch railing in front of me. Besides, by this point, almost everyone was still gathered around the railcar, staring inside at the two dead giants instead of looking in my direction.

With one eye on the crowd, I unscrewed the black cap on the plastic container. The acrid smell of gasoline wafted up to me. I smiled. I'd seen some generators in among the building supplies. Of course, they'd need gas to run. Maybe luck wasn't going to completely abandon me tonight.

I didn't have time to be sneaky or particularly creative, so I kicked over the plastic container. The gasoline slopped all over the porch and dribbled off the side like butter dripping off a hot biscuit. Then I raised the lantern over my head and dashed it down onto the gas-soaked, wooden porch.

WHOOSH!

The gas ignited at once, the bright heat of it flashing in front of my eyes and sucking the moisture out of them. I wasn't the only one who noticed my sabotage. Elektra LaFleur's head snapped around in my direction, her gaze drawn by the rapid spread of the fire.

"There!" the other assassin screamed, green lightning flashing in her hand. "There she is! Get her!"

Fuck. I'd hoped to slither back into the shadows while everyone else was distracted by the pretty flames. Not going to happen now. At least everyone was looking in this direction, instead of at Finn and Natasha sneaking out of the opposite side of the train yard. Still blinking orange spots out of my vision, I vaulted over the porch railing and ran out into the waiting darkness, moving away from Finn and the girl.

A few shots rang out, but none of them came close to hitting me. I didn't even feel them kick up any gravel around my feet. Not surprising. Most people couldn't shoot their way out of a paper bag, much less hit a moving target in the dark. Even if someone had gotten lucky and put a round in my back, I was still wearing my silverstone vest, which would catch any bullet that came into contact with it.

Still, not wanting to chance it, I forced myself to run faster. Off to my right, several giants started to give chase. No worries there. Giants might be strong, but they weren't the quickest creatures around. I had no doubt that I could easily outdistance all of them with my current pace.

But there was one person that I couldn't outrun—Elektra LaFleur.

I glanced over my shoulder long enough to see the other assassin sprinting after me, running just as fast as I was. She was quick, I'd give her that. Green lightning flashed in both of her hands now, illuminating her way and letting her keep me in sight. I could feel the raw, elemental power in the eerie lightning, the shocking, deadly electrical charge of it, even though I was a hundred feet ahead of her. She was so fucking *strong*, even stronger than I'd realized before. That little jolt she'd given me at the Pork Pit earlier today was nothing compared to the pure, pulsing energy she held in her hands right now.

But most importantly, Elektra had one advantage that I didn't—we were running through a yard full of metal rails, and metal would easily conduct her lightning.

Elektra knew as well as I that lightning can move a hell of a lot faster than humans. That's why she dropped to her knees and slammed her green, glowing hands down onto one of the metal rails, unleashing her lightning, and sending it sparking toward me. The deadly electricity zipped along the rails, jumping from one to another, until the whole train yard glowed with its shocking power.

I didn't have a chance of outrunning the lightning, but I had my own magic, my own elemental power. I just hoped it would be enough to save me.

I dropped to my knees in the middle of a set of rails, careful not to touch either of them, curled into a ball, and grabbed hold of my Stone magic, pulling it up through my veins and onto my skin, head, hair, eyes, making them all as hard and solid as granite. After all, you can't electrocute a rock—

The lightning slammed into me.

For a moment, my vision went completely green, that bright, peculiar, eerie shade of green that was the same color as LaFleur's magic. Her cruel elemental power smashed against my body, wanting to zip through me the same way that it had all the metal rails around me. But I gritted my teeth and pushed back with my Stone magic, keeping the lightning at bay, keeping it from breaking through the hard shell of my skin. Because if it did that, I'd be dead, fried to a crisp just like that dwarf had been by Elektra the other night. Another bug zapped by her electrical power.

But that didn't mean it still didn't fucking *hurt*.

Maybe it was because I'd never been up against an elemental with electrical magic before. Maybe it was because LaFleur's power was just as strong as my own. Hell, maybe her power just worked in its own unique way. Because despite my Stone magic, I still felt every bit of the lightning, felt every bit of the static charge of it crackling around me and trying to fry me from the outside in. The jolt of it over and over again made my heart beat so hard that I thought my whole chest would explode from the pressure. I was still getting electrocuted. All my Stone power was doing was keeping it from killing me outright.

I don't know how long I huddled there, using my Stone magic to block the electricity humming around me, my mouth open in a terrible, silent scream that just wouldn't come out. Sweat poured down my face, and my whole body shook from the effort. But finally, my vision cleared, and the green lightning zipped farther down the metal lines and finally sparked away into nothingness.

Still holding on to my Stone magic, I drew in a deep, shuddering breath. Green-gray smoke wafted up from my body, choking me, and the silverstone in my vest felt as hot and heavy as an anvil hung on my chest. The once-solid metal sloshed around inside the fabric like water. The silverstone had absorbed all of LaFleur's magic that it could before dissolving into its liquid form from the sheer heat of it. It took a lot of raw elemental power to melt silverstone—a whole hell of a lot. My vest had just saved my life, had just kept me from getting fried to death outright.

But the fight wasn't over yet. Legs shaking, I got to my feet and stumbled on. Behind me, I heard Elektra scream with fury and surprise that I was still standing, still running, still breathing.

Elektra's magic had dazed me more than I would have liked, which is why I didn't have any particular plan in mind, other than to just run until I got away from her. But the assassin was in much better shape than I at the moment and closing fast, given that I'd almost been fried by her electrical magic.

And then, somehow, I heard it, even above the blood pounding in my ears and the slap of my boots on the loose gravel—a train whistle. Getting louder and louder with each second.

Sweetest fucking sound I'd ever heard.

I forced my legs to move faster, to pump harder, until my feet barely touched the ground. I veered right over to the edge of the train yard. I was running across the upper level, the flat plateau where the old depot was located. But there was a lower level to the yard too, some thirty feet below me, the place that all the trains passing through Ashland used these days since the depot had been closed. The lower rail yard was a straight shot through the city, do not pass go, do not collect two hundred dollars. On the far side of the lower level, the black waters of the Aneirin River rushed by, keeping time with the trains that chugged alongside it.

The whistle sounded again, a harsh scream in the night air, and five seconds later, I saw it. A train churned this way, moving through the lower level of the yard, a line of cars snaking along behind it like the sections on a fat, metal caterpillar.

The train was moving much faster than I was, and the

front engine car drew up next to me in seconds. I grabbed hold of my Stone magic again, using it to harden my skin once more. And when one of the train's many cars passed below me, I jumped.

It felt like I hung in midair for several seconds before finally falling.

I slammed into the top of one of the railcars. It was a thirty-foot fall, and since my body was already so hard and heavy with my Stone magic, I actually made a dent in the thick metal, a perfect, Gin-shaped groove with arms and legs spread out wide like a cartoon character. Wiley E. Gin.

For a moment, I just lay there and breathed, grateful that I'd timed the jump just right and landed on top of the car, instead of slipping in between two of them and getting run over by the relentless, churning wheels. I doubted even my Ice and Stone magic would have let me survive that.

But the train wasn't moving quite fast enough.

Ten seconds later, Elektra LaFleur popped into view, running parallel on the level above me, powerful green lightning crackling in her hands once more. LaFleur stopped and reared back, ready to throw another ball of her deadly electricity at me.

By this point, I was weak, dazed, and utterly drained. I wasn't sure I could bring enough Stone magic to bear to ward off LaFleur's power again, especially since my silver-stone vest was liquefied and the metal car I was lying on would probably conduct her electricity that much more. So I did the only thing that I could.

I rolled out of the Gin-shaped groove, toppled off the

side of the car, and fell another fifty feet into the Aneirin River below.

As an assassin, provided you live long enough, you're sure to experience déjà vu from time to time. When you kill someone the same way that you have a dozen people before. When you use the same disguise to get close to a target. When you feel your latest victim's warm, sticky blood coat your hand.

I'd done another swan dive into the Aneirin River a few months ago, when one of my hits had turned out to be a trap, so I was familiar with exactly how chilly the river actually was. But I'll be damned if the water wasn't that much colder tonight. My mind, hell, my whole body, immediately went numb from the shock of it. The bitter chill surprised me, making me stupid and sloppy enough to open my mouth, and water poured down my throat, the icy, bone-rattling cold of it further freezing me from the inside out. The water also cooled down the melted silverstone in my vest, turning it heavy and solid once more, while the force of the fall peeled the black ski mask off my head.

Gagging on the fishy-tasting water, I forced my legs to kick upward in a steady rhythm, and a few seconds later, I broke the surface. The swift current had already pulled me several hundred feet away from LaFleur, although I could still see the green spark of her lightning flickering, getting farther and farther away with every second.

I wondered what would happen if the assassin threw her lightning at the river itself, if the whole length of it would light up with her electrical magic. I shuddered at the thought. Maybe she was too far away or maybe, like me, she just didn't have that much juice left. But more seconds passed, and no lightning came arcing toward the river, something I was infinitely grateful for.

I was too dazed to do much of anything but go with the flow of the water. I drifted maybe a mile downstream before I finally saw a rocky outcropping I thought I could swim to. So I drew in a breath, turned my head, and flailed that way, making my arms and legs go through the motions, even if I couldn't exactly feel them at the moment.

I didn't quite reach the rocks, but I managed to get into shallow enough water to wade up onto the shore. I fell onto my stomach in the frozen mud and frosted cattails, panting from the effort, entirely disconnected from my own body. I didn't feel anything anymore—not even the cold that I knew had invaded my body and was slowly killing me.

I don't know how long I huddled there before I managed to summon up the strength to roll over onto my back and fumble with one of the zippers on the front of my vest. At this point, my whole body shook from the cold, even though I didn't actually feel it. My hands trembled from the force of it, but apparently the message just wasn't reaching my brain, because it wasn't registering as an actual physical sensation to me. I didn't feel anything but numb. Completely numb. Or maybe dead, if this is what being dead felt like. I'd helped a lot of people get that way over the years, but I hadn't actually been on the receiving end of things myself—yet.

But the really weird thing was that the spider rune scars on my hands were glowing.

A small circle surrounded by eight thin rays, one embedded in either palm, and they were both as bright as the lights on Owen Grayson's Christmas tree. The runes glowed with a cold, silver light—the kind of light that flared whenever I used my Ice magic. But . . . I wasn't doing that right now. At least, I didn't think that I was. Or if I was, I didn't know why or how.

It kind of freaked me out, since the last time that my palms had glowed like this was when I'd finally broken through the silverstone embedded in my hands. The metal had been absorbing my Ice magic until I'd forced myself to blast right through it and had brought an entire coal mine down on top of myself and the men who were trying to kill me.

But this? Now? I had no idea what was going on. I stared at my glowing palms another minute.

Fuck. This couldn't be good.

But I put my wonky magic out of my mind. I managed to unzip the pocket on my vest and pull out my cell phone. I squinted at the glowing screen, which meant that I still had a signal. Somehow Elektra LaFleur's magic and my swim in the river hadn't completely fried the device. Better than a Timex and much more useful right now. It took me three very slow, concentrated tries before I managed to hit one of the numbers on the keypad and then send the call.

He picked up on the third ring. "Hello?"

But it wasn't Finn's voice on the line—it was Owen's. I must have hit the wrong number on my speed dial, because I'd wanted to call Finn, not Owen.

"Ow . . . Ow . . . Owen," I managed to get out through

my chattering teeth—teeth that I couldn't even feel at the moment.

"Gin? Where are you? Are you okay?" Concern filled his voice.

"T-tr-train yard. I-I—jumped in river. Down—downstream now. Finn—Finn has the girl."

I knew that I wasn't making a lot of sense, but I just couldn't think. I couldn't move, I couldn't do anything. My whole body, my mind, everything was just numb. Dead and numb.

"Are you hurt? Where are you?"

The phone slipped from my deadweight fingers and plopped onto the muddy riverbank.

"Gin? Gin?"

Owen's voice was the last thing that I remembered hearing before the world went completely cold, dead, and black.

❋ 19 ❋

"Gin!" the hoarse, worried whisper roused me out of the liquid blackness I'd been so peacefully drifting along in. "Gin! Are you out here?"

The sound of my own name startled me the rest of the way awake, and my eyes snapped open. At least, I thought that they opened. I certainly wanted them to. But since the world still remained pitch-black, I wasn't quite sure about that.

After a moment, the events of the night filled my mind, vague flickers and flashes of images that should have made more sense to me than they did. McAllister and LaFleur eating at the Pork Pit. Me sneaking into the rail yard. Finding Natasha. Torching the old depot to create a distraction. LaFleur's eerie green lightning racing along the metal rails toward me. That last one made me shudder. Her power had hurt so much—

"Gin!" the voice called again.

And now someone was out here looking for me in the dark—but was it friend or foe?

"We've looked everywhere," a second voice said. "She's not here, and she's not answering her cell."

A woman. That was a woman talking.

My mind wasn't working quite the way it should, but I knew I didn't want a woman to find me. Didn't want Elektra LaFleur to find me. I shuddered and curled into an even tighter ball, barely daring to breathe. If the other assassin discovered me now, she'd finish me off with her lightning. Then LaFleur would go after Bria, Finn, and everyone else I cared about, and there would be no one to stop her. I wouldn't be around to stop her—

"Let me concentrate," the first person rumbled again. A man, given the deep pitch of his voice.

Some small part of my mind frowned. That voice sounded . . . familiar. Why? Why did it sound so familiar? Why did I like the deep, rumbling sound of it so much? Why did I want to call out and answer it?

I felt a bit of magic surge to life somewhere nearby. But it wasn't LaFleur's crackling electrical power or Mab Monroe's red-hot Fire magic. Surprisingly, this magic felt similar to my own Stone power—cold, still, calm, comforting. Not exactly the same, but it wasn't the complete wrongness of another element either.

"This way."

Something rustled over my head, and I heard heavy footsteps. Someone's boots squished in the mud, getting closer and closer with every step. I tried to bring my hand up to my vest to grab one of the silverstone knives hidden in the zippered pockets, but my hand just wouldn't work. Wouldn't move, wouldn't grasp, wouldn't do anything but lie by my side like a dead fish. No part of my body worked. It dimly occurred to me once more that I couldn't feel anything—not my fingers, not my toes, and especially not anything else in between.

"There! There she is!"

Someone rustled through the cattails I was lying in, sending clumps of dirt raining down on my face, but I didn't even have the strength to reach up and brush them away. I got the sense that someone was standing over me, though, looking down at my cold body.

"Why—why are her hands glowing like that? With that silver light?" the woman whispered in an awed tone.

"I don't know," the man rumbled. "Go start the car and turn the heat on full blast. Now."

Another pair of footsteps scurried away, hurrying back up the muddy bank. Again I tried to summon up the strength to move, to protect myself, or even to just open up my eyes and see exactly what this new threat was. But I just couldn't do it. I couldn't do anything right now.

Strong arms lifted my body up out of the frozen mud. I breathed in, and a rich, earthy scent filled my nose. His aroma, the one that always made me think of metal, if metal could ever have any real smell to it.

"Owen?" I mumbled.

At least, I thought that I mumbled his name. My lips were so cold and stiff that I didn't actually feel them move. I tried to open my eyes again but found I couldn't. Something had glued my eyelids together. Ice probably, frozen in my lashes, from my foolhardy swim in the Aneirin River.

Silence.

Then a warm hand smoothed down my cold, wet hair. "Hang on, Gin. Just hang on—"

The world went black once more.

I don't really know what happened after that. I was dimly aware of riding in a car, someone's hands yanking at my heavy, wet, ice-crusted clothes. Every once in a while, I woke up long enough to hear people talking. Odd bits of conversation I probably should have understood but that just made no real sense to me.

"I'm driving as fast as I can."

"Use that cloud knocker."

"Put her in the tub."

"She's so *cold*."

Sometimes I thought that I heard Owen's voice. Other times I could have sworn it was Eva Grayson talking. But what would the brother and sister be doing at the train yard? I'd gone there to meet Finn, not them. I just couldn't make sense of anything.

Slowly, the cold receded from my body, an inch at a time, and warmth enveloped me once more. My fingers and toes and everything in between started to tingle as my circulation was slowly restored. I gritted my teeth as the fiery needles stabbed me one after another in an unrelenting wave.

"It's okay now, darling," a soothing voice whispered. "You can let go of your Ice magic now. You're safe, Gin. Relax. Just relax."

So I did and drowned in the darkness once more.

*   *   *

The next time I tried to open my eyes, I was actually able to do it, with no problems or struggles of any sort. After a few seconds, the world snapped into focus and I realized I was lying in a bed. Above my head, puffy white clouds drifted across a cerulean blue sky on the fresco on the ceiling. The dreamy clouds comforted me, and I let out a quiet sigh. Safe. I was safe now. Because only one person I knew had her ceilings painted like that—Jo-Jo Deveraux.

Somehow I'd gotten from the muddy bank of the Aneirin River all the way across town to the dwarf's house. I wasn't too concerned right now with exactly how that had happened, just the fact that I was safe and warm and could actually feel my arms and legs again. I wiggled my fingers and toes and was pleased when they all responded to my internal command. Looked like I hadn't lost any digits to frostbite or hypothermia, no doubt thanks to Jo-Jo's healing Air elemental magic. Good. It would be hard to hold on to my silverstone knives with no thumbs.

A faint scuffle sounded, and I lifted up my head.

Over the mound of blankets that covered me, I spotted Natasha standing at the foot of the bed. The little girl had been cleaned up since the last time I'd seen her in the train yard. Her dark brown hair had been pulled back into a ponytail, and her face was free of the grime and tears that had covered it. The puffy bruise was gone from her cheek, and I didn't see any other injuries on her. Jo-Jo had probably used her Air magic to get rid of those, as well as heal me.

Now the girl was dressed in what looked like one of Sophia Deveraux's black Goth sweatshirts, given the fact that it was covered with bloody broken hearts. Matching sweatpants and socks completed the ensemble. Sophia might be a dwarf, but the sweatshirt still reached down to the girl's knees, looking like a dress on her thin frame. The legs on the sweatpants had been rolled up several times too.

"Hi," I croaked.

Instead of answering me, Natasha stared at me a second longer, then turned and ran out of the bedroom.

I put my head back down on the pillow and lay there in bed for a few minutes, just letting myself adjust to being alive, awake, and in one piece again. Slowly moving my body, flexing my fingers and toes and making sure that everything was in more or less working order. Jo-Jo had outdone herself again, because I felt almost as good as new, except for the bone-deep weariness that made me want to curl up and sleep for eight more hours. But that was just an aftereffect of being magically healed by the Air elemental, nothing more. Especially since I was pretty sure I'd resembled an ice cube by the time the dwarf had gotten her hands on me last night.

The most important thing was that Elektra LaFleur hadn't killed me yet. And now that I knew that my baby sister, Bria, was on her hit list, I was even more determined to end the other assassin's existence.

Which I wouldn't accomplish by staying in bed all day. So I sat up and threw off the blankets. I really must have been frozen when I'd gotten here because I had on not one, not two, but three sets of flannel pajamas—along with five pairs of wool socks. I looked like a marshmallow with so many heavy, dense layers covering my body. I shook my head and got to my feet.

I took a step, stumbled, and almost did a header into the cherry dresser next to the bed. My feet might still be attached to the rest of me, but apparently they weren't accepting orders just yet because more needles of pain flared to life deep in my muscles. I gritted my teeth and planted my hands on the wooden dresser, waiting for the sensation to pass. I was damned if I'd collapse back onto the bed. Not while LaFleur was still breathing. Not while the assassin had her sights set on killing Bria.

"You shouldn't be up yet," a low voice drawled.

I looked up to find Owen Grayson standing in the doorway, a steaming mug of something clutched in his hand.

Owen looked just as tired as I felt. His blue-black hair was rumpled, stubble covered his face, and shadows darkened his violet eyes, as though he hadn't gotten much sleep last night. He was dressed casually in a thick, black turtleneck sweater that highlighted his broad shoulders, but mud covered his boots and stained the knees of his jeans.

I frowned. "Why is there mud all over your clothes?"

"Because I'm the one who found you last night," Owen said. "You called me. Don't you remember?"

I had a vague recollection of hitting Owen's number on my speed dial instead of Finn's but that was all. I concentrated, and more flashes of light and sound swam up in my mind, filling in some of the blanks from last night.

"I called you, and you came looking for me," I said. "But how did you find me? I didn't exactly give you directions."

Owen leaned against the doorway and took a sip from

his mug. The smell of sugary-sweet hot chocolate made my mouth water. "No, but I called Finn, and he told me where you were and what the two of you had been doing. When you called me, you said that you'd jumped into the river and were downstream. I told Finn that, and he was able to guess where you might have washed up. So I got in the car and went looking."

"And Eva was with you too, wasn't she? I remember hearing her voice."

Owen nodded. "She wouldn't let me go without her, and I thought that the two of us searching would be better than just me."

I shook my head. "But even if you had a general idea of where I was, it would still take hours to search the riverbank, especially in the dark. So how did you find me?"

Owen walked into the room and picked up something from the nightstand on the other side of the bed. Sunlight streaming in through the window glinted off the edge of one of my silverstone knives.

"These," he said. "I knew that you had to have at least a couple of them left on you, not to mention the metal melted into your hands. So I just concentrated and focused on finding any silverstone in the area. They led me right to you."

Of course. Owen had what he considered to be a small elemental talent for metal, which was an offshoot of Stone, although I knew that his magic was anything but weak. The bottom line was that Owen could sense, control, and manipulate metal just the way that I could Ice and Stone. Still, it must have taken every bit of magic he had to specifically sense the silverstone in such a big area, especially with all the cans and other metal debris that littered the riverbanks.

"That's why you look so tired, isn't it?" I murmured. "You used up all your magic to find me last night."

Owen shrugged as though it was nothing. But it wasn't nothing to me. Besides Finn and the Deveraux sisters, I couldn't even remember the last time someone had cared enough to come looking for me when I was in trouble. I was so used to being on my own for so long, always being the tough, strong, capable one, that I'd forgotten how nice it felt to have someone else look out for me.

To have someone else care about me.

And just like that, the fragile strings of my feelings for Owen joined together, all the tangled threads wrapping around and weaving their way through my heart. Scary and painful in some ways, but necessary in others too.

Ignoring the needles still tingling in my legs, I managed to walk around the bed. Owen put his mug down and opened his arms. I stepped into his embrace. For a moment, I just laid my head against his chest, breathing in his rich, earthy aroma. Then, when I felt steady enough, I stood up and pressed my lips to Owen's.

Maybe it was my frame of mind or the fact that I'd almost frozen to death last night, but I felt so much in our kiss. Owen's lips against mine, his body flush with my own, his tongue slowly stroking against mine. The familiar passion sparked to life deep inside me. The feel of Owen, the smell, the taste of him, heated me in a way that all the wool socks in the world just couldn't.

But it wasn't just my body he'd affected. As much as I'd tried to fight it, warmth had blossomed in my heart for him too, unfurling one small, fragile petal at a time. And the emotion had only been strengthened by what he'd done for me last night. For coming to my rescue when I needed him the most, for helping me when I couldn't help myself, for saving me when I couldn't save myself.

Some time later the kiss ended. We stood there in the middle of the bedroom, our arms wrapped around each other, breathless. For the first time, I didn't try to ignore what I was feeling or pretend that things were only physical between us. They were much more than that now.

"Well, now," Owen murmured against my lips. "That makes it all worthwhile."

I drew back and arched an eyebrow. "Really? I wouldn't have figured you for a man who could be so easily bought off with a mere kiss. Even if there was a good deal of tongue action involved."

A wicked grin spread across Owen's face, softening the scar on his chin and making his violet eyes sparkle with a sly light. "Well, if you have something else in mind, I'm open to suggestions."

I jerked my thumb over my shoulder. "There is a bed in this room."

"Yes, I had noticed that," Owen said. "I also happened to notice that you have on about a closet's worth of clothes."

"You don't like the marshmallow look?" I quipped. "Or perhaps you're just not up to the challenge of getting through all my many layers of woolen chastity?"

Owen's eyes narrowed, and his lips quirked up into a sly, sexy smirk. "Oh, baby. You have no idea what I'd do to get through those layers and down to the good stuff."

I pressed a soft kiss to the side of his mouth then put my lips up against his ear. "Then why don't you show me?"

Owen's hands slid down my back before coming around to the front of my body. Our eyes met and held as he undid the top button on the topmost flannel shirt I was wearing—

Someone let out a not-so-discreet cough. I looked over Owen's shoulder to see Finnegan Lane standing in the doorway, a cup of chicory coffee in his hand and a knowing grin on his handsome face.

"Well, it looks like someone's feeling better," Finn drawled.

✳ 20 ✳

I sighed and looked back at Owen. "Rain check?"

He leaned forward and pressed a quick kiss to my lips. "I'll hold you to that."

And I would have been holding him, if I'd had my way. But Finn was here now, no doubt to check on me, and I knew that the others would be wondering how I was doing as well. The romantic reunion and thank-you-for-saving-my-life sex would have to wait until later. I sighed and stepped out of Owen's embrace.

By this point, most of the pins and needles had vanished from my legs, but I still wasn't rock steady on my feet, which is why I held on to the polished banister as the three of us went downstairs.

Since it was Sunday, Jo-Jo's beauty salon was closed, but that's still where I found the middle-aged dwarf, painting Natasha's fingernails a sweet little-girl pink. Vinnie held his daughter on his lap, his hands around her waist, his head perched on her shoulder, as if he couldn't quite believe she was back here with him instead of dead and buried. Rosco, Jo-Jo's basset hound, was snoozing in his basket in the corner as usual, his fat, stubby legs twitching with some sort of dream.

The three of them looked up at the sight of me standing in the doorway. Vinnie got to his feet and set his daughter back down in the cherry red salon chair. Natasha gave me a tiny smile, then held out her other hand so Jo-Jo could paint the rest of her nails. She seemed to be doing well, all things considered. At least she was safe now and back with her father, where she belonged.

Vinnie came over and stood in front of me. He looked just as tired as I felt, although his seemed to be more of a happy relief than anything else. The Ice elemental hesitated, then held out his hand. I took it, and we shook. His palm felt cool against mine.

"Gin, the Spider, whatever you call yourself, anything you ever need, anything I have, it's yours," Vinnie said in a low voice. "All you have to do is ask."

The bartender didn't owe me a thing for saving his daughter, not one damn thing. Rescuing the little girl from the horrors and death that had awaited her at the train yard had been my pleasure. But even more than that, I thought that Fletcher Lane, my murdered mentor, would have been proud of me for doing it. The old man had had a bit of an altruistic streak, helping people with certain messy problems. Pro fucking bono, as it were. Of course, I hadn't known about Fletcher's side business until after he'd died, but I still thought the old man would have approved of my actions last night.

"Whatever you want," Vinnie said again. "It's yours."

I would have told Vinnie that we were square, but I knew his fatherly pride dictated that he find some way to pay me back. And as much as I was starting to enjoy following in Fletcher's pro bono footsteps, I was never one to turn down a favor.

"I just might hold you to that."

He returned my stare. "I hope you do. I really hope you do."

"Daddy?" Natasha said in a soft voice, interrupting us. "Aren't my nails pretty?"

The little girl held out her hands for us to inspect. Vinnie gave me another smile, then turned, went back to his daughter, and hugged her close once more.

"They're beautiful, honey. Just beautiful," he whispered against her hair.

And they were.

Jo-Jo settled Natasha in the downstairs den with some chocolate chip cookies that I'd baked yesterday at the Pork Pit, a glass of milk, and some old *Scooby Doo* reruns on one of the cable networks. Vinnie sat on the couch with his daughter, giggling right along with her at the slapstick antics on television.

The rest of us—Jo-Jo, Finn, Owen, and I—retreated to the next room over, the kitchen, which was one of my favorite rooms in the house. A rectangular butcher's block table surrounded by several tall stools took up most of the area, while appliances done in a variety of pastel shades ringed three of the walls. Runelike clouds, Jo-Jo's symbol, could be found everywhere in the room, from the place mats on the table to the dish towels piled next to the sink to the fresco that covered the ceiling.

My eyes went to the cloud-shaped clock on the wall. Just after one in the afternoon, more than twelve hours since I'd taken my swan dive into the Aneirin River. My thoughts turned to all the time I'd lost—and what might have happened while I'd been unconscious.

"What about the Pork Pit?" I asked Jo-Jo.

"Sophia's covering for you," the dwarf replied, bustling around the kitchen, pulling plates, silverware, and more out of the drawers and cabinets.

I nodded. The Goth dwarf knew just as much about running the barbecue restaurant as I did. I only hoped she wouldn't have to work too hard today, prepping all the holiday orders, since I wasn't there to help her.

Jo-Jo reached for an oven mitt and opened the stove door. The mouthwatering smell of fresh-baked lasagna drifted out to me, and I scooted off my stool.

"Here," I said. "Let me help you with that."

Jo-Jo gave me a hard stare with her clear, almost colorless eyes. "You just sit back down right now, darling. I can cook for you today. I was doing it for years before you came along, Gin."

Properly chastised, I sank back onto my stool.

Jo-Jo dished up the lasagna, along with a Caesar salad and some garlic breadsticks. The others had already eaten. Good thing, since I attacked the food with unrestrained gusto, going back for three helpings. Then again, it had been the better part of day since I'd last had a meal.

When I was finished, Jo-Jo cleared everything away. In the den, Natasha had finished her cookies and milk and was now taking a nap. Vinnie snored along with his daughter. Not surprising. He'd been through just as traumatic an ordeal as she had, when he thought he'd lost her.

"So lay it out for me," I said, once everything was squared away. "What happened last night? And what's been going on while I've been out of it?"

Finn took a sip from the mug of chicory coffee that he'd set down on the counter. By my count, that was the third cup he'd had since I'd woken up. "After you ran back into the train yard, I told the kid to stay put and hung around for a few minutes, covering your back. Which was considerably easier to do once you started that fire. It lit up the whole depot like it was the Fourth of July. I popped a couple of the giants and dwarves who were headed your way. I looked for LaFleur and Mab, hoping to take them out too, but I didn't have any angles on them. So I did all the damage that I could, then grabbed the girl and got the hell out of there."

I thought that the goons had been shooting at me last night, but it had really been Finn, picking off a few more of Mab's men, trying to add even more confusion to the scene.

"I got the kid back to my car," Finn continued. "I drove around, trying to figure out where you might be, or how I could help you, but you were already gone, and I had no idea where. At least not until Owen called me. I told him where to start looking for you, while I brought Natasha over here. Jo-Jo patched her up, and Vinnie hasn't let his daughter out of his sight since then."

I looked at my foster brother. "Thank you for that."

Finn shrugged. "You're the one who did all the heavy

lifting. I just killed a couple of Mab's men and drove the girl over here."

I nodded.

"As for the aftermath," Finn said. "Well, things have gotten *really* interesting in the last few hours."

"How so?" Owen asked.

Finn stared at him. "Well, for starters, that little fire that Gin started? It completely gutted the old train depot. Mab won't be building any kind of nightclub there any-time soon."

"It was just a little gasoline," I said. "Surely, it didn't do that much damage."

Finn raised his eyebrows. "A little gasoline mixed with paint and all that other flammable shit that was lying around the depot. You started a four-alarm fire. The whole place went up like kindling, and Mab's men freaked when they couldn't contain it. They had to call the fire department to come out and handle it. Evidently you could see the flames and the smoke a mile away."

I frowned. "Why didn't Mab just take care of it her-self? Fire's her element. Surely, she could have put out the flames or at least helped contain them."

Finn shrugged. "Maybe, but apparently she was too busy screaming at Elektra LaFleur for failing to kill you and bring back your head to care that her building was burning to the ground right in front of her. Rumor has it that Mab was a wee bit upset with her hired gun."

Despite the fact that I'd almost been electrocuted and frozen to death last night, I couldn't help but grin. Maybe it was petty of me, but I loved thwarting Mab's best-laid plans.

"According to my sources, you've become LaFleur's

number one priority," Finn said, taking another sip of his coffee. "Mab wants you dead yesterday, Gin. And if Elektra can't get the job done in the next few days, then Mab's going to show her how it's done—starting with Elektra."

I nodded. I'd expected nothing less after last night's escapade. I'd infiltrated Mab's newest little fiefdom, snatched Natasha right out from under her nose, burned her potential nightclub to the ground, and escaped from her assassin. Not a good night to be Mab. A great one for the Spider, though.

Finn had already told me that the other power players in Ashland had been sniffing around Mab, ever since I'd killed Jake McAllister in the Fire elemental's own home a few weeks ago. For the first time in a long time, the city's other underworld sharks sensed weakness around the Fire elemental, a weakness that they wanted to exploit. And now all this had happened.

A few more nights like this one, and I wouldn't have to make a run at Mab. Her other enemies would do it for me. Not that they would succeed, of course, as Mab was no pushover. But my small victories would make them bold enough to try. That was something, at least.

I thought back to all the things that I'd overheard Mab and Elektra talking about last night in the railcar. Finding the Spider. Killing the Spider. Doing the same to Gin Blanco. And most importantly, murdering my sister, Bria. There was only one way I could prevent all of that from happening—I had to kill Elektra LaFleur. I'd been planning on doing it anyway, and I might have taken my shot at her last night, if I hadn't had Finn and Natasha to think about.

But taking out the other assassin had morphed into a

necessity. LaFleur was one of the best, and now she was on Mab's ticking timetable. The assassin would torture and kill anyone she thought might know who I was in order to find me. Which meant there were three people in the most danger right now—Roslyn, Xavier, and Bria.

Roslyn and Xavier because Mab suspected they were somehow connected to Elliot Slater's death and Bria because, well, she was her. The woman that Mab thought was destined to kill her. So Roslyn and Xavier had to be warned, and Bria, well, I wasn't sure what to do about her. I knew that Xavier would help watch my sister's back, since the giant was her partner on the Ashland police force. But there were just too many other times, too many other places, someone like LaFleur could get to her, kill her. There was really only one way to solve this particular problem.

"Well, then," I murmured. "I guess I'll just have to kill LaFleur first."

"And how are you planning to do that?" Jo-Jo asked.

"Yeah," Finn chimed in. "How are you going to do that? Because my sources tell me that Mab's holed up on her estate and that she's not coming out until Elektra brings her your head on a silver platter. The train yard was tricky enough. They weren't expecting you to know about it, much less actually show up there. But Mab's mansion is locked down tighter than Fort Knox. There's no way you're getting close to the Fire elemental on her own turf. And apparently, LaFleur's in there with her as well."

I thought about everything I knew about Elektra LaFleur. All the information in that file that Fletcher had compiled on her. All my interactions with her over the last few days. How she thought, how she killed, the things she seemed to want out of life. I thought back to the conversation I'd overheard between her and Mab, the one where they had talked about all the people the Fire elemental wanted dead.

"Oh, I don't think I have to worry about getting into Mab's estate," I said, echoing the words I'd told Sophia just last night. "Sooner or later, LaFleur's going to come to me."

Owen frowned. "Why do you think that? Do you think she knows who you really are?"

I shook my head. "No. There's no way she got a good look at me last night. Not in the dark with everything that was going on. Even if she did, I was wearing that ski mask, at least until it got ripped off when I fell into the river. But Elektra will come to the Pork Pit sooner or later."

"But why?" Finn asked, his walnut-colored brows drawn together in confusion.

I told the two of them about everything I'd heard Mab and Elektra talk about in the railcar—namely, the untimely demise of one Gin Blanco, soon to be followed by that of Bria Coolidge.

"So you're going to set yourself up as bait," Owen said. "Okay. I guess I can understand that. But how do you know that LaFleur will show? She's supposed to be hunting down the Spider, not spending her time assassinating you."

I shrugged. "There's no guarantee that she'll come after me. But I was an assassin for a long time, and I ran into more than a few of my comrades over the years. Some of them were like me and Fletcher. They killed for the money or because it was a job that they were good at."

Finn, Owen, and Jo-Jo all nodded.

"But LaFleur's different," I said. "She kills for the thrill of it. Because it amuses her. That's why she toasted the dwarf at the docks. Because it gave her a charge, at least for a few minutes. She doesn't think that Gin Blanco, simple restaurant owner, is any kind of threat to her at all. Hell, she bragged to Mab that killing me wouldn't take up more than half an hour of her precious time. LaFleur will want, no, she'll *need* some kind of little victory after letting me get away from her last night. Some little something she can take back to Mab that she accomplished, that she got right. But even more than that, she'll need a kill for herself. Something to quiet that twitchy itch in her if only for a few hours."

"And you think that Gin Blanco will be it," Owen said, the worry loud and clear in his voice.

I nodded. "I do. Jonah McAllister wants me dead in the worst way. He just doesn't want to get his hands dirty doing it. LaFleur will be all too happy to do the job for him."

We sat in the kitchen in silence. In the den, Natasha's cartoon played on, the high jinks and *yuk-yuk* laughter sounding cheerily obscene next to the grim reality facing me—kill or be killed. But like it or not, it was the story of my life. It had been ever since I was thirteen. So far, I'd been the one who'd done the killing, and it was a tradition I planned to continue.

"Say that she does come for you, that she comes to the

Pork Pit to murder Gin Blanco," Owen said. "What are you going to do?"

I stared at him with my flat gray eyes, letting him see the cold violence that always lurked there in the depths, just below the calm surface. "My plan is simple really. Kill the bitch before she kills me."

✳ 21 ✳

We stayed in the kitchen for another ten minutes, hashing out how things might go down when LaFleur came to the Pork Pit to murder me. Not much to hash out really. I'd kill her, then Sophia would help me dispose of her body. Simple, efficient, deadly. Those were always the best kinds of plans.

Finn and Owen offered to watch the restaurant, to be lurking in the shadows waiting to provide backup when LaFleur called, but I turned them down. I did my best work alone, when I didn't have other people to think about, when I didn't have other people to worry about. If I had one second of distraction, one second of hesitation with LaFleur, I'd be the one who ended up dead instead of the other assassin.

Finn and Owen didn't like it, but they understood my reasoning. When they realized that I wasn't budging or changing my mind, the two of them reluctantly relented to my decision and left the kitchen. Finn went off to call Roslyn and Xavier and tell them to lie low and watch their backs for the next few days, while Owen checked in with Eva to give her an update on how I was doing.

I stayed behind in the kitchen with Jo-Jo. The middle-aged dwarf had remained silent during most of Finn's debriefing, but now she turned her pale, colorless eyes in my direction.

"What's bothering you, darling?" Jo-Jo said.

I sighed. In addition to her healing skills, Jo-Jo also had a bit of precognition. Most Airs did, since their magic let them listen to and interpret all the feelings and emotions that swirled along with the wind. It was just another way in which the dwarf's power was the opposite of mine. Jo-Jo's elemental Air magic gave her glimpses of the future, while my Stone power let me see into the past and what had happened in a particular place.

Thanks to Jo-Jo's precognition, I never could really hide anything from the dwarf, so this time I didn't even bother to try.

"Elektra LaFleur and her electrical magic," I said. "She's strong, Jo-Jo. So *strong*. Maybe even stronger than I am. LaFleur almost got me last night, almost broke through my Stone magic and fried me alive right there in the rail yard with her electricity. And even though she didn't kill me, her magic—it hurt so *much*. It took every bit of strength that I had to keep going after she blasted me with it that first time."

"You're worried she might kill you," Jo-Jo said in a soft voice.

I shrugged. "It's a distinct possibility. She almost got

me last night. Hell, I would have frozen to death anyway if Owen hadn't found me and brought me here."

Jo-Jo gave me a thoughtful look. "I don't know about all that, Gin."

I stared at her. "What are you talking about?"

The dwarf took a sip of the hot chocolate that she'd made while I was arguing with Finn and Owen. "You don't really remember much about last night, do you?"

I shook my head.

"I didn't think so," Jo-Jo replied. "Sure, you were in bad shape when Owen brought you in, but you weren't nowhere near close to dying."

I frowned. It had certainly felt like I was dying, especially since I hadn't been able to feel any part of my body, there at the end. "What do you mean? I was half-frozen to death, from what I remember."

"Oh, you were definitely that," Jo-Jo agreed. "But not because of the river or LaFleur weakening you with her electrical magic. The frozen thing? You did that to yourself, Gin."

Unease curled up in my stomach. "What do you mean?"

Jo-Jo tilted her head to one side and stared at me with her clear eyes. "I mean that when Owen brought you into my beauty salon last night, you were holding on to enough magic to turn this whole house into a block of solid elemental Ice."

I blinked. I didn't remember doing anything like that. I didn't remember doing much of anything except drifting in and out of consciousness. "But I couldn't have done that. I couldn't feel anything, anything at all, not my fingers, not my toes, and certainly not my Ice magic."

Jo-Jo shook her head. "Maybe that's what you think, maybe that's how it felt to you. But somehow, you were using your Ice magic. A lot of it. More than I've ever seen you use before."

This time I shook my head. "I don't think so. If anything, I should have made myself move, should have made myself get up and start running and stay warm until I could get somewhere safe. Not turn myself into a human Popsicle."

That's what I'd done the last time I'd taken a late-night plunge into the cold depths of the Aneirin River after leaping off one of the balconies of the Ashland Opera House. That had been a few months ago when Brutus, aka the assassin Viper, had tried to kill me before I'd stiffed him instead. Brutus had managed to sneak up on me and put a gun to the base of my skull. All the other assassin had to do to kill me was just pull the trigger, but Brutus had wanted to gloat first about getting the drop on me. I'd kept him talking and had managed to turn things around. In the end, I'd left Brutus's body in the opera house and made my getaway.

For a second, Brutus's face flashed in front of my eyes. A short, stocky, Asian man with a black ponytail, a rune tattoo of a viper curling up his neck, and a scar slashing down his face to meet it.

I frowned. Thinking about the other assassin reminded me of something, of some small memory, of something that had to do with Elektra LaFleur—

"No," Jo-Jo said, making me lose my train of thought.

"You were too wet, too cold, for that, and you instinctively knew it. So you did the only thing that you could. You grabbed hold of your Ice magic and used it to insulate your body, to wrap yourself in the cold until someone could come and find you and get you warm again. You've heard stories about kids up north falling into frozen lakes, getting fished out, and then miraculously being resuscitated a few hours later, right? With almost no damage whatsoever?"

I nodded.

"Well, that's what you did. You used your Ice magic to lower your body temperature enough to preserve yourself," the dwarf explained. "Those spider rune scars on your hands were glowing as bright as cold stars with your elemental power. I had a hell of time getting you to let go of it enough so that I could start healing you. Gin, you plumb wore me out last night."

Jo-Jo Deveraux was one of the strongest elementals I'd ever met, certainly the strongest Air healer. She was the kind of elemental that even someone like Mab Monroe would think twice about taking on. And somehow I'd tired the dwarf last night fighting her Air magic with my own Ice power?

I just didn't believe it. More importantly, I just didn't *want* to believe it. But Jo-Jo had always claimed I had more raw elemental magic than anyone she'd ever seen before—including Mab. I'd never been comfortable with that thought, and once more it made me shiver, even in the bright, cheery warmth of the dwarf's kitchen.

Because really, when it came right down to it, the cold, hard, rocky truth was that my mother and sister had died because of my elemental power. Because of what I could do with it. To say that I had some guilt about that would be an understatement. Ever since I'd found out that I was the cause for all of this, for all the misery and suffering in my own life, I'd felt sick over it. Just—sick.

Still, despite what Jo-Jo and even Mab thought, I wasn't foolish enough to think that I was the greatest elemental power that had ever been born. There was always somebody stronger out there, somebody quicker, tougher, smarter. All you had to do was be unlucky enough to meet them, have an off day, and then you got dead.

"I told you that your Ice magic would only get stronger since you overcame the block of having that silverstone in your hands," Jo-Jo said in a soft voice. "I'd say that it's the equal of your Stone power now. It was what saved you last night. And it's what will help you kill Elektra LaFleur. Don't be afraid of it, Gin. Don't be afraid of yourself."

I didn't meet the dwarf's eyes, but another shiver swept through me just the same.

Because it was too late for all that now. It had been ever since the night Mab had murdered my family.

Jo-Jo went into the den to put some blankets over Vinnie's and Natasha's still-sleeping forms. The dwarf agreed with me that the two of them needed to stay out of sight for the next few days, which meant they'd be bunking here for a little while longer. At least until I'd dealt with LaFleur—one way or another.

I took a long, hot shower and put on the spare set of clothes Finn had brought over for me earlier. Then I went back downstairs, fully intending to head over to the Pork

Pit for the rest of the day, help out Sophia, and see if La-Fleur came by for her inevitable visit.

To my surprise, Owen was waiting downstairs in the kitchen.

"I thought you were going home to Eva," I said.

"I'm going to go right now," he said, getting to his feet. "And you're coming with me."

"I am?"

Owen nodded. "You are. You need to rest, Gin. At least for one more day before you put yourself out there as bait for that assassin."

I raised an eyebrow. "And you're, what? Offering to take care of me for the rest of the day?"

Owen nodded again. "Night too," he said in a husky voice. "If you'll let me."

I stared into his violet eyes, looking once again for any hint, any sign, that he'd finally wised up. That Owen had finally realized how cold, violent, twisted, and emotionally distant I really was, and that he was finally ready to pretend he'd never met me. But there was nothing in his gaze but warm acceptance—and stubborn determination to watch out for me, even if I didn't want him to. Even if I didn't think I deserved it. Even if I didn't think I was actually worthy of someone's time, consideration, attention, and sympathy.

The tangled threads around my heart tightened a little more.

Just for Owen standing there in Jo-Jo's kitchen and caring enough about me to try to delay my inevitable death at least one more day. The realization, the sheer force of it, took my breath away, and I had to reach out and put one hand on the kitchen table to steady myself.

"So," Owen said, "are you coming along peaceful-like, or am I going to have to hog-tie you and put you in the car?"

"Promises, promises, sheriff," I quipped. "You have no idea how much I like being tied up."

A slow, lazy grin spread across Owen's chiseled face. "Well, maybe that's one of the things we can talk about in greater detail—at my house this evening."

The grin dropped from his face, and he was serious once more. "What do you say, Gin? Come home with me. Even if it's only for today."

Please. He didn't say the word, but we both heard it in the rough, raw tone of his voice. And try as I might, I couldn't stop the silken threads wrapped around my heart from quivering in agreement. From wanting to enjoy just one more carefree day and night with Owen, before I focused all my attention on the deadliest enemy I'd ever faced.

"All right," I said in a teasing tone, trying to lighten the mood and the unfamiliar, uncomfortable emotions flooding my chest. "But only if we can talk about that tied-up thing in much greater detail."

"Oh," Owen said, another grin creasing his face. "I think we can arrange that."

❋ 22 ❋

Sometime during the night, Finn had gone back to the train yard and retrieved my car from the discreet location where I'd parked it. So I was able to follow Owen back to his house in my own set of wheels.

An hour after our talk in the kitchen, I was safely ensconced in Owen's massive bed, with several pillows behind my back and several more blankets piled on top of me, even though I was no longer cold. Owen had also started a fire in the stone fireplace in the corner of the bedroom, and the flames danced merrily, bathing the room in a pleasant, cheery glow. It was late afternoon now, and outside, the long winter shadows had already started to stretch over the landscape, blackening everything they touched. But in here, everything was bright and warm and cozy.

After seeing how I was doing, Eva Grayson had gone out to do some last-minute Christmas shopping with her best friend, Violet Fox. So Owen and I were alone in the mansion. After starting the fire, Owen had told me to sit tight and then disappeared into some other part of the house, saying that he had a surprise for me. As a general rule I didn't like surprises. Not many assassins did. But I was willing to make an exception just this once.

A few minutes later, Owen stepped back into the bedroom, carrying a large wrapped box that was obviously a Christmas present. Fat, blue snowmen covered the paper, grinning up at me like fools, while a wide red ribbon topped off the whole thing.

Owen sat down on the bed next to me and put the box in my lap. "Merry Christmas, Gin."

"Oh." There I went again, being a conversational genius.

I stared at the box, then looked up at Owen. "But I don't have your present yet. At least, not with me."

I winced at the lousy lie. The truth was that so much had been going on these last few days that I hadn't given any more thought to what I might get Owen. He was a millionaire in his own right with a slew of successful businesses, so it wasn't like he really *needed* anything. Still, I wanted to get him something—something meaningful, special. But what could it be? Somehow, I didn't think that a light-up Christmas sweater or a cheesy holiday tie would cut it.

"That's all right," Owen rumbled. "I thought I would give these to you early. You might find a use for them before Christmas."

Now I was curious, eagerly so. Fletcher Lane might not have been my blood father, but the old man had passed his rampant sense of curiosity on to me. In fact, it was the one trait that always seemed to get the best of me, no matter how hard I tried to squash it.

Still, I hesitated. "Are you sure you want me to open it? Right now?"

He nodded.

"Okay."

I plucked the fat bow off the box and placed it on top of Owen's head. He playfully grumbled at me, but left the red ribbon where it was, a streamer trailing down each side of his chiseled face. Then I ripped into the snowman-covered wrapping paper, shredding it with my nails. The box was solid and much heavier than I'd thought it would be, and a moment later I realized why. It was actually a silverstone case—the slick, fancy kind that a banker like Finn might use to carry around a large sum of cash.

"Go on," Owen urged. "See what's inside."

I popped the clasps on either side of the case and opened it up. Inside lay a tray of thick black foam—and five silverstone knives. The metal winked at me in the firelight.

"They're beautiful," I said in a low voice.

And they were. The knives were similar in design to the ones that I always carried, but I could tell that these were exquisitely made, even more so than my usual weapons. I plucked one out of the foam, turning it this way and that, getting a feel for the weapon.

Light but strong, thin but sharp, beautiful but deadly. The knife felt like a natural extension of my hand even more than my old, familiar weapons did. It was as though Owen had somehow measured my hand from every conceivable angle and then designed a blade just for me.

The metal winked at me again, and I realized that a symbol had been stamped into the hilt. I peered more closely. I recognized it immediately, of course.

A small circle surrounded by eight thin rays. A spider rune.

My rune. My knives.

"Do you like them?" Owen asked, his violet eyes light and hopeful in his face.

For a moment I couldn't answer him. I was just so touched and slightly stunned by the thoughtfulness of his gift and all the work that had so obviously gone into the knives. Even with Owen's elemental talent for metal, it would have taken him hours, maybe even days, to make each one of the weapons. No one had ever given me something so personal, so perfect before. And the fact that it was Owen who was giving them to me . . . Once again, I let myself truly hope that things would be different with us, and that our relationship wouldn't end in disaster like my last one.

"They're perfect," I whispered. "Absolutely perfect. But when did you have time to make them? We've only been . . . together a few weeks."

Owen shrugged. "I started thinking about the design a while back when I realized just how much you liked knives."

I stared at the silverstone weapons glinting in the black foam. "And you're giving them to me now, giving them to me early, because of LaFleur, aren't you?"

"I am."

Once again, I stared into Owen's eyes, searching for any sign, any hint, that he was somehow disgusted by my plan to kill LaFleur. That deep down, he simply abhorred who I was and the bloody violence I was so easily capable of dishing out without hesitation or regrets of any kind.

But there was nothing in his gaze but understanding. And I was beginning to think that was all there would ever be. That Owen would never show the disgust and disappointment my previous lover, Detective Donovan Caine, had. That Owen would never leave me as Donovan had because of my being the Spider. However crazy it was, Owen understood me—and he fully accepted what I was and the things I had to do to keep the people I loved safe.

"You know," I said, my voice thick with emotion that I couldn't quite hide. "You didn't have to stay at Jo-Jo's last night. And you didn't have to listen to Finn and me talk about the best way to kill LaFleur this afternoon. If you'd left me there, I would have understood. If you don't want to know anything about what I do when I go out late at night, I would understand that too."

Owen gave me a faint, slightly sad smile. "Still comparing me to Donovan, eh, Gin?"

I shrugged. "I was an assassin for a long time, Owen. I might be retired, but part of me will always be the Spider. Always be ready, willing, and able to do what I have to do, no matter how violent or bloody it is or who I have to hurt in the process. These last few weeks with you have been great. All I'm saying is that I understand if the novelty's worn off and you want to get off the carousel ride now before it kills you."

"I admit that you being an assassin has certainly made things . . . interesting," Owen said in an honest voice.

"But I also think you're the most fascinating woman I've ever met. Strong, caring, and fiercely loyal to the people that she loves. I'm no choirboy, Gin. And I don't expect you to be one either. I'm a lot of things, but a hypocrite isn't one of them."

He stopped and drew in a breath. "As for the knives, I made them because I knew you would like them. I knew you would use them. And I made them because I wanted you to have the best damn weapons available when you do go after Elektra LaFleur, Mab Monroe, or whoever's on your hit list at the moment. I want you to come back to me, Gin—in one piece. Always. That's why I made the weapons for you. Because if I can't be there, then at least they can. And they're the best damn pieces I've ever made because I made them for you."

I might have been sleeping with Owen for the past few weeks, but I hadn't let him get close to me. Oh, I'd told him all about my past, about the night that Mab had murdered my family, about Fletcher taking me in off the streets and teaching me how to be the assassin the Spider, even about Bria being back in town and all the conflicted feelings I had toward my sister. But I hadn't let him get close to me, hadn't let him have any real piece of my heart.

Maybe it was time to change that.

I put the silverstone knife back in the case, closed the lid, and set it down on the floor beside the bed. Then I threw off the blankets, scooted over to Owen, wrapped my arms around his neck, and pressed my lips to his.

The things I was feeling weren't subtle, weren't safe and small and cautious, and neither was my reaction to Owen.

My tongue plunged into his mouth, hot and demanding, even as I crawled up and straddled him, rocking back and forth, telling him exactly what I wanted, exactly what I needed—him. Now. Always.

After a second of hesitation, Owen growled low in his throat and responded in kind, his tongue dueling with mine for control. A minute later, we broke apart, already breathing heavily. But the kiss had done nothing to quench my desire for him. If anything, it had only made my need flare that much brighter, that much hotter. I already felt close to exploding. Or perhaps that was because of everything I was feeling—things I just couldn't put into words. Not now, maybe not ever. But I could show him how I felt—again and again and again.

I moved in to kiss him again, but Owen held a finger up to my lips.

"Wait, wait, are you sure you feel up to it?" he murmured. "We don't have to—"

I rocked forward again, slowly grinding against him. Then my hand dropped to his stomach and moved lower, stroking him through the thick fabric of his pants, showing him exactly how up to it I felt.

Owen reached for me, and our lips met again. We spent a long time just kissing, just exploring each other's mouths, reveling in the other's scent, taste, feel, touch. Finally he reached for me, ready to take things to the next level, but I slid off the bed. I wanted this to last, to be something special, if only for tonight. Because I knew it might be my last, if LaFleur had her way.

My eyes locked with Owen's, gray on violet, both

gleaming with heat, passion, need, desire. I stretched my arms up over my head. And then I started to move.

I did a slow, sinuous striptease for him, curving my body this way and that, shedding one piece of clothing at a time as I went along, letting the fabric float away to the floor. Owen sat back on the bed and enjoyed the show, although the desire burned that much brighter in his gaze, with every bit of myself I revealed to him.

Finally, when I stood naked before him, I held out my hand. He took it, and I pulled him off the bed and up to his feet. Owen started to gather me in his arms again, but I moved around him, still teasing. Sliding my hands this way and that across his chest. Touching him here, then there, lower, harder, softer, gentler, until the muscles in his neck bulged from the strain of standing still.

I moved behind him, running my fingers through his thick, black hair, before pressing a soft kiss to the side of his neck.

"Let me undress you," I murmured in his ear.

Owen nodded and lifted his arms over his head. I made quick work of his sweater, socks, and pants, and soon, he stood there before me wearing only a pair of black silk boxers. They hung low on his lean hips, a dusky trail of hair dipping down below the waistband. I stepped closer to Owen, who watched me through hooded eyes. He knew the teasing game I was playing, and he was enjoying it just as much as I was.

I hooked one finger in the waistband of his boxers, then lightly snapped them back against his skin.

"Hey, now," he growled. "Don't damage anything you might want me to use in a few minutes."

"Oh, don't worry," I said. "I'll take extra good care of you tonight."

I leaned forward and slowly slid his boxers down his legs. Owen stepped out of them and kicked the silk across the room. But I was already moving forward, putting my mouth on his thick length, sucking gently, then harder, my nails running every which way on and around him.

"Gin," he rasped, his hips automatically pumping forward. Owen braced a hand on the nightstand to keep himself in check.

"Now, now," I said in a soft voice. "Good things come to those who wait."

I continued my teasing for several more minutes, bringing him to the edge again and again but not pushing him over it. Owen groaned with delight.

But finally, he had had enough of my teasing. He grabbed my arms, pulled me to my feet, and picked me up. I locked my legs around his waist. He maneuvered me up against the closet wall and gave me a wicked, wolfish smile, his violet eyes as bright and beautiful as I had ever seen them.

"My turn," he rasped.

His lips dropped to my neck, kissing me there, as one of his hands went down between my legs. I opened myself to him, and he slipped a finger inside me, pumping back and forth in a quick motion that drove me crazy with need. He added another finger, and my pleasure only increased, to the point that it was almost painful.

I threw back my head and clenched myself around his fingers, tighter and tighter, trying to find my release. But Owen was just as good at this game as I was, and he wouldn't let me slip off the edge any more than I had let him before. After several sweet minutes of torture, he pulled me away from the wall and lowered me to the bed.

"You stay right there," he murmured.

Like I had any intention of going anywhere right now.

I took my little white pills, but Owen grabbed a condom out of the nightstand and covered himself with it for extra protection. He reached for me again, but I grabbed his shoulders and made him sit up on the bed. I did my slow grind again, moving up and down on his lap. He wasn't satisfied to just watch this time. His hands were everywhere on my body, even as his head dipped lower and his mouth latched onto one of my nipples, scraping the taut bud with his teeth until I groaned with pleasure.

Back and forth we moved on the bed, first with me on top, then Owen, ours hands and mouths all over each other, taking every single ounce of pleasure the other had to give—and then some.

Finally, we came together, Owen sliding inside me, my hands on his back, urging him to go deeper, harder.

"Yes," I breathed against his neck. "Yes."

Then we both went over the edge—together.

Afterward we lay there in bed, a loose tangle of arms and legs. I felt more sated and loved—physically and otherwise—than I had in a long time. For once, all the soft things that I was feeling, all the tender emotions in my heart, didn't scare me. Not now. Not with Owen. And I had a feeling they never would again.

And most importantly, I could tell he felt the same. It was in the way he kissed me, the way he looked at me, the way he held me, even now, his fingers sliding through my hair, my head on his chest, both of us curled together, each one enjoying the other's warmth and the simple, quiet pleasure of just lying here.

"So I've been thinking about your idea for Christmas," I murmured, lightly running my nails across his broad, muscled chest. "About having a holiday party here."

Owen raised an eyebrow. "And?"

I drew in a breath. "And I think it's a good one. I've already asked Bria to come."

Owen didn't say anything for a moment. "Are you going to tell her then? That you're really her sister?"

I nodded. "I think so. Things are getting too complicated with LaFleur and Mab. I can protect Bria better if she knows the truth. I just hope she can accept who and what I am—and what I plan on doing to Mab."

Owen's arms tightened around me, and he gathered me close once more. "If Bria Coolidge is half the woman you are, then I think she'll understand everything you've been through. You said yourself that she came back to Ashland to find you, to investigate the murder of your mother and older sister."

That was the conclusion I'd drawn the night I'd broken into Bria's house to keep Elliot Slater and his giants from killing her. Finn had snooped around after the fact and had found something interesting in Bria's office—a dry-erase board that contained every known detail about the murder of our mother, Eira, and older sister, Annabella. It looked as if Bria had come back to Ashland for the sole purpose of trying to bring Mab to justice for what the Fire elemental had done to our family.

But that hadn't been the only thing on the murder board. Bria had also had a picture of one of the spider rune scars on my palms taped up there, courtesy of Fletcher. After he'd died, from beyond the grave, the old man had arranged to have a photo of Bria delivered to me so I would realize she was still alive—and he'd sent her one of the scar on my palm in return so she would know the same. I supposed Fletcher had wanted us to find each other—one way or another.

I hoped that Owen was right about Bria accepting me and my dark, murky past, but I couldn't get rid of the tight ball of unease that twisted my stomach. Finding out that your long-lost sister was also a notorious assassin who was going around town killing bad guys wasn't exactly the stuff dreams were made of. So I decided to focus on other matters, starting with the man beside me.

I trailed my hand down Owen's chest, drawing a series of loose circles, before going lower and taking him in my hand.

"Round two?" I suggested, sliding my nails up and down his thick length.

Owen grinned and pulled me even tighter. "I think I'm up for that."

I responded by lowering my lips to his once more.

✳23✳

I spent the night with Owen. But this time, I didn't get up and sneak out of bed early the next morning. Instead, I woke him up for round three before I had to leave to go to the Pork Pit. After that, it was business as usual at the restaurant.

At least, as much as it could be when I was expecting an assassin to drop by sometime during the day and try to kill me.

Given the fact that Elektra LaFleur had almost succeeded in doing that very thing two nights ago, I took a few extra precautions. More than the ones that were part of my daily routine, anyway. I might long to kill the other assassin, but I wasn't going to be stupid about things either. Fletcher had taught me better than that.

For starters, I had on one of my many silverstone vests, hidden underneath my blue work apron and a bulky black sweater that obscured the lean shape of my body. And I had Owen's oh-so-thoughtful Christmas presents secreted on me as well. A knife tucked up either sleeve, one in the small of my back, and two more stuffed inside my boots.

Early that morning, before the Pork Pit had opened, I'd walked around the interior of the restaurant twice, slowly, looking at it from every angle, thinking what I would do if I wanted to kill the owner of such an establishment. The best way to get in, the easiest way to get close, the weapons I might use. All the things that assassins had to think about if they wanted to get away after the fact. All the things I'd thought about as the Spider for so many years that were just second nature to me now.

Despite Mab's edict to make it look somewhat like an accident, given what I knew of LaFleur, I doubted the other assassin would care exactly how she killed me, as long as she got to use her electrical magic. Hell, I doubted she'd even be that quiet about things. I imagined LaFleur would be perfectly happy to barge in through the front door of the Pork Pit, fry me with her green lightning, and stroll right back out when I was dead and charred. I couldn't fault her for that. Sometimes the direct approach was the best.

I only hoped she'd wait until the restaurant was deserted before she made her move. Collateral damage was one thing I'd always avoided as an assassin. Call me a sentimental fool, but I didn't want some innocent family's Christmas to be ruined because Mommy happened to be in the wrong place at the wrong time.

When I'd thought about things and how they might play out, I flipped the sign on the front door of the Pit over to *Open*.

Now all that was left to do was wait for LaFleur to show.

And then we'd dance.

The day passed quietly. Well, as quietly as usual, considering the fact that Sophia Deveraux and I were still busy cooking all day long, trying to keep up with all the take-out and holiday party orders that just kept pouring in, despite the fact that tomorrow was Christmas Eve. Normally, I helped wait tables as well as dished up food, but today all I did was cook. Catalina Vasquez and the rest of the waitstaff took over the slack.

Finn dropped by about five that afternoon. As always, he wore one of his designer suits. A Christmas green one with a red candy cane–striped tie that would have looked ridiculous on anyone else. As soon as he sat down at his regular seat at the counter, Sophia poured him a cup of chicory coffee. The Goth dwarf gave Finn a fond smile and patted his hand. Finn grinned and winked back at her. Even gruff, tough Sophia wasn't immune to the legendary charms of Finnegan Lane.

By that time, the take-out orders had started to slow down, and Sophia and I had put together all the party trays for the day. The various members of the waitstaff who'd come into work today were all in the back of the restaurant taking their break, so I decided to take one too and talk to Finn about the latest goings-on in Ashland.

"Anything new?" I asked, putting a few of the pumpkin-raisin cookies I'd baked fresh this morning on a plate and sliding them over to him.

Finn, of course, had two cookies before he bothered to answer me. "Not much, according to my sources. Mab's still holed up on her estate, and LaFleur's still supposed to find the Spider and kill her as soon as possible."

"Same old, same old."

"Same old, same old," Finn agreed.

"What about the others?" I could take care of myself, but everyone else was vulnerable, especially where La-Fleur was concerned.

"Everybody's okay. Vinnie and Natasha are still tucked away at Jo Jo's house, and Roslyn and Xavier are watching their backs. Xavier is also keeping an eye on Bria during their shift together like you wanted him to," Finn said. "There's been no sign of any of Mab's men or LaFleur hanging around the salon, Roslyn's house, the police station, or even Northern Aggression. Everything's quiet so far."

I nodded. "So far."

I doubted it would stay that way through the rest of the night. But when Elektra LaFleur came calling, I would be ready.

And then the assassin would finally die.

But nothing happened the rest of the afternoon and on into the evening. Not a damn thing. Nobody came into the restaurant who looked like she didn't belong. No strange phone calls, no weird take-out orders, nothing.

Finn left to go see what else his snitches had to tell him, and we made a plan to meet at Jo-Jo's later on to try to figure out what to do about Vinnie and Natasha, since the two of them couldn't stay hidden at the dwarf's house forever.

"LaFleur?" Sophia asked, wiping down the back counter.

The waitstaff had left for the evening, and the two of us were alone in the restaurant. I stared out the storefront windows, but the scene hadn't changed since the last time that I'd looked two minutes ago. People still moved back and forth outside on the sidewalk, although the crowd had thinned out after rush hour. Now folks tucked their chins down into their coats and hurried on to their destinations as fast as they could, desperate to get out of the December cold.

I turned to Sophia and shrugged. "Looks like she's not going to show. She must be busy chasing the Spider's ghost tonight, instead of plotting to kill Gin Blanco."

The Goth dwarf grunted and went back to her wiping. It didn't look like anyone else was going to drop by, so we started closing down the restaurant for the night. Turning off the French fryer, doing the same to the griddle and the ovens, putting the leftover food into the refrigerators—all our usual routines.

When all that was done, I grabbed the day's trash, opened the back door of the restaurant, and stepped outside into the alley behind the Pork Pit.

The crackle of electricity in the air immediately told me she was here.

I could feel Elektra LaFleur's elemental magic leaking off her like water dripping from a faucet. Some elementals were like that—they constantly gave off magic, even when they weren't consciously using their power. They just oozed magic at all times. That's why I always felt red-hot needles pricking my skin whenever I was in Mab's proximity. The Fire elemental radiated power just like LaFleur was doing right now.

Even if LaFleur hadn't been dripping with elemental power, my own Stone magic would have clued me in to the fact that something was wrong in the alley. Instead of their usual slow, clogged murmurs, the bricks of the restaurant had taken on sharp, muttered notes of worry. Something had disturbed the stone, and I knew exactly what it was—the twisted, shocking intentions of the assassin lying in wait for me. The new, harsh vibration over-powered the bricks' usual sighs of contentment.

My eyes scanned over what I could see of the alley. Dumpsters, the backs of other buildings, and a small crack barely big enough for a child to squeeze into, an old hiding place of mine back when I'd been living on the streets. Slushy puddles of oil and other stains coated the alley floor like glossy black varnish. But I'd give LaFleur credit. She was just as good at hiding as I was, because I didn't immediately spot her lurking in the shadows. Still, I knew she was there—and I was more than ready for the assassin.

I put the trash bags in the Dumpster, banging open the metal hatch like I didn't have a bloody care in the world, but when I closed it and turned around, ready to go back inside the warmth of the restaurant, there she was, standing in the alley behind me.

Elektra LaFleur.

She wore the same dark green peacoat that she'd had on the last time she'd come to the Pork Pit, along with a pair of black pants and stiletto boots. That seemed to be her outfit du jour. LaFleur could afford to be a little more colorful with her wardrobe than I could, since she just fried people with her electrical magic and didn't get up close, bloody, and personal as I did with my knives. As always, her emerald headband held back her black hair, and the white orchid tattooed on her neck gleamed like a ghost in the semidarkness.

She gave me a wide, toothy smile, as though us two gals had just run into each other shopping at the mall. "Remember me, Gin?"

"How could I forget?" I murmured, staying where I was, my arms loose by my sides, knees slightly bent, my weight on the balls of my feet, gathering my strength for what was to come.

Evidently LaFleur thought that I would be surprised, at the very least, at her just popping up out of seemingly nowhere. Maybe she was hoping I'd immediately scream, run, or do something else stupid like that, because her crimson lips turned down into a pout, as though I was ruining all her fun. Too damn bad.

"You don't seem surprised to see me," she finally said.

I shrugged. "Jonah McAllister hates me. I figured he would send someone like you after me sooner or later. I see he decided on sooner."

I suppose that I could have strung her along, played the little game, and danced to the same old boring tune. I could easily have pretended to be nothing but a restaurant owner, an innocent, helpless woman with a smart mouth that had gotten her into trouble with the wrong people. But I was tired of running and hiding. From Elektra LaFleur, from Jonah McAllister, and most especially from Mab Monroe.

Elektra raised an eyebrow. "Someone like me?"

"An assassin," I clarified. "That is what you do, isn't it? Kill people?"

Her eyes narrowed in thought, and she tilted her head to one side, studying me. "It is. But what I'm wondering now is how someone like you could possibly know something like that."

She wasn't the first person to ask me that. Nobody ever thought someone like me, Gin Blanco, could be someone like the Spider. I looked like such a nice, simple, sweet gal—from a distance anyway. Up close, the perpetual winter in my cold gray eyes tended to shatter that particular illusion, along with many others.

I shrugged again. "I run a restaurant. I hear things. Word on the street is that you're Mab Monroe's newest little minion."

Anger flashed in her gaze at my mocking tone. "I'm nobody's fucking minion."

I cocked an eyebrow, surprised by the sudden unexpected show of emotion, especially since I'd never seen her be anything but smug before now. "Really? Because it looks to me like you're standing here in the middle of this dirty, dingy alley ready to kill me on someone else's order and dime. Isn't that the very definition of the word *minion*?"

She stood there, considering my words. "You know, I suppose it is. But my pay is much, much better than that of any mere minion."

Elektra let out a low chuckle. Elemental power crackled in her pealing dulcet tone, like an electrified church bell. It made me grind my teeth together, even as that primal little voice in the back of my head started up its chorus once again. *Enemy, enemy, enemy.* Or maybe it was just the constant, static feel of her magic snapping up against my skin that put me on edge—and the very real possibility that I wouldn't be able to overcome a frontal assault by her, no matter what Jo-Jo Deveraux said. No matter how much Ice and Stone magic the dwarf claimed I had.

"You know, you're far more interesting than you appear, Gin. Or is it Jen? I wasn't quite clear on that. Call it a quirk, but I always like to know exactly who I'm killing."

"It's Gin. Like the liquor." I quipped my usual line.

"Ah. Thanks for clearing that up."

We stood there in the alley staring at each other. Elektra brought her finger up and tapped out a pattern on her crimson lips, as though she was considering something important. Green sparks of lightning flickered like fireflies in the air around her. She wasn't even trying to hide her power now. Arrogant bitch. She never even considered the possibility that I might have magic of my own. Sloppy, sloppy, sloppy of her.

"I am rather surprised that you haven't started screaming for help yet, Gin. Or tried to run away, at the very least. Not that it would do you any good." She nodded at something over my shoulder. "I brought along a few friends just in case you were quicker than you looked."

I glanced behind me. Sure enough, three giants stood at the far end of the alley, blocking the exit. They stood like I did, hands loose and ready by their sides. So even if LaFleur had missed me with her lightning, the rest of Mab's men would have stepped up to finish the job. I had to admire the assassin's thoroughness. She'd thought of almost everything—except the fact that I was the Spider and just as deadly as she was.

"It is good to be prepared," I quipped and turned back to face the other assassin. "You just never know what kinds of difficulties you might run into in your line of work."

A thoughtful light flared in Elektra's eyes. "You sound like you have some experience in these sorts of things."

"I wouldn't exactly say *experience*," I said. "Although I do seem to be getting the stuffing beat out of me on a regular basis."

Elektra smiled. "Oh, yes. Jonah told me all about that beating he had Elliot Slater give you a few weeks back. I would have loved to be there for that. Although, if I'd been Slater, you wouldn't have walked away after the fact. How did it feel, though? To be Jonah's little bitch? To know he's the reason you're going to die in this filthy alley tonight?"

I rocked back on my heels and clasped my hands behind me, as though I was considering something. I used the opportunity to palm one of my silverstone knives—one of the five that Owen had made for me. My thumb traced over the hilt, right over the spot where Owen had stamped my spider rune into the metal. The weapon felt cold, hard, and comforting in my hand, the way it always did. Maybe even more so tonight, because it had been a gift from Owen, his way of helping me take down LaFleur.

"Actually, I think you know all about being Jonah's little bitch," I said. "After all, you're the one fucking him, not me. Tell me, do you just bend over and take it? Or do you have to do all the work? Because McAllister strikes me as being a lazy bastard in bed."

Green rage sparked in LaFleur's eyes, along with her

magic. "I don't take anything from anyone, bitch. I do who and what I want, when I want."

I shrugged again. "Could have fooled me. I can't imagine another reason why you'd let McAllister fuck you. Oh, wait. I forgot. That's what *minions* do. Do whatever and whomever they're told. Personally, I would have asked for more money at the very least. But then again, I suppose I just have higher standards than you do."

Elektra's face showed no more emotion at my taunts, but green lightning flickered to life in her curled hand. The color of it matched the cruel glow in her eyes. Temper, temper, temper. I'd gotten to the other assassin and made her angry. I only hoped it was enough to make her reckless, to give me a sliver of an advantage.

"You know, Gin, I was going to make your death relatively quick, if not entirely painless," she said in a pleasant, benign tone, as though she were talking about the weather or some other banality. "Now, I think that I'll just make it *hurt*."

"Bring it on, bitch," I said and palmed another one of my knives.

Surprise flashed in the other assassin's eyes at the cold venom in my tone, but it wasn't enough to make her think twice about what she was here to do. She held out her hand, and the lightning intensified, growing from a few small, flickering sparks into a solid ball of power. Even across the alley, I could feel the raw elemental power that she controlled.

I only hoped my own would be enough to overcome it.

I reached for my Stone magic, ready to use it to harden my skin, to make my body as tough as the brick of the buildings around us. But before LaFleur could throw her ball of lightning at me, before we could start our deadly, final dance, the strangest thing happened. The back door of the Pork Pit swung open.

And Detective Bria Coolidge stepped out into the dark alley.

❊24❊

"Gin? Are you out here? It's Bria," my baby sister called out. "I wanted to talk to you about the Christmas party you mentioned to me the other day."

Bria stepped out into the alley in between us, and the door banged shut behind her. I was in front of her, while LaFleur lurked in the shadows behind her.

Before I could move, before I could do anything, before I could even shout out a warning, the assassin struck. Quick as lightning, she grabbed Bria by her shaggy blond hair and pulled the other woman up against her chest. LaFleur hooked her arm around Bria's throat, placing her in a chokehold.

"Detective Coolidge," Elektra purred. "So good of you to join us this evening."

But my sister wasn't going down without a fight. Bria went into immediate attack mode, lifting up her boot, probably to smash it down onto LaFleur's instep before pivoting and throwing the other woman over her shoulder.

Before she could do any of that, Elektra brought up her hand, the ball of green lightning still flickering there, and shoved it into Bria's face. My sister had to jerk back to keep the elemental magic from burning her cheek.

"Ah, ah, ah," LaFleur warned. "I wouldn't do that if I were you. Unless you want me to melt that pretty face of yours right off."

Bria's blue eyes narrowed. Despite the tenuous position that she was in, she wasn't afraid—not the least little bit. Instead, I could see her thinking about things, calculating the angles and the chances of succeeding, just as I would have if our positions had been reversed. My sister's gaze cut to me, then to the three giants standing in the alley behind me. She knew as well as I did that the odds weren't with her. Not while LaFleur had hold of her, the assassin's electrical magic an inch away from her eyes.

"Who the hell are you?" Bria spat out. "What do you want?"

"Why, your untimely demise, of course, along with that of good ole Gin here," Elektra said. "You were actually next on my to-do list tonight, detective. How very thoughtful of you to come to me instead. Now I can double my fun. Your death will go a long way toward my employer having a very merry Christmas."

"Mab," Bria snarled. She knew as well as I did that the Fire elemental wanted her dead in the worst possible way. She just didn't know exactly why. "You work for Mab Monroe."

"Correct," LaFleur said in a cheery tone. "I work for

Mab. And you know what she's hired me to do, specifically? Make sure that the two of you quit breathing. Immediately."

The lightning intensified in LaFleur's hand, until the glow from it lit up the whole alley. For a moment, I thought she was going to kill Bria right then, right there. I narrowed my eyes and studied the other assassin, wondering how I could distract her long enough to give Bria a fighting chance to get away from her—or at least out of the immediate vicinity of Elektra's lightning. I'd only get one shot, one second of opportunity before LaFleur fried my baby sister with her elemental magic. I'd come too far, suffered through too much, killed too many people, to let Bria die. Not now, not ever.

But to my surprise, the lightning flickered and dimmed in LaFleur's hand. Oh, she still had enough power in her to give Bria a good, sharp jolt, but the magic wouldn't kill her now—probably.

I couldn't help but wonder what the other assassin was up to. If it had been me, Bria would have been dead thirty seconds ago, and I'd be dying on the ground right now. Never hesitate, not for a second, not for any reason whatsoever. That's what Fletcher Lane had taught me.

But LaFleur hadn't gone for the kill shot, even though she'd had it. I had a sinking suspicion I knew why—and what the other assassin was going to say next.

"You know, I haven't had a lot of fun these past few days," LaFleur murmured. "I think I'll change that tonight. Starting with the two of you."

Of course. LaFleur wanted to play with us first before she killed us. Because that's what she did to people.

Because she'd let the Spider slip through her fingers and wanted someone to take her anger out on. And her proclivities might just be the death of me and my sister tonight.

LaFleur let out a low whistle, and the giants who'd been standing at the end of the alley stepped up to join the party. "Boys, put these two ladies in the limo."

I managed to slip my silverstone knives back up my sleeves before LaFleur or the giants spotted them. The oversize goons reached for me, and I jerked and flailed around, pretending that I was desperately trying to get away from them, even though I really wasn't. No way was I leaving Bria behind. But my jerky movements had the desired effect, and one of the giants shoved me against one of the metal Dumpsters in the alley.

I crashed into it with a loud bang, moaned for show, and slumped down to the alley floor. While I was curled into a ball, I slipped my silverstone knives out of my sleeves once more and slid the weapons underneath the Dumpster.

I didn't want the giants to grab hold of my arms and feel the weapons tucked up my sleeves. Right now, LaFleur thought that I was just a defenseless cook. I didn't want her opinion of me to change whatsoever. Every second she thought me weak was another second I had to escape and save myself and Bria.

Besides, sooner or later, Sophia would come out into the alley to see what had happened to Bria and me. When she realized that we weren't back here, the dwarf would start looking around. She'd find the knives and realize something bad had gone down. She'd call Finn and get the cavalry charge rolling—provided Bria and I lived that long.

LaFleur shook her head. "Oh, *now* she starts blubbering. How disappointing. Pick her up."

Two of the giants plucked me off the ground. The third moved over to help Elektra with Bria. The giant yanked my baby sister's gun off her belt, then ran his hands over the rest of her body in a slow, suggestive way. Bria's lips tightened, but she didn't respond to his leers. The giant found her backup gun strapped in an ankle holster and removed that one as well, along with the cell phone in her jacket pocket and her keys.

I held my breath, but the two giants holding on to me didn't bother to search me for weapons. I suppose they considered the cop more of a threat than the cook. It was a mistake that was going to cost them their lives. I was glad I'd ditched the two knives, though. The way the giants had their hands clamped on my arms, they would surely have felt the blades through my sweater. But the fabric was bulky enough to at least hide my silverstone vest.

When the giant finished searching Bria, the four of them marched us out of the alley, with LaFleur keeping a close eye on the proceedings, the ball of green lightning still flickering in her hand. She wasn't going to drop her magic until we were secured. Maybe not even then.

LaFleur had a limo waiting two blocks away, well out of sight of the storefront windows of the Pork Pit. The giants shoved Bria and me inside the back, then crowded in after us. The few people still moving out on the street ducked their heads and walked even faster when they spotted us. In Ashland, giants shepherding people into the back of a car was never a good thing.

"Cuff them," LaFleur called out from the street.

The giants produced a couple of pairs of handcuffs and clamped them on our wrists, shackling our hands in front of us. Mistake number one. It's much harder to get free if your hands are behind your back.

While the giants were busy settling themselves into the limo, I looked at the metal, which had a peculiar glint that could mean only one thing—it was made out of silverstone. Which meant that I'd have to use my elemental magic to somehow break through the metal chains before I could get free to do anything else with my hands—like carve up LaFleur and the giants with the three knives I still had on me. Fuck. My being an elemental was something else that I didn't want LaFleur to know about just yet. Not until it was too late.

"Don't worry, Gin," Bria said in a low voice, trying to reassure me. "Everything's going to be fine."

I just stared at my sister and the determination blazing in her blue eyes. If she only knew that I was the reason all this was happening in the first place. That I'd thumbed my nose at Jonah McAllister once too many times. That I was the Spider, the assassin who was going around killing Mab Monroe's men. That I was the one with the Ice and Stone magic Mab had so desperately wanted to snuff out. That I was the reason why the rest of our family was dead. I wondered if Bria would be so eager to rescue me then. Probably not.

But I had a bad, bad feeling she was going to find out all that and more before the night was through.

Elektra LaFleur climbed into the limo and sat across from us. One of the giants was next to her, with the other two crowded in on either side of Bria and me. Elektra tapped on the roof of the car with her fist, and the limo pulled away from the curb.

Elektra regarded the two of us a moment before reaching into the small wet bar housed in the back of the limo. She pulled out a crystal glass and poured herself a couple of fingers' worth of a pale blue liquor.

"Gin," LaFleur said, toasting me, before taking a long pull on the cold drink.

I hoped she choked on it.

"Where are you taking us?" Bria demanded.

Elektra leaned back against the limo seat and smiled. "Somewhere nice and deserted where no one will hear you scream, detective."

Bria didn't say anything, but her eyes narrowed. Her whole body tensed, as though she was getting ready to launch herself across the seat at the other woman. I reached down and put a hand on her thigh, warning her. Bria's head snapped around to me, and I gave a small shake of my head. *No,* I was telling her. *Taking her on is suicide right now. Don't do it. Don't you dare.* My sister frowned, but she seemed to get the message in my sharp gaze because her body relaxed the slightest bit.

"Aw," Elektra pouted over the rim of her glass of gin. "I was really hoping that you'd be stupid enough to try something, detective. But don't worry. I'm going to shock the fight right out of you, among other things."

Bria opened her mouth, but before she could let out another angry retort, someone's cell started chirping.

LaFleur rolled her eyes, then dug in her coat pocket, pulling out a small silver phone.

"What!" she snapped into the receiver.

I couldn't hear the voice on the other end, but it had to be Mab by the way that LaFleur suddenly straightened up in the black leather seat.

"I was just getting ready to call you with an update, Mab," Elektra said, confirming my suspicion.

My lips tightened. Damn and double damn. If Elektra told Mab she had Bria and me, the Fire elemental would probably want to meet the assassin wherever she was taking us just so she could watch Bria's death in person. Just so she could be sure it had actually happened this time. And then we'd both get dead—in a hurry.

I had to do something to prevent that from happening. Elektra and her giants would be hard enough to take out. I didn't want to have to face Mab tonight too. Not when Bria was here in the line of fire with me.

"Minion," I said in a mocking voice just loud enough for the other assassin to hear. "You're nothing but Mab's little minion and Jonah's little bitch. Who are you going to roll over and open your legs for next, Elektra? One of the giants here?"

Bria frowned and stared at me, obviously wondering what I thought I was doing, antagonizing the other assassin. But I couldn't think of anything else to do. Elektra had showed me her temper once before in the alley. It was the only real weakness I'd seen in her so far—one that I was desperately trying to exploit any way I could.

Elektra's green eyes narrowed, and she regarded me for a long moment. Then she straightened up. "You know what, Mab? I'm getting rather tired of your constant need for updates. All you need to know is that I'm working on it. I'll call you back when it's done and not a second before."

Then she snapped her cell phone shut and tossed it down onto the seat between her and the giant. A moment later, it started ringing again. Elektra regarded it with a venomous look.

"Aren't you going to get that?" one of the giants rumbled. "Mab doesn't like it when her calls get ignored. Trust me. I know. I had to have Air elemental skin grafts for a week after she got done with me."

Elektra snorted. "Fuck what Mab wants. In case you haven't noticed, I'm busy doing her dirty work right now. So she can wait. Unless you'd like to answer the phone and tell her yourself? Although I have to warn you, it will be the last thing you ever do. Because I don't like it any more than Mab does when people disobey me."

Lightning flickered in LaFleur's green eyes, bringing the promise of death along with it. The giant swallowed and stared at the window. The phone rang five more times before Mab's call went to voice mail. Elektra glared at it again before pouring herself some more gin.

I breathed a quiet sigh of relief. One problem solved.

Now I just had to figure out how to get my cuffs off, get Bria to safety, and kill LaFleur before Mab came looking for the other assassin.

All in a night's work for the Spider.

* 25 *

We rode for about fifteen minutes, the limo twisting and turning through the downtown area like a large black beetle scuttling ever closer to its ultimate destination. Nobody said anything, but the giants kept their eyes on Bria and me the whole time, ready, willing, and eager to slap us around if one of us tried to do something stupid.

Now that we were captured and officially on the way to our deaths, LaFleur seemed to have lost interest in us. The other assassin drank more of her blue gin and stared out the window the whole time.

With every passing mile, I could feel Bria's body getting tenser and tenser against mine. I could almost see the wheels turning in her mind as she thought of and discarded various ways to overpower and escape our captors. Several times, she glanced at the limo door, as if she was thinking about leaping over the giant and flinging herself out of the vehicle.

While I admired my sister's bravado, I didn't bother doing the same. It wouldn't do us any good to try to make a break for it. Not while we were all squished together in the back of the limo. LaFleur would only have to touch one of us with her electrical magic, and it would zip through all of our bodies like chain lightning. I had no doubt that the other assassin was perfectly fine sacrificing Mab's giants, as long as Bria and I weren't breathing in the end.

Finally, the limo slowed, then stopped. The giants yanked us out of the car, and I found myself standing in the old train yard once again. The limo had pulled into the very center of the yard, and metal railcars surrounded us on all sides. The smell of smoke wafted over to me, and I looked over my shoulder.

The crumbled, blackened remains of the train depot still smoldered, despite the cold. Finn had been right when he'd claimed that I'd started a four-alarm fire, because virtually nothing remained of the structure but mounds of flaky ash. Here and there, warped pieces of metal stuck up out of the gray ash, gleaming underneath the portable spotlights that had been set up around the depot. I guess the metal had just been too thick and dense to completely melt with the rest of the building.

A cold smile pulled up my lips. Well, that was one thing I'd done right these past few days. If nothing else, I'd delayed Mab's plans for her twisted nightclub and bought Roslyn Phillips and Northern Aggression at least a few more months of business.

Then my eyes fell to all the metal rails that crisscrossed through the train yard and stretched out like greedy fingers in every direction—metal that could conduct LaFleur's electrical magic faster than I could slit her throat with one of my silverstone knives. Even now, I remembered the pain of her electrical power slamming into me. It had hurt like nothing else I'd ever experienced. Worse than being stabbed, worse than being shot. Hell, even worse than being beaten by Elliot Slater.

The smile dropped from my face. I was really starting to hate this place.

Elektra raised an eyebrow. "I'm afraid this is the end of the line for you girls."

"Wow," I said. "Did you come up with that little bit of witty repartee all on your own? Or has Jonah McAllister been giving you tips in between blow jobs?"

Elektra regarded me for a moment. Then she backhanded me across the face as hard as she could. Despite her petite frame, the assassin had plenty of strength in her muscles. But worse than the sheer force of it was that she put some of her magic into the blow, and I felt the static shock of her power all the way down to my bones. Just for an instant, but the jolt was more than enough to make me stagger back and my heart race from the electrical discharge. Fuck. She was so *strong*. I was really going to have to figure out some way to keep her electrical elemental magic from killing me before I stabbed her to death.

Elektra eyed me. Satisfied that I was properly cowed, she jerked her head at the giants.

"Put them in the railcar while I get some things ready for our special guests," she snapped. "And I want one of you on every side of that damn railcar. If the Spider's lurking out there tonight, she's not getting her hands on these two, understand?"

The giants nodded. There were four of them now, including the limo driver, who'd stepped out to join the other three. Right now, they were more afraid of LaFleur than the nebulous danger the Spider presented. I had to admit I was a little disappointed. After my performance here the other night, you'd think that the giants wouldn't be so quick to discount the Spider and what she could do to them. But they were faced with a more immediate danger in LaFleur, so that's what they chose to focus on. I suppose I couldn't blame them for that.

Still, the irony of the situation wasn't lost on me. Oh, the bloody irony. If I'd been alone, I would have laughed long, loud, and hard over the absurdity of it all.

Because what Elektra LaFleur didn't realize was that she had already captured the Spider—and the assassin was planning to kill me and my baby sister before the night was through.

LaFleur disappeared into the shadows, probably to go get some kind of power tools or other sharp objects that she could torture Bria and me with. I'd needled her too much for her to just blast us with her electricity. No, the assassin really wanted to make it hurt for as long as possible before she finally went in for the kill shot with her elemental magic. Or maybe she was just going to get a couple of white orchids that she could leave on our bodies after the fact. Didn't much matter either way. She'd left us alone with the giants. Mistake number two. Never take your eyes off your target.

The giants marched us deeper into the train yard, leading us over to the same car they'd been holding Natasha in when I'd rescued her. Had it just been two nights ago? Somehow, it seemed like a lifetime. Especially since tonight might be the end of mine and Bria's.

The giants forced us up the steps and into the railcar. Someone had removed the table and cards because the inside was empty now—except for the brown bloodstains on the metal floor and the matching spatters on the silver walls. Mab's men hadn't gotten around to mopping those up just yet.

My eyes slid to the back window, already thinking of how Bria and I could escape. But several solid two-by-fours covered up the hole, bolted into the metal. The giants had already fixed that part of the car, making it prisoner-ready once more. We wouldn't be getting through those boards, not without making noise that would easily give us away. I might want to kill LaFleur, but I'd rather know that Bria was safe first. Telegraphing every single step of our escape was one way to ensure that it wouldn't happen at all.

The giants slung us down in the middle of the railcar. The metal floor was as cold as ice, even through the thick fabric of my jeans. My breath frosted in the air. The temperature had already dropped into the low teens tonight.

"Don't move," one of the giants growled before the four of them trooped outside.

The door slid most of the way shut, but it didn't make that particular, heavy *click* that would tell me the giants had fully sealed us inside. Hmm.

Bria started to scramble to her feet, but I put my hand on her arm and held her in place on the metal floor beside me.

"Wait," I whispered. "Just wait."

Bria frowned at me in confusion but did as I asked. Ten . . . twenty . . . thirty . . . I didn't even get to forty-five seconds before the door rolled back once more and one of the giants stuck his head inside, checking on us and making sure we were exactly where he'd left us. Just like I'd thought he would.

Satisfied that we were going to stay put, he nodded, pulled his head back outside, and slammed the metal door shut. This time, the latch did *click* into place. I didn't think they'd actually locked us in, since I didn't hear an iron bar or anything else bang down on the outside, but they'd shut the door until LaFleur returned and told them to open it. Or until I figured out a way to make them open it.

"How did you know that he would look back inside?" Bria asked in a low voice.

"Because I've been dealing with suspicious bastards like that since I was thirteen," I murmured.

Bria stared at me a moment longer, then started twisting her handcuffs, trying to find some way to break the metal. I thought about telling her not to bother, since the handcuffs were made of silverstone, but decided against it. Better that she was focused on trying to escape than the horrors that waited for us with LaFleur otherwise. Still, part of me was proud of my sister because she was thinking about escape, just like I was, instead of curling into a ball, giving up, and waiting for her death.

I took a few moments to study every part of the rail-car, from the floor to the ceiling to the walls to the door that I knew at least one giant was guarding. Not much to see. Bria and I were the only things inside, and the giants hadn't been stupid enough to leave anything helpful in here, like power tools. I didn't know how long LaFleur would mess around before she came back and started torturing us, but one thing was for sure—I needed these handcuffs off long before then.

I stared at the metal linking my hands together. They were ordinary handcuffs, except that they were made of silverstone. If I'd been by myself, I might have tried using my Ice magic to flash-freeze the cuffs, then snap them off. But Bria was here trapped with me, and using that much magic was sure to bring LaFleur running. So I'd just have to be a little more circumspect. Small and quiet was always better than big and flashy anyway. Being the Spider had shown me that.

So I drew in a breath and reached for my Ice magic. Once again, I was surprised by how easily it came to me now and how much stronger it seemed, even since my swan dive into the river the other night. My power was growing just as Jo-Jo had said it would. I hoped the dwarf was right about all the other things she'd told me about my magic—namely that I was the strongest elemental she'd ever seen.

Because I was going to have to be to kill Elektra LaFleur and keep Bria safe.

I grabbed hold of my magic. The silverstone cuffs around my wrists immediately responded, absorbing my small trickle of power before I could even think about using it.

"Gin?" Bria asked, stopping her own struggles with the handcuffs as she sensed me using my power. "What are you doing? Do you—do you have *magic*?"

I didn't answer her, mainly because I couldn't do that and concentrate on my power at the same time. The silverstone snapped around my wrists made it hard—so *hard*. Every time I grabbed my Ice magic, every time I tried to form the particular shape that I wanted with it, the handcuffs would absorb all my power before I could even get started.

I glared at the cuffs around my hands. Such a small thing, but they were keeping me contained, just as La-Fleur had wanted them to—and she hadn't even realized I had elemental magic to begin with.

I had a shitload of silverstone melted into my hands when I was a kid, and I'd overcome that block, blasted my way right through it when I'd needed to the most. I could get through this one too. These measly handcuffs were nothing compared to the silverstone that Mab had seared into my palms the night she'd murdered my family. *Nothing.* I wasn't going to die because I was chained, and I sure as hell wasn't going to let the same thing happen to Bria.

But that didn't mean I couldn't make things a little easier on myself. I grabbed the handcuffs and slid them down my arms as far as they would go. Not far, but it gave me another two inches between the magical metal and my palms, where I would release my magic.

Once again, I reached for my Ice magic, and a cold silver light flickered in my palm, centered on the spider rune scar there. I immediately felt the handcuffs come to life, as the silverstone metal hungered to absorb my magic. I gritted my teeth against the constant power drain, focused, and forced my Ice magic away from my palm, trying to move it up into the very tips of my fingers, which was as far away from the silverstone cuffs as I could get it.

It worked.

Slowly, snowflake-shaped crystals spread up my fingers, and the cold, silver light began sparking there on the tips of my fingers instead of farther down in my palm. A small thing, but it took all the control I had to do it with the silverstone cuffs on my wrists continuously soaking up my magic. Quickly, before I lost the thin grasp I had on it, I forced the magic into the particular shapes I wanted—two slender Ice picks.

When they were finished, I let go of my Ice magic, let out a long, tense breath, and wiped the cold sweat from my forehead. Such small, simple shapes, but those had been the two hardest things I'd made with my elemental power. *Ever.*

"You're an elemental?" Bria asked, her blue eyes narrowing. "With Ice magic?"

"Yeah," I said, grabbing the Ice picks and working on my handcuffs with them. "Just like you are."

Bria frowned. "Just like me? How do you know that I have Ice magic, Gin? I've never done any magic in front of you."

"Yes, you have," I said in a gentle voice.

For a moment, I flashed back to our childhood. Bria had loved using her magic when we were kids, making all kinds of Ice sculptures and flowers and other shapes just because she could. Just because she found it fun and entertaining. I wondered if she still did that. I wondered a lot of things about my sister—including how horrified she was going to be with me before the night was through. Hell, before we even got out of this metal car.

The picks did the trick, and the handcuffs popped open. Although I wanted nothing more than to sling them away, I forced myself to set them down quietly on the floor. I stood up, and Bria did the same.

"Where did you learn how to do that?" Bria asked, curiosity in her voice. "Even I have a hard time doing that sometimes."

"Finn," I said. "The man can pick a lock like you wouldn't believe. Now hold out your hands, and I'll help you slip out of yours."

She obeyed, and I used my Ice picks on the cuffs. A few seconds later, the lock clinked open, and the silverstone cuffs popped off Bria's hands. I scooped them up, along with the other pair, and stuck them both in the back pocket of my jeans. I didn't know what I might do with them, but I'd learned a long time ago how to improvise and turn even the simplest things into deadly weapons.

Bria stood there, rubbing the circulation back into her wrists. I drew in a breath, my heart starting to squeeze in on itself. Because now it was truth time—whether I was ready for it or not. I couldn't do what needed to be done, couldn't make sure that we both lived through the night, without revealing exactly who and what I was to Bria.

Without telling her I was the Spider.

"I need you to listen to me, Bria."

She looked at up at me, still massaging her wrists. "Okay."

I drew in another breath. "Some things are going to

happen tonight, probably in the next few minutes, that you aren't going to like very much. I know you're a detective, a cop, that you've spent your whole adult life protecting people. But I need you to turn off that part of you tonight. I need you to do exactly what I say when I say it, with no questions asked and no hesitation. Do you think you can do that for me?"

Bria frowned. "What are you talking about, Gin? You've got Ice magic, sure, but what do you think you're going to do against four giants? Not to mention LaFleur. If I still had my guns, we could probably get past the giants and get away before LaFleur came to see what all the commotion was about. But we don't have any weapons, other than our magic. I'm pretty strong for an elemental, but I can't take out four giants with my magic. At least, not all at once."

"You don't have to. I'm going to do it for you."

Her brow wrinkled as she tried to puzzle out what I was saying. LaFleur could come back at any second, and we didn't have any time to waste. So I decided to make it easy for her. I reached down, drew the two silverstone knives out of my boots, and twirled them in my hands. There wasn't much light in the railcar, but Bria spotted the weapons at once—and realized exactly what they were and whom they belonged to.

Emotions flickered in her gaze. Shock. Surprise. And slowly, comprehension.

I gave her a second to stare at the knives before I tucked them up my sleeves. Seconds ticked by, and my sister just looked at me, like she'd never seen me before. Like she wasn't sure she wanted to right now.

"Let me see your hands," Bria finally said, her voice thick with emotion.

"Bria—"

"Let me see your fucking *hands*." She ground out the words through her clenched teeth.

There was no going back and no hiding anything. Not now. She knew.

Bria knew who and what I was.

I drew in a breath and let it out, preparing myself for what I might see in her face. For the horror and disgust that I was almost certain to see there. Then I slowly held out my hands and turned them up toward her, so that she could see my palms—and the two spider rune scars branded into each one of them.

A small circle surrounded by eight thin rays. The same rune that Bria wore on that ring around her index finger.

Bria's blue eyes widened in shock, and all the color drained from her face. "Genevieve?"

"Hi there, baby sister," I said.

❋ 26 ❋

"Genevieve," Bria whispered again. For a moment, her body swayed side to side, like she might faint. Her blond hair glinted with the motion.

I shifted on my feet. "Actually, I prefer Gin now."

"Genevieve Snow," she repeated, as though I hadn't said a word. "You're Genevieve Snow. You're my . . . sister."

"In the flesh," I said in a light tone.

"And the Spider." Bria's voice was flat, hard, cold. Her body quit swaying, and her spine snapped upright once more.

"And that too."

We didn't say anything. Bria moved over to the opposite side of the car, to the spot where Natasha had been huddled, as though she couldn't stand being close to me. Maybe she couldn't, now that she realized who I was and all the bad, bloody things I'd done.

"You're the woman who's been going around town killing Mab Monroe's men," Bria said in a dull tone. "All those men the last few weeks. And Elliot Slater and all those giants up at his mountain mansion before that. How many has it been since you started? Or even since I've been in town? A dozen? Two?"

The accusation in her voice hurt me worse than if she'd hauled off and delivered a stinging slap across my face, but I made myself stay calm, cold, detached, just the way Fletcher Lane had taught me. I would survive this, just the way I had so many other unpleasant things over the years. Even if I was about to lose my own sister—again.

I shrugged. "I quit keeping count a long time ago."

"Why?" she asked. "Why did you kill them all? Why are you . . . what you are?"

I knew that these were the questions Bria would ask me when she finally found out I was the Spider, the ones she'd demand answers to. But the truth was far too twisted and complicated to get into—at least tonight. And I couldn't help the hurt that pierced my heart at the look on her face—the absolute shock and the sheer horror of realizing what I was. Of knowing that her long-lost sister was a brutal killer. Maybe it had been a pipe dream, but I'd wanted Bria to accept me the way Owen had. But as I looked into her hard blue gaze, I knew she didn't—and probably never would.

There was no time for hurt feelings. No time to dwell on the past or the sea of emotions between us. No time to give into sloppy sentiment and shattered hopes and dreams. All that mattered now was surviving—and killing LaFleur before the assassin told Mab that we were here and at her mercy.

So, as tough as it was, as much as I just wanted to sit down with Bria and explain everything to her, as much as I wanted to beg her to love me the way I loved her, the way I'd always loved her, I forced my feelings aside and embraced the coldness in my heart once more. The cold, hard, black part of me that had let me survive so much over the years—the murder of my family, living on the Southtown streets, becoming an assassin, and all the ugly, bloody, terrible things I'd had to do in between just to survive.

"Look," I said. "I know we have a lot of . . . things to discuss, but there's no time right now. We need to get out of this car and out of the train yard before LaFleur comes back. At least, you do."

"And what are you going to do?" Bria asked in a cold voice. "Stay behind and kill her?"

"You'd better believe it," I snapped.

My sister gave me a hostile look. Evidently she didn't care for my brutal honesty. Too damn bad. Because I'd gone through too much as a kid to save her life only to let her die now on this cold December night.

So I reached around and drew my third knife out of the small of my back. I walked across the railcar toward her. Bria tensed, as though she thought I was actually going to use the weapon on her. That hurt me more than anything else she'd said or done. I might be a monster, but I wasn't that kind of monster. And I never would be. She should have known that. She should have just—*known*.

But I forced the feeling aside, buried it under my determination to get her out of here—no matter what. Surprise filled my sister's face when I held the weapon out to her hilt first.

"Have you ever used a knife?" I asked.

She stared at me for a long moment, then shook her head. "No. Not like you have."

I nodded. I'd expected as much, which meant I was going to have to do all the heavy lifting here tonight. Maybe it was better that way.

"All right. If things go according to plan, you won't have to use it anyway," I said. "But it's better to have a weapon than not, so take it."

Bria stared at the silverstone weapon in my hand as though it were a copperhead that was going to lash out and bite her.

"Take the knife," I ground out the words. "LaFleur could come back here any second, and we don't have time to argue about it."

She hesitated a moment longer, then took the cold weapon from my hand, careful not to let her fingers brush against mine. My heart twisted in my chest at the small, deliberate slight, but I ignored it, the way I had so many other emotions over the years.

"All right," I said. "Here's what we're going to do."

It took only two minutes of screaming and pounding on the metal wall before the giant standing guard out front opened the door to the railcar. About time. I was getting hoarse at that point—and wondering if he was going to be dumb enough to fall for something so old, so clichéd. If the giant didn't, if he kept the door closed, then I was going to have to go with my plan B, which was to use my Ice magic to blast through the two-by-fours bolted over the busted-out window.

But just when I was about ready to stop screaming, a click sounded, and the door creaked open.

The giant had fallen for it after all. Sloppy, sloppy, sloppy of him. But I wasn't complaining too much. Not tonight. No, tonight I'd take every bit of luck I could get and go back hungry for more. Even if luck was always a capricious bitch who'd screw me over the second that she could.

As soon as the door opened wide enough, I nodded at Bria, who nodded back. Then I drew another breath deep into my lungs, preparing myself for what was to come.

"Let me out of here!" I screamed and flung myself past the giant through the open door of the railcar and down onto the loose gravel that covered the train yard. "That bitch is crazy! She's got a knife! Two of them!"

The giant, who'd started to swivel toward me to grab me, instead snapped his attention back to Bria, who stood in the middle of the car, a silverstone knife in her hand. He stood there, mouth open, eyes wide, wondering what was going on and what he was supposed to do about it.

He never had a chance.

I hopped back up onto my feet and slithered up next to him. Then I grabbed a fistful of his shirt, yanked his head down to my level, and slit his throat with one of my knives. I turned my head, so the warm, sticky, arterial spray of blood caught me only on my cheek instead of going into my eyes and momentarily blinding me.

One down, three to go.

The giant started choking and gurgling, spewing more blood all over my face, neck, hands, and clothes. His hands went to his throat, the way they always did, trying to stem the blood loss even though it was already too late. He went down on his knees and collapsed against the side of the railcar, down for the count.

I looked up at Bria, who was staring down at the dying giant. Shock and horror and disgust filled her face, but I had no time to think about what she was feeling right now—or what she thought of me, her long-lost, big sister Genevieve. I was pretty sure I knew anyway—and it was nothing good.

Of course, the other three giants had heard the commotion of my screaming and their dying friend. They all abandoned their posts around the other sides of the railcar to come and investigate. I palmed my second knife and sprinted to the left just in time to catch one of them coming around the side of the car.

One, two, three.

I made two deep slashing cuts across the giant's chest, digging the blade in as far as I could. The giant screamed in pain and swung at me, but I ducked and pivoted out of reach. When his fist went wide, I stepped back in range. My boot slammed into his knee, which buckled under the sharp assault.

The giant lurched forward, and I stepped into him and cut his throat as well. More blood spattered onto me, but I ignored the sensation. I pivoted again, this time out of the way of the giant's falling body, and turned to face the new danger.

The third giant—the one who'd been stationed on the back side of the railcar—had also decided to come around this way. He stopped short at the sight of his buddy already on the ground and bleeding out.

"What the hell—"

Last fucking words he ever said. I hopped up onto the back of the downed, dying giant. Using him as a stepping stool, I reached up and slammed my first knife into the third man's heart. He too lashed out at me with his fist, but I ducked under the slow blow, came up inside his arms, and stabbed him again in the stomach, ripping into his guts with my knife, before shoving my shoulder into his chest.

The attack took him by surprise, and he screamed again and lurched back away from me. His feet skidded on the loose gravel. For a moment, his massive arms windmilled crazily in the air. Then, screaming and blubbering all the while, he went down in a pile of twitching limbs, joining his friend.

And then there was one.

I turned around to find the fourth giant, the one who'd been driving the limo, standing at the far end of the rail-car. He was a little smarter than his friends because instead of charging at me, he fumbled in his suit jacket for the gun strapped in the holster there.

I sprinted forward, but the giant was faster.

He yanked out his gun, raised it, and fired at me.

Crack! Crack!

The sounds echoed through the train yard, booming like thunder against the metal rails. If LaFleur hadn't heard the fight before, she sure as hell knew something was wrong now.

The giant's aim was true, and two bullets *thunk-thunked* into my chest. They would have killed me—if I hadn't been wearing my silverstone vest underneath my sweater. The magical metal easily caught the bullets and kept them from punching through my heart. I grunted at the hard, bruising impacts and kept running at the giant. He backed up, wondering why I hadn't gone down yet.

That hesitation cost him his life.

My knives flashed silver in the moonlight, and, a minute later, he joined his other three dead and dying friends on the ground.

When I was sure the giants were no longer a threat, I raced back to the middle of the railcar. Bria still stood inside, looking as shocked as ever at the dead bodies littering the gravel like empty beer cans.

I palmed one of my knives so that I had a free hand and held it out to her. "Come on, come on, get down from there! We have to get out of here."

Bria stared at my bloody fingers a moment before shaking her head, leaning forward, and grabbing my hand. I helped her down and started to lead her away from the railcar.

But the sharp, static crackle in the air told me that it was already too late.

I glanced over my shoulder to see Elektra LaFleur standing in the doorway of the other railcar, only fifty feet away from us. The assassin's eyes met mine, and a smile curved her face.

"Run," I told Bria.

My sister stood there behind me, clutching my silverstone knife in her hand, unsure of what to do. Uncertain about whether she wanted to stay and make a stand with me or slink off into the darkness, find a phone, and call Finn as I'd told her to while we'd been plotting our escape.

LaFleur hopped down out of the railcar and sprinted in our direction, green lightning already flickering in her hands.

I grabbed Bria's coat and yanked her forward so that her face was right next to mine. Our eyes met. Blue on gray. And I let her see just how cold and hard I really was deep down inside. I let her see all the black, twisted ugliness inside me, every last bit of it, because I knew it was the only way to save her life right now—even if the knowledge would make her hate me forever. It was worth it to save her. Everything I'd ever suffered for her had always been worth it.

"Run," I ground out the word. "You fucking run like your life depends on it because it does. If she gets past me, and you're still here, you're dead. *Dead.* Do you hear me Bria? Now run, and don't you dare look back. Don't make all this—don't make everything that I've ever done for you—count for nothing. Or I'll kill you myself, baby sister. Do you understand me? Do you?"

I shook her once and shoved her away. Bria stared at me another second, as shocked, disgusted horror filled her face at my screamed words until there was no room for anything else. She backed up one, two, three steps—more afraid of me than anything else in the world right now.

What little was left of my heart broke in that moment.

But my harsh words had the desired affect, because Bria turned around and ran, disappearing into the darkness. She didn't look back. Good. I didn't want her to.

At least, that's what I told myself, even if I didn't really believe it.

Footsteps crunched on the gravel. I forced my mind

away from Bria and focused once more on the matter at hand—killing Elektra LaFleur before she could do the same to me and my sister.

But Elektra was smarter than her giants. Or maybe she was just that much more arrogant. Either way, she didn't keep coming until she crashed into me. Instead, the other assassin stopped about ten feet away. Her eyes went to each one of the giants on the ground around the railcar, then to the bloody knives I still clutched in my hands.

"Well, Gin," Elektra said in a calm voice. "I have to say you're just full of surprises. Or would you rather I call you by your other name . . . Spider?"

I shrugged. "Doesn't much matter to me since you're not going to live to tell anyone about this little encounter."

Instead of being cowed by my threat, given the fact that I was pretty much covered in blood from head to toe and brandishing two silverstone knives, LaFleur laughed. The crackling peal in her voice made me grind my teeth together. I was going to enjoy silencing that sound—forever.

Already I could feel LaFleur pulling her electrical elemental magic around her, bringing more and more of it to bear. The hair lifted on my arms and the back of my neck at the feel of it. Once again, I was struck by just how fucking strong her magic was, just how much raw power she had, but I pushed that thought aside. Thinking about how powerful your opponent was was a sure way to get dead. Weaknesses. I needed to focus on the bitch's weaknesses, not her strengths.

Elektra reached up and wiped a small tear from the corner of her eye. I'd made her laugh until she cried. Too bad I couldn't make her die the same way.

"I'm glad that you find your own impending death so amusing," I said. "Although in this case, laughter will not be the best medicine. Nothing's going to save you."

Elektra smiled at me. "You certainly are confident, Spider. Then again, so was my brother. Right before you killed him."

My eyes narrowed. "Who the hell was your brother?"

Elektra tilted her head to one side. To anyone else, she would have seemed the figure of easy confidence. But I could see the tightness in her face, the calculations taking place in her eyes. She was looking for weaknesses, just like I was. Waiting for the right moment to lash out at me with her magic. My hands tightened around the hilts of my knives.

"You probably knew him best as Viper," she said. "Or maybe Brutus. He had a lot of names."

In the file of information that he'd compiled on her, Fletcher Lane had said that LaFleur came from a family of assassins. The file had even mentioned a brother. I'd just never expected it to be him, Brutus, aka Viper, the assassin I'd killed a few months ago at the Ashland Opera House. A man's face flashed in front of my eyes, and I remembered his tattoo—the one of a snake crawling up his neck, the one he had taken his assassin name from. One that was eerily similar in design to Elektra's orchid, now that I knew what I was looking for.

"That fucking neck tattoo," I spat out. "I should have known. I thought I'd seen it somewhere before."

She gave a delicate shrug of her shoulders. "Family trait. We all have one. Our parents decided Brutus should have a snake, even though I was older and wanted to be called Viper. But they thought it was a more manly symbol. They were rather sexist that way."

I put the pieces together in my mind. "So what? That's your secret motivation? You came here to Ashland, you took Mab's contract to kill me, just to get revenge for your brother? For Brutus? The bastard double-crossed me. He tried to hit me when I was trying to hit someone else. He got exactly what he deserved."

Elektra let out another crackling laugh. "Oh, please. I couldn't care less that you killed Brutus. He was nothing to me. But I'll admit he was a good assassin, which made me curious as to who had murdered him and how. We were always competing with each other, you see. Who could do the most hits, who could get to the hardest targets, who could command the highest price. So when this little job in Ashland came up, I thought, why not come and test myself against Brutus's killer? Why not take on the great Spider? And so here we are."

"And so here we are," I murmured.

We stood there staring at each other, our eyes locked, green on gray. Neither one of us looking away, neither one of us moving a muscle, neither one of us even breathing. At this moment, we were just like two gunslingers out in the middle of a dusty, deserted street, ready for a duel at high noon. Only one of us would walk away, and I was determined it was going to be me.

"Well," Elektra said in a light, happy voice. "I suppose we should get on with things. Before Detective Coolidge gets too far away, and I have to chase her down. I really hate running, especially in these shoes."

There was no way she was getting past me. No way

in hell she was putting one finger on my baby sister. No matter what I had to do, no matter what I had to sacrifice to keep that from happening.

"Bring it on, bitch," I snarled.

Elektra LaFleur gave me another smile. Green lightning flashed to life in her hand once more.

And then we danced.

* 27 *

LaFleur reared back and threw her ball of green lightning at me. The other assassin wasn't messing around anymore. Now that she knew I was really the Spider, she was going for the kill shot first. Smart of her.

But I was expecting it. I dived forward, tucked into a ball, and rolled back up onto my feet, all in one smooth motion. The lightning sailed over my head and streaked off into the darkness. My momentum carried me within arm's reach of the other assassin, and I slashed at her with my silverstone knives, trying to end this with two swift cuts.

But she was expecting my move as well and caught my wrists. We stood there, her hands locked onto my arms, see-sawing back and forth, with me trying to plunge the knives down into her body, and her holding my hands back. LaFleur was just as strong and determined as I was. Neither of us could get any kind of real advantage, merely grappling the way we were. So Elektra decided to up the ante.

She smiled, and lightning flashed once more in her green eyes.

I was able to grab hold of my Stone magic and use it to harden my skin the split-second before she slammed her elemental magic into me, using her hands like two conduits.

This wasn't the first time I'd been blasted by magic. A few months ago, I'd gone toe-to-toe with Alexis James, an Air elemental who liked to use her power to flay people alive, to force oxygen under people's skin and strip it from their bones one slow inch at a time. That's what Alexis had done to Fletcher when she'd tortured and killed him inside the Pork Pit. She'd tried to do the same to me when we'd had our inevitable confrontation at the old Ashland rock quarry. But Alexis James hadn't been as strong as Elektra LaFleur.

I felt every bit of the other assassin's power surge into me, crackling against my own, arcing around me like lightning attracted to a metal rod, trying to break through the protective shell of my Stone magic. Even though my Stone power was blocking her attack and keeping the electricity from killing me outright, it didn't do anything to stop the pain of it from filling my body. And it still hurt so fucking *much*, the shock of it arcing and arcing through my body as though I were holding on to a power line. I'd been wrong before when I'd thought you couldn't electrocute a rock—because that's exactly what was happening to me right now. My muscles spasmed, my teeth clattered together, and my whole body twitched and cramped and screamed from the agony of the electricity zipping through me again and again and again.

My silverstone vest absorbed some of the other elemental's magic, growing heavy and warm against my chest, as the metal sucked in the electrical power coursing through it. But the vest didn't take in enough juice to keep me from screaming over and over again.

And, of course, LaFleur had finally sensed my magic since I was using so much of it just to ward her off. Just to keep breathing. Just to keep my heart from stopping and my skin from catching fire.

"Well, she's an elemental to boot," Elektra muttered. "Another surprise. But it won't save you, Spider. Nothing will. Not from me."

And then the bitch snapped up one of her hands and punched me in the face.

It was the proverbial straw. I stumbled back at the sharp blow, and one of my knives slipped from my hands. My twitching, spasming feet skidded on the gravel, just like the giant's had earlier tonight, and I went down on one knee. LaFleur came at me. One, two, three. Hard, bone-cracking blows, all with the extra oomph of her electrical magic behind them. One knocked the other knife out of my hand. The second caught me in the stomach. And the third connected with my jaw, shattering my concentration on my Stone magic.

Green sparks sputtered like fire from her clenched fists every time she hit me. And on the third, final blow, her power finally broke through my own.

For a moment, my vision went pure, hot, pulsing green as LaFleur's magic coursed through me, and I screamed again as the electricity seared every single nerve ending in my entire body. I convulsed once, twice, three times, before I fell to the ground, my limbs twitching violently from the unexpected burst of energy. If she'd been going for the kill shot then, I would have been dead.

But instead of finishing me off, LaFleur actually let go of me—and more importantly, her electrical magic. Her third mistake. When you've got someone down, don't stop until she's good and dead.

"Out of Stone magic already? *Tsk, tsk, tsk.*" Elektra clucked her tongue against the roof of her mouth and walked around me in a tight circle. "Disappointing, Spider. Very disappointing."

I was too busy trying to get my spasming limbs under control to come up with a witty response. But I did manage to reach one of my hands around my body to the small of my back. Somehow, I made my still-twitching fingers wrap around a bit of metal there.

"I don't know how much you know about me, Spider, Gin, whatever you want to call yourself," LaFleur said, still circling around me. "But unlike you, I don't use weapons to kill. It's so . . . ordinary. So *common*. Don't you think? Instead, I like to use my electrical magic to finish people off. It's so much more visceral that way. Not to mention that I enjoy the light show as well. But I bet you've already guessed that little fact about me, given the way you're writhing around on the ground."

"Yeah," I rasped. "I'd noticed that about you."

Elektra smiled, then slid her hand inside her green jacket, which she was still wearing. I knew exactly what she was reaching for. The bitch thought that she'd already won. How wrong she was.

Sure enough, Elektra drew a single white orchid out of

the depths of her coat. I don't know how she had managed to keep it from getting smushed during our struggle, because it was just as soft, white, and exquisite as the others I'd seen her with. Maybe she used her electrical magic to make the petals perk up just the way she wanted them to. Didn't much matter either way. She was going to be dead in another minute, two tops. My fingers tightened around the bit of metal in my hand behind my back, getting ready to make my move—

Crack! Crack! Crack! Crack!

Elektra reacted immediately to the whine of bullets zipping through the air and threw herself down to the ground, rolling, rolling, rolling across the loose gravel to make herself a smaller, harder target to hit. Just the way I would have done. The white orchid that she had been holding flew out of her hand and twirled to the ground like a helicopter.

My head snapped up, and I spotted Detective Bria Coolidge standing about fifty feet away, her arms up and loose, her feet hip-width apart. A classic shooter's stance. Somewhere along the way, my baby sister had gotten a gun—one that she'd turned on LaFleur. I couldn't deny the fact that I was happy to see Bria, even if I had told her to get out of here.

Bria advanced toward us, taking aim at LaFleur, who'd used her momentum to roll back up into a low crouch. A dark stain marred the right shoulder of the other assassin's green coat, slowly spreading outward. Bria had winged LaFleur with one of her bullets.

And my sister wasn't done. Even though the assassin was still moving, she leveled the weapon at LaFleur's chest and pulled the trigger.

Click.

Empty. The gun was empty already. Another reason I rarely used guns. They always ran out of bullets too quickly for my liking.

Bria cursed, threw the gun away, and reached around behind her back, coming up with the silverstone knife I'd given her in the railcar. She hesitated a moment, then chucked the knife at LaFleur, who had started toward her. To Bria's surprise and mine, she actually hit the assassin. LaFleur jerked to one side, but not before the blade sank into her shoulder—the same shoulder that had already been pierced by Bria's bullet.

But instead of shrieking from the pain, Elektra LaFleur let out a low laugh, the power of her electrical elemental magic still crackling in her voice. She wasn't close to being dead. Not yet. More of the damn eerie green lightning flashed to life in the assassin's hands, and she threw the ball of elemental power at Bria.

My sister's eyes widened. She hurled herself to one side out of the way of the ball of energy, but it hit the ground where she'd been standing. The lightning slammed into the rails and zipped along them, heading straight for Bria. A second later, a muffled shriek filled the air, and I saw my sister's body twitch and convulse on top of the metal. The lightning flickered around her for another two seconds, before sparking up into the night. I watched, my heart in my throat, my breath completely gone.

"Come on," I whispered. "Come *on.*"

Bria didn't get up, and she didn't move.

My heart felt like it was being ripped in two inside my chest, and I wanted nothing more than to scream and scream and scream. But I couldn't do that. Not until LaFleur was dead.

Once she realized that Bria was down, LaFleur walked back over to me. Then the assassin pulled the blade out of her shoulder, just the way her brother, Brutus, had done once upon a time, when I'd wounded him with one of my knives. Elektra dropped the weapon. It landed on the ground three inches away from my left hand.

Her fourth and final mistake. The one that was finally going to cost the assassin her life. Never, ever leave a weapon within arm's reach of an assassin, especially not the Spider.

"Uh-oh, Gin. Looks like Detective Coolidge didn't take your advice and was stupid enough to come back to try to rescue you."

Elektra smiled down at me, her green eyes glowing as smugly as a cat's in her face. She was oh so pleased with herself.

"Well, I don't think that little jolt I just gave her was enough to kill the detective, but it will keep me from running after her at the very least. Mab's going to be so happy when I tell her that I've killed the two of you. And in one night. I'll have to make sure that she gives me a bonus for killing the elusive Spider—"

And that's when I made my move.

With my still-twitching left hand, I reached out, snatched up the fallen knife, and slammed it into her foot, driving the blade all the way through her fucking stiletto boot to the other side. Elektra hissed with pain and tumbled to the ground beside me, clawing at the knife. She pulled it out and tried to turn it on me, but I slapped it away from her.

With my right hand, I yanked the silverstone handcuffs out of the back pocket of my jeans. Then I grabbed one of her flailing arms and snapped the cuff around it. Elektra hissed again, this time with surprise, and jerked her arm back, but not before I clinked the other cuff around my own left wrist.

"What the hell—" she sputtered.

"Here's another thing I've noticed," I snarled in her face. "I don't have to live to win. I just have to make sure you *die*."

Elektra screamed with fury then, threw herself on top of me, and unloaded on me with every single thing that she had. All her green lightning, all her electrical power, all her elemental magic. The silverstone cuffs around our wrists absorbed some of her power, but not enough to make a difference. The cuff grew hot against my wrist, as did the vest on my chest, as the pieces of silverstone started to heat up from all the energy pouring into them. The vest wasn't going to be enough to save me. Not again. Because now, LaFleur was going for the kill shot, and she had all her attention and energy fixed on me.

Instead of reaching for my Stone magic, this time I grabbed hold of my Ice power, pulling it up through my veins, sending it into every single part of my body just the way I would my Stone magic. Instead of hardening my skin like my Stone power did, my Ice magic had a very different, very surprising affect.

It made me cold to the touch—and completely, utterly numb.

Ever since Elektra had unloaded her electrical magic on me the first time in the train yard, I'd been thinking about her power—how much it had just *hurt*, even though I'd used my Stone magic to insulate myself from it. She'd done the same thing with it to me again tonight. Hurting me, even through the shell of my Stone magic. So I'd known there wasn't any point in reaching for my Stone power again.

Maybe it was using my Ice magic to help me break out of the silverstone handcuffs, but somewhere along the way tonight, I'd started to think about what Jo-Jo had told me. About what I'd done the night I'd fallen into the Aneirin River, about how I'd used my Ice magic to wrap myself in the cold, to preserve my body from the harshness of the elements. I'd felt nothing that night, not even the cold seeping into and shutting down my body.

The simple fact was that LaFleur's magic just hurt too much. I couldn't concentrate on killing her when I was busy thinking about how much agony she was causing me, how her electricity was frying me one cell at a time. So this time I'd decided to use my Ice magic not to feel anything at all.

It was a long shot—but it *worked*.

I didn't feel anything. Not hot, not cold, and certainly not the other assassin's electrical magic slamming into my body again and again and again. Oh, my vision went green the way it had before, but that's because LaFleur was lighting us both up like we were a Christmas tree. She was using everything she had against me.

Through it all, I held on to my Ice magic. I didn't know how much damage she was doing to me, how badly she was frying my skin or burning me, and I didn't care.

All that mattered was keeping her here shackled to me so that she couldn't hurt Bria any more. All that mattered was stopping the other assassin—for good.

While her lightning crackled around me, Elektra also used her free hand to hit me. Over and over and over again, she slammed her tight fist into my face, my chest, and every other part of me that she could reach.

But because of my Ice magic, I didn't feel any of the blows. Not a one.

Still, I had to do something. Sooner or later, I would exhaust my magic, and I didn't know if it would be before or after Elektra ran out of juice herself. Somehow I pushed her away as far as I could, then rolled over onto my hands and knees, half-dragging Elektra with me. A steady burn of light caught my eye, and I stared down. My left hand was open, and the spider rune scar on my palm was glowing a bright silver, just like it had that night in the coal mine when I'd finally broken through the block of the silverstone metal in my hands.

I looked past it to my goal—the silverstone knife that I'd slapped away from Elektra. The only one I had left. But the only problem with not being able to feel my body was that I seemed to have zero control over it as well. It was like I was floating above myself, watching all this happen to someone else, and not being able to affect the outcome one bit.

Fuck that.

I needed that knife, and I was going to get it, numb body or no numb body. So I stared at my fingers harder than I had ever looked at anything in my life, willing them to move with the force of my gaze, to curl up, to just *twitch*.

And somehow they did.

Even though I couldn't feel them, I somehow made my fingers move, just by the sheer force of my mind. My thumb inched closer to the dagger, dragging the rest of my hand along with it. I got one fingertip on the weapon, then another, then another. All the while, LaFleur kept hitting me, kept raining blows onto my back and head. I ignored her the way a dog would a flea jumping around on its ass. The assassin wasn't important right now. Getting my hands on my knife was all that mattered.

Twenty agonizing seconds later, my hand closed around the hilt of the silverstone dagger. I might have only imagined it but I could have sworn that I felt the spider rune stamped on the hilt sear my skin with a magic that was even colder than my own.

Meanwhile, LaFleur was still trying to fry me with her electrical magic, even as she kept pummeling me with her free fist. I drew in a breath, concentrating one last time, gathering my strength for this one last thing.

And then I rolled back over and shoved the knife into her side.

It was an awkward blow and certainly not one of my best, given the fact that we were shackled together. Fletcher would have shaken his head sadly at my utter lack of form. But it got the job done. Most anything would, if you put enough muscle behind it. And even though I couldn't feel my arms, I knew that I'd driven the knife into her with everything I had.

Just because my body was numb didn't mean that I couldn't still hear things—like Elektra LaFleur's howl of rage. The wounds in her foot and shoulder might not have slowed her down much, but a knife in the stomach is a little more serious, especially given just how deep I'd shoved it into her. For the first time, real, raw pain filled her voice.

More importantly, she finally lost her grip on her electrical magic. The green lightning flashing around our bodies vanished in a shower of sparks, as though a firecracker had just exploded over our heads. I'd hurt her bad. But I didn't stop, not even for a second. Even though I still couldn't feel my own hand, my own fingers even, somehow I pulled out the knife.

And this time, I buried it in the bitch's heart.

Elektra let out a final shriek. Her body convulsed once, twice, three times, just as mine had done when she slammed her electrical magic into me. That damn eerie green lightning flashed around us once more, slamming us both into the gravel. Elektra's final death blow. Then her limbs slackened, and all the fight drained out of her body.

We were still shackled together, with me now on top of her. I stared down into her pale, shocked face.

"You know what, Elektra?" I rasped through my cold, numb, dead lips. "You should have killed me the second you had the chance. Instead, you talked yourself to death, you arrogant bitch. Just like your brother Brutus did."

I don't know if she heard me before the last of the green lightning finally flashed, flickered, and faded from her eyes, and she was still.

* 28 *

When I was sure that Elektra LaFleur was dead, I let go
of my Ice magic.

Pain immediately flooded my body, cutting through
the cold numbness, but I didn't care right now. I flopped
over onto my back, scooting as far away from her as I
could, given the handcuffs that still bound us together.
The metal had weakened from the heat of LaFleur's
magic, but the cuffs hadn't completely melted. Something soft brushed against my fingers, and I turned my
head to the right.

Elektra LaFleur's orchid, the one she'd planned on
dropping on my body, lay on the ground next to me.
Somehow the flower had survived being crushed during
our fight. A breeze whistled through the train yard, ruf-
fling the delicate white petals. I shuddered and turned
away from it.

I lay there on the loose gravel, riding the waves of

pain, and watching the green-gray smoke puff up from my body and drift away like ribbons unfurling into the night sky.

But I couldn't rest yet. Not until I'd checked on Bria. Not until I knew whether my baby sister was still alive.

I didn't have long to wonder. Just as I started to force myself to sit up against the pain, footsteps crunched on the gravel behind me, and a second later, Bria's face came into view above mine. Dirt smeared her features, along with a few scrapes and bruises from where she'd thrown herself onto the gravel, and her shaggy blond hair was a static-charged mess. One of her blue eyes twitched, and similar spasms zipped down her throat and into the rest of her body, making her arms and legs jump ever so slightly. But other than that, she was fine. She'd just been jolted by Elektra's magic, not killed outright.

I let out a quiet sigh of relief. My sister was fine for one more night. Which made everything I'd just been through worthwhile, including the pain that kept flooding my body like a river relentlessly rising inch by inch. I gritted my teeth and pushed it away as best I could.

"Are you all right?" Bria asked in a soft voice.

Her gaze locked onto the macabre smoke drifting up from my body. I could smell it, of course. But for once, the acrid stench didn't bother me and didn't trigger any old, unwanted memories. Maybe that's because I was still alive and LaFleur wasn't.

"I'm still breathing," I rasped. "That's good enough for now. Help me up, please."

Bria gave me her hand and pulled me up into a sitting position. Despite my attempts to ignore the pain from my injuries, it took me a moment to get my breath back. My wrist was also still cuffed to LaFleur's, and her arm flopped against my own. Dead weight, in every sense of the word. Elektra's green eyes stared sightlessly up into the night sky. Blood still oozed from the stab wounds on her chest and stomach, and the warm, coppery scent of it filled my nose.

I didn't have any magic left, not even enough to make another Ice pick so that I could unshackle myself from her dead body. I just sat there and stared dully at the handcuffs.

"Let me help you with those."

Bria must have sensed what I was thinking, because she held out her hand and reached for her own Ice magic. A blue light flickered in her palm, and the familiar caress of her elemental power flowed over me like a cool, refreshing breeze, washing away the static remains of LaFleur's electricity. Somehow, Bria's magic made my injuries, my pain inside and out, just a little easier to bear. It felt so good, so *right* that it made me want to weep.

A second later, Bria had two Ice picks in her hand that looked identical to the ones that I'd made earlier tonight. She crouched down beside me and went to work on the handcuffs. It took her a couple of minutes and a few soft curses, but eventually the silverstone clinked open, and LaFleur's dead arm fell back to the ground to join the rest of her.

Bria sat back on her heels, crouching there in the cold beside me. She stared at me, then at the dead assassin beside me. I couldn't read the emotions flashing in her eyes—or maybe I just didn't care to tonight. Maybe I was just afraid of what I would see.

"What are you going to do now?" I asked.

She knew what I was asking—if she was going to arrest me and turn me in for being the Spider. For killing Mab's men and all the others I'd murdered over the years.

Bria sighed and ran her hand through her hair. Green static crackled around her fingers. She shuddered and dropped her hand. "I'm going to call in and report that I was abducted tonight by someone claiming to be an assassin. That she was going to torture and kill me before the Spider intervened. Mainly, that the assassin is dead and that I was locked in a railcar the whole time and didn't see a thing."

"You're not turning me in?" I whispered.

Bria looked at me. Without a word, she shook her head. I didn't ask her why. I didn't think she even knew the reason herself. But that wasn't the only issue between us.

"And what about us? We're sisters, Bria."

"You're . . . It's just . . . I can't . . ." She sighed. "I don't know, Gene—Gin. I just don't know. I need some time to think about things. You're not exactly what I expected to find when I came back to Ashland. None of this has turned out the way I thought it would."

"What did you think would happen?"

A humorless smile lifted her lips. "I thought I'd charge Mab Monroe with the murder of my mother and older sister and see her dragged away in chains, for starters. But that's not going to happen now. Neither is the picture-perfect reunion I'd imagined having with my big sister, Genevieve."

There was no real judgment in her voice, no condemnation in her tone, just weariness, the same weariness I felt right now. But her words still *hurt*. I knew that my being the Spider was the thing that stood between us. My deadly skills might have saved us tonight, but they were also tearing us apart now. Maybe forever.

All I wanted to do right now was put my arms around Bria and make sure she was really okay. Tell her—no, *promise* her—that everything was going to be okay, just as I had when we were both little girls and she skinned her knee or lost her favorite doll.

But we were both too old for such childish things now, and there was just too much between us. Too much history, too much emotion, too many things left unsaid and undone.

Bria's eyes met and held mine. With all our feelings shining there inside for the other to see. Her shock. My hope. And no resolution to either one in sight.

Then my baby sister got to her feet and stalked off into the darkness to make her call.

I sat there huddled on the cold, loose gravel, slowly moving my body and cataloguing my injuries while I waited for Bria to come back. Elektra LaFleur hadn't beaten me as badly as Elliot Slater had, but the other assassin hadn't pulled her punches either. My face had already started to bruise and swell from where she'd hit me, and not all of the blood on me was hers. A slow, steady trickle of it slid down my face from a cut that she'd opened on my left cheekbone. Ugly, nasty, electrical burns also covered most of my exposed skin, especially on my hands and arms.

But I could still move, still walk, talk, and breathe, so

I wasn't too concerned. Jo-Jo Deveraux could heal anything short of death. I might hurt like hell, but I'd live until I got to the dwarven Air elemental healer.

A few minutes later, Bria returned. She clutched a small silver cell phone in her hand that she passed down to me.

"Here," she said in a quiet voice. "That's LaFleur's phone. I got it out of the back of the limo where she left it. I didn't want to go digging through the giants' pockets to find theirs."

I didn't have to ask her why—because I'd slashed into the men with my silverstone knives, filleting them like fish, until there was probably more blood on the ground around them than was still left in their bodies. Even now, I could hear the gravel of the train yard muttering all around me, the stones whispering of all the dark, ugly, bloody things that had been done here tonight.

"I thought that you might want to call your friend Finnegan Lane first," Bria said. "Before I do my thing."

"Thank you," I said and dialed Finn's number.

It rang only once before he picked it up.

"Where the hell are you!?" Finn screamed in my ear. "We've been looking everywhere for you!"

I winced at his voice blaring out at me. "I'm fine. I'm back at the train yard. LaFleur jumped me behind the Pork Pit and decided to take me for a little drive tonight."

"Well, I hope that you had the good sense to kill her for interrupting your evening," Finn sniffed. "And for making us worry."

"I did. But I wasn't the only one that she nabbed. Bria's here with me."

Silence. I could hear Finn thinking through the phone. He knew that in order to kill LaFleur I'd had to show Bria who I really was—and exactly what I was capable of.

"And how is she taking the news?" Finn finally asked.

I looked over at my sister, who was crouched down and examining LaFleur's body, along with my silverstone knife, which was still stuck in the assassin's chest. "Well, she hasn't screamed and run away yet. I suppose that's something."

"Sit tight," Finn said. "We'll be there in ten minutes."

"Don't worry," I said in a wry tone. "I'm not going anywhere."

I hung up the phone and held it back out to Bria. "He'll be here in ten minutes. It'll take the po-po at least twenty to get here. So go ahead and make your call, if you want."

She nodded. Bria started to take the phone from me, but before she could touch it, the cell started ringing. My eyes narrowed. I hadn't given Finn the number, and there was only one person I knew of who would have a reason to call LaFleur right now.

So I snapped the phone open and answered it. "Hello, Mab."

Silence.

I waited a few seconds. After it became apparent that she wasn't going to answer me, I decided to initiate the conversation.

"Your girl LaFleur's dead," I said in the cheeriest tone that I could manage, considering the fact that I'd almost been electrocuted tonight. I stared at the other assassin's body. "And growing colder by the second."

"*You.*" Mab's voice was dark, cold, and ugly in my ear.

"Me," I replied, a bucket of sunshine in comparison. "You've been busy since the last time we talked. When was that? Oh, yeah. The night that I killed Elliot Slater at his quaint little mountain retreat."

More silence.

Bria just stared at me, listening to my side of the conversation with the Fire elemental. My sister's mouth tightened into a thin line.

"I have to admit that you gave me a good fight this time," I said. "Hiring LaFleur to come to Ashland to try to kill me was an inspired move, since it was so obvious that none of your own men were going to get the job done. Too bad you backed the wrong horse. Again. But that seems to be a bad habit of yours. One that I'm going to end very, very soon."

"So you killed LaFleur tonight," Mab snarled. "So what? It's not going to save you in the end, Spider."

"Probably not," I murmured, staring up at Bria. "But it sure as hell was fun."

I hung up the phone and passed it back to Bria. It started ringing again the second that she touched it, but she waited until it had stopped before turning away from me, flipping it open, and calling in her kidnapping.

While she did that, I picked up one of my wayward knives and used the hilt to draw my spider rune into the gravel right next to LaFleur's body. Mab already knew I'd been here, of course, but I wanted to drive the point home to her, so to speak.

A few minutes later, just as Bria was finishing up her call, a pair of headlights popped into view at the far end of the train yard. By this point, I'd managed to get to my feet and retrieve all of my silverstone knives, so I palmed one of the weapons, just in case the vehicle held more of Mab's men. Bria didn't have a weapon; she picked a long piece of pipe up out of the junk in the train yard and held it down by her side. She came up to stand beside me, even though she didn't look at me.

Tires crunched on the gravel, and a large silver SUV rolled over to us. The doors opened, and Finn got out of the passenger's side. I expected Sophia Deveraux to hop out of the driver's seat, but to my surprise, Owen slid out of the vehicle instead.

The two men jogged over to us. Owen stopped in front of me, his violet gaze sweeping over my body, but when he realized that I was in more or less one piece, some of the tight concern in his face faded away.

I held up one of the bloody knives he'd given me for Christmas. "You should give me presents more often. Because this one worked like a charm."

Owen shook his head and just smiled at me.

Finn was a little more practical about things. Once he looked me over and made sure that I was okay for the time being, my foster brother directed his attention to Bria.

"Detective," he said. "You're looking well this evening, all things considered."

"Lane," Bria replied in a cool voice, crossing her arms over her chest. "You're acting as smarmy as ever."

Finn grinned, his green eyes twinkling. He loved a challenge, especially when the current object of his affection so obviously hated him. Or at least hated him knowing that she was attracted to him. Even after everything that had happened tonight, a spark of interest filled Bria's face as she stared at Finn before she managed to hide it. Finn saw it too, which made his grin widen that much more.

"We need to leave," I said, interrupting his leering at Bria. "Bria's called the cops and told them about her . . . kidnapping this evening. And lucky intervention and rescue by the mysterious Spider."

Finn and Owen stared at me, then at Bria. My baby sister shifted on her feet, but she met their curious gazes head-on.

"The cops will be here any minute," she said in a cool voice. "So I suggest the three of you leave before they arrive—or I decide to change my story."

Owen came over and gently put his arm around me to help me to the SUV. Finn stayed where he was. He looked at Bria, then back again at me, a more hopeful look on his face now. I shook my head, telling him that nothing had been resolved between the two of us.

Bria saw the exchange and frowned. Our gazes met and held again. So many emotions shimmered in her bright blue eyes. Shock. Relief. Weariness. And just a touch of fear. The last one saddened me more than I'd thought possible. I didn't want my baby sister to be afraid of me. I wanted her to see the hope and longing that filled my heart. I wanted her to know I would never, ever hurt her. I wanted her to accept me, if only for this one brief moment.

Whatever Bria saw in my face, it wasn't enough to break through this wall between us—a wall I'd built brick by brick, body by bloody body, as the Spider.

"Come on, Gin," Owen said.

His arm tightened protectively around me, as if he could somehow shield me from having my heart broken by my sister. It was already too late for that, though.

"We need to get you to Jo-Jo's," he finished. "You're hurt. You need to be healed."

Bria was the only one who could really heal me right now, who could soothe this fierce ache in my heart. But apparently my sister wasn't interested in having anything else to do with me, because she turned away from my hopeful, searching gaze.

There was nothing I could do but accept her decision—at least for tonight. So I nodded and let Owen help me over to the waiting SUV. Finn followed us.

Bria stood there next to Elektra LaFleur's body and watched us disappear into the night.

* 29 *

Owen loaded me into the front of his SUV and drove me over to Jo-Jo's. Once we got there, Finn took his own Aston Martin back to the train yard, to keep an eye on Bria from a discreet distance and see how the cops and Mab Monroe reacted to the latest strike by the Spider. I wanted someone that I trusted nearby in case things didn't go as Bria thought they would. If worse came to worse, Finn would charge in and get my sister out of there—whether she wanted to go or not.

Owen put his arm around me again and helped me up the three steps to Jo-Jo's wraparound porch. Before he could use the knocker to bang on the door, I grabbed his arm. I tilted my head back and stared up at him.

"You didn't have to come with Finn, tonight," I said.

Owen looked down at me, his violet eyes flashing like amethysts in the semidarkness. "Yes, I did. Because I care about you, Gin. A lot."

He didn't use the L-word, but there was a catch in his voice that told me that he was thinking about it. Maybe Eva had told him that would also be too much, too fast. I smiled at the thought.

"What's so funny?" he murmured.

"Nothing. Nothing at all."

His arms tightened around me, and I felt the warmth of his body sink into my own. It felt good. It felt right. For a moment, I just stood there and wondered at the soft concern filling his face. I didn't know how or when or even why it had happened, but Owen truly cared about me, bloody knives and all. He'd shown it to me over and over again these past few days, but for the first time, I let myself believe in him—and us.

"There's nothing I can do that's going to drive you away, is there?" I murmured.

Owen flashed me a sly grin. "Finally figuring that out, are you?"

I nodded.

His grin deepened. "Well, it sure took you long enough."

We stood there on the porch another moment, just holding on to each other, before Owen helped me inside and back into the salon. Jo-Jo was there waiting, along with Sophia.

I sat down and leaned back in one of the cherry red salon chairs like I'd done so many times before. Jo-Jo raised her hand, and her Air elemental magic filled the room as she started to heal me. For some reason, it didn't bother me as much as it had before. Oh, her magic still felt like she was pricking me with thousands of sharp needles all at the same time, but it didn't make me grit my teeth the way it usually did, and the silverstone scars on my palms didn't itch and burn nearly as much.

Maybe my nerves had been fried a little more than I'd thought by LaFleur's electricity. Or maybe it was because anything would have felt good in comparison to the jolts that the other assassin had given me tonight. LaFleur might be dead, but I'd remember the crackling power of her magic forever, another little scar on my psyche to go along with all the others that were already there, all the other people I'd managed to kill by skill or magic or sheer luck, like Alexis James, Tobias Dawson, and Elliot Slater.

"There," Jo-Jo said about three minutes later and dropped her hand. "All done."

"That's it?" I asked, surprised it hadn't taken her longer to patch me up. "That's all?"

The dwarf shrugged. "You weren't beat up as bad as you usually are. Those electrical burns were nasty, but not nearly as deep as they could have been."

I frowned. "But what about LaFleur's magic? She blasted me with her electrical power over and over. I thought she was going to kill me with it."

"And you used your Ice magic to counter it," Jo-Jo said, her colorless eyes boring into mine. "She might have got a couple of good licks in on you at first, but then you wised up, and your magic blocked most of hers. I've been telling you all along that you're strong, darling. When are you finally going to believe me?"

For once I didn't shiver at her ominous words. Instead, I sat there in the chair and thought about things. Maybe when I killed Mab Monroe and lived to tell the tale—maybe then I'd believe the dwarf and her claims about just how strong my elemental magic was. But there was a lot more story to be told before then. Many more things needed to be put in place before Mab and I had our final dance. Tonight I was just happy the other assassin was no longer a threat.

An hour later, Jo-Jo, Sophia, Owen, and I were in the kitchen, while Vinnie and Natasha were sound asleep upstairs. Neither one of them had heard Owen bring me in, and I'd asked Jo-Jo not to wake them. They needed their rest.

Jo-Jo had just finished making us all some hot apple cider when Finn came strolling in through the kitchen door. He, of course, turned his nose up at the cider and opted to pour himself a cup of chicory coffee instead.

"So how did things go at the train yard?" I asked. "Is Bria okay?"

"I was actually surprised," Finn said, taking a sip of his coffee and leaning against the nearest counter. "The po-po had already arrived by the time I got back to the train yard, instead of taking their sweet time like they usually do. Anyway, the cops were there, lights blazing, guns drawn, sweeping the area for evidence, and blah, blah, blah. Bria talked to them for a long time, showed them all the bodies, the usual drill."

"Was Mab there?" I asked.

Finn nodded. "She showed up about an hour after Bria called it in. Since it was her property, they let her look at the bodies. They were her giants, after all, members of her security force."

My hands tightened around my mug of cider. "Then what did Mab do?"

Finn shrugged. "Not much. Like I said, she poked around for a little while, then she left. Bria was still there talking to the other investigators so Mab couldn't get to her. At least, not without killing twenty cops along with her. And, of course, the press had also shown up by that point, and all the reporters were clamoring for interviews with Bria, since she was the latest person to be saved by the Spider."

"You think that Mab will go after Bria again?" Owen asked.

I thought about it. "Eventually. But I don't see how she can right now. Mab's had too many losses, too many setbacks in a row. After what happened tonight, I wouldn't be surprised if some of her own men turned against her or maybe even just defected outright. The other underworld sharks like Phillip Kincaid are definitely smelling the blood in the water. Mab will have to work on shoring up her own organization first before makes another run at Bria. I think I've bought her some time, at least."

I was determined to kill Mab long before she set her sights on Bria again—no matter what.

It was late, and I didn't feel like driving home, so I spent the rest of the night in one of Jo-Jo's guest bedrooms— the same room I'd woken up in just the day before. I was wiped out from everything that had happened tonight, but I wasn't too tired to dream . . .

It took longer than I thought it would to navigate through the ruined rubble of my house. There were fires everywhere.

Busted water pipes that gushed like geysers, broken, splintered glass that cut into my bare feet, electrical wires that sent up showers of blue and red sparks in all directions.

I still couldn't believe I'd done all this with my Ice and Stone magic. That I'd somehow managed to collapse my own house and cause all this destruction with my screams of rage and pain and fear. I hurried on as fast as I could, picking my way over the piles of rubble, ignoring the sharp rocks that sliced my feet and the raw, fresh agony of the silverstone metal that had been melted into my hands. I'd stopped long enough to rip away part of my nightgown, soak it in cold water, and wrap the scraps around my palms, but they still hurt so much, sending a fresh, pulsing wave of pain through me with every beat of my heart. But no matter how much I hurt, no matter how much pain I was in, I was determined to find Bria and go—somewhere. Just get away. Before the Fire elemental found us and killed us both.

Finally I stumbled out of the house and into the garden in the courtyard outside the kitchen. An hour ago, it had been a beautiful spot, with thick stands of flowers and plants and trees and bushes, all arranged around a gurgling stone fountain. But part of the house had collapsed onto the fountain, smashing it to pieces.

And that wasn't the worst thing I saw. A man's arm stuck out of the rubble there, his blood a bright crimson against the white, pulverized marble.

I stopped and looked at the arm. Whoever it was attached to had to be dead, even though blood still dripped off the ends of the fingers. And I realized that I'd caused this too. That I'd used my magic to crush someone to death, even though that hadn't been my intention at the time. The thought made my stomach twist, and for a moment, I thought I might vomit. But I swallowed down my hot, bitter, sour bile and moved on. I'd feel guilty later. Right now, all that mattered was finding Bria.

I slipped past the bloody arm and crushed fountain and headed for the far side of the courtyard, where a set of stairs climbed up to the second level of our house. The stone stairs were actually hollow underneath, with a secret chamber inside. A couple of months ago, I'd dragged a table, some chairs, and Bria's favorite doll house into the chamber so we could be comfortable in there while we played. It was also my favorite place to come whenever Bria and I were playing hide-and-seek, because she never thought to look for me in there. But then again, she was only eight.

After I'd seen the Fire elemental murder Mother and Annabella, I'd snatched Bria out of bed, put her in the secret chamber, and told her to stay there until I came back to get her. Nobody knew about the hollow stairs but our family, so no one would find Bria there. At least, I hadn't thought they would until I'd heard my baby sister scream.

I rounded another wall of rocks, and the staircase came into view. I looked up and froze, my heart plummeting to my feet like a cold, lead weight that had been dropped off a bridge.

Because instead of the hollow staircase, all I saw now was a pile of rubble.

"Bria?" I whispered.

She didn't answer me.

"Bria!" My voice grew louder, sharper, as the panic set in.

I hurried over and dropped to my feet beside the rubble, trying to dig through it, trying to claw my way through the stone to get to Bria, who surely had to be trapped underneath. But the rocks were far too heavy for me to move by myself. Only one thing to do. So I stood up, wiped my tears away, and lashed out with my Ice and Stone magic, just like I had before when I'd been tied down to the chair.

One by one, I blasted the rocks out of my way, not even caring that the flying shards stung my face like bees. Blood ran down my hands and cheeks, mixing with my own hot tears.

Finally, I found the thing that I was dreading most. Because instead of Bria, instead of my baby sister smiling up at me out of the rocks, all I saw was blood.

So much blood.

Too much blood for anyone to lose and still live.

Bria was dead. I'd brought her out here and hidden her so that she would be safe from the Fire elemental and her men. She probably had been—until I'd used my Ice and Stone magic. Until I'd lost control and lashed out with it without thinking. I'd caused our whole house to crumble—right on top of my baby sister.

I'd killed my own sister with my magic.

My knees buckled, and I crumpled in the rubble, screaming once more, this time with grief. Bria was dead . . . dead . . . and I'd killed her—

I woke up with my mouth open in a silent scream and cold sweat dripping down my face. For a moment I was back there again, trapped in the rubble of my own house, slowly realizing that I'd killed my younger sister even while I'd been so desperately trying to save her. It was as fresh and raw to me as if it had just happened.

Then I remembered who I was. Where I was. And that I was safe now. And so was Bria.

I flopped back against the pillow and turned my head, my eyes going to the phone resting on the nightstand beside me. I reached for it. I thought that I'd lost Bria once back then, and I'd carried the guilt of her supposed death with me ever since. I wasn't letting her go a second time, no matter what it took for her to accept me. No matter how long it took.

The phone rang three times before she picked it up.

"Hello?" She sounded as wide awake as I was right now, despite the late hour.

For a moment, I found myself searching for words, the way I always did whenever I called her. I drew in a breath and forced myself to speak.

"It's Gin," I finally said. "Can we talk?"

✳ 30 ✳

The next day was Christmas Eve. The Pork Pit wasn't officially open for business, so I'd given all of the wait-staff the day off with pay, but Sophia and I had a few last-minute orders to see to before we closed down for the holiday. And I had some last-minute shopping to do, because I still hadn't decided on a present for Owen, and time was running out.

In between cooking and giving people their party orders, I kept one eye on the clock on the wall, counting down the hours until my visitor arrived. Finally, three o'clock rolled around. At one minute after, the front door opened, causing the bell to chime, and she stepped into my restaurant.

Detective Bria Coolidge. My baby sister.

She looked as cool and professional as ever in her long coat, sweater, jeans, and boots. Her badge glinted a warm gold on her leather belt next to her gun. She stood in the doorway, as if she wasn't quite sure what she was doing here. That made two of us.

Sophia and I both looked over at her. Then the dwarf turned her flat, black eyes to mine and gave me a small, encouraging nod.

"Back," Sophia grunted in her broken voice, disappearing through the swinging doors to give us some privacy.

I wiped my hands on a dishrag, stepped around the counter, and approached my sister. "I'm glad you came."

Bria just shrugged, as though she didn't trust herself to speak yet.

I locked the front door behind her so we wouldn't be interrupted. We settled ourselves at one of the booths next to the storefront windows—the same booth that Jonah McAllister and Elektra LaFleur had sat in when they'd come into the restaurant a few days ago. This time, though, the irony didn't bother me. Because LaFleur was dead, and I wasn't.

"Do you want anything to eat? Something to drink?" I asked.

Bria shook her head and looked at me, clearly wanting me to go ahead and say whatever was on my mind. Okay. I could do that. I hoped.

I drew in a deep breath and slowly let it out. And then, I started, telling her all the things I'd longed to for so long now.

"I called you so late last night because I had a dream about you—about the night that Mab murdered our mother and Annabella," I said in a low voice.

Bria frowned, as though she didn't quite believe me. "You had a dream? About me? About that night?"

I nodded. "I've been having them a lot lately. For a couple of months now. Only they're not really dreams, so much as memories of that night. Last night, I dreamed about when I went to find you, after I used my magic to collapse our house. I remember picking through the rubble, trying to find you in that secret playroom under the stairs, but realizing that the stairs had collapsed along with the rest of the house, and finding only blood instead. So much blood."

My voice dropped to a whisper, and I had to swallow once before I was able to go on. "I woke up screaming then, because I thought you were dead, that I'd killed you with my magic. It's a dream I've had a lot over the years."

Something flashed in Bria's blue eyes. It might have been guilt, but I ignored it. If I didn't get the words out now, I didn't know if they would ever come to me again.

So I sat there and told Bria everything.

How I thought that she'd been dead for the last seventeen years until Fletcher Lane had left me a folder of information about my family's murder with Bria's picture inside. How I'd searched for her with no success, and then had been startled to discover that she'd come back to Ashland on her own—as a detective with the police department, no less. How I struggled with how to tell her who I really was and all the things I'd done in the meantime to protect her from Mab. All the people I'd killed to keep her safe.

And then I told her the real reason our mother and older sister had died that night—because Mab thought a member of the Snow family, a girl with both Ice and Stone magic, was destined to kill her someday.

"She thought that I was you, didn't she?" Bria asked. "That I had both Ice and Stone magic?"

I nodded. "From what I've been able to piece together, yes."

"And that's why she wants me dead now." Her voice was cold and flat. "Because she thinks I'll kill her one day with my magic."

I nodded again.

To my surprise, Bria threw her head back and let out a short, bitter laugh. "Well, I suppose that serves me right for being such a coward in the first place."

"What does?"

"Because I ran away that night," Bria said in a low tone. "Like the coward that I was."

I frowned. "What do you mean?"

Bria drew in a deep breath. "That night, when you hid me in the playroom under the staircase, I got scared sitting there in the dark all by myself. So I went back inside the house to try to find you, even though you told me not to. And I saw—I saw Mab torturing you. I didn't know who she was at the time, but I saw her and Elliot Slater duct-tape your spider rune medallion between your hands, and I heard her ask you all those questions about me."

This time Bria was the one who had to stop for a moment.

"And I—and I heard you scream when she heated the rune and it melted into your hands. I didn't know what to do. I wanted to help you, I wanted to use my Ice magic, but I was just so scared, so terrified that I couldn't get it to work. So I—I just ran. I ran away. Out of the house and back toward the secret playroom. I thought that what was happening to you was my fault for leaving and that if I went back there, everything would be okay. Stupid, I know."

Guilt and self-loathing gave her lilting voice a harsh, ugly tone. It looked as though I wasn't the only one who had carried around the emotional baggage of that night for all these years. I didn't blame Bria for what she'd done. There was only one person at fault in all of this—Mab Monroe. And she was going to pay for what she'd done to us, more than she'd ever imagined.

Bria wouldn't look at me, so I slowly reached over and took her hand in mine. Her fingers felt as cold as ice against my own.

"You were eight years old, Bria. Just a kid. There was nothing you could have done to help me, nothing you could have done to stop Mab."

She stared at the tabletop. "You were just a kid too, Gene—Gin. And look what you did. You sat there, and you didn't say a word about me. Not one word. And I know how much Mab hurt you. I heard your screams all the way outside the house, even after I went back out into the courtyard. I had to put my fingers in my ears to block the sound."

We didn't say anything for a few minutes. Instead, we just sat there, staring at our hands stacked one on top of the other.

"What happened then?" I finally asked. "After you— left?"

Bria shrugged. "I don't remember a lot of it. I ran back through the house for what seemed like forever, stopping to hide every time I saw one of Mab's men search-ing for me. But finally I made it all the way back to the staircase where you'd told me to wait before two of Mab's men spotted me. One of them grabbed me, and I started screaming."

I remembered the sound of her screams that night. The awful, awful sound. The one that always made me wake up in a cold sweat.

"Anyway, I don't really know what happened after that. I guess it was you and your magic, because the house started to collapse right on top of us. Part of it fell on one of the giants and buried him."

That must have been the one whose arm I'd seen near the fountain.

"I jerked away from the other giant, ran past the stair-case, and managed to make it out of the courtyard. But he wasn't as fast as I was. I saw the staircase fall and crush him to death." She gave me a tight smile. "I know it's hor-rible now, but at the time, I remember thinking that his blood squirted out of him just like juice from a tomato. I imagine that's whose blood was on the rocks you found. His, not mine."

It wasn't any more horrible than all the things I'd done as the Spider, but instead of telling her that, I just nodded.

"Anyway, I just kept on running, going deeper and deeper into the forest around our house until I collapsed. After that, things get a bit blurry," Bria said. "All I re-ally remember is that sometime later, this man found me out there in the middle of nowhere. I don't really remem-ber much about him, just that he had the greenest eyes

I've ever seen. All slick and shiny-looking, like glass or something. Anyway, he took me . . . somewhere. Fed me, bathed me, and made sure that I was okay. The next thing I knew, I had a new mom and dad. They were wonderful people, Gin. I think you would have liked them. But it wasn't—the same. It wasn't ever the same."

I looked over at the wall beside the cash register and the photo of Fletcher Lane that was hung there. In the faded picture, a young Fletcher held up the catch from his fishing trip, beaming proudly at the camera. Somehow, I knew that the mystery man that Bria was talking about was him.

And once more, I was stunned—simply stunned. The old man had found Bria all those years ago? Had given her to her foster parents? Why? Had he been looking for me as well?

More importantly, had he known about Mab's attack on our family? Had he been there that night? Had Fletcher been there as the assassin the Tin Man, as one of Mab's men? That horrible thought slammed into me with the force of one of my own silverstone knives, slicing my heart in two. Had the old man in some way been responsible for the murder of my mother and older sister?

For a moment, the world tilted crazily, and I couldn't breathe. I just couldn't *breathe*—

"You're not the only one who has dreams," Bria said in a low voice, cutting into my troubled thoughts. "Last night in the train yard, I was doing just what you wanted me to—getting out of there. But I couldn't stop thinking about that night and how I had acted back then. And I decided that I didn't want to run away again."

Somehow I pushed my speculations about Fletcher aside and concentrated on her once more.

"Is—is that why you came back for me last night? Because you felt guilty about running away all those years ago?"

Bria bit her lip and nodded. "I was a coward once before when my big sister needed me. I didn't want to be one again. Especially over an arrogant assassin like Elektra LaFleur. So I ran back to the giant you had killed, the one with the gun, picked it up, and circled around behind her. The two of you were struggling, so I couldn't get a clear shot. But then she started using her magic, and you collapsed at her feet. I thought she was going to kill you, and I just—lost it. That's why I started shooting. But I didn't think to check to see how many shots were left, which is why I ran out of bullets before I could kill her."

"Believe me," I said in a wry tone. "I was grateful for the shots you took. It distracted her long enough to let me do what needed to be done."

Bria nodded and lifted her eyes to meet mine. "And that's what you specialize in, isn't it? Because you're the Spider."

I stared at her. "Does it bother you? The fact that I used to be an assassin? The fact that I've decided to go after Mab and make her pay for all the evil things she's done? For what she did to our family, to us?"

Bria didn't say anything, but I could see the struggle in her face. She hated Mab as much as I did, but my sister was still a cop. She still believed in things like law, order, justice. She'd spent her whole life believing in them and fighting against people like me. She couldn't just put all that aside because she'd found out that her long-lost sister was a notorious assassin. No matter how much I might want her to.

"So you really are the Spider?" she finally asked.

I nodded.

"And how many people have you killed over the years?"

I didn't want to push her farther away, but I wasn't going to lie to her either. Not anymore. So I shrugged. "I quit keeping count a long time ago. You wouldn't want to know anyway, not really."

"No," she said in a thoughtful tone. "I wouldn't want to know. Not really."

We didn't speak for several moments.

"So what now?" I asked. "We've both been searching for each other for weeks, and we both want Mab to pay for what she did to our family. So where does that leave us?"

Bria hesitated. "You have to understand that I've spent my whole adult life being a cop, Gin. That I was raised by a cop, a good one. Rules, procedure, the law, all of those things mean something to me. I don't think that they do to you."

I shrugged again. No, they didn't, because I had my own rules, my own procedure, my own law. But I didn't think that Bria wanted to hear about the Spider's cynical, bloody, violent worldview right now.

"I should be turning you in for everything you've done, including killing Elektra LaFleur and Mab Monroe's men, even if they deserved it," Bria said. "But I just can't seem to bring myself to do it. I don't know why."

Her reluctance to rat me out wasn't much, but it was a place to start.

"Well, I know what I want," I said. "You're my sister, Bria. I want what I've always wanted—a relationship with you. You back in my life in some way. I want to get to know you and see how much you're like the little girl I remember, the one I used to play all those games with, and have such fun with. Don't you want that too? After everything we've been through? After all these long years we've been apart?"

Bria let out a tense breath. "I thought I did before I found out that you were the Spider. Now, I just don't know."

Her words didn't surprise me. I'd expected this conversation to more or less go the way it had. But her lack of commitment hurt me, wounded me deep down in a way I couldn't even begin to describe. Probably the same way that my doubt and hesitation did to Owen. He'd never said anything to me about it, but I could tell that Owen wanted something from me that I just wasn't ready or able to give him. Just as Bria wasn't ready to give me her love and trust. Not now, maybe not ever. Irony. Out to get me once again.

"I need some time to think about things, Gin," Bria said, running a hand through her blond hair. "I mean, it's not just you. After I left the train yard last night, I called Xavier and told him what had happened. Xavier's my *partner*, for crying out loud, and he knew more about you, about who you are and what you do, than I did. Or do. Or whatever. I feel . . . betrayed. By him, by you, by the whole situation. I can't just snap my fingers and forget everything that I am just because I know who you are now."

"I understand," I said in a quiet voice.

And I did.

Once upon a time, I'd been a happy little girl with a mother and two sisters who had loved her. But fate or destiny or even simply circumstance had turned me into a killer. It was a choice that I'd embraced and something that I'd had to do in order to survive. I knew this. Rationally, I knew it, but it had still taken me a long time to adjust to the fact that I'd never be that carefree little girl again.

And neither would Bria. In many ways, my sister was just like me. She might believe in the law and in justice, while I put my faith in my knives and my will to use them, but deep down, we were more alike than she realized. We both did what needed to be done to protect the people we cared about. I just got more blood on me along the way. I wondered if Bria would ever realize that. I hoped she would. I hoped—for a lot of things. Too many things, really.

"Well, my invitation still stands," I said.

Bria frowned. "What invitation?"

"The one to the Christmas party tomorrow at Owen Grayson's house. I'd like you to come, if you would."

Bria immediately shook her head. "I don't think that would be a good idea, Gin. I just need some time to think about things. How much time, I don't know."

I nodded, accepting her request. After all, I was the Spider, the assassin whose rune was the symbol for patience. I'd wait for Bria—for however long it took.

"All right. I'll be here, whenever you're ready," I said. "In whatever way that you want me to be."

And then there was nothing left for us to talk about, not today, so Bria slid out of the booth and got to her feet. I did the same and unlocked the front door for her.

She put her hand on the knob and twisted it as if she was about to leave. But for some reason, she turned and faced me once more.

"Whatever issues there are between us, whatever bad things we've both done over the years, I want you to know that I'm glad you're alive, Gin," Bria said. "I'm glad you're alive."

It sounded like she was saying good-bye—forever. But before I could call out to her, before I could try to get her to stay, Bria opened the door, stepped out into the cold evening, and walked away.

Taking the last piece of my childhood, and maybe even my heart, with her.

✸ 31 ✸

That night, I couldn't sleep. Part of it was Bria, of course, and everything that had been said between us. But mostly, I couldn't stop thinking about what my sister had told me—about the man with the green eyes who'd found her wandering around in the forest after Mab had murdered our mother and older sister.

So I got out of bed, headed downstairs, and went into Fletcher Lane's office.

I clicked on the light and stood in the doorway, staring into the room in front of me. The old man's office had always been something of a mess, with papers and folders and pens scattered everywhere, from his battered desk to the bookcases that hugged the walls to the filing cabinets on either side of the door. Supposedly there was some kind of method to the madness, although I'd never quite gotten the grasp of it. Fletcher had always claimed that there was no need to lock his office, because if someone ever broke in, she'd give up trying to find what she was looking for out of sheer frustration. The only reason I'd been able to find LaFleur's file was because it had actually been in one of the filing cabinets in its proper place.

Even though he'd been dead for a couple of months now, I just hadn't had the heart to clean out Fletcher's office yet. I supposed that part of me wanted to keep everything the way that it had been the day he'd died, as if that would somehow bring him back. The air even still smelled faintly of him—like sugar, spice, and vinegar swirled all together.

But the old man wasn't coming back, and I wanted answers. So I drew in a breath, stepped into the room, and started going through the stacks of papers.

An hour later, I was ready to give up, just as Fletcher had intended. Because I'd found nothing. No files, no papers, nothing that gave me any clue as to why the old man had rescued Bria or how he'd even known she was in trouble in the first place. Once again, Fletcher had kept secrets from me, and now, since the old man was gone, I doubted I'd ever get the answers to my questions.

Tired and disgusted, I headed toward the door. I reached over to flip the light off to go back to bed when something winked at me from one of the bookcases. I looked over and noticed a crystal paperweight sitting on the shelf—one that I'd never seen before. Of course, I hadn't been in Fletcher's office for quite some time before he'd died. Curious, though, I walked over to the bookcase. It took me only half a second to realize that the paperweight was shaped like a small circle surrounded by eight thin rays.

A spider rune. My rune.

But the real kicker was the slim folder underneath the glinting crystal.

Unlike the other manila folders that littered the rest of the room, this one was the same dark brown as the bookcase, which made it practically invisible, along with the fact that most of it had been shoved back and under the books on that particular shelf. It looked like something Fletcher had just put on the bookcase and forgotten about, but I knew it was more than that. The spider rune–shaped paperweight told me as much. Fletcher had left it here for me to find. It was just my own fault that I hadn't bothered to look for it—until now.

My hands shaking just a bit, I slipped the folder off the bookshelf. *For Gin,* the old man's handwriting scrawled across the front in silver ink. I stared at the words a moment, then went over, sat down behind the desk, opened the folder, and started to read.

It was all there, written down in black-and-white.

Everything Fletcher Lane had observed about my family, every open door and unlocked window at our mansion, every single plan he'd made to get the job done when Mab had hired him, had hired the Tin Man, to assassinate my family.

I read the words, and it was almost like I could hear Fletcher's voice in my mind, patiently explaining things to me.

It started out like any other hit, the old man wrote. *I was to kill your mother, Eira Snow, and leave you and your sisters unharmed. I would have done it too. But Mab changed her mind and wanted the three of you dead as well. You know that I don't do that sort of thing.*

"No kids," I whispered in the utter silence of the office. "Ever."

Part of the assassin code that the old man had taught me—the same one he'd lived by for so many years. And apparently, the reason Bria and I were still alive today.

I kept reading. There was more—so much more. Fletcher chronicled it all. How he'd used his various contacts to tell Mab that he didn't murder children. How he told her to hire someone else to do the job. How she'd threatened to find and kill him for turning her down. And finally, how Mab had sent some of her goons after him, while she went to our house to murder my family.

Even as an assassin, I couldn't stand by and do nothing, not while innocent children were being targeted. So I tried to stop it; the old man's handwriting spelled out the words.

But I was detained by some of Mab's men. By the time I got there, it was too late. The mansion was fully engulfed in flames, and Mab was gone. But I found some tracks leading away from the house, and I knew that someone had survived. I found Bria early the next morning, wandering around in the forest, babbling about how she'd run away and how her mother and sisters were dead. So I took her and hid her until I could find a good home for her.

I thought that you were dead, Gin, until you showed up in the alley behind the Pork Pit all those weeks later. You know what happened after that.

I did the best I could for Bria—and for you, Gin. Keeping the two of you apart was the best way I knew to keep you hidden, to keep you safe from Mab, to give you time to grow up, to give me time to train you to be the Spider, the assassin you needed to be to finally defeat her. I hope you know that.

I hope you can understand everything I did. I hope you can forgive me someday.

"I know you did your best, Fletcher," I whispered. "I know you did."

There was more—so much more. But the tears in my eyes blurred the words too much for me to read them. At least for tonight. So I closed the folder, laid my head down on the desk, and stared at the spider rune–shaped crystal paperweight until the sun rose over the eastern mountains.

The next day—Christmas—we all gathered at Owen's mansion.

Me, Finn, and the Deveraux sisters, who brought Vinnie and Natasha Volga along with them. All crowding into Owen's downstairs living room, along with Eva and the two people that she'd invited over for the holiday celebration—her best friend, Violet Fox, and her grandfather, Warren T. Fox. Xavier was there too, with Roslyn Phillips, who'd also brought her sister, Lisa, and young niece, Catherine.

They were all in the living room, drinking my special Christmas punch, shaking the presents that they'd bought for each other, laughing, talking, smiling.

The only person I cared about who wasn't here was Bria.

I hadn't heard from my baby sister since our talk at the Pork Pit yesterday. Xavier had pulled me aside earlier and told me that she was working today so that some of the other cops could spend the holiday with their families. I could have told the giant that Bria had a family too, if only she'd realize it, but I held my tongue. No need to ruin Xavier's day.

I spent the morning in the kitchen, whipping up a Christmas lunch that would have done any Southern hostess proud. A tart but sweet cranberry sauce, roasted vegetables, fluffy mashed potatoes with plenty of real, fattening butter, sour cream, and cheddar cheese in them, and for the centerpiece, there was an enormous, spiral-cut ham with a brown sugar glaze. And then there were the desserts. I'd made a little something for everyone, from yummy fruit pies and warm berry cobblers topped with vanilla bean ice cream, to sweet sugar cookies and rich, chewy fruitcakes. I had a crowd to feed, and I'd outdone myself with all the dishes.

I might not be the most demonstrative person when it came to telling people how I felt about them, how much I cared about them, but I could sure make them a meal that they'd never forget.

We'd already eaten, and now I was back in the kitchen, washing the dishes while the others opened their presents. Of course, the ones most excited by the gifts were Roslyn's niece, Catherine, and Natasha. The little girls tore into the wrapping paper, barely pausing to admire the pretty packages before destroying them to get to what was waiting inside. The squeak, squawk and squeal of new toys filled the air.

"Here's the last of the dinner dishes," Owen said, carrying a final set of plates into the kitchen and dumping them into the sink. "You want me to dry while you wash?"

I wiped my hands off on a dish towel and turned to face him. "Sure, after you open your present."

Owen raised an eyebrow. "A present? For *moi*?"

"Yes, for you."

I reached across the counter, grabbed the present I'd put there earlier this morning, and held it out to him. The gift was wrapped in candy-cane-striped paper and had the small look of a jewelry box.

Owen took the box and carefully shook it, but no noise came from inside it.

"You didn't think I'd make it that easy for you, did you?" I said in a teasing tone.

He grinned. "I had hopes."

"Go ahead. Open it."

Owen shook the box one more time before tearing into it just as Catherine and Natasha had done in the other room. He ripped off the paper, popped open the box, and paused, staring at what was inside the small container.

He fished out the item and held it up for me to see. "A key?"

"I admit that it isn't nearly as nice or as inspired as the new silverstone knives that you made for me," I said. "But I have been busy these last few days."

Owen stared at me with his violet eyes. "And what does this key go to?"

My heart, because you've proved yourself worthy of it. That's what I thought about saying, that's what part of me wanted to say to him. But I didn't. I might not have much experience when it came to this relationship business, but I knew it was too soon for that. Especially since I was still processing this new warmth I felt for Owen and how best to handle it—and him.

"It goes to Fletcher's house," I said. "My house. It occurred to me that you've never been over there while we've been together. I thought you might like to see it sometime. Anytime that you'd like."

"I see."

I stared at Owen, wondering if it was enough, if maybe I should have gotten him something more substantial—like a holiday tie or a light-up Christmas sweater.

Then he looked up at me, a slow smile spreading across his face, softening his features and warming his violet eyes, and I knew I'd done the right thing. "One question. Are you going to try to kill me the way you probably do all of your uninvited guests? Because I'd hate for my first visit to get off to a bad start."

"Oh, I think I can make an exception for you," I replied in a teasing tone.

Owen joined in my soft laughter. He drew me toward him, and our lips met in a hot, long kiss that made me wish the party were already over so we could be alone—

The doorbell rang, the merry chime echoing through the house.

Startled, I drew back from Owen, looking in that direction before my eyes went back to his. He nodded, telling me that I should go get it. We both knew there was only one person it could be. Only one other person knew I was here today, that we were all gathered here today. Only one other person had been invited.

So I walked to the front door, drew in a breath, and opened it.

And there she stood, her cheeks pink from the December cold and the thick flakes of snow that swirled around lazily in the air. Detective Bria Coolidge. My baby sister. She wore her long coat as she always did and held a small wrapped box in her hand, about the same size as the one I'd just given to Owen.

"Gene—Gin."

"Bria."

We stood there staring at each other before I remembered my manners and stepped back.

"Come in. Please."

Bria hesitated, then stepped inside. I hurried to shut the door behind her before she could change her mind and leave. The sounds of the others' laughter drifted down the hall to us, along with the holiday music that someone had popped into the entertainment system. The soft strains of "I'll Be Home for Christmas" filled in the silence between us. Bria stood where she was just inside the foyer, uncertainty flashing in her blue eyes.

She drew in a breath, much as I had a moment ago. "Here," she said, holding out the present. "This is for you."

I took the small box from her. "Wait here. I have something for you too."

I went into the kitchen, retrieved the other special present that I'd brought with me today, and stepped back into the hallway. Bria hadn't moved an inch from where I'd left her. She stood tall, still, and frozen, like she was afraid to move, like it would somehow hurt her.

I held out the square wrapped box, and she took it from me. We stood there, both staring at the presents in our hands.

"Well," I said in an awkward voice. "I guess we should open these."

Bria let out a weak laugh. "That is what people do."

We each tore into the wrapping paper. Bria was in more of a nervous hurry than I was, because she got to her present first. She opened the top of the box and pulled out a snow globe, which I'd found during my last-minute shopping yesterday. I'd managed to get to one of the malls an hour before it closed, then had spent the rest of the evening prepping my Christmas feast.

Bria held the globe up so that snow swirled through the scene—two young girls sitting on the rim of a fountain in a beautiful garden.

"I saw that and thought of you," I said. "Thought of us. Do you—do you remember the courtyard where we used to play?"

She bit her lip and nodded. "I do."

We didn't say anything, each of us lost in our own memories of the past. Some good, some bad, some best forgotten.

"It's beautiful," Bria said. "Thank you. But how did you know that I like snow globes?"

I hesitated. "I saw some of them in your house a few weeks ago, the night Elliot Slater attacked you."

"The night you came in and saved me from him," she finished.

I nodded.

Bria looked at me. "You know, I never thanked you for that. Slater would have killed me that night if it hadn't been for you."

I shrugged. "I was just doing what anyone would do."

"No," Bria said. "You were doing what a sister would do. Something I finally realized today. Now, open your present. Please."

I hesitated before lifting the lid on the tiny box she'd given me. A small piece of jewelry lay inside—a ring. A thin silverstone band with a tiny spider rune stamped in the middle of it. I recognized it at once. It was one of the three rings that Bria always wore on her left index finger. My ring.

"I can't take this," I said. "This is yours. Your ring. I've never seen you without it."

Bria shook her head. "It's not really my ring. It's yours. I had it and the others made the day I graduated from the police academy. It's what I wore to remind myself of you, to remember my promise to come back to Ashland someday and find a way to make Mab pay for taking you and Mother and Annabella away from me. But now that you're here with me, I don't need the ring anymore. I want you to have it. Please, Gin?"

There was nothing I could do but put it on. To my surprise, the ring slipped easily onto my right index finger. It fit perfectly.

"Well," Bria said, shifting on her feet, that uncertain look filling her face again. "I should go. It sounds like you have a party to get back to in there."

She turned toward the door, but I grabbed her arm. I tried not to notice how she tensed at my touch. Time, I told myself. It would just take some time.

"Stay," I said. "Please. It would mean a lot to me."

Bria hesitated, but after a moment, she nodded. She took off her coat and put it on the rack with the others. Then, our shoulders not quite touching, we walked down the hall and into the living room. The others stopped their conversation as we stepped into the room. They all knew what Bria meant to me, what having her here meant to me.

"Everyone," I said in a loud voice. "This is my baby sister, Bria."

Nobody said anything for a moment. Then everyone moved forward at once, welcoming Bria to the party and into our little family. Forever.

I stepped back out of the way and let the others talk to Bria. She turned first one way then another, saying hello to everyone. Roslyn, Xavier, the Deveraux sisters, the Foxes, the Volgas. This went on for quite a while, but I was content to just stand aside and watch. Finally the others gave Bria some breathing room, and she wandered over into the corner, probably just to find a moment's peace before jumping back into the fray.

And that's when Finnegan Lane finally made his move.

"You know, we're going to be seeing a lot of each other now," Finn said in a smooth voice, sidling up to her.

Bria gave him a cool look. "Just because you're Gin's foster brother doesn't mean I have to be nice to you."

"No, it doesn't, although I imagine it will make things easier for Gin if we at least try to get along."

Bria snorted, not buying Finn's lame line for a second.

Instead of being offended, Finn just grinned at her. "You're not going to make this easy for me, are you?"

Bria's blue eyes narrowed, but once again, I saw a hot spark of interest glittering in her gaze. Whether she wanted to admit it or not, she was attracted to Finn. "No. I think you're the kind of man who's had it far too easy over the years, especially when it comes to women. At least, that's the rumor I've heard."

Finn clutched his hand over his heart. "Oh, detective. How you wound me."

Bria snorted again.

"Well, then, I guess it's a good thing that I've got tradition on my side," Finn said, his grin widening.

Bria frowned. "What are you talking about?"

Finn pointed up at the ball of mistletoe hanging over their heads. It took Bria a second to realize what the mistletoe was—and what Finn intended to do next.

Before she could protest or step back, Finn grabbed her, pulled her into his arms, dipped her low, and soundly kissed her. The motion surprised my sister, and she didn't even have time to put up a token struggle. Not that she would have anyway.

Because after a moment, her hands, which had been windmilling in the air, settled on Finn's broad shoulders. Her fingers dug into his muscles, and I couldn't tell if she was trying to push him away or pull him closer. For his part, Finn was kissing my sister for all he was worth, holding her close in a way I'd never seen him do with another woman before.

"Well, that could be interesting," Owen murmured in my ear. "How do you feel about that?"

Finn and Bria broke apart, still holding on to each other and both breathing heavy. Finn put Bria back up on her feet and gave her another suave smile, although his face was faintly troubled, as if he'd enjoyed that kiss a little more than he'd thought he would. As if he'd felt a little more than he'd thought he would—maybe even a little too much for comfort.

Bria glowered at him and turned away, but not before

I saw a small, almost triumphant smile curve her lips as well.

"I think Finn may have finally met his match," I said.

Owen put his arms around me, and I leaned my head against his chest.

"Merry Christmas, Gin," Owen said in a quiet voice.

But was it really merry? I might have killed Elektra LaFleur and ended the threat that the assassin posed to us all, but I hadn't accomplished my ultimate goal— eliminating Mab Monroe. Until the Fire elemental was dead, we were all still in danger, no matter how safe we might feel right now.

Then I looked out at the people in the living room. Finn, the Deveraux sisters, Eva Grayson, Roslyn and her family, Xavier, the Foxes, Vinnie and Natasha. And Bria, finally back in my life after so many years gone. Everyone smiling and laughing. Everyone warm, loved, and happy. For this moment, for this one day, everything was perfect, and I knew I couldn't wish for anything more. Today, I'd take what happiness I could get. Tomorrow, I'd get down to the business of taking out Mab—once and for all.

"Merry Christmas, Owen," I said in a soft voice, echoing his sentiment.

And it was.

Turn the page for a sneak peek at the next book
in the Elemental Assassin series,

SPIDER'S REVENGE

Jennifer Estep

Coming soon from Pocket Books

❋ 1 ❋

Old habits die hard for assassins.

And I planned on murdering someone before the night was through.

That's what I did. Me. Gin Blanco. The assassin known as the Spider. I killed people, something that I was very, very good at.

Tonight I had my sights set on my most dangerous target ever—Mab Monroe, the Fire elemental who'd murdered my family when I was thirteen.

I'd been plotting the hit for weeks. Where to do it, how to get past security, what weapons to use, how to get away after the fact. Now, on this frigid night, I'd decided to finally carry out my deadly plan.

I'd been on the prowl for hours. Three hours, to be exact. Each one spent out in the bitter February frost, after having climbed my way up the side of a fifteen-story mansion, one icy foot at a time. Hard bits of snow pelted my body, as I tried to keep the shrieking wind from tearing me off the side of the house. It wasn't the most comfortable that I'd ever been during one of my hits, but it was necessary.

Too bad Mab knew I was coming for her.

Oh, I hadn't expected it to be *easy*, but slipping past the massive net of security, first in the snowy woods around Mab's mansion, and then closer to the house itself, was a bit more problematic than I'd anticipated. The whole area was teeming with giants the Fire elemental employed as her personal bodyguards, not to mention nasty land-mines and other traps strung through the trees like invisible spiderwebs. Of course, I could have dropped the giants, killing them one by one as I went along, but that would have resulted in the alarm being raised, and the security net tightening that much more.

So instead I'd opted for a silent, nonlethal approach—at least for now. It had taken me an hour to work my way through the woods, then another one to get close enough to the mansion to slither up the stairs to a second-floor balcony and then heave myself up onto part of the roof that sloped down there. After that, things had gotten easier, since there were no sensors, alarms, or giants posted on the roofs that covered the various parts of the massive structure. Not many people bothered with such things above the second floor, since most folks weren't brave or crazy enough to climb any higher, especially on a snowy night like this one.

I wasn't particularly brave or crazy, but I was determined to kill Mab.

A strong gust of wind slapped and then backhanded

the mansion, screaming in my ears and hurling more frozen snow off the eaves and onto me. The chunks pounded my body before disappearing over the side of the roof and dropping down into the eerie silver dark of the night.

I grunted at the hard, stinging impacts. As an elemental, I could have used my Stone magic to protect myself, could have tapped into my power and made my skin hard as marble so that the rocklike wads of snow would bounce off my body like bullets off Superman's chest. But elementals can sense when others of their ilk are using their powers, and I didn't want to give Mab any hint I was here.

At least, not before I'd killed her.

By this point, I'd worked my way up to the sixth floor, where the mansion's blueprints had indicated there was a particularly large dining room. According to some chatter that my foster brother Finnegan Lane had picked up from his various spies, Mab was hosting a fancy dinner party this evening. Finn hadn't been able to determine what the party was for or even who had been invited, but that didn't much matter. Mab was getting dead tonight— I didn't care who was in the room with her.

I'd been in position for more than an hour now, outside the dining room window, laying flat on a part of the roof that plateaued before sloping down at a severe angle and dropping away to the ground far below. But really, the worst part of the night wasn't the guards, the cold, the snow, or even the icy, treacherous climb—it was having to listen to the stones around me.

People's emotions, actions, and feelings sink into their

environment over time, especially into the stones around them. As a Stone elemental, I could hear those emotional vibrations in whatever form the element took around me, from loose gravel in a driveway to the brick of a building to a marble sculpture. The sounds, the murmurs, the whispers that reverberated through the stones let me know what had happened in a particular spot, what sort of people had been there, and all the dark, ugly, twisted things that they'd done in the meantime—or who might be lurking around in the here and now, trying to get the drop on me.

Fire, heat, death, destruction. That's what the stones of Mab's mansion murmured of, punctuated by sly, smirking, confident whispers of power and money—both things that the Fire elemental had in abundance. But the most disturbing thing, the sound that made me grind my teeth, was the cackling of maniacal madness that rippled through the gray stones. Wave after wave of it, as though the rock had somehow been tortured until it was just as broken, burnt, and dead as Mab's many victims.

After a minute of listening to the stones' wailing cries, I blocked out the damned, disturbing noise and got on with more important matters, like checking my weapons. As always, I carried five silverstone knives on me—one up either sleeve, one against the small of my back, and two more tucked into the tops of my boots. The knives were my weapons of choice on most jobs because they were sharp, strong, and almost unbreakable. Just like me.

But Mab was a Fire elemental, which meant that she could create, control, and manipulate fire the same way I could stone. And Mab wasn't just any *mere* Fire elemental—she was rumored to have more raw magic, more raw power, than any elemental born in the last five hundred years. She could easily fry me alive with her magic before I got close enough to even think about plunging my silverstone knives into her burning black heart.

I'd decided to play it smart and keep a healthy distance between us, just in case things didn't work out exactly as I'd planned tonight. So I'd brought another weapon along with me—a crossbow. It looked like your typical crossbow—heavy, substantial, deadly—made even more so by the rifle scope that I'd mounted above the trigger and the six-inch-long, barbed bolt already in firing position. Since it was made out of silverstone, a particularly tough magical metal, the bolt would rip through anything that it came into contact with—glass, stone, flesh, bone.

The crossbow currently sat on the window ledge, with the barb pointing inside. I'd been in firing position for more than fifteen minutes, and all I had to do to release the deadly bolt was pull the trigger.

Good thing, as people were starting to arrive for dinner.

The black velvet drapes had been drawn on either side of the window, letting me see into the dining room. Closing the drapes was something most folks didn't bother with above the second floor. Sloppy, sloppy, sloppy of Mab's bodyguards not to see to a pesky little detail like that.

I'd actually been inside Mab's mansion once before, when I'd been stalking another target a few months ago, and the dining room before me was just as opulent as I remembered the rest of the house being. The room was a hundred feet wide, with a ceiling that soared high above it. Gold and silver leaf glinted in elaborate patterns on the ceiling, while several chandeliers dropped down from it and glistened like jewel-colored dewdrops above a polished ebony table. Three dozen place settings of fine china covered the table, along with matching flatware. Silver buckets filled with ice, champagne, and other expensive liquors were spaced down both sides of the table, so that everyone could have easy access to the booze.

For the last ten minutes, tuxedo-clad giants moved through the area, bringing in plates, napkins, liquor, and everything else that may be needed. My gaze drifted over to a buffet table that had been set up on the far side of the room. Mab and her guests were dining on lobster tonight, among other delicacies.

Finally, one of the giants opened the double doors at the end of the room, bowed his head, and held out his arm, ushering the guests inside. Time to get the party started, in more ways than one.

Most of the guests drifted in individually, although a few were coupled up in groups of two or more. Men and women. Old, young, fat, thin, black, white, Hispanic, dwarves, giants, vampires. There was more variety to the crowd than I'd expected. Usually, all of Mab's business associates looked the same—middle-aged men with more money than common sense and all the greedy, twisted appetites to match.

But these people were different. Oh, they all looked like I'd thought they would—dressed to the nines in tuxedos and evening gowns, with expensive jewels, perfect makeup, and coiffed hair to match. But they didn't act like I'd thought they would. They didn't mingle together, they didn't start drinking and eating, and perhaps most telling, they didn't even bother talking to each other. Instead, all the singles, couples, and tight-knit groups stayed to themselves, leaving several feet of distance in between each one of them. Curious. Most curious indeed.

Through the rifle scope, my eye went from one face to another, trying to get a sense of exactly whom Mab had invited to her shindig and why they were acting so strangely. I might not care what their names were or how much money they had, but I did want to know if any of them fancied themselves tough guys who might be a threat to me. Not that I was planning on sticking around after I took out Mab, but it never hurt to be prepared. Fletcher Lane, the old man who had been my mentor, had taught me that, among many other deadly things.

Despite their tuxedos, gowns, and glittering jewels, every single one of the men and women had a tense, coiled, predatory air about them, and they all gave one another the same flat, hard stare, as if they were all competing for the same prize and would do anything to get it. A few of them actually eyed the silverware, as if they were thinking about picking up the knives, spoons, and forks, and thinning out the crowd a bit before the show got started.

I frowned. Mab did business with all sorts of unsavory characters, but something about the people inside the dining room bothered me. Maybe because they all reminded me . . . of me. Gin Blanco. The Spider.

Before I had time to think that thought through, the

double doors opened again, and Mab Monroe stepped into the room.

The Fire elemental strolled through the tense crowd until she reached the middle of the room. Everyone turned to stare at her, and what little conversation there was had stopped, like a radio that had been turned off mid-song. Like her guests, Mab had dressed up for the evening, in a long sea-green gown that complimented her pale skin. Her coppery red hair was piled on top of her head, each artfully arranged strand dripping down the sides of her face like so much blood. But the most striking thing about Mab were her eyes—two bottomless black pools that seemed to suck up all the available light in the room instead of reflecting it back. Even the bright chandeliers overhead seemed to dim as she had passed underneath them.

The severe V in the front of Mab's gown showed off her creamy décolletage, as well as the necklace that she wore. A flat gold circle encased the Fire elemental's neck, accentuated by a ruby set into the middle of the design. Several dozen wavy golden rays surrounded the bloodred gem, and the intricate diamond cutting on the metal caught the light and reflected it back, making it look as if the rays were flickering.

The flamboyant ruby-and-gold design was much more than just a mere necklace—it was a rune. A sunburst. The symbol for fire. Mab's personal rune, used by her alone. Runes were how elementals and other magic types in Ashland identified themselves, their families, their power, their alliances, and even their businesses to others.

I had a rune, too. A small circle surrounded by eight

thin rays. A spider rune. The symbol for patience and my assassin name. Actually, I had two runes—one branded into either palm. The marks had been put there by Mab the night she'd murdered my family. That's when the Fire elemental had tortured me by duct-taping a silverstone medallion shaped like the spider rune in between my two hands and then superheating the metal with her magic until it had melted into my flesh, marking me forever.

The sight of Mab and her flashing sunburst necklace made the spider rune scars on my palms itch and burn, the way they always did whenever I was around the Fire elemental, but I didn't move from my position. Didn't rub my hands together to make the uncomfortable sensation go away. Didn't let out a tense sigh. Hell, I didn't even blink.

Killing Mab was much more important than the memories that filled my mind or the pain that they brought me, even now, seventeen years after the fact. Now was not the time to be sentimental or sloppy. Not when I had a chance to kill the bitch, to finally end our family feud— once and for all.

Inside the dining room, Mab turned in a circle, her black eyes roaming over her guests, sizing them up just like I had.

"I'm glad to see that you all could make it."

The Fire elemental's voice was low, soft, and silky, with just a hint of a rasp to it. Still, despite her gentle tone, a clear undercurrent of power and authority crackled in Mab's words.

Thanks to Finn and his ability to get his hands on absolutely anything, I'd opened the dining room window earlier and fastened a small bug inside underneath the windowsill. The bug's receiver, which I'd stuck in my ear several minutes ago, let me hear Mab loud and clear.

"I wasn't sure exactly how many of you would show up on such short notice," Mab continued. "But I'm most pleased by the turnout."

I frowned. Turnout? What was the Fire elemental up to, and who were these mysterious people that she'd invited to her mansion? I had a funny feeling that they weren't the tame businessmen and businesswomen that I'd expected to find.

A woman stepped forward, separating herself from the pack. She wore an evening gown like all the others, but the garment was just a bit too big for her thin, wiry frame. The fabric was slick and cheap, and the mint-green color was faded, as though she'd been wearing the dress for years, pulling it out of the depths of her closet for special occasions just like this one. She had to be seventy if she was a day, and her skin had the dark, nut-brown look of someone who'd spent her entire life out-doors, working under the burning sun. Her iron-gray hair had been pulled back into a tight bun, which set off her sharp, angular face, and her eyes were a pale, washed-out blue.

The woman was one of the guests who'd come in with someone else. A young girl of about sixteen stood off to her right, dressed in a low-rent pink gown with a poofy ballerina skirt, which made it look like a prom dress. The girl was as light as the woman was dark, with long molasses-colored hair shot through with honey-blond highlights. Her hazel eyes were wide and innocent in her lean, almost gaunt face, and the girl kept glancing from side to side, obviously awed by all the lavish furnishings.

"Well, there was really no choice in the matter, Mab." The woman's voice was low, pleasant, friendly even, as though she was talking to some stranger on the street and not the most dangerous person in Ashland. "Not with the generous payout you were offering. I'm surprised that more people didn't show up to try to collect."

The others in the room nodded in agreement. My eyes narrowed. Payout, for what? And how were they going to collect? Was this some kind of business deal? Or something else . . . something more sinister? Something to do with the Spider, perhaps?

It wasn't out of the realm of possibilities. Not too long ago, Mab had hired an assassin named Elektra LaFleur to come to Ashland, hunt me down, and kill me. Of course, I'd taken care of LaFleur instead. Still, ever since then, I'd been waiting for the Fire elemental to do something, anything, to try to find the Spider again. Mab wasn't the type of person to give up, especially when I'd been offing her men, thwarting her best-laid plans, and generally thumbing my nose at her for months.

But everything had been quiet since I'd killed LaFleur in the city's old train yard. Even Finn and his many spies hadn't heard a whisper of what Mab might be planning, which worried me more than if I knew that the Fire elemental had dispatched every man at her disposal to track me down.

Somehow, though, I knew that the quiet was about to end tonight—in a big, big way.

"And you would be?" Mab asked, staring down her nose at her guest.

The woman bowed her head respectfully, although she never took her eyes off the Fire elemental. "Ruth Gentry, at your service."

"Ah, yes, Gentry. Well, I appreciate your honesty," Mab said, returning the thin woman's pleasant tone. "You have a stellar reputation, as does everyone else in the room. Which, of course, is why I asked you all here tonight."

The Fire elemental had peaked my curiosity with her strange words, and I paused, wanting to find out exactly who the mystery people were. Curiosity was often an emotion that got the best of me, but for once, I forced it aside. I was here to do one thing—kill Mab. Everything else could wait.

"I hope you all had a pleasant journey," Mab said, looking at her guests. "As you can see, we'll be dining on the various dishes that my chef has prepared. . . ."

I tuned out the Fire elemental. Slowly, I reached forward until my fingers closed around a tiny, clear, almost invisible suction cup on the window in front of me. I gently pulled on the cup, and a small circular piece slid out of the window. A glass cutter was among the tools I'd brought with me tonight, tucked away in the zippered pocket on my silverstone vest. Earlier, I'd used it to carve an opening in the window. I wanted a clear shot at Mab and not one that might be distorted by my crossbow bolt punching through the glass.

I put the glass down beside me on the snowy roof. Then I slid my crossbow forward, until the tip of it, the end with the bolt, just protruded through the hole in the window—aimed right at Mab.

One of Mab's giant bodyguards, who was pulling double duty as a waiter tonight, came over to stand beside her, as though he had an important message for her. The Fire elemental ignored him and kept talking to her guests about how they'd discuss business after dinner. Too bad she wasn't going to even make it to the first course.

I waited a few seconds to be sure that the giant wasn't going to interrupt or step in front of Mab, then scooted forward even more and put my eye next to the rifle scope. The Fire elemental wasn't that far away from me, maybe fifty feet, but the scope gave me a crystal clear view of her face.

I aimed for her right eye, which looked blacker than ink. I'd only get one shot at her, and I didn't want to waste it on a chest wound that might not put her down for good. Mab might have more magic than any other elemental in Ashland, but even she wouldn't be able to survive a crossbow bolt through her eye, especially since the silverstone projectile would keep on going until it blasted out of the back of her skull. Hard to recover when half your brain matter was missing.

Despite all the people I'd killed over the years, all the blood I'd spilled, all the sudden, violent, brutal deaths I'd caused, my finger trembled just a bit as I set it on the crossbow's trigger. My heart raced in my chest, picking up speed with every single beat, and a bead of sweat trickled down the side of my face, despite the cold. I drew in a breath, trying to calm my nerves and quiet myself. Trying to go to that cold, dark, hard place that I'd been to so many times before—the shelter that had gotten me through so many terrible times in my life.

Because this was the hit that truly, finally mattered—the only one that ever had. For my murdered family, for my baby sister, Bria, for me. It wouldn't make things right, it wouldn't erase all the horrible things I'd suffered through or the equally bad ones I'd done myself, but killing Mab would keep the people I loved safe. And I hoped it would bring me some kind of peace too.

I hadn't been able to stop Mab years ago, when she'd murdered my mother and older sister, but I could kill her now. Everything that I'd ever done—living on the streets, becoming an assassin, honing my deadly skills—had been leading up to this one moment, this final confrontation.

I let out my breath and pulled the trigger.